I can't take the crazy think any longer.
I've never told anyone this before.
It's my crazy-think story.

E. W. Summers was born in New York and grew up in both New York and Pennsylvania. After a graduate degree in writing from the Johns Hopkins University, E. W. Summers now lives in Maryland and teaches English in the public school system.

Crazy Think

E. W. SUMMERS

MICHAEL JOSEPH
LONDON

MICHAEL JOSEPH LTD

Published by the Penguin Group
27 Wrights Lane, London W8 5TZ
Viking Penguin Inc., 375 Hudson Street, New York, New York 10014, USA
Penguin Books Australia Ltd, Ringwood, Victoria, Australia
Penguin Books Canada Ltd, 10 Alcorn Avenue, Toronto, Ontario, Canada M4V 3B2
Penguin Books (NZ) Ltd, 182–190 Wairau Road, Auckland 10, New Zealand

Penguin Books Ltd, Registered Offices: Harmondsworth, Middlesex, England

First published 1997
1 3 5 7 9 10 8 6 4 2

Set in 11½/13½pt Monotype Bembo
Typeset by Rowland Phototypesetting Ltd, Bury St Edmunds, Suffolk
Printed in England by Clays Ltd, St Ives plc

A CIP catalogue record for this book is available from the British Library

ISBN 0 7181 4184 9
ISBN 0 7181 4289 6

For Josh, Tish, Jim, Cari, and, of course, Charlie.

Chapter One

IT was two o'clock in the morning and, for the third night in a row, I hadn't been able to sleep. It reminded me of being a kid, all those nights I lay awake protecting my sister Claire from the bogeyman. It didn't make any difference that I was far from the farm, a thirty-five-year-old man on his own. Richard Cory Hayes. Managing partner in my own accounting firm. Living at 411 East 88th Street, New York, New York. The bogeyman still lurked outside my doorway.

The following day I was to give my statement in preparation for Claire's trial for the murder of her husband.

That's what my insomnia was all about.

'It's the past you've got to think about, Richard,' her lawyer Boyce told me in his high-rise office the day after the murder. The past could save Claire. 'Think about why a girl like Claire would marry an abusive guy in the first place. Why would she stay married to him? Why not get a divorce? Why'd she have to kill him?' We'd looked at each other across his glass-topped mahogany desk.

'I don't know if I can make an outsider understand,' I'd said.

'I don't think you have a choice if you want to help your sister.' Boyce folded his hands on top of his desk. 'If you want to help your sister' hung between us.

Although Claire must have had her doubts at the time, I

had wanted them both to believe that there was no question I'd do whatever it took to help her. Talk to my brother and sisters about the past. Go backward in time to 37 Brookfield Court, our big family home in Waterton, New York. Even to the farm.

Since the murder, it's been hard to talk about the farm.

My younger sister Claire's story, like my own, begins at the farm. That's what the murder has made me realize. What began this story happened years ago, but the event that set off its climax occurred on a warm October night in New York City five years ago . . .

It was after ten, the October night Claire called five years ago.

I was still up, which wasn't that unusual. Ever since my ex-wife Johanna left me, I puttered around my studio apartment pretending to work on the book I was writing about making audit practices more profitable, but really thinking about the night she left.

'You know something, Richard? I've always been afraid of you,' she'd said, just before she moved out. We stood facing each other in our tiny apartment, a dusting of fading sunlight casting shadows. She's an artist, and the sun shadows gave her oil paintings an eerie glow. 'You're like a slow-ticking bomb waiting to explode.'

I took a step in her direction.

She put up her hands as if to ward me off.

Because it hurt so much, that gesture infuriated me more than the remark and I moved closer, towering over her. 'What's that supposed to mean?'

As if I didn't know

'I'm leaving. Now. Tonight.' She didn't answer my question. 'My brother is meeting me here.' Her voice held a warning, but she didn't need to caution me. I didn't want to know her answer.

Afraid of what she might say

I didn't hang around to chat with my soon-to-be-ex-

2

brother-in-law; I slammed out and headed to the gym where I beat the crap out of a heavyweight bag. I'd had one in the garage at Brookfield Court when I was a kid, and even as an adult I savored the feeling of power that smashing one gave me. That night, I feared it was the only power I had; I surely didn't have the power to keep my wife from leaving me. I didn't even know how to tell her I was sorry.

I was lonely after she left. Many evenings I sat, sipping beer, in my one chair in front of my one window, a large expanse of cracked yellowed glass covering an entire wall. Last summer I saw a fat man, who appeared to be about my age, in it.

His window was always open, and I'd hear strains of a Gordon Lightfoot tape, the man singing along, his voice cracking and breaking as if he were an adolescent. I filled out imaginary income-tax returns for him, so I didn't have to feel ashamed that when I heard Johanna had left me for some guy named Ed, I'd mailed her sketches but smashed my old farm fishing-tackle box filled with her half-empty paint tubes.

When Claire called, the night of John's death, I hadn't even pulled my couch into a bed yet. Although it was a Sunday, I'd gone into the office and the day had vanished in a haze of paperwork. By the time I got home at 9 p.m., I was exhausted. I felt old and gray and depressed, and surprised myself with my reflection in the bathroom mirror. Tall, broad-shouldered. No wrinkles, my blond hair wasn't thinning. Blue eyes clear, no red lines to prove my sleepless nights.

I decided to take a walk.

I shrugged into sweats and headed outside. It was dark, the sky overcast but nice, one of those October evenings without a chill. I walked across First toward Second, thinking I'd stop by a coffee shop I liked on the corner of 75th and Second. I sat in my usual corner, leaning my head against the window. Lucy, the waitress for my table, brought me two warm bagels and sat beside me for a moment.

'So,' she said. 'I guess she didn't come back?'

I shook my head.

3

'You know what I did when my first husband left?'

'What did you do?'

'I bought the cheapest plonk by the case.'

I laughed. She left me to my bagels and I went back to window watching, but I wasn't seeing New York's Upper East Side hustle. I was watching my mother hide her wine on the porch off the kitchen in our family's Brookfield Court house. She's in her red and white checked house dress. She's furtive and gasping from the weight. It's funny, I don't know if she's a big woman or not. I don't know how my ex-wife or Claire might compare to her if they stood side by side. I always think of her as big. Bigger than me. I see a muscle twitch in her arm as she moves her case of Carlo Rossi. The porch is dark; it's a chaotic porch cluttered with bicycles, lawn mowers, empty boxes we use to pack our stuff to go to the farm. There's the boot collection, tall green rubber boots, short brown boots, heavy laced boots, and his toolboxes are out there, too. When he hollers for a Phillips head, you better know which toolbox to go for. For a long while there are empty bottles for the milkman to collect each morning on the porch, and she leaves the milk card with its square boxes carefully checked: three quarts milk, two orange juice, two tubs cottage cheese. The cases of Carlo Rossi take up one whole corner.

'Another bagel?' Lucy startled me, and I shook my head.

'I've got to get home,' I said. I did not like taking trips down Memory Lane. It felt more than wrong to me, it felt illegal. What was past was past.

It was still warm outside. The East River is only a few blocks east, and I felt that curious dampness that tells you a body of water is nearby. I used to feel it on the farm as a kid. Our ponds and creeks aren't the East River, but we felt the same mist. Gracie Mansion, the mayor's home, is set close to the river with lots of maple and oak and walnut trees surrounding it. On any October night, their branches are so thick with leaves, the mansion's hidden from view. That night, the breeze sent their leaves on a slow dance to my neighborhood. In the gleam of street lamps, I could just make out their colors – poppy red, pumpkin orange, egg-yolk yellow. No different from the colors staining the farm's Blue Ridge Mountains. Claire and I, I thought, are probably the only persons in New York who might be thinking about those mountains.

At home, I considered doing the dishes, but decided against it. As I was considering my business partner Mary's advice to call one of her cousin's nieces for a date, the phone shrilled. For a minute, I let myself hope it was Johanna. Had she discovered Ed was a loser?

It was my sister Claire.

'I've killed John,' she told me. 'I shot him. There's blood everywhere.' A full thirty seconds passed before she started to scream. Then the line went dead.

Stunned, I stood holding the phone. Claire? Silent Claire? Claire the shadow girl who followed me around the farm? When I drove the tractor, she sat beside me. When I strung barbed wire, she held the staples. When she got scared at night, she crept into my bed. Even in family pictures, Claire stood a little behind the rest of us like a shadow. I'd always thought she'd settled in New York because I was here. I had the sense of being zapped into unreality, as if I'd sped into a new dimension. I failed to picture my frail sister killing a man six or seven inches taller than she, maybe a hundred pounds heavier. I knew she'd been in therapy, but although we spoke once or twice a month, I never asked her why.

Afraid of what she might say

I felt nothing for John.

I couldn't get hold of any tangibles for a solid minute, maybe more. I'm not sure I could have spit out my name had someone asked. But I'll tell you this: Claire's phone call had blown the lid off my depression. Now I was angry, angry at being forced to take action. Probably nobody likes to be forced to do something, but I know I hated it worse than other people. It's as if my whole being rebelled. Still, I had always

5

been the one in the family who looked out for the four younger kids. All else vanished from my mind but that familiar, overpowering need to take charge of the situation, but I didn't know what to do, and I was angry at finding myself in that position. Should I call the police? 911? And then, like a drumbeat deep within my brain, I heard Boyce Regner, Attorney at Law, Boyce Regner, Attorney at Law. Had I seen his name on a business card? Heard it at a party? I didn't know and didn't care. I snatched up my phone directory and searched for his name, praying there'd be a home listing for him.

There was. He answered. I explained the situation and how Claire's screaming still echoed in my ears. 'She's been seeing a Dr Glassman, a therapist associated with the Psychiatric Institute of Manhattan,' I told him.

His response was to the point: 'Don't touch anything in the apartment. Take her directly to the Psych Institute. Meet me in the lobby. Get there as fast as you can.'

Something distasteful buzzed in my brain when he said Psych Institute, but I didn't waste time trying to figure it out. I jogged out of my building to the Lexington and 86th Street subway station, taking the train to Astor Place. I sat on a slick brown seat, feeling like Dustin Hoffman in *Marathon Man*. I thought about that guy in the Dallas Tower, Charles somebody or other, and how he murdered his mother and his wife, headed for the tower and zapped twenty-two more people. I thought about the guy in Canada, the one who opened fire in a university, walking quietly from room to room, spraying people with bullets. I had a glimmer of how they felt. The scary thing was, I knew that at some time in my life I'd felt the same way, but I didn't know when or why. It was a flash of insight I didn't want. I sensed that, after tonight, nothing in my life would ever be the same.

When the train screeched to a halt and the doors slid open, I hurried into the smelly subway pit. Up the steps, out of the sticky underground air into the starless night. Moving, moving,

moving. Claire and John's Washington Place apartment was only a few blocks away. I ran down Waverly Place, skirting Washington Square Park, closed and eerily silent, hung a left at MacDougal, a right onto Washington Place.

John and Claire lived on the third floor of a three-story building divided into three apartments with Benjamin's Beauty Salon on the street floor. I jerked my keys to her place from my pocket with trembling hands and opened the first of three locked doors. Then the second. The steps leading to their apartment were skinny and winding, shiny linoleum covering them. Around and around I went, finally reaching their landing. John's trash littered it. Golf clubs. Books, magazines, skis. A collection of baseball hats.

I pressed my ear to the door. Silence. No neighbors lurked in doorways, either. I'd been careful to check on my way up the stairs. A gunshot in New York doesn't bring people outside; it sends them under the covers. Remember Kitty Genovese? At least my sister didn't have to worry about witnesses. I pushed the door, and it opened. I knew I was functioning on adrenalin. I thought of Bonnie and Clyde and the scene in the movie when the Texas Ranger and his men spray them to death. I wanted to be the ranger. I wanted to kill somebody, too.

Jesus

Not Claire, never Claire, just somebody. I heard my heart in my ears. That same feeling of nonreality persisted. I took a deep breath and stepped inside. I didn't need to go any further than the front room. It was about the size of my parents' walk-in closet at 37 Brookfield Court. Claire had a table squeezed into the room to use for her art. A couch sat crushed against a wall. A stereo system occupied a homemade three-decker table in a corner. They had a bedroom, a bathroom that couldn't hold two people, and a postage-stamp kitchen. Spacious by Village standards.

I saw my sister curled into a fetal ball in a corner of the couch. What must be her pajama bottoms lay bunched on the floor. Her top was opened. Clearly torn. Long tangly hair hid her face. She looked like a little girl.

John's body draped across most of the couch. His pants were off, but he wore a tight white T-shirt with a V-neck like my father always wore. I wore crew-necks. The thick wet smell of fresh blood filled the air. I remembered it from those days when my father and I went hunting. We'd kill deer and gut them while they steamed. I didn't see a gun anywhere. For all I knew, she may have tossed it behind the sofa or out the window to be discovered by an earlymorning jogger.

'Claire?' I whispered.

She lifted her head. Each feature in her face broke my heart. Those staring hyacinth-blue eyes with their long lashes; the nose that I'd always teased her was crooked; her colorless lips. She looked no different than she had twenty years ago when she'd crept into my room in the dead of night. As vulnerable and as innocent. She didn't look like a killer.

I took a step toward her.

'He won't bother us anymore.' She spoke in the hesitant voice of a small child.

I felt a vivid slash of fear push through my sense of non-reality. Jesus. Whom was she talking about?

As if I didn't know

My ears throbbed. 'You're sick,' I whispered.

'Look what I've done.' Claire flung a thin arm toward John. She put a pillow to her face and peeked from behind it at her husband. She looked up at me, eyes huge and swimming with something I couldn't identify. I saw her fingers pluck, pluck, plucking at the pillow's fringe. She pulled the pillow close against her chest, the same way she'd clung to her teddy bear when we were little. 'He doesn't own us anymore, does he?' she said, staring at him.

Chilled, I knew she was wading into waters I had no intention of putting my feet in. She set the pillow on her lap and began twisting each individual fringe. I remembered, when we were kids, she'd twist her dinner napkin until all that remained were shreds of colored paper. Those ripping, tearing fingers looked strong, and for a moment, I was afraid of her.

Afraid of what she might say

She sat up straight now, the pillow tossed to one side. Her torn pajama top slipped off her shoulder, and I saw blue and yellow and green bruises. That bastard. Claire had once confided that John hit his mother, had blackened her eye, but I hadn't listened hard enough. I hadn't wanted to.

Poor Claire. I felt a pulse in my jaw, the vein in my forehead.

I saw the white lace of her pale pink pajamas ripped. I saw her small breast and its pink-tipped nipple. I smelled the rank, dank smell of body odor that comes with fear. I didn't know if it was Claire or me. Her sudden movement knocked John's body to the floor. The thud sounded loud as a shotgun blast. My little sister grinned, a face-splitting grin. 'Ding, dong, the witch is dead, witch is dead,' she warbled.

I looked at her, unable to speak. There was a ringing in my ears. I felt as if I might be sick. Add vomit to the other smells in the place. I kept looking at her and I wanted this night to have never been. I wanted to erase it. I wanted her to disappear. I wanted her to be silent. We'd all wanted her to be silent. And she had been. For years. Guilt overwhelmed me. I tried to put my hand out to her, but nothing happened. My arm swayed at my side, a dead weight. 'Poor Claire,' I said at last. My throat hurt. Her song died away.

At last my arm came unglued and I stretched my hand toward her. She flinched and with a little whistle of a moan, slouched back onto the couch. She looked like a bundle of tattered clothes awaiting Good Will. 'Don't touch me,' she hissed, her arm up to protect her face.

Like Johanna

I continued to stand zombie-like in the room. I don't remember finding Claire's bathrobe and slippers, calling a taxi, shoving Claire in, hurtling across town to PI, as the locals call the Manhattan Psych Institute. We must have sat together in the lobby, leaving the receptionist to guess which one of us was the crazy, until Boyce Regner got there. I know I felt like a terrified kid – what if the doctors made a mistake and committed me?

I do remember meeting Boyce. He stepped through the glass doors and into the room, a tall, dark-haired man between thirty-five and forty. He wore jeans, a red T-shirt, leather bomber jacket, and the same kind of sneakers I did – Nikes. I stood to greet him and realized we were on eye level, that we probably could have exchanged clothes. After a pause, he shook my hand with a firm, warm handshake that matched his brown eyes. I sensed an intuitive compassion about the man.

He'd already contacted Dr Glassman. They'd worked together before. He told me not to worry about the arraignment or Claire's formal incarceration in PI, that he'd take care of everything including the bond hearing. He'd notified the police; they'd meet us at the apartment as soon as Claire committed herself to the Psych Institute. He told me he didn't plan to set foot in the apartment until the cops were there, too. 'I don't want any question of evidence tampering or obstruction of justice on my part. The way I see it right now, it's not going to be a question of guilt,' Boyce said, 'but a question of her not being criminally responsible for the killing. It'll be a not guilty plea.'

While I knew everything he'd done had to do with his perception of how to best handle the case, I felt he'd shown concern for my sister as well, and I liked him for it. Made me feel like I'd done the right thing in calling him. Besides, it was much easier for me to focus on Boyce than to confront the reality of what Claire had done or my own irrational fear of the law. We stayed by her side, filling out forms, finally handing her over to a nurse with a kind face. She unlocked a door and the two of them stepped into an adult care unit. The nurse relocked the door. Claire didn't look back.

Three police showed up outside Claire and John's apartment. One of them big and bumbling, his hands covered with dense black hair; one slim, dark with a thick Hispanic accent; one a woman, thick-waisted, clearly at home in the manly uniform. Her manner was abrupt, accusatory. She was a woman. She ought to have some understanding as to what had happened here. I'm not sure why I thought the police would understand when I, Claire's own brother, was having difficulty accepting what she'd tried to tell me when I first arrived and saw the bloodbath.

After the cops got done with their questions and pictures and settled down to wait for the medical officer to arrive and pronounce John officially dead, Boyce and I decided to go around the corner to Humphrey's, an all-night bar and grill tucked into the basement of a building similar to Claire's.

I must have been in shock because I felt nothing at all. I was a robot. I had not witnessed my sister's confusion, I had not heard what she said, I had not seen what was left of my brother-in-law. I was barely conscious that this was a lawyer by my side. We traipsed down the cement steps. I knew I couldn't face one of Humphrey's thick bloody hamburgers, but I could do with a beer and some chips. Boyce was hungry, too. John's death fueled our desire to eat and we couldn't stop. Wings, chips, beer, celery, carrots dipped in creamy ranch dressing stung with garlic, more wings and beer disappeared in amazing quantities at our corner table. It was more than half an hour later before the two of us sat looking at each other with empty mouths. I felt like a huge fat bear, stuffed and ready for hibernation. I knew without a shred of doubt that what I wanted was to go into hiding. I wanted to stop being on watch. Even as that thought came to me, I felt something inside me tighten up. A faraway little boy's voice whispered in my ear: *You are on watch for the rest of your life.* Go away! I wanted to shout. I'm not going to get dragged into the past.

'Waiter!' I called. 'Bring me another Heineken.'

Boyce put his hand on my arm. 'You've had enough, Richard,' he told me, and his voice held a sympathetic note.

'This must be really hard on you,' he added, and again that note of sympathy was there, only stronger. 'You're doing a great job holding it together.' He kept his hand on my arm. I thought about shaking it off but didn't. This man's unexpected gentleness triggered a sudden sense of loss inside me so great, I couldn't speak. It overwhelmed me, shocking me with its intensity. I didn't understand where it was coming from. I was supposed to be Richard, elder brother of Max, Elizabeth, Claire, and Tina. Protector. I didn't cry when my beloved great-grandmother Munsy died. I didn't cry when Buddy, my childhood dog, died. I don't remember shedding a single tear throughout my childhood. I didn't cry when Johanna left me. What was I doing at Humphrey's with a man I scarcely knew, a lawyer, no less, tears threatening to drip down my face?

His hand was warm and soothing on my arm. 'It's obvious from meeting you both that there's a lot more to this than your sister pulling a gun and zapping her husband.' He patted me, and for one wild second I had a sense of what it might have been like to have a loving father, one who listened when I spoke. Then I felt guilty. I remembered trekking off to the Episcopal church each week as a kid and having the fifth commandment drummed into my head: *Honor thy father and thy mother.* I'd always thought of Jesus as sitting at the right hand of God, the Father Almighty.

My father was God.

Jesus Christ, where is this stuff coming from? I swallowed hard, not wanting these thoughts. I hadn't been to church in over sixteen years. I straightened up and stopped the self-pity. I shook off Boyce's hand.

Boyce cleared his throat. 'I'm going to need Dr Glassman's help. I'm going to need Claire's help, and Claire's going to need your help, Richard.'

I nodded and turned away from him. A voice from the past was in my ear, using almost the same words as Boyce: *I think we better take her to the emergency room. Richard, you come with me to help.*

I pressed my hands to my head. I couldn't tell who was speaking or if the trauma of the evening had set off some strange reaction in me. I thought it was one of my parents' voices and for some reason it gave me the shivers, as if I was a little kid seeing adults do something they shouldn't.

Richard, you come with me to help

I turned back to Boyce, shoving away the voice. I slammed my hand on the table, knocking over a salt shaker. I grabbed it and slapped it back down so hard it fell again. 'So what is it I'm supposed to do?' I said.

'Come by my office tomorrow afternoon about four o'clock. Be prepared to give a statement. Support your sister.'

'This whole thing sucks,' I said.

'It sure does,' said Boyce.

At home, I lay on my unopened sofa bed for hours, unable to sleep, unable to get up and go to work, unable to do anything. I kept hearing the voice: *Richard, you come with me to help, Richard, you come with me to help, to help, to help . . .*

My parents had done the best they could, all of us kids knew that. How many kids have a farm like ours? How many kids have a mother who can sing and play the organ, any tune you want because she plays by ear? She and I play duets, too, me on my trumpet, she on the piano. Claire's too shy, and Tina's too little, but Elizabeth, Max, and I are all members of Saint James Episcopal Church's Little Blue Choir and our mother brings home those blue choir vestments each week, never entrusting them to the ironing lady but washing and ironing them herself so that on Wednesday afternoons we return from school to the ironing board and a sea of royal blue. Wednesday evenings when my dad has medical staff meetings, my mother and we kids relax. She finishes ironing and hangs our choir vestments on padded hangers around the kitchen like angels. She makes spaghetti with the sauce we like, the sauce without meatballs, just ground up hamburger meat and not much seasoning. Instead of a salad, she cuts up bits of carrots and cucumbers and she peels off their skin. For dessert we bake brownies, using her rich grandmother Munsy's recipe. Tina's a bundle of baby stuff, teddy bears and diapers, and a pacifier we all have to keep track of, but the rest of us work together on Munsy's brownies. Even Elizabeth. She's reading a book, *Nancy Drew* or *Pollyanna*, or *The Five Little Peppers and How They Grew*, but she reads the recipe to us as well. My mother takes charge of the double boiler, two gleaming white pots with black-trimmed edges. I pour sugar into the chocolate mixture while Claire watches and Max stirs and we lick our fingers like crazy. There's a naughty feel about those evenings, a secretive feel, as if we're doing something we shouldn't, and yet, what would that be?

I must have dozed at last because the phone blared and I started awake. It was my partner Mary, worried about me. I took a deep breath. 'I'm sorry I haven't been into the office today,' I said, and then I told her what Claire had done.

'I'll call my friend Boyce Regner,' she said immediately.

'What? You know Boyce?'

'Richard, of course I know Boyce. We're in a Host Your Own Murder club. You know, the game? I was a witness for him two years ago in that case where the college boy killed his girlfriend.'

'You were?'

'Richard, don't you remember? Hal and I were sitting at the table next to them at the Green Garden Café on West 57th and saw her flop into the Nacho cheese dip and heard the crackers crunch against her jawbone. It's all I talked about for months.'

Now I remembered. That's how I knew his name the night before. He must have recognized my connection to Mary right away. I realized I blocked out a lot of her Boyce conversations because I'd never liked the whole idea of the law. Ever since I was a kid, I'd had this idea of it as a huge force out to destroy you.

'I'm a little slow today, Mary,' I said.

'Oh, Richard, I'm sorry. Let me hang up and call Boyce right now. We just had lunch last week.'

'I called him last night. He's got her in PI and he's taking care of the bond hearing and arraignment,' I said, as if Claire's legal situation neither frightened nor intimidated me. 'I'm going in to see him this afternoon.'

When Mary said, 'What can I do to help?', I snorted, a sound that started as a laugh and almost turned into a sob. I already knew the only thing my mother would be concerned about was how it would affect her. *What will the neighbors say* I didn't see her worrying about Claire, much less me. More than ever, I would have to take charge, do Claire's talking for her, do my own talking as well. Damage control, I thought. I knew I'd have to talk to my parents within the hour, too.

'I think the next few months are going to be tough,' I said.

'Me, too,' said Mary. 'Thank God it's October and not March.'

An accountant after my own heart.

Boyce A. Regner, Attorney at Law. The letters were gold, edged in black across the mahogany door. As I stood outside the office late that Monday afternoon all geared up, I noticed every whorl of wood, every rich, dark shade. I couldn't think of a single time in my life when I'd felt this peculiar blend of fear, anger, and longing to set matters straight. I'd had time to get myself under control. I'd spent an hour at the gym, pounding the heavy bag.

The reception room had a cool, uncluttered look. The door to what was obviously the inner sanctum opened and a woman came out. She looked classy. She smiled at me and sailed out the outer door. I'd barely had time to recover from this when another woman beckoned me into Boyce's inner chambers.

I straightened my shoulders and headed inside.

This time he wasn't in blue jeans: he wore a pair of carefully pressed brown wool slacks, beige shirt, and a good-looking blue sport jacket with gold buttons. It was the type of look that people like my father and his friends had, the look I had, the look that said Wasp and got you into places like the Waterton Country Club. Even though he was a lawyer, I have to admit there was a sense of familiarity about him.

Boyce's office was nothing like his reception area. The place where he worked turned out to be what he called 'pure Boyce'. 'My wife says that, too,' he told me, 'and I can't tell if it's a compliment or not.' He had original artwork, and bookshelves holding more than law books lined the walls, floor to ceiling. *Absalom, Absalom* sat on one shelf alongside *Of Mice and Men* and a thick book of American poetry. One wall had his diplomas and I noted he'd graduated *summa cum laude* from SUNY Albany with a Bachelor of Arts degree and he'd gotten his Juris Doctor degree from the University of Michigan. Not quite Colgate, I thought, with a certain degree of satisfaction. Colgate was my alma mater, my father's alma mater, and my mother's father's alma mater. And not Yale Medical like my father, either.

We shook hands.

'I spoke to my parents this morning and told them about you and what happened with Claire and John,' I said, right off the bat, letting him know who was in charge. 'I also called PI. They wouldn't let me speak to Claire. I'll let you know when I do.'

'Claire,' said Boyce. 'That's why we're here.' He motioned me into one of the leather armchairs facing his desk. A spray of fresh flowers bloomed from a clear glass vase on one of the bookshelves. 'I've been out to see her, Richard,' he said.

I pulled at the knot on my tie. This was not going the way I'd planned.

He cleared his throat. 'Richard, she's telling me a pretty garbled story.'

the silent shadow

'She keeps talking about thirty-seven Brookfield Court,' he continued, 'and a place she calls the farm. She's talking years ago, I think.'

There was no way he could realize how incredibly ironic the situation was or have any idea that Claire had spent most of her life as silent as a corpse compared to the rest of us kids and now it was she spilling her guts. How dare she start blabbing about our family? If anyone was going to tell about the family, it would be me. It had always been me. There'd even been a few times in junior high and high school when guidance had called me in to discuss Max or Claire. It had made me feel as if I could be counted on not only to give the correct version of events, but to help map strategy for dealing with my troubled younger brother and sister.

'You'll need to hear my point of view, too,' I said.

'Absolutely. Every detail you can remember. It's the past you've got to think about, Richard. Think about why a girl like Claire would marry an abusive guy in the first place. Why would she stay married to him? Why not get a divorce? Why'd she have to kill him?' We looked at each other across his desk.

'I don't know if I can make an outsider understand,' I said.

'I don't think you have a choice if you want to help your sister.' Boyce folded his hands on top of his desk. 'You've got to remember anything that will corroborate Claire. I'll tell my secretary we'll be meeting tomorrow for your statement.'

Corroborate Claire? I didn't know what she was saying and I wasn't sure I wanted to. Every detail I could remember? Jesus Christ. I'd spent most of my life trying not to remember. Now some stranger comes along and tells me he wants every detail.

The pendulum on an antique clock tick-tocked loudly.

Boyce's phone shrilled, but he didn't pick it up. He looked at me, but I couldn't read his expression. He said, 'I may be filing a Notice of Incompetency. I'll have to decide soon.'

'What does that mean?' Why is it that lawyers have to talk this jargon? Accountants don't. We use terms like financial statement, tax return, estate planning. No secret meanings. It is what it is. 'Notice of Incompetency?' I said.

'Basically what it says is that Claire may not be competent

to assist in her own defense.' Again, that unreadable look from Boyce. 'If I decide to enter a plea of not criminally responsible by reason of insanity, I've got to do that pretty soon. It's a defense that has to be raised early. The judge'll order a psychiatric evaluation.'

'So – what are you saying?'

'I'm saying, if that's the route I go, don't underestimate your importance in your sister's defense. And, if it's not, you're probably even more important.'

Back to the old corroboration.

'I've got to bring up something else, too.' Boyce looked at me. 'My fee. This isn't going to be cheap, and there's no guarantee.'

I felt the heat in my face and the pressure of having to explain and defend my parents and, at the same time, protect my sister. I hated the bind I was in. And hated the hazy uneasiness I felt at being in a law office.

'My parents will pay for this,' I said.

Chapter Two

TUESDAY dawned bright and cold. Gone was the warmth of just two nights ago, the night John had died and I'd taken a casual stroll on the Upper East Side, enjoying the feel of leaves drifting over from the mayor's mansion. I'd been awake most of the night, worried about giving my statement. My stomach was in an uproar, and my mind raced from the farm to Brookfield Court and back to the farm again, the word corroboration lingering in my brain like a malignant tumor.

Had it been this cold on the farm in late October? Yes. The farm mornings were the coldest mornings in existence, yet some of the happiest, too. I loved the farmhouse. I still love it. It's small, nothing special, built in the 1700s, the foundation big old stones that mice nest between, running in and out like it's a fancy hotel. It's got a stone wall around it, stones still firm and in place and stone steps leading to the front door. Our maple tree grows big on the far side of the stone wall but hangs heavily into the yard, its branches thick with green leaves and climbing branches, and we climbed the stone wall and from there we stepped right onto the tree. From the top you can see for a long ways – clear to the quarry on the far side of the Steam Hollow Road.

I almost smiled through my shivering, remembering the way we kids bundled straight from beds with flannel sheets, long johns still on, and into another layer of clothes. The upstairs where we kids slept is something they keep meaning to fix up but don't. There's only one bathroom, it's on the first floor, right off my parents' bedroom, and there's a door opening into the kitchen, too. Claire and Elizabeth hate having only one bathroom and the way my father barges in whenever he feels like it, but nothing at the farm bothers me. For me, going to the farm is like coming to life, after being nothing but a wax figure in the Waterton house.

Fires heat the place, and it's never warm enough. I'm always the first kid dressed and downstairs and I race into the living room and hover in front of the blaze in the stone fireplace. The living room is a big room, running the length of the house, tattered Oriental rugs on the floor so threadbare they've got rugs beneath them.

No matter how early I get downstairs to check on the fire, my dad is up before me, rekindling its flame. If he's in the room, I'm set to carrying wood from outside to the fireplace woodbin, but if he isn't around, I stand silent as Claire, hands stretched toward the fire's warmth.

Today, in New York, there was no fire, no farm, no brothers and sisters. Just me, needing to haul myself out of my warm bed and into the shower. I wanted to feel fresh, sharp, in control, but I just couldn't get up yet. I rolled onto my back and lay there for a bit.

Today I'd give Boyce my statement. Tuesday, October 17. My father's birthday.

He'd be sixty-five years old today, and I'd sent him a card, but my guess was that the family wouldn't be doing any big-time celebrating, 'under the circumstances' as my mother referred to Claire's sojourn in the Manhattan Psych Institute in the brief conversation I had had with her the day before, after seeing Boyce. She'd said she and my father weren't certain whether to mention 'Claire's situation' to anyone outside the family. I'd told her I'd be giving a statement the next day, but I didn't know if she was listening or if she'd tuned out. Both my parents had a way of tuning out what they didn't want to know.

I wasn't surprised she referred to what had happened to Claire as 'Claire's situation'. When we were kids, they dealt with our peccadillos the same way: Max's repeated school suspensions; Elizabeth's desire to leave home to go to college in Europe; Claire's and my drug and alcohol days. All dismissed – not as youthful indiscretions, dismissed as nothing, non-events.

Tina's suicide.

I yanked at my pillow, wanting to bury myself beneath it. Tina was my baby sister, the afterthought in the family. Lay down in my parents' bed after breakfast one morning when she was barely twenty years old and used my father's .357 to blow out her brains. No one talked about it or her. She was only seven when I left for college. Now she was nothing but an empty space in my heart, a picture removed from atop my mother's piano, an ash-filled vase locked inside the family vault.

With a fast jerk and wild fling of covers, I got up. No time to dwell on the past, I told myself. Enough of that at Boyce's office. I stripped off my boxers and T-shirt and stood naked in the middle of the room. I flexed my shoulders, stretched my neck, took a deep breath. If Boyce wanted to hear about the family, today was his lucky day.

I sat in Boyce's waiting room at 8.45 a.m. sharp. Boyce's door opened, and out came the same woman I'd seen yesterday. She was really pretty – slender, blond shoulder-length hair, an air of quiet confidence. He followed her out and put his hand on her shoulder. 'He won't win on this, Sam,' I heard him say.

'Are you sure?' She had to look up to talk to him, and I sensed a certain frustration in her demeanor. Had Boyce let her down at some point in the past? Told her she'd win and, instead, 'he' did – whoever 'he' was?

Boyce dropped his hand. 'I told you at the time, nothing is carved in stone, Sam. But we were a hundred percent right as far as the law's concerned. The judge had no business making that decision. I told you, you should have appealed. We would have won.' No question her words frustrated him. It was in his voice, in the way he stepped back from her, in the way he cleared his throat when he finished.

'I'd had enough.' The woman's voice was low and assured. 'All this has dragged on and on. I want the whole thing over this time. Forever.' Sam — I assumed that was her name — didn't sound whiny or pissed off, just certain of what she wanted. And what she wanted was for her legal problems, whatever they were, to be over.

I knew exactly how she felt. What felt different was that she didn't seem diminished by Boyce's status as lawyer. It looked to me as if she knew how to push Boyce's buttons, and for reasons I didn't understand I'd always thought of lawyers as all powerful. I don't like admitting it, but I know that's why I resented having to answer to Boyce. It didn't matter that maybe I sort of liked the guy; he was a lawyer.

This time it was she who touched Boyce's shoulder. 'I'll take care of the financial statements by next week,' she said. 'Don't worry. See you in court.'

A quick smile to me, a wave to the secretary, and she was gone.

'Richard, everything's all set,' said Boyce, from his office doorway. 'The court reporter ought to be here by nine thirty. I want to talk with you before she gets here.'

I cleared my throat with an authoritative kind of growl to sound as tough as I could. I wiped my still damp hands on my pants and followed Boyce into his office. Like the night of the murder, I felt curiously detached from my surroundings, as if I had stepped into an episode of *Twilight Zone*.

'I'm going to be honest with you, Richard.' Boyce's voice was soft. 'I haven't made up my mind what we're going to plead yet. Temporary insanity's always risky. So is not criminally responsible. Right now in New York's political climate it's riskier than usual. Manslaughter's a possibility, but I can tell you, whatever we do, you're vital. Claire is too unstable right now. She's lacking credibility.'

'What's she telling you?' My gut clamped tight with tension.

'About Brookfield Court,' said Boyce. 'About the farm. She's telling me a pretty wild tale about your dad.'

I felt that curious detachment again, a pulsebeat of anger lurking beneath. 'What?' I asked, my words seeming to come from far away. 'What's she saying?'

Boyce looked right at me. 'That's not important right now, Richard. What's important now is your story of life in the Hayes family. We're going to piece together Claire's puzzle. Starting at the beginning.'

Boyce's intercom bleeped: 'Edna Morgan is here. She's all set.'

I trailed Boyce out of his office, nodded abruptly at Edna Morgan, and followed both of them into a big windowless room with an oval table in the middle. No comforting Oriental rugs here. Instead, Boyce had installed thick, navy-blue carpet. Dark textured paper on the walls. Edna, the court reporter, plunked herself at the head of the table, a machine propped in front of her.

Boyce closed the door.

I wished I was anywhere but in this conference room. It reminded me of my dad's den – a curiously dark, dank little room in the otherwise spacious Brookfield Court house. The walls were painted navy and had a thin stream of gold wallpaper running along the molding. Part of his extensive gun collection served as wall adornments. His rare three-barreled shotgun was mounted over the door. Deer heads decorated the remaining walls. The only furniture was his desk, a swivel chair and a long, low couch slipcovered in a navy-blue plaid. It's where we had our little father–son talks that, until I'd stepped into Boyce's navy-blue conference room, I'd pushed right out of my mind.

23

One conversation came back to me as vividly as if I was in that den. He's sitting in his swivel chair, wearing a suit and tie. I'm about thirteen years old and I'm standing. Already I'm pushing six feet, but I feel like a midget. My heart's pounding.

'So,' my dad says, 'your mother tells me you attended a sex-education class today at school.'

I'm gangly and clumsy and sweaty. My dad and I might hunt together, but we don't talk about this kind of stuff. I can't believe he said the word sex at all. I want the floor to open up and swallow me. I want to run outside and play ball. Even though I know this is all for my own good.

'Right,' I say, looking at my feet, ashamed.

'What did you learn?' He's using what my brothers and sisters and I call his empathy voice, the one where he leads you down a path of kindness and then calls a sudden halt. Bam! You've walked into a wall. Max says he does it on purpose, but I don't think so.

'I don't know.' Me and my buddies Jay and Chris laughed ourselves silly afterwards, Chris putting his hand to his dick all through English class, closing his eyes and looking wildly excited every time Ms Little turned her back.

'You must have learned something,' he says, the empathetic tone disappearing.

'Masturbation,' I say. 'I learned about masturbation.'

'You don't want to masturbate,' my father says to me, as I stand before him. 'You can become addicted and then you won't be able to have a proper relationship with your wife.'

'Okay,' I mumble, and start to fumble my way to the closed door and he says, 'I want you to sit in this chair, Richard, until I tell you to leave.'

I sit, the specter of masturbation looming between us.

'Richard?' A note of irritation laced Boyce's voice. 'Edna's ready. Let's go. Begin at the beginning.'

I saw Edna Morgan poise her fingertips over the recording machine. I saw Boyce look at his plain gold watch.

I wished my brother Max, the family soothsayer, was here.

24

He'd severed ties with the family after Tina's death, unwilling to talk even to me, but I knew what he'd say: 'So, you're going to tell our story, Richard?' He'd laugh. 'Yeah, right. And some judge is going to buy it. Give me a break. You going to tell him about Munsy's money? How about King of the Mountain? You going to tell about the H-Man?' I could picture him saying, 'What about the farm? Think a New York City judge'll believe that farmhouse?'

Edna stared at me.

Boyce grinned. 'Give it to me. Mom and Dad Hayes. Thirty-seven Brookfield Court. The farm. Claire, Max, Elizabeth, Tina. The whole gang.'

Okay, Claire, I said to myself, this one's for you. I didn't think about the possibility of doing it for myself. I knew I'd be walking a fine line between saying what might be best for Claire and, on the other hand, what my parents expected me to say. I think it was this balancing act that set off the anger which had thumped inside me ever since Claire's phone call. Besides, as far as I was concerned, the past was past, over, *finis*.

And lawyers had no place in our lives except as overseers of trusts or estate planning or property exchanges.

And there was no room anywhere for a mental institution.

Thump . . . thump

'You all set, Edna?' I said, biting the bullet. 'I'll start with my dad. Jack Hayes.' I closed my eyes, looking toward a past I thought I'd put behind me.

'He's graduated from Yale Med School, an obstetrician gynecologist,' I said, 'a guy who makes lots of money, a big practice, chief of staff, an important man around the southern New York state town of Waterton, population forty thousand tops. My mother Bev comes from a long line of important people – mostly judges scattered around New York state. Everyone in town knows Bev and Jack. On the outside, they lead this life like they're supposed to: big house, children, social life, church every week.'

'What's the Waterton house like?' Boyce said.

I'd made the visit home three years ago for Tina's funeral, but I didn't need that visit to jog my memory.

'It's a typical big suburban house in an upscale neighborhood,' I told him. 'The address is thirty-seven Brookfield Court. Lots of shady maple trees, all the houses red-brick and two-story. Max and I take care of our yard with its grassy acre, but others in the neighborhood hire gardeners.'

By now, we'd removed our jackets and loosened our ties.

'Anything ever go on in that Waterton house that the neighbors might have talked about?' Boyce spiked out that question as if he was Pete Rose sliding across home plate. I felt defensive as hell. This was my family he was talking about, and I thought I should set the tone, not him. After all, my family was paying him; he was working for us.

Thump

I tightened my tie. 'I don't know. I guess there was tension between Bev and Jack.'

Boyce softened his tone. 'Was your father ever violent? Did he hit your mother?'

With a sense of foreboding, I wondered again what Claire had been telling him. I'd never been to a therapist, but I figured they kept their voices calm to try to get you to confide stuff you didn't want to – just like Boyce. My father might have been a bit of a bastard, but he was still my father.

Honor thy father and thy mother

'For God's sake, Boyce,' I said, 'the man was human, if that's what you mean.'

Boyce looked at me. 'Remember anything specific? Christmas? A particular birthday or dinner hour?'

A birthday. Sure I could tell him about a birthday. 'My mother bought him a tie for his birthday one year,' I said, feeling less pressured. 'She sends away to a mail-order place for a tie that says, "Damn, I'm Good." When she shows it to us, Elizabeth exchanges a look with me and says, "Are you sure it's a good idea, Mom?" and, after a pause, my mother says, "It's a joke, right? It'll be okay." Claire says nothing,

26

Max laughs, and we all look at my mother. She looks back and then she says, "Damn, I'm Good," and we burst into laughter before I challenge my siblings to a quick game of red-light, green-light which I win.

'She sets it in a fancy box at his place at the dinner table. We kids sit straight in our assigned seats, not an elbow in sight, and from the record player come the muted strains of *Camelot*. She's got the heavy brocade drapes opened so neighbors can look in and see the happy Hayes family. The whole room smells of rich gravy and browned potatoes. I watch my father and force myself to swallow chunks of roast leg of lamb and bits of jiggly mint green jelly.'

As I told Boyce the story, I realized I was getting almost as agitated as I'd felt on that long ago birthday, fearing my father's unpredictable temper.

I am on watch

I pushed down my cuticles, squeezing my knuckles. 'We're waiting for him to open Mom's present,' I said. 'I look at Claire. Two spots of bright color bloom bright on her white face. I feel Max and Elizabeth's eyes on me. Tina's got her hands wrapped around her plastic bottle. I touch my spoon with the tip of my right baby finger, a signal we've worked out that says, "It's going to be okay."

'He opens the thin oblong box. Off comes the lid. Beneath crisp red tissue paper lies the tie – navy blue with red letters: "Damn, I'm Good, Damn, I'm Good, Damn, I'm Good." I glance at my mother. Her eyes are bright, but I see her lips trembling. So's her hand on the sherry glass. It's so quiet that when Tina's bottle slips from her chubby fingers it lands on the floor with a shotgun blast.

'Still he says nothing.

'I watch him finger the tie. It's lined in blood-red silk.

'He leans toward my mother. My teeth clench. Then I see he's kissing her on the cheek. "I am, aren't I, Bev?" he says. She smiles back at him. There's love and a tentative sense that it might reach as far as my seat at the table. The moment smells

27

like warm cinnamon buns and I think the love might ooze sugary white frosting across the room. He stretches his arm toward me . . .'

I stopped talking. I could barely breathe. Boyce raised his arm, extending the water pitcher toward me. I put up a swift hand to protect myself. Jesus, for a minute I'd thought he was going to haul me off and smack me. I might just as well have been at the dinner table twenty odd years ago. It wasn't just Boyce's raised arm, it was the whole scene, the tension, the not knowing what might happen.

Anything might happen

'My father laughed and tousled my hair,' I told Boyce, taking a deep breath. I wanted him to see how kind my dad could be, how much my imagination might have distorted reality. "You're not scared of an old man, are you?" he says, with a grin that shows his gold bridge. "You think your wife will give you a tie like this one day, Richard?" he adds, and we kids smile at each other, but there's an undercurrent to his voice, and I wonder why I don't feel so good.

'Later, Max tells me it's a sex thing, but Elizabeth says it was a challenge. "You know," she says, "like the male gorilla's always got to establish his turf? He just wants to make sure you understand who's the head gorilla." And surprisingly Claire speaks up and says, "That's what Max said, a sex thing."'

Boyce made a sound like a snort. 'Max sounds pretty smart to me, Richard.'

I looked at him.

'Claire doesn't sound incompetent, either.' There was something in Boyce's voice I couldn't identify, but I did know it wasn't sympathy for me.

No one at this table was going to tap a spoon with his baby finger at me.

Anything might happen

I don't know what Edna did for lunch, but Boyce hurried off to a luncheon meeting. I called Mary and asked her to meet me. When she was upset with her husband Hal or one of her many relatives, she'd blow off steam to me, and right now I felt like blowing off steam. Boyce and his questions had pissed me off, and I guess I was still angry with Claire, too, for forcing me into this position. Why couldn't she have just walked out? Johanna did, and it was a lot easier. My parents might not talk about my divorce, but silence was a whole heck of a lot easier than stirring up all these wiggling worms from the past. I could almost see Max exploding into the limelight with some spectacular crime of passion, but Claire?

'So,' Mary said, as soon as we settled at our booth at Verymore's, a place midtown with good hamburgers and thick chicken sandwiches, 'did Boyce ferret out the family secrets? Is the Hayes family wrung inside out? Is Jack a cross-dresser and Bev really a man?'

I wasn't taken aback. I'd known Mary a long time. We'd worked together at Hammond, Hammond, and Dailey before we left to set up our own accounting firm. Although she was a good twenty years older than I, we got along great. I liked her because she'd never been a kiss-up at Hammond's, she had great technical knowledge of tax law in contrast to my audit expertise, and she was as dedicated to our clients as I was. She brought in a lot of business through her devotion to the Catholic church, her clientele from Hammond's, and her huge dysfunctional family. Mary wasn't somebody to wallow in life's tribulations, and she'd had enough herself that her comments about mine made me laugh. The thing that amazed me was the readiness with which Mary'd spill her childhood stories. I parceled mine out, careful to edit. One of my family's rules was that you kept family business to yourself.

'You know what?' I said. 'I just might be able to get through giving my statement, save Claire, and keep my parents from having a breakdown because their kids betrayed the family secrets to a lawyer, of all people.' I took a bite of hamburger. 'I've just given Boyce background stuff so far, and he hasn't pushed too hard. Not that he's got any right to, anyway. He

29

says Claire's spilling her guts, but maybe he's saying that to get me going. Who knows?'

'What is your problem with lawyers?' A glob of chicken fell from Mary's sandwich onto the checkered tablecloth. 'Oh, I know you've told me that ever since you were a kid, you've had this thing, but it's ridiculous at this point. You must realize that, Richard. They're professionals, just like you or me. More professional. They've got more education and they make more money, so what is it?'

At that moment, the door to the restaurant swung open with a blast of chilly air. Boyce and three other men entered Verymore's. Our booth was second from the door, certainly within earshot. I could see him; Mary had her back to him. My mouth full of hamburger, I shook my head at her, hoping she'd be quiet.

'You're being an ass, Richard,' announced Mary, and there was no doubt Boyce heard her and recognized her voice as well. He looked right at me and grinned while Mary kept up her spiel: 'You're stuck on some long ago distrust of lawyers and here's your poor sister needing you to get over it. For God's sake, Richard, Claire's gone and murdered her husband. She's got to be desperate. She needs you to tell the truth, all of it, without your usual deletions. Boyce is her attorney, not your enemy, you idiot.'

'You tell him, Mary.' A hostess was seating Boyce's cronies, but he stood beside our booth, a big smile on his face. I felt incredibly stupid.

Mary burst out laughing. She motioned to him to squeeze in beside her and he did. 'So here you are, Mary,' he said, 'involved in another murder. What is it with you, anyway?'

She just shook her head. 'Designing my own office How to Host a Murder,' she said, still laughing. 'Looks as if I'm one up on you, Boyce.'

I continued to sit there feeling stupid.

'Oh?' said Boyce. 'You mean you killed John?'

'Framed Claire, too,' Mary told him. 'Wanted to get ol''

Richard here on the hot seat.' She must have seen the look on my face, then, because even though she laughed again, she leaned across the table and touched my arm. 'Sometimes I think it's better to laugh, Richard, that's all.'

No one understood Mary's sense of humor better than I did, and I know I should have agreed with her, laughed, set everyone at ease, but I couldn't. A tense little silence settled over our booth. I saw Mary and Boyce look at each other.

Boyce glanced at his watch and stood up. 'Nice seeing you, Mary. Call me. We'll do lunch.' Then that grin again. 'Keep reading Richard the riot act,' he said. He couldn't get that grin off his face. 'We'll chart new territory this afternoon.' With a wave, he headed across the restaurant to where the men he came in with were seated.

Now it was Mary's and my turn to look at each other. I knew she was getting ready to say something, maybe an apology, maybe more of the same. I don't know. I set my hamburger down on the plate and turned away from her to look out the window. I felt the heat in my face. It may have been anger; it may have been embarrassment. Maybe both. Or maybe a sense of the situation being out of control.

'I'm sorry, Richard, if I embarrassed you. You know I'm right though.' Mary's voice was gentle. 'Open up to Boyce. He's a good guy. I know him. Don't be a jerk. Don't hold anything back if it'll help Claire.'

I thought about how much like my brother Max Mary sounded. Full of advice. Maybe all this heart-on-your-sleeve shit works for them, I told myself, but I'm doing this my way.

I turned around and looked straight at Mary. 'So,' I said, 'have we heard anything back on the bid from Flaherty Corporation?'

She started nodding in that way she has, a way that makes me feel about ten years old, and I swear, if she'd said one more thing about Boyce or Claire or me or my family, I would have gotten up and left.

'Well?' I said.

I watched her register my anger and I could almost feel her deciding to let me lead her away from Boyce and the family. We spent the remainder of our lunch chatting calmly about a corporate financial statement I was working on, a long-outstanding bill from a divorcée who had the money to pay, and an estate that had been in litigation for over a year. By the time she'd eaten her last bite of chocolate amaretto cheesecake and I'd scooped the last glop of chocolate mint chip ice cream from a parfait glass, an amicable, even productive, atmosphere reigned.

She got up to leave first. I told her to leave the tab, I'd get it. She laughed at that. 'You mean, Hayes and Lintini'll get it, don't you?' She pulled on leather gloves and gave me a long look. 'Behave yourself this afternoon, Richard,' is all she said, though, before hurrying off to the subway. Thick red lipstick stained her water glass. My mother always blotted her lips with Kleenex. As I watched her gray-suited figure sway away, I wondered what life might have been like had she been my mother.

Boyce still sat across the room when I gathered my coat, paid the tab, and left.

I thought it would be unbearably awkward to sit down opposite Boyce in his conference room that afternoon. I feared he might laugh or clap me on the back and say something like, 'That's some partner you got there, ol' buddy!' But he didn't mention our lunch meeting at all. Edna, Boyce, and I simply settled down to business. Within the hour, I felt we three had been together for years, each other's habits already ingrained. About three o'clock, he switched from Waterton to the farm.

Relieved, I loosened my tie. I liked talking about the farm. 'The farm,' I said, 'was separate from the rest of our existence. No doctoring, no cocktail parties, no neighbors, no assigned table seats, no silver napkin rings. The farm's in the foothills of the Blue Ridge Mountains. He bought it and all the land surrounding it when I was almost three. A thousand acres. Elizabeth was one year old, Claire a baby, and Max and Tina weren't born yet.'

'How did it fit in with your everyday existence?'

'They had a schedule set up,' I said. 'We visited the farm every other weekend, fall, winter, spring. In the summertime, my mother and the kids lived at the farm while my dad stayed in town and practiced medicine.'

'Where is it exactly? How far from Waterton?'

'It's in the Steam Hollow Valley on the Steam Hollow Road, four hours or so from our place in Waterton,' I said. 'It's not much – a white farmhouse, a weathered gray barn at the far end of the meadow beyond the backyard, dilapidated sheds, a new machinery barn right next to the house. Hurricane Hazel blew down the old barn and we kids played in the wreckage before the new one was built. A rickety staircase led straight from the ground to nowhere, and we liked the idea of a random staircase out in the open air.'

Once started on the farm, I didn't want to stop. When did I ever get a chance to tell somebody how much I loved that place? Who in my current life was interested? Johanna never was. She grew up in Manhattan and had no interest in farming whatsoever. Here was someone demanding to know about it. I let down my guard a little. 'Right inside the front door is the kitchen,' I said. 'The table's the centerpiece, but there's a back section to this room and there's a stove, dark brown and shiny and it opens from the top only. You put coal in it and a hot fire burns and heats the house in winter. That's in addition to the fireplace in the living room where we keep a roaring fire when it's cold. Sometimes my dad sizzles steaks and potatoes in the fireplace and afterwards we pop popcorn in a mesh popcorn-popper cage and it's the best popcorn in the world.'

'You sound like a kid,' said Boyce. He'd loosened his tie, too.

33

I realized that there was no one in the world, except maybe Max and Claire, who knew what the farm had meant to me. 'Claire loves it, too,' I said.

'I think you're right, Richard.'

Feeling less defensive, I took a deep breath and said, 'One time Max and I were alone at the farmhouse fooling around in the living room. In town, we're not allowed in the living room, but at the farm, it's okay. My mother even lets us play my great-grandmother Munsy's huge old pump organ that's pressed against one wall.

'That afternoon, Duke Ellington and his band are blasting away on our old Victrola. Outside, the wind's blowing fierce and wild, and that's the way both Max and I feel. Max is doing a dance routine he's invented that takes him from one end of the living room to another, and up and over the couch, a chair and the organ bench, as well. It's early spring and through the windows we see leaves doing a crazed dance of their own. Cootie Williams bursts into the "East St Louis Toodle-oo" and chills thrill my whole body. I spend hours that afternoon aching to imitate Hootey on my trumpet, seeking to replicate those piercing sounds as Max tippety-tap-taps his way around the room. Sweat drips into my eyes, onto my trumpet. Max removes his shirt and pants, turning into a blur of white jockey shorts.

'We never hear my father's Land Rover spin into the gravelly drive. Nor his footsteps through the house. Only his silence in the living-room doorway. He looks at us, saying nothing at first. "You two remind me of your mother," he says at last, and turns on his heel. Max manages another pirouette or two around the room, raising his arms high above his head, middle fingers pointed to the sky, but I wipe off my horn and lay it in its coffin-like case.'

I looked at Boyce. Something in his face made me say, 'The guy didn't like music that much. Not everybody does. It's not a crime.'

Boyce said nothing.

'Dancing isn't exactly something a dad wants for his son. You've got to admit that.'

'Claire says he didn't support her painting. She says your great-grandmother Munsy was the only adult in the family who acted as if what you kids wanted mattered. She says Munsy'd invite you kids to visit and give you free reign of her house.'

I had to smile. Munsy'd lived in a rambling mansion, a house on the Susquehanna River with four sets of stairways that Claire, Max and I spent hours chasing each other up and down whenever we visited. She had a cook named Alice who made us anything we wanted for lunch – grilled cheese or chili dogs, macaroni and cheese or the best turkey tetrazzini in the land. Munsy'd tell us endless stories about the past, often the same one five times straight beginning each time as if she'd never told it before. Her creaky voice sounded just fine in my ears, like an A sharp on my trumpet.

I felt safe at her house.

Boyce's voice interrupted my thoughts. 'Claire says Munsy had a lot of money and that when she died some fifteen years ago, your parents said little or nothing about her death to you kids. She says they didn't even have a funeral, only a small memorial service without so much as a eulogy.'

'That's the Episcopalian way, isn't it?' I said, trying to hide my anger at Claire's talking to Boyce. It seemed unbelievable to me that Claire was telling Boyce all this private family information.

'Claire told me that Munsy was one of the early investors in IBM, Richard.'

The only place Boyce could have learned that fact was from Claire. He wasn't bullshitting me. The silent shadow had turned into a veritable blabbermouth. I tightened my tie, cleared my throat, wanting to get back on safe territory. I could describe the farm indefinitely. Munsy was an unresolved issue for me, and ever since I was a kid I'd had a vague unpleasant idea that Munsy and money were tied up together and money was something I'd been taught that polite people don't discuss. Clients were one thing: I was terrific at advising them about their money and discreet as hell besides. My family's money was an entirely different matter. My parents refused to have me do their income taxes; they had their own accountant. Talk of money had always been taboo at our house. That silent Claire had broken that inviolate rule with Boyce, not only an outsider but a paid outsider, put me back on the defensive. How dare she?

What else had she told Boyce

'Claire says Elizabeth thinks Munsy left you kids her money.'

I could feel my face getting red. 'Jesus, Boyce,' I said, a sarcastic note creeping into my voice. 'What makes Claire such a reliable source? Miss P I herself. It's been my experience that heirs have to be notified. Max took the money my father'd set aside for him years ago when he left home. There wasn't much. Max, with his big mouth, would have said something if there was. I'm sure of that.'

'Maybe the estate got settled after Max took his money.'

'Still, as heirs, we would have to be notified.'

'Not if you all were minors. Claire says Elizabeth says you were. She says the will may have stipulated you have to be twenty-five before inheriting it. She says they've talked about it quite a bit over the years.'

This whole discussion was beginning to piss me off. I didn't want to think about it or what it might mean. I couldn't believe all this talk of money was going on among family members and I didn't know about it. Beneath my anger, I suppose I was hurt, too. How was it that my sisters were talking to each other about this family stuff and not to me?

'So what?' I demanded. 'What difference does it make? It was a long time ago.'

'So, there should have been plenty of money to support anything any of you wanted to do. Your music, for instance,' Boyce said, looking straight at me.

'Look,' I said, an edge to my voice, 'I thought you wanted

36

me to describe the farm. Munsy has nothing to do with the farm.' I felt my shirt sticking to my back. This business of Munsy and her money had gone as far as I intended it to go. Like all the rest of Claire's and my story, Munsy's death was unfinished business.

'Right. The farm. Keep talking,' said Boyce.

I couldn't erase the feeling that this talk of Munsy was a portent of something disagreeable, so I wasted no time launching into further description of the farm: 'There's two doors off the kitchen,' I told Boyce. 'One leads into what ought to be a dining room, but it's not. It's my parents' bedroom. There's a pistol on top of his dresser, shotguns hanging on walls, a well-oiled twenty-two hooked by wires over the bed frame.'

I knew I was talking too fast, giving irrelevant details, but I felt pressured, and I wanted to keep control of the situation.

'Tunnels run the length of the house,' I blurted, 'but the only way to get to them is through a secret closet at the top of the stairs. The tunnels have chamber pots and water pitchers. Max and I haul out two chamber pots, clean them and keep them under our beds.

'I remember one time racing upstairs to grab my fishing pole and catching Max flinging piss from his pot out the window. It hissed straight into the gutters and down, spraying straight into my father's precious grape arbor. Max snatched my piss pot out from under my bed and tried handing it to me, but I wouldn't take it.'

Honor thy father and thy mother

For a second, I wondered how it might have felt to dump piss on my father's grape arbor.

'Sounds like a place in the sun, Richard,' Boyce said. 'Dancing, pissing, the best food in the world. What else did you tell me about? Crackling fires? Secret tunnels?'

'Don't push me, Boyce.' My damn tie was choking me.

I saw him put his hand on Edna's to stop her everlasting clickety-click-clacking. 'Let's take a break,' he said.

Edna had that machine folded up in an instant. 'I don't work past three thirty,' she said, 'unless you want to pay overtime fees.'

'I don't.' I needed to get out of there. Boyce and I shook hands and I agreed to continue the next day at 9 a.m., but I didn't hang around to chat. I was out the door quicker than Edna and walking fast toward home. All I seemed able to focus on was Claire's big mouth. I knew I was supposed to be feeling sorry for her and I did, but I also felt rage: How dare she dredge up the past like this?

How dare she

As I hurried uptown, I remembered only one other time in my life when I'd felt so angry with Claire. It came to me in a flash from the past, a memory I'd thought disintegrated long ago. I'd always felt bad about my anger that night, yet here it was swallowing me up again, as fast or faster than my feet led me home.

It's a cold February Friday night. Dad has gone out to the farm earlier in the day to get fires going and pump primed.

Mom takes us kids out of school at lunchtime and drives us to the farm in that smelly old station wagon with the dog Buddy and the food in those cardboard cartons she used time after time and this time she had a cake too. A yellow sheet cake with thick fudge frosting. She serves it up on paper plates at the farm on Friday nights. I love that cake. It oozes right through those skinny plates, leaving an oily spot on the bottom. Butter, I guess.

We get there about five and the Steam Hollow Road is icy and Mom nearly wrecks a dozen times and snow's piled up high on either side of the road like a fence. We can't see over the snow. Just snow and cold and our tires sliding back and forth and Mom's hands white on the wheel.

It's one of those Fridays when Dad broils a steak over the fireplace and Mom pulls corn-on-the-cob out of the freezer to surprise us. The living room smells of steak and burning wood and all our faces flush with the heat. Everyone has eaten a piece of that buttery cake and, one by one, I toss the paper plates into the fire. Mom sits close beside Max on the couch, her head on his shoulder. I don't care: Dad likes me the best. I know it.

I know it for sure after supper that night when the whole family is enjoying the fire, toasting marshmallows, and watching Dad out of the corner of their eyes as he drinks a Jim Beam, then two, then three. We're holding our breath now, waiting to see if the good dad disappears, the bad dad taking his place.

Tonight is different. My mother gathers glasses and silverware, heads for the kitchen. An 'Oh, no' sweeps from the kitchen into the living room, and my dad motions me to go see what's the matter. We've run out of water. Back I go to the living room to tell my dad. I'm a little afraid – will he be angry? Will he and I have to storm from the house, trudge up the creek to the spring and check on the elaborate water-pumping system he's rigged? It's so cozy here at the house and so cold and dark outside.

'No water, Dad,' I say from the living-room doorway.

I see everybody avert their eyes. I know they're trying to avoid danger, but no problem tonight. This is how I know I'm Dad's favorite: He chuckles, sips his drink, and says, 'So, Richard, want to go up to the spring on your own? Might be iced over and you'll need a pickax to get it flowing again.' He waits a beat and says, 'Or do you want to go down in the cellar and haul up a bucket of water to get us through tonight? We could check out the spring in the morning.'

Use the cistern in the basement? Me? We kids are rarely allowed in that dark, dank cellar. He's never let anyone but himself near that round wooden tub he built to store extra water for emergencies. A thick sheet of clear plastic covers the vat to keep out spiders and coal dust and rats and dirt that sifts through the floor above it, and he's got the buckets stored upside down and covered with clear plastic as well.

'Me?' I say. 'You want just me to go down there?' I look

around at the other kids to see if they're paying attention. See, Max, I want to say, he's trusting me to go down in that cellar. Let Mom lay her head on your shoulder all you like: I'm the one assigned the manly duties.

My father takes another swig of his drink. 'No, Richard,' he says, smiling widely, 'I want the other kids to sit on the steps and watch you. I want them to see how to get a water bucket in an emergency.'

Wow! 'Okay,' I say, and motion to the others.

I have to admit, I'm a little scared. I have to go down into the basement to get to the light switch. It is dark and smells of coal from the coal bin, a black pit in that already dank cellar. The cistern is around the corner beneath the rickety staircase and as soon as I open the door to go down into the cellar, I hear the steady tink, tink, tink of dripping water. Elizabeth, Max, and Claire are hot on my heels.

I do not want to go down those shaky steps in the dark, but I do. The air is damp and I'm certain a rat will leap on me or a cobweb choke me with its sticky thread. Still, I make it down the steps, past the coal bin to the outside door. I can hear giggling from my brother and sisters, which really angers me. I push open the outside door and step into the night for a breath of fresh air. It's cold, maybe 20 degrees outside, and a nasty chill wind sweeps through the valley. The moon's a sliver above the huge oak with the wooden swing dangling at the end.

'Richard! Come on!' It's all of them hollering for me.

I snap the light switch. Nothing. I try again. No luck. I'll have to get the water in the dark. I don't think about a flashlight; I just want to get out of this cellar. I am getting angrier by the minute.

I close the outside door and move slowly past the coal bin once more and take cautious steps around those ratty stairs to where I know the cistern is. The plastic sheet catches me in the eye and as I reach to push it away, I feel its slick dampness and wonder if my hand is coated in slime. I push away the

40

sheet and grab a bucket and feel around the vat until I find the spout.

'Hurry up! Richard! Hurry up!' It's Max and I'm certain I hear Claire's voice chiming in as well.

'I'm coming!' I holler, in the meanest voice I've got. I move back toward the stairs, both hands clutching the bucket. It's really scary in this stupid cellar, and I want to get out as fast as I can.

The staircase is completely dark. Someone's closed the door into the house so that no light shines down to help me. I hear giggles and I feel the rage swelling inside me. How dare they make fun of me?

I reach the door and balance the water pail on the top step. I feel the heat in my face as I push against the door. They've locked me out. I hear them laughing. *How dare they*

I smash my fist against the door. Once, twice, again. 'Open it,' I demand, and soon it swings open, and I step into the house carrying my bucket. Claire and Max and Elizabeth all grin at me.

I want to kill them.

Instead, I hurry to the kitchen with my fucking bucket and hand it to my mother, who is busily wiping off counter tops, and I turn to my brother and sisters who have followed me into the kitchen and say, 'We're playing King of the Mountain,' and Max says to me, 'You look just like Dad with that vein popping out on your forehead.'

I want to punch him, but I see my father coming around the corner from the living room, so I don't. I want to punch Claire and Elizabeth, too. I watch as my father moves into the kitchen and slings his arm around my mother.

'I said we're playing King of the Mountain,' I hiss, and grab ice skates from the huge cardboard boot box by the kitchen door. I've got matches in my pocket and firewood's already stacked by the pond's edge.

Out the back door I slam and across the rickety wooden bridge my dad and I built the summer before, clitter-clatter, and I'm now at the edge of the lower pond, its ice a pale gray gleam in the night. Up, up, up the hill we go, our breath a poof of white mist and we're there – at the upper pond. Only the stars and the moon light it for us and it's a sweep of smoothness, no stones or rocks or brambles.

I get a fire blazing in no time, our eyes adjust to the dark and it's into our skates and out onto the ice. I've not spoken to any of them. It's cold and the cold is in our mouths and eyes.

I stand at one end of the pond and I holler out, 'I'm King of the Mountain. Catch me if you can!' And there's a skitter of skates and frost on the ice and we Hayes kids are all over the pond. Claire's the only one as fast as I am.

That night, the night Max and Claire and Elizabeth laughed at me, no one catches me. I'm so angry inside I want to bust. I keep flashing my long silver blades and I bend down low, my arms behind me and I fly around that pond as fast as Zorro, screaming, 'I'm King of the Mountain, I'm King of the Mountain,' and I can feel the heat in my face and around and around I go, King of the Mountain.

No one can catch me that night. Claire doesn't even get close, and so I decide it's time for jumping the barrels Dad brought up there for us a month or two ago, but first I tell Max to build up the fire until flames dash across the sky and Elizabeth says it's a message from God.

The heat in my face is burning me and I challenge Max and Claire and Elizabeth to barrel-jumping and I know Elizabeth and Max don't want to but I know they're afraid to say so. I see it in their faces but I don't care. They help me set up barrel one and no one is having the slightest trouble seeing. In fact, the night light dazzles me. I feel as if I need sunglasses. All four of us jump the first barrel with room to spare.

We line up two barrels now, side by side in the center of the ice and one at a time we hurtle across the ice and whoosh! Up and over! Only this time Elizabeth and Max crash and I can tell Max has really hurt himself. Good, I think.

Now it's Claire's turn. I always make everybody go ahead

of me, so I'll have an idea of the competition. I make the rules and the younger kids follow them.

Claire gears up for the big jump and she's cold, I can tell. She's cold, clean through her Eddie Bauer jacket with its mouton fur collar, and I know that if I was beside her I'd see that her lips are blue and her face white and her ears aching and she'd have that ice-cubey feeling inside her forehead. She bends down and flies over the ice and right over both barrels, landing on her feet, and skates off to the fire side of the pond in triumph. I'm hot on her heels and I manage the same jump, same landing, and I join her at the fire. I look at her and she looks away.

Now it's three barrels and in a scrape of ice and a blurry dash we're both up and over with room to spare. My lungs are starting to hurt with the effort and the cold. I hope Claire's are, too. I do not want to lose.

Claire gets over four barrels and I don't and I start to hate her in that moment and I scream, 'I hate you! I hate you!' at her and my voice is echoing through the Steam Hollow Valley like a treed coon's deathcry and Claire looks at me as if her world has crashed down around her feet and I half expect the ice to crack and crumble and her to fall beneath its depths, only that doesn't happen. She's a sphinx, and all I can think is how dare she beat me?

Which is exactly what I was thinking these many years later. How dare she jockey me into this losing position? I'd slowed to a normal pace and I paused now to catch my breath. I really felt sick, my own anger sickening me. I wanted to help Claire. I loved Claire. How had things managed to go so wrong? How had the past surfaced after so many years like some Spanish galleon decayed beyond repair?

By the time I got to my apartment, it was all I could do to manage all those steps. I felt very old and out on a limb and like I'd like to be anybody but who I was.

How dare she

★

One message lit my answering machine. My mother, rattling on about the stress of 'Claire's situation', and she hoped I'd remember when I talked to this lawyer that whatever I said reflected on the whole family. In the background, she had the same old record player she'd played when we were kids squawking show tunes mercilessly.

God, I realized in a rush, I hated show tunes. She'd dripped their syrup over my whole life. I unplugged the damn answering machine and glared at it. Would I ever be able to get her voice out of my ears?

Whatever you say reflects on the whole family, the whole family, family

Chapter Three

B Y the time I staggered up my apartment steps from a run, it was dark. My hands and feet were ice, my chest burning with the heat of the run, and the tip of my nose numb. My feelings were numbed by then, too. I would just have to keep putting one foot in front of the other and get through the mire Claire had created when she murdered John.

I could hear my phone ringing through my locked door and fumbling with my keys, I managed to walk inside, just in time to hear the click as someone hung up.

I took a shower.

I'd no sooner stepped dripping onto the bath mat when the phone jangled again. I wrapped a towel around my waist and snatched up the receiver.

'Yo, bro,' I heard.

I laughed, unbelieving. 'Max?' I hadn't heard from him in over three years. He'd disappeared into San Francisco's nether world after Tina's death.

'None other than the Belle Dame Sans Merci.'

I laughed when he used that nickname. Elizabeth had given it to him when we were kids because he would never give an inch. We didn't know the poem, but we liked the sound of the name. It fit Max. I'd try to explain that the reason Dad pushed him so hard about his math was because he wanted him to get into a good college. Max said it was because Dad had to feel powerful. Max never granted Dad the benefit of the doubt. Never acknowledged all the money spent on private tutors. Part of me had resented every penny they'd spent on him. I'd at least have been grateful.

After my laugh, we were silent. It had been a long time since we'd spoken, and we'd parted angrily when he refused to attend Tina's funeral. 'I'm not coming to help Bev put on her show of a family united in its grief,' he'd said. 'I refuse to play John-John to her Jackie Kennedy. Tina knows I loved her, Richard. And she's dead now. Dead, get it?'

'The family needs to be together,' I'd told him.

'What family?' Max had demanded. 'Don't you think Tina's killing herself is what this family is all about? Jesus, Richard, she's been killing herself in small pieces for years.'

'What do you mean?' I'd asked.

'You know exactly what I mean. The boating accident. The car wreck last summer. The overdose freshman year. She slit her wrists three times, starting when she was twelve years old. She's left notes all over the fucking house for Mom and Dad and all they say is "I'm sorry" as if she had to apologize for her mere existence.'

'She was only seven when I left for college,' I'd said. 'You can't blame me.' I'd felt to blame, though. Felt as if I'd failed in my job as eldest brother.

'You asshole,' Max had shouted. 'This isn't about blaming you. It wasn't your responsibility to raise her. Don't you get it?'

I wasn't angry anymore. I avoided my feelings about Tina's death as much as I could, and while I remembered Max's words, I never did get it. But I missed him. I lost him and Tina at the same time. He'd sent me postcards from time to time; he was no longer an undertaker, but a full-fledged member of a dance troupe. About a year after Tina's death, my mother had a minor heart attack and Max sent me a card of the Wicked Witch melting. I missed him a lot.

'I had an interesting chat with Claire today,' Max said at last. 'She called me from the Cuckoo's Nest.'

So Claire had called Max and not me. I was hurt and angry, too. I'm the eldest. I'm in charge. I'm the one who rescued her. Why would she call Max and not me? Boyce hadn't told me she was allowed calls out. I'd pictured her in a locked cell. 'How'd she know how to get hold of you?'

'She has my number.' I wasn't prepared for how hurt that made me feel. He hadn't given me his number. These siblings of mine were freaking me out. I thought their first allegiance was to me – King of the Mountain. What was going on?

'Don't go getting all worked up, Richard. It's different with Claire. She's not my heterosexual big brother.' In a less flip tone, he added, 'She's not jealous of Bev's fixation on me, and she's not hung up on preserving the parents.'

I sat on the sofa bed, feeling damp and chilly. My towel was a lump of dank green terrycloth. 'So I guess she spilled her story,' I said. 'Are you coming for the trial?'

'C'mon, Richard, you think a faggot brother's going to help Claire? Make her valid on the witness stand? Believe me, at this point in my life, there's no more hiding who or what I am, and I don't go anywhere without Todd. He's my mainspring, big bro, and a screaming queen and I love him that way. I'm sending a written statement, that's it.' Max paused. 'You're in kind of a bind, aren't you?'

'What do you mean?' I felt myself getting defensive. Max did this to me as a kid, too. I hated it when he challenged me. That lump of towel on my lap felt like a giant's hand right between my legs. I shifted position, but the hand seemed to follow me. I shivered.

'Gimme a break, Richard. You've got to testify about Jack and Bev, and that's against your grain. You always wanted to pretend they did things the way they did for a reason. You've always had Jack on a pedestal. He's a son of a bitch, face it.'

'Maybe.' The chills vanished. I was hot, my face flushed. I was glad my apartment was dark. I felt less exposed. Max didn't mention it was against my grain to have anything to do with legal procedures. Didn't he know how difficult for me just talking to Boyce was?

'Maybe, my ass,' said the Belle Dame Sans Merci. 'Don't you remember the time he smashed the bowl of Cheerios over your head so hard the little round Os went flying straight to the ceiling and stuck in a pattern that looked like a sick dinosaur? Give me a reason for that, big brother. What about the time he smacked Claire in the face and you jumped to her defense? Remember how you shouted, "But she didn't do anything – you'll have to fight me!" and he nearly killed you with those iron fists of his. Don't you remember?'

I could barely swallow. I hated this kind of pressure. I'd had enough pressure when I was a kid to last me a lifetime. In high school we'd had to formulate a life's goal for careers class and mine had been to never feel crushed in a no-win situation again. The way to do that was to take control of my life. Why couldn't Max understand that you can't control your past? Why rake it up? What was the point? Why not remember the good? And there was good, despite whatever Claire was telling Boyce, despite Max's memories, there was good.

'Don't you remember the dad who taught us flying grasshoppers make great bait because they flap around on top of the water attracting bass?' I managed to say. My voice didn't sound like me. 'Don't you remember him lying in that hammock under the maple trees at the farm reading *Uncle Wiggily and Charlie and Arabella Chick* to us?'

'No,' said Max. 'I don't remember that dad.'

'Max,' I said, after a bit. 'I'm doing my best.'

'I know you are,' said my brother. 'Claire says you're in the midst of giving your statement to her lawyer.'

'Will you give me your phone number, Max?'

Silence. Then he said, 'I'm working too hard to survive myself, bro. I can't have you upsetting the old apple cart.'

'Max, I wouldn't try to . . .' I started to say.

'Don't, Richard. It's not your fault.'

'I love Claire. You know that.'

'Of course I know that.'

'I love you, too, Belle,' I said.

We hung up, and I didn't know if we were closer to understanding each other or not.

I sat in the dark for a while, naked and confused. Max and I had shared so much over the years, it was hard to believe that in many ways we were so far apart from each other. We shared the same memories. He'd once sent me a Christmas card with a typed message saying, '. . . we shared a childhood of inexorable sadness. We are in the foundations of one another's souls, big bro.' I'd memorized it. Whatever I was as a person, Max had had a hand in it. If I was really honest with myself, though, I knew I was afraid of Max and his vision of our world. I had been ever since I could remember. As a kid I used to hold my breath, worried about what he might say in front of other people.

whatever you say reflects on the whole family

My mouth had a metallic taste to it as I sat in the dark considering Max, the nubby sofa cushion scratchy against my bare skin. He'd always been a storyteller, the sibling who'd say anything about the family, always talking fast and loud and laughing. Everyone who listened, laughed. I had laughed, too, but I can remember how detached I felt from our frantic laughs, and how much I wished he'd stop. For some reason I remembered the fear of being arrested. Somehow fearing that his fast talk would result in an arrest – mine. I pictured being locked up, the key thrown away. I don't know why. Once, he and I and three of my friends from school were sitting out in the backyard at Brookfield Court. Nobody's home but us and my dad, who's in his den cursing and paying the bills. My mother is probably getting her hair done and who knows where the girls are. Ballet? Piano lessons? Girl Scouts? It's springtime, and the forsythia rages across our back fence like wild dandelions and the sun shines hot and warm. I bring out

49

my cassette player and the sounds of Herbie Hancock on the electronic keyboard mingle with the buzz of distant lawn mowers and the slurp of boys guzzling Kool-Aid. We take off our shirts and are glancing self-consciously at each other's hairless chests when this kid named Bo announces he has to whiz.

'Can I use your bathroom?' he says, already unzipping his fly.

'Better not.' Max starts to laugh. 'My dad'll hear you pissing and come in and knock you around. He's a soundless pisser himself.'

We all look at him. 'What are you talking about?' I say.

'Didn't you know?' says Max, looking straight at me. 'Oh, yes,' he says. 'I'm in that lavatory the other day, the one next to his sacred den and my pants are down around my ankles and my hand's on my dick and I'm doing my thing, spraying a little around the edges and all, and bam! The door snaps open, bouncing back and forth a time or two, and guess who? Yep,' says Max, 'it's Dad. That old vein is beating in his forehead and he says, "I told you not to make so much noise when you're going to the bathroom." I mean I'm like freaking, you know?'

All of us nod. Me, too.

Max says Dad told him that his own father taught him to go silently, that it was impolite to make noise, to let others know you were relieving yourself. 'And, then,' says Max, 'he whipped down his fly and gave me a silent pissing demonstration, the red vein beating time in his forehead. Then he closed his pants and departed.'

We all laugh nervously. Bo never does go to the bathroom. Max keeps giving demonstrations, though, and we all have to pee when he's done we're laughing so hard. So we line up and whiz into the bright yellow forsythia.

From the dark of my one room, the fat man's apartment was lit up like Fifth Avenue at Christmas. A picture of the Last Supper hung on his far wall, bright with garish reds and oranges. I made out Judas Iscariot leaning close to Jesus, whispering, his robes a slash of green.

I wanted to cry, but I got up and went into the bathroom and brushed my teeth. I put on clean shorts and a white T-shirt. A crew-neck. I thought about strolling down to the coffee shop for a jolt of Lucy, but I stayed home alone instead and sipped a glass of stale beer.

I lay awake in my opened sofa bed for a long time. By now I'd finished four beers and felt soothed, a little sentimental. Max was wrong, I thought, feeling older, wiser, somehow superior. There had been good in our childhood. You just had to allow yourself to let it be good. Snug under the quilt on my sofa bed, I let myself sink into the past. I pictured the dinosaur on the kitchen ceiling at 37 Brookfield Court, but not as clearly as I remembered the smell of my father's chainsaw. Like it or not, Max, I thought, we're part of the Hayes family.

I put my hands under my head, my pillow a white cloud beneath me, and let myself remember the excitement of the winter weekend when I learned to use the chainsaw at the farm, a year or two before the night my brother and sisters laughed at me about that stupid water bucket, and the memory swallowed me up.

It's a long ago Friday and Mom's picked us up at school around noon. My dad's at the farm, he left right after breakfast, and now my mom and me and the other kids cruise down the Penn-Can Highway to Pennsylvania. Another couple hours on the road and the Blue Ridge Mountains rise all around us, naked trees scary in the dusky late afternoon.

I want Mom to hurry, hurry, hurry, and she's fiddling with the radio dials now. Thump! We've hit a pothole on the Steam Hollow Road. My mother doesn't say a word. She's found the religious radio station out of Pallstead, the teeny tiny town near our farm, that she loves. A burst of Aunt Bee spouting a Christian homily fills the car. We pass the reservoir. From the road it's no more than a black blot, and a few stars are already out for the evening shining into its blurry blackness. Old Man Pott's shack appears in the dusk, a flush of pine trees growing to the rear.

On both sides of the road is our land. He's got a thousand acres and it's all posted. Nobody can be on it but us. We come to a hill and, from the top of it, I can look straight down at the farmhouse. Tonight, its chimneys are smoking and my dad's got the outside lights on for us.

Swish! We're down the hill and pulling into the driveway. I'm out of the car and searching for my dad. It's a careful search. I don't want to take him by surprise, and I don't want him taking me by surprise.

Up the stone steps I got to the kitchen, taking care not to slam the door or track in dirt. No sign of him, but there's an empty glass on the table. Bourbon, I think. He only drinks when we're at the farm, never in town where he might have a patient. I can't tell if he's had one glass or two or three. I tiptoe through the house, peeking into the living room to see if he's fanning the fire.

He's not there.

I look in the bathroom with its big old tub that stands high on clawed feet with slick rounded edges. The toilet works only if the pump's been primed and I'm thinking maybe he's working on the pump, but it's already primed and water's dripping from the sink faucet. I hear Mom calling me to help unload the car. If he hears her calling me and I don't go help, I'll be in trouble; if he's not around and can't hear her, I want to find him.

I hear someone breathing. I jump. It's only Claire. Her eyes are wide and she's hunched. 'Where is he?' she whispers.

'I don't know,' I say, and touch her shoulder. I know her. She wants to know where he is so she can stay away from him. With me, it's different. I want to help him with the pump and the wood. I know how to hammer a staple into a fence post to hold barbed wire taut. I know how to prime a pump.

'Listen,' I say. We both stand still. Off in the distance, there's a grinding noise. It gets louder, then softer, then stops altogether. We keep listening and it starts again, louder this time.

'It's the saw,' I say. 'He's using the chainsaw!' I turn to Claire. 'He's got to be up at the barn. Come with me.'

She shakes her head.

'You'll be okay.'

She just looks at me, and I look away. Much as she wants to follow me, I see in her eyes that her fear of him is greater. Her eyes seem to say I should keep away from him, too, and it makes me kind of mad. I don't like the pressure.

'I'll see you later,' I tell her abruptly, and I hurry from the house, out of the door. I bump into Max.

'What are you doing?' he says.

'I'm going to help Dad. You better stay and help Mom.' I know I'm sounding superior, but, after all, I am the eldest son. Besides, Max is Mom's favorite. He looks at me and says, 'You two gonna compare dick sizes or what?' and I give him a push and head toward the barn without looking back.

I don't need a flashlight. I know the way in my heart. You cut through the part of our yard that's mowed and walk right into the meadow. It's about a quarter mile to the barn and there's nothing but me and the night sky and the dry hard ground beneath my feet.

'Richard!' My mother's voice fills the night, but I don't answer. After a bit, she stops calling. My breathing is loud and the quicker I move, the louder it gets.

I hear our dog Buddy bark a series of short sharp yelps. I picture him dancing around my dad and the saw, his stub of a tail wiggling his whole butt. The chainsaw shrieks across the meadow. It wipes out the labored sound of my own breathing.

I'm still two hundred yards away, but the saw's fumes leak clear across the night. My nose twitches at the smell of burning gas and oil. It's the smell of exhaust from a car that's not running right, that smoky, black exhaust streaming from the tail pipe that always makes my mother say, 'Something's wrong with that car ahead of us.'

I see him. He's got a light bulb rigged outside the barn, and his six-foot frame is no more than a dark shape in front of it. The sawhorse is out, and he's got a tree limb snug inside it. I know his right foot's pressed to the tree limb, both hands clutching the giant chainsaw. It's all smeary shadows from where I'm standing, taking in the scene, checking it out. I see jagged saw teeth as he lifts it between his legs. They're black against the yellow light. I hear its roar. I edge closer to my dad, feeling the way I think a deer might, poking his wet nose toward an unfamiliar salt lick. Crunch, crunch go my feet.

A dog barks in the distance.

The light bulb's casting light high into the night sky. Beams flash around my dad in a twelve-foot radius. The sky is orange. It's yellow. Blue.

My heartbeat's a thump in my ears. I creep forward, not wanting him to know of my presence yet. Now I see there's no light bulb at all. It's a raggedy-flamed fire.

He lifts the saw again and its teeth rip into a log. I come forward, knowing he'll need me to stack the wood. What I want to feel is the power of that chainsaw warm against my own fingers. Fresh-cut logs roll near his feet smelling crisp as sliced apples.

The saw's still grinding when I step out of the shadows into the light. The heat is intense, the odor of burning gas and oil overwhelming. His face is sweaty. But I see it's the good kind of sweaty, the kind of sweaty he gets from tossing bales into the hay wagon or hauling water from the spring to prime the pump. I like the smell of his working sweat. Dial soap laced with bay rum and warm skin. Sometimes, he uses Lava. My mother says his bay rum smells like bourbon, only sweeter. A man's odor, she says. One day I want to smell like that, too.

When the saw sputters and dies, I take a step forward, closer to him and the heat of the fire, and say, 'It's me, Dad. Richard.'

He turns to face that thirteen-year-old me, the saw held

54

tightly between his legs, aimed straight out. He's wearing a red flannel shirt sprinkled with sawdust. He's got on the heavy canvas hunting vest with slots for bullets edging its bottom cuff. Bullet tips poke out. I want to tell him I'm afraid they'll blow up in the heat, blowing him and his chainsaw sky high. I don't say anything, though. He's still looking at me, and I realize how big and dangerous that saw is. All he has to do is jerk on the starter rope and it'll burst into activity and it's pointed at me. Orange flames fill the sky. Buddy yelps from somewhere behind the barn.

I take a step backward. Then another. That saw is so big.

'It's me, Dad,' I whisper.

For a moment, we two stand our ground. All around us is our farmland, all one thousand acres of hills and trees, meadows and hayfields, ponds and creeks and secret pools. It's to my right, to his right. To my left and his left. It's the strip of blue mountains behind him and the hardened meadow ground behind me. It's the black-as-pitch barn and the blueing fire sizzling in jagged flames of orange and yellow sparks. Pole-shaped logs lying on the ground between us. Chainsaw with its blade poised to penetrate any object that gets in its way.

I can't move or breathe. Part of me thinks this moment is what we've been moving toward since the day I was born. He's top gorilla. Nervous sweat breaks out on my forehead. I might be thirteen years old, but I know danger when I smell it. No amount of burnt exhaust or dry wood chips disguises it. My dad's taken me deer hunting ever since I was seven. I can smell a deer's fear before my dad can. It smells of damp matted grass and it's cold as pond water beneath winter's sheen of ice. It's unpleasant, too, with an aftertaste like vomit.

Pop! A twig crackles in the fire, snapping into the starry sky and the moment passes. I watch him set down the saw and brush the back of his arm across his forehead. His fingers touch the bullets' tips. He steps toward me. I want to flinch, but I don't.

'Hey, son,' he says, and his face softens into a smile. In the fire's flickering light, I see his eyes that are just like mine – hyacinth blue like Claire's and set deep in his face. They're smiling at me and so is his mouth. He's got perfect teeth except for the one gold bridge, and my dad tells me if I'm lucky, I'll be like him. He doesn't have one filling. I've already got three. When he smiles the way he is now, his eyes matching his teeth, I melt inside and feel loved. Special. I'm his eldest son, the one he teaches to aim a rifle at a deer's heart and whiz an arrow straight from the bow to the bull's eye. I know how to drive a tractor, build a doodlebug, and now, I think, he'll let me hold that saw.

'Hey, Dad,' I say, and take a step forward. We smile at each other, and I can't help but be proud. Claire should see us now, I think. She'd see he's not so bad. Yet part of me knows it's different between him and her, but I can't put my finger on why. I think of Max, and a mean part of me is glad that it's me my dad likes.

'I'm glad you're here, Richard.' He tousles my hair. Sawdust from his gloves sprinkles my face. 'I need help stacking these logs. We'll need them this weekend.' For the first time I notice the Land Rover off to one side, its hatch wide open. I lean down and pick up a log, then another. Before I know it, I've got the back of the Land Rover filled with wood. Sawdust scratches my eyes and my nose feels dry with the smell of wood chips. I know if I blow my nose, gray will come out.

'I'll show you how to start the saw,' he says. This is what I've been waiting for him to say. I stand right next to him at the sawhorse. The crack of the saw's power smacks into the night. I'm holding it now, forty pounds of spinning blade, and it's between my legs. I bring the sharp edge down to the log resting in the sawhorse and zap! A piece of log rolls off. There's nothing to this, I think. My muscles are growing on the spot.

Within an hour we're finishing up, stacking wood outside the barn, wrapping the saw in a canvas cover, setting it inside the barn on a shelf. I drag the sawhorse into the barn, too, and lock up. He's put a special padlock on the outside door and only he's got a key, but tonight he lets me use it. Together we snap shut the back of the Land Rover.

'What about the fire?' I say.

We turn and face it. Nothing exists in that moment but me and him and the fire's warmth and the black blot of night. In the distance a horse neighs. Nearby I hear the scuttle of what's probably a woodchuck scampering into his hole. Sawdust is under my feet and dusting my jacket. My thumb throbs, and I know I'll have a blister on it tomorrow. My dad moves nearer to me and rests his hand on my shoulder. 'Let's let it die out by itself,' he says. He pauses, and I sense he's got more on his mind. I know better than to say anything. After a bit, he says, 'Your grandfather taught me to build a fire.' He clears his throat and tightens his grasp on my shoulder. I sense he needs me there beside him. 'He taught me to put a circle of stones around the outside so it couldn't spread. One time without warning he took my hand and forced it onto one of those hot stones. He told me he wanted me to see how hot a fire was.' My dad looks at me then, and I sense he is a boy again, not my dad at all. 'I never understood his doing that,' he says to me. 'I knew a fire was hot. It took weeks for my hand to heal.' He drops his hand from my shoulder.

I'd always remembered him telling me that story about his dad, I'd hung onto it for dear life at times. One summer afternoon, Claire and I were canoeing in the upper pond, just the two of us, and I told her Dad's story. We made it around the pond three more times before she said anything, and then she said, 'If he knows how much it hurts, why does he do it to us?' and I'd practically jumped down her throat saying, 'He's never burned our hands! How dare you say that?' and she didn't say anything else.

I'd never told Max about Dad's hand. I wished now that I had. I wished Max had come with me that evening to the barn, that he'd stood at the fire's edge with us. I wish he'd grown cold like I had, that a chill from the mountains had swept through him, same as me. I remembered knowing my teeth were going to chatter before long and how I'd rubbed my hands together to warm up and stomped my feet, too. I remembered patting my dad's hand, and his touching my hand to his cheek. I wished Max had been there to see that.

'Let's go,' my father says. 'Your mother'll be angry if we're late for dinner.'

We hop into the Land Rover and he drives it right into the meadow toward the farmhouse. The ground crunches under the wheels and the headlights blaze a path. Buddy bounds alongside us. Swaths of gray smoke curl from the chimneys into the sky and I feel happy. His gloved hand rests on top of the gear shaft thrust up between us.

I had felt so proud and pleased with myself.

I sat up in bed now, swinging my feet to the floor. The hardwood was cold against them and I pulled on a pair of heavy socks and a sweatshirt, too. I wanted to call Max and say, 'Look, Dad taught me to use the chainsaw one night at the farm and he didn't hit me or yell at me, or humiliate me. He told me about his own dad, he made me feel good.' My hand was on the phone when I remembered I didn't have Max's number. I sat for a long time with my hand on the receiver, and I heard Max's Belle Dame Sans Merci voice just as if I'd called him.

'That's great, Richard,' he said. 'He didn't hit you, or yell at you, or humiliate you. That's good. Now here's one for you. I have at least ten friends and you know what? Not one of them is afraid of his dad! That's right, big bro! Did it ever occur to you, not everyone is afraid of his father? That maybe it's not a normal, run-of-the-mill, everyday feeling? Ever think about that, Richard? That not everybody is grateful for a crumb of kindness every ten years? I know another ten people who – guess what? You'll never guess this one – but! Their dads never hit them. Not once! Not even a little slap in the mouth!'

'Shut up, Max,' I said, and crawled back under the covers. From where I lay, I could see the street lamps dimming, and dawn creeping across the October sky. Max's thoughts seemed as real as my own.

Could it really be only two days since Claire had murdered John?

I couldn't sleep.

Chapter Four

BEFORE going to Boyce's the next morning, I stopped by the office. I felt as if I'd been gone a year, not just a couple of days. It was early, about seven thirty, and I didn't expect to see Mary. I was generally the early bird, and she usually arrived a half-hour or so after me. I had wanted to surprise her, take care of some things, and leave them completed on her desk as if an elf had arrived in the night. I'd never been absent from work before, and I felt guilty leaving her with all our obligations.

But Mary was already at her desk, a cup of coffee steaming at her left hand, a cigarette in her right.

'Are you in for the day?' she asked.

I shook my head. 'Boyce wants me back. I don't know what he's driving at, but I've got to help Claire, so that's that.'

'That's right, you do.' She gave me a look.

'I'm not getting into this with you, Mary,' I said.

'Fine, don't.' She shrugged, a shrug that seemed to say, 'You're going to do things your own sweet way, no point in my saying a word.' She pushed a sheaf of papers toward me.

With a sigh of relief, I reached for Carvalho and Ahearn Inc.'s tax projections for the next year and spent the next hour happily estimating tax liabilities.

At eight thirty sharp, I piled the completed work on

Mary's desk. We exchanged a rueful smile and she gave me a thumbs up.

I was off to Boyce's.

I didn't shell out for a taxi but walked the ten blocks to Boyce's office. It only took me twenty-two minutes. I stopped in the foyer of his building to catch my breath. It was one of those huge, open foyers with beige marble floors and scattered gold couches and glittery mirrors instead of walls. I settled onto a couch and took some deep breaths. People hurried past me clutching briefcases.

Someone sat down next to me. I looked the other way, not wanting even the semblance of a conversation. I was feeling pretty defensive about the upcoming meeting with Boyce, and the last thing I desired was small talk with a stranger. Whoever it was sighed, and started wiggling.

I looked.

It was the woman I'd seen in Boyce's office – Sam – and she was trying to get on her coat while holding a folder of papers. She looked every bit as attractive as she had upstairs in Boyce's office. Blond, blue-eyed, slim, well-dressed. The barest hint of a flowery perfume emanated from her. Azaleas? Lilies? The smell reminded me of the farm in springtime.

I jumped to my feet, the way my mother'd taught me to in the presence of women or my elders. 'May I help?'

At first, I thought she might not look up or answer me.

'Sam?' I ventured.

This time she looked up. 'Hey,' she said. 'I know you from Boyce's office, don't I? I just came from there.' She held out her bulging folder.

'I'm on my way to his office right now.'

'Sit down,' she said, 'or help me up or something. I don't want to break my neck looking up at you.'

I dropped back onto the sofa cushions. By now she had her coat on, folder in her lap. She stuck out her hand. 'I'm Sam Saunders.'

Her handshake was firm, her skin soft.

I couldn't believe it. On my way to get raked over the coals by Boyce, this beautiful woman was talking to me. 'I'm Richard Hayes,' I told her, hoping this scene was not a dream.

She smiled. 'I know. I asked Boyce's secretary who you were.'

Wow. 'What'd she tell you?' I figured my grin must look really stupid, but I couldn't get it to go away.

'Not much. Just your name.' She laughed. 'She said Boyce would kill her if he knew she'd breathed one word about a client, but she told me you're single. Divorced.' She looked at me. 'I am, too. Divorced.' A quizzical look crossed her face, making her appear vulnerable. 'When I married, I thought it would be for life,' she told me. 'I wasn't brought up to think divorce an option.'

'My wife left me,' I said. 'No option there.'

'Mmm,' said Sam.

Awkward silence.

Clitter-clatter of a woman on high heels moving past.

I caught another whiff of Sam's perfume. Again, I thought of the farm and wondered if she loved the wild bloom of flowers in springtime the way I did. I swallowed hard and said, 'Your perfume reminds me of my family's farm and all the wild flowers growing around it. I've always loved the smell of flowers.'

She gave me a big smile. 'Me, too. We had a sunken garden in our yard when I was growing up. My favorite part was a section bursting with tiger lilies and lilies of the valley and yellow and white daffodils all smooshed together.'

'Tiger lilies? Orange or yellow?' I had a lump in my throat.

'Orange,' said Sam.

Just like at the farm.

'I've got to go,' Sam said then. 'I'm due back at work by nine thirty.'

I'd completely forgotten the time.

62

I jumped to my feet again. 'I'm supposed to be in Boyce's office at nine,' I said.

This time Sam rose, too. 'Oh, yes, Boyce,' she said. 'He's quite a guy, huh?'

'I guess,' I said.

'He's done a great job for me.'

I stood there, uncertain.

She leaned down, gathering up her folder with its overflowing papers. 'Financial statements and stuff,' she said. 'My settlement agreement – revised for the hundredth time.'

'Sam?' I said. 'Could I call you sometime?'

She seemed to think for a minute, then she nodded, saying, 'I'm in the book. S. Saunders, Leroy Street.'

I shook her hand again, not sure what else to do, and then hurried off to the elevators, my heart pounding.

All too soon I was back in the stuffy blue room with Boyce and Edna, Sam and her breath of fresh air forgotten. That defensive feeling of mine was back in full force, and I didn't like it and I didn't know what to do about it, so as Boyce and I faced each other and Edna scratched away on her recording device, I said, 'In some ways my dad was a hero. I remember times when we were at church and the cops would come and escort him, sirens blazing, to the hospital.' Maybe Max refused to acknowledge the good, but Max wasn't here, was he?

'Cut the bull, Richard,' said Boyce. He wore a gray suit, pale blue shirt, a bright red power tie. 'You think I haven't contacted Waterton General Hospital? You think I haven't looked into your dad's history pretty carefully? You think I don't know about the malpractice suit in nineteen sixty-five? Or the one in sixty-eight? Or the three in nineteen seventy-four?'

'What are you talking about?' I took care not to shout, but my face was hot. His words and attitude caught me off guard. I felt this way when Max challenged me, but I was always bigger than he was. I could beat him up.

'He's been reported to the state medical board seven times, Richard. Don't tell me you didn't know that.'

I was stunned. 'Claire's locked in the nut-house,' I blurted. 'How would she know? I've never heard anything about this.'

'Claire didn't tell me this. I've had my clerks looking into him ever since I checked Claire into the Psych Institute.'

'You're checking out the guy who's paying you,' I said. 'That's nice, Boyce, real nice. You've got him paying you to crucify him.' I was on my feet now, staring at the bookcase, my back to him, hands plunged into my pockets. No question about it, Boyce had hit my buttons. Maybe I came honestly by that negative feeling for the law. 'This is a man who anonymously paid for a new suit for the preacher at the farm. He visited his mother every single week in the nursing home until she died. He paid for Tammy Watkins' baby's funeral.'

I felt just the way I had as a kid when my father pushed me to the wall. One time, a lamp in the living room at Brookfield Court had mysteriously shattered. My dad lines us up in a row and demands a confession. No one confesses. I feel lifeless, like a mannequin in a store window. I don't know what I expect him to do; I don't know what I myself would do if I was the father. I have to believe what he does is right. He's my father. *Honor thy father, honor thy father, honor thy father* He turns to me. 'Which one shall I punish?' he asks. I shake my head. 'Which one?' I swallow and look at Elizabeth, Max, Claire and Tina. The girls are out. Max grins at me, waggling his eyebrows like Groucho Marx.

'Me,' I say. 'Punish me.'

'Is this a confession?'

'No.'

He slaps me hard in the face. 'Did you do it?'

'No.'

Slap.

'Did you do it?'

'No.'

Slap.

'Did you do it?'

'Yes.'

I'd felt so incredibly pressured by him that day, pressured to tell who did it, pressured to take the heat, pressured to save the others. The funny thing is, I no longer remembered if I broke the damn lamp or not, what I remembered was the sense of pressure and my thinking that I must have done it or he wouldn't have punished me.

That incredible sense of pressure is what I felt right now.

'You're acting like a little boy who wants to believe his daddy is God, Richard.' Boyce's voice cut through my thoughts. 'Here's what one woman reported to the board: Her name's Robin DeSantos. She's thirty-three, a mother of two, and her family doctor recommended your father, the town's Yale-educated gynecologist, for a hysterectomy. She says the operation went fine, but that a few days later her sutures tore open. Dr Hayes put her under anesthesia and sewed her up. A few days later, the stitches tore again. This time Dr Hayes redid the stitches without anesthesia. It was excruciating. When she went in for her final checkup, Mrs DeSantos says your father told her her husband would appreciate his handiwork because he'd sewed her up tighter.'

I kept my back to Boyce. Edna clicked away and I ignored them both. I hadn't counted on this when I'd so blithely said I'd do whatever it took to help Claire. I wanted to tell Boyce that, sure, my father's temper got out of hand, sure he'd smacked us around. I understood enough about psychology to know that she'd married a violent guy because that's what she knew. But this medical stuff, this was something different. I'd never heard a whisper of medical malpractice suits at home. In no way was I prepared for this.

'There are women who without him would never been able to have children,' I said.

'Here's another one.' Boyce's voice was loud and he enunciated each word. 'In nineteen sixty-seven he told a patient she had genital warts, performed painful surgery, said she could never have children, then told her she had cervical cancer. The doctor she went to for a second opinion told her there was nothing wrong with her. The second doctor was right.'

Those blue walls in Boyce's room stared straight back at me. Boyce's words triggered old memories, hurried conversations between my mother and father, hushed words behind closed doors. For the first time, I remembered their lawyer, a short, gray-haired guy in great shape bustling in and out of our house for a while, and I remembered my father's vicious remarks about lawyers. One time I came home from school early with a sore throat. I felt really shitty and more or less slithered into the house and up the back stairs to my bedroom. My parents must have been in their bedroom or hallway or somewhere nearby because I overheard my dad saying something like, 'Those fucking bastards'll gouge you out of your last dollar,' and then my mother's voice saying, 'I don't like it when you talk that way. My father was a lawyer, you know that, and my cousin's recommending Harrison, he's the best with this sort of thing, and you need him . . .' I don't know what was said after that, the fear in my mother's voice sent tremors through me. I remember a wild slamming sound as if Dad had closed a door really hard. Later, I discovered he'd put his fist through the wall just outside their bedroom. Another time I heard her whispering on the telephone to my father, and the hissing sound of her whispers seemed to go on forever: 'God, Jack, don't get angry, that's the worst thing you can do, you've told me that a million times, don't get angry, Jack . . .'

don't get angry

I didn't know what was going on or why he needed a lawyer and neither of them explained any of it. Elizabeth told me Mom had had an illegal abortion and that Dad had done it. I thought she was crazy, but I recalled thinking that maybe it was true. They had enough kids, surely they didn't need another one; he was doing the best thing for the family. Then I never thought about that odd time in our life again.

Until now.

'He was still practicing medicine right up until two years ago, Boyce,' I said to the wall. 'He was on the staff of two hospitals. He was a member of the credentials committee of the Waterton County Medical Association. He won an award for community service.'

'He was a big fucking fish in a small pond,' said Boyce. 'Nobody wanted to touch him. The board said no witnesses, no case.'

'How do you know about it?'

'One of my clerks found a nurse from his office who felt like talking.'

'Maybe she's a liar.'

'She's willing to testify.'

'To what?' I swung around to face Boyce. He stood so we were eye to eye.

'That your father's a fucking pervert.'

I wanted to punch him. His empathy was nothing but a false trail. Just like Max liked to say about my father's empathy voice, the one leading you down a path of kindness and bam! Smack! A wall.

'What's that got to do with it?' I demanded.

'Everything,' said Boyce.

We stared at each other. Eye level. Nobody around here was bigger than anyone else. Edna's fingers lay still.

'I'm Claire's attorney.' Boyce's voice was soft, but there was no mistaking its intensity. 'And there isn't anybody, anywhere, who's going to stop me from doing my best to represent her. I'd like to have you on her side, Richard. If you're not, and make no mistake about this, the prosecution will chew you both up and spit you out. Claire's going to be so much spittle.' He put his face so close to mine, his breath dusted my face. 'You see, Richard, I believe Claire, and I don't think there's a soul on this earth other than you that's able to corroborate her story. Tina's dead. Elizabeth's vanished. Max is out in San Francisco kissing men. Sounds to me like you put your nuts on the line a time or two as a kid and got 'em chopped.'

I took a step closer to him. Our noses touched. I heard Edna rustling in her chair.

In that moment I hated Boyce. I hated myself for deluding myself that he was sympathetic, a lawyer different from other lawyers. I'd let myself trust him, and the funny thing was, I realized, even in the heat of the moment, I didn't want to let go of that trust. Some survival instinct deep within told me that this might be my last chance and Boyce was the key. If I didn't trust him, I'd probably never trust anyone. From the beginning of time, my parents had told us never to trust anyone who wasn't family. Facing me was the ultimate juxtaposition: Trust a stranger, destroy the family, and save Claire. And yourself, said a voice within me.

'I've got to take a walk,' I said, and flung myself from the office. Rather than wait for the elevator, I raced down the stairs and onto the street. I didn't know where I was going. I got three blocks downtown and then raced back to Boyce's. Up the steps I charged to his secretary's desk. 'Tell Boyce I'll be back in an hour,' I panted. 'Don't let Edna escape. I'll be back. I'll pay for the time.' Then I was out the door again, but breathing easier. I would be back. Deep in my heart, I knew there was no more running away.

I sat down on a bench in south Central Park. I shivered, but I wasn't ready to go back. Usually at this end of the park, hot dog vendors hawked their goods, balloons floated heavenwards, bicyclists hogged the sidewalks. Not today. Too cold. Cold as Boyce.

Your father's a fucking pervert

God, I wanted to punch a heavy bag. I imagined the one in our garage at Brookfield Court and pictured myself pounding it. A right, a left, a right. The bag turned into Boyce, then my dad. Jesus. I hated this chaotic feeling. This sense of being out of control, as if my moorings had been cut and I had to free float.

68

I had to get my thoughts organized before I could deal with Boyce again.

So what now? I asked myself. Do I tell Boyce everything? There was no way of knowing how much Claire had told him. I didn't want to tell him something Claire hadn't already said. No point in spilling more dirty laundry than necessary. I wanted this to be neat and tidy – a completed tax return. I wanted to sign on the dotted line and have the past finished with; I wanted as little damage as possible.

I laughed a loud laugh that caused a couple hurrying past me to stare. Claire's husband is a slab of dead meat, Claire's in the nut-house, and I'm worried about damage control. I put my head in my hands. I was thinking just like my mother. She'd always had a way of seeing only what she wanted to see in the light she wanted to see it in. I thought of those alcohol-hazed nights when Max and I would meet on the back stairs like two imbeciles, laughing, tripping over our own feet, burping loudly, sometimes making it halfway up the steps only to crash down to the landing again. My parents had to have heard us, but neither ever appeared in the hallway to see what the heck was going on.

Once I staggered into their bedroom. My father's out, probably at the hospital, and my mother lies in solitary splendor in their big bed. She's enough to give me the DTs on the spot, and I'm glad Max hasn't fallen into the room with me. His sick humor would be my undoing. As it is, I look at that thin figure lying there under the merciless light of the reading lamp. Purple drapes hang at all four windows. Thick, pleated drapes that make the room even darker than night. Furniture presses against every wall. Two dressers, a vanity; an antique glass cabinet, once used as a breakfront, serves as a gun cabinet. Pistols lie on the shelves; shotguns and rifles line the rest. Shorn of make-up, her face looks a sickly white, the way I picture a corpse. Max, who wants to be an undertaker, hangs out at Debose's Funeral Home after school and he's told me all about the waxy white look of corpses.

69

Her eyes are open, she's reading a hardback Taylor Caldwell. Her eyes are blue, pale blue, and her nose sticks out, sharp and pointy, enough like my own that it's scarier than ever looking at my corpse mother. Her lips are a strip of pale pink blending right into her face. Her hair is squashed with a black spider-web hair net anchored to her head with long thin bobby pins. She's flat on her back, *Captains and the Kings* clutched in her hands, and I see she's wearing that ratty faded pink nightgown I hate. The women in *Playboy* look nothing like this. Are there two species of woman? I wonder.

I'm fifteen; she's got to be thirty-eight if she's a day. She's taken more trips out to that porch of ours for a tipple of wine than I know, maybe more than she knows, but she doesn't bat an eyelash when I come roaring into her room, hollering, 'Hello, hello, hello.' I don't know why I do it, I just feel like talking about my evening. And now here is my sweet mother awake.

'So, Mom, what'd you do tonight?' I shout, in that loud voice a drunk uses. Fumes swirl above my head in wild abandon.

Mom doesn't bat an eyelash. Her voice is slight, a tad martyred. 'I read the paper,' the corpse says, and I see her lips crack open. 'Diane Millbury's father died,' she says, adding, 'I don't think we need to go to the funeral, but we should send flowers.'

Diane was my father's nurse until she retired. I haven't seen her in three years. 'Flowers, yep, we'll send her flowers for her hair,' I say, and do a little soft shoe all around the room, bowing and sweeping in front of the gun cabinet – totally unlike my sober self. I run to her bathroom and puke. The smell of Southern Comfort nearly suffocates me and I puke again.

Mom lies in bed and I hear the rustle of a page.

For a long time I keep my head over the toilet bowl, wanting more than anything else in the world to cry. I know I don't know why and I don't cry, either.

Sitting on that cold park bench in Central Park twenty years later, I knew why I wanted to cry. I just wanted her to see me, I thought. I wanted her to ask me what was wrong. I don't know that I could have told her, but it would have been nice to have a mother who acknowledged the reality of my existence.

When did they ever see you

She never did.

I looked up to see that same couple hurry back past me and realized time was passing, but I wasn't ready for Boyce yet: no, I'm in the kitchen at Brookfield Court, it's 6 p.m., the sacred dinner hour, and we're all in our assigned seats.

It's dark outside so it must be winter and inside it's winter, too. A chill is in the air. I stay silent, proud and protective at my end of the table. Uncertainty laces that ugly sixties kitchen with its green linoleum floor, its red and green curtains and ambulance-white appliances. Mom's got the sterling silver set with every fork in its correct spot, and in the center of the table is a lazy Susan of their pills – Miltown, aspirin, multi-vitamins, Sinequan, bottles of dark syrupy medicine, too. Plus a jar of mixed pills, shiny, robin's egg blue Nembutal, sunny yellow Dalmane, chartreuse and muddy brown Librax, and capsules of Phenobarbital, bright red on one end, clear with powder showing through on the other. And we're using paper napkins. I know Munsy would freak if she knew my mother used paper napkins, but we do.

We're all at our schizophrenic table, Dad's exhibiting bon-homie, I know he's getting ready to quiz Max on his lack of algebra achievement for the day, and he's wearing that black suit, starchy white shirt and thin dark tie. No 'Damn, I'm Good' today. Mom's back is looking martyred as she bends over the hot stove, ladling gravy into the silver gravy boat, scooping mashed potatoes from the pan into a big bowl. Down onto the table comes the food and, as always, my parents serve our plates. We bow our heads. Dad says the blessing: 'Bless O Lord this food to our use and us to thy service, in Christ's

71

name we ask it. Amen.' Believe me, I don't mention that he left out the part about 'make us ever mindful of the needs of others.'

'Amen,' we say, and look up. I'm trying to determine the source of the chill and can't. But I tighten up, keep my elbows out of sight, frown at Max, and try to be invisible.

Anything might happen

Dinner's over. Elizabeth ventures a remark or two about American history. Tina and I keep silent. My father pokes Max a little about algebra, but no big deal. He asks Claire a question about trigonometry and then goes off on a tangent about some incompetent nurse at the hospital, not noticing that Claire hasn't answered. Elizabeth clears dishes from the table to the sink. I start to relax.

Out comes dessert. A big bowl of pistachio pudding. It's greener than Librax. My father starts to laugh, so we all do. I mean we're having a good time. The pudding's green as toothpaste and jiggly and we're laughing and all of a sudden Mom's on her feet, screaming at Dad. He's up and in her face. She picks up the pudding, slams it back down. Smash goes the bowl, splatter goes the pudding, green, glass, spraying everywhere. No one's hurt, so far, but we're dead quiet. Still, I'm afraid to look at Max, afraid he'll make me laugh. I don't know what they're saying to each other, I just see faces close and red and throbbing, and then swoop – her coffee cup's in her hand and from there it's in his face! My mother has thrown her coffee into his face! Part of me's ready to dissolve into green laughter and a wild hurrah and part of me is a corpse.

What's going to happen? The other kids are looking at me. Claire edges from her seat, crouches behind mine. I touch my spoon with the tip of my right baby finger, but I'm mistaken. Everything is not okay.

In the flash of an eye, my father raises his hand toward my mother and she runs shrieking from the room. She's in the hallway, now she's in the living room.

Elizabeth creeps up the back stairs, clutching Tina's hand,

Claire right behind them. I want to follow, put my arms around them, tell them it's okay, I'm King of the Mountain, but I don't. What about my mother? Max and I slither down the hallway to the living room. Dad's sitting on her, her arms pinned by his knees and his face is against her face. Their noses are touching, faces red as her Sunday lipstick. She's screaming, but it's more whiny now, and I can see he's not punching her, but he's got her stiff hair in his hands. His words are smoosh in her face. I don't want him to know we're there. I'm wet with fear and the not knowing. I see Max run into the den and I hear him lift the telephone receiver and dial a number.

Before Max has even hung up the phone, my father's up and out the door. He's a human flash into the Land Rover, the garage door buzzes with electricity and zoom! Out into the night he goes.

My mother sits up, uses the back of her hand to wipe away tears and then stands up. No blood drips onto the rug.

The front doorbell rings. Max is still in the den, but I see his shadow in the doorway. I'm in the hallway. Neither of us moves. Mom races to the door in a girlish skip and flings it open. It's our next-door neighbors, Mr and Mrs Silvers. Mr Silvers is a step ahead of Mrs Silvers. Her face is a concerned orb over his left shoulder. He clears his lawyer's throat and says heartily, 'Can we come in a minute? Just taking a stroll.'

No one ever takes a stroll in our neighborhood and stops by for a casual chat, it isn't done. But Mom opens the door and in they come. I see him looking around and Mrs Silvers' eyes are everywhere. They sit side by side on the couch. Mom sits across from them on the chair with the matching ottoman. She shoves that out of the way, though, and keeps her feet side by side, no leg-crossing for her. She's animated, all choppy arm and hand movements, a smile splitting her face, which is pink and flushed, her hair tangly. I'm amazed at what I see in Mr Silvers' smile at her. She seems so devoid of *Playboy* appeal to me.

73

'So,' he says, all chipper and neighborly, 'everything going okay for Jack at the hospital?'

'Oh, yes,' chirps my mother. 'He was just named Chief of Staff again.' She smiles. 'Somebody sure thinks he's doing something right.'

'And what about you? What do you think, Bev?' Mr Silvers is downright offensive, I think, and I want to rush to my mother's side and defend both her and my father.

I stay, sullen and confused, in the hallway. Max's shadow remains motionless, but I swear I feel its confusion as well.

My mother goes coy on the neighbors. 'I think Jack's wonderful,' she says.

It's not long before this ridiculous charade is over and my mother and I and Max are back in the kitchen cleaning up green glop. No one says anything. I hear a rustle and see Elizabeth crouched on the bottom step of the back stairs, Tina in her arms, Claire almost hidden behind her. My mother stays animated and chirpy, like Mr Silvers has somehow given her a much-needed shot in the arm. Max's face is long as a city block and glum as a rotted plum. Finally he says, 'Why didn't you tell them, Mom?'

'Tell them what?' she says, with another gay swipe at a dish with the dish towel. She reminds me of Mary Tyler Moore in *The Dick Van Dyke Show*.

'You know.'

'No, I don't.'

I realize a lot quicker than Max that tonight didn't happen. What my mother doesn't want to know or see, she doesn't, and I felt sick all these years later, a thirty-five-year-old man, knowing I wasn't so very different. Claire killed her husband. She'd told Boyce the reason lay in the past – at 37 Brookfield Court and the farm – and I didn't want to see it. Like my mother, I wanted to pretend it never happened.

I continued to sit on that hard park bench. I was scared at the realization I might be like Bev. I supposed I loved my mother, but I don't think I liked her much. Thinking of myself as King of the Mountain had always made me feel I was more like my dad – strong, a powerful person, someone to reckon with. The other kids looked up to me.

Didn't they

I thought about Max refusing to give me his phone number. I thought about Claire calling him, not me. I remembered the way she flinched when I moved toward her the night of John's murder. Jesus.

Boyce's conference room looked bigger and brighter to me when I returned exactly one hour later.

'Time's running out,' said Boyce, right off the bat, not giving me a chance to let him know I was ready to talk. 'Tomorrow I've got to be in court and I'm not sure about the day after.' This was Boyce number three – not compassionate, big-brother Boyce, not hardass prosecution Boyce, but down-to-business Boyce. 'I filed the Omnibus Motion today for Discovery and Inspection.' He looked at me. 'I had an interesting call while you were out,' he said.

'Who?'

'Wilson Brown, John's father. All the way from Blueberry, Maryland.'

I felt Munsy's presence in Boyce's office at that moment. She liked to say things like 'I can feel bad tidings, Richard. There's a goose on my grave.' No question, John's father would be a goose on my grave. I'd met him only once, at the wedding weekend, a short, squat, overweight man, red face laced with spider veins. He'd made an off-color remark about Claire's small breast size in front of John, Claire, and me that made me want to punch him, but John did nothing. Claire seemed oblivious.

I swallowed. The thump of my heart was back in my ears. 'What did he want?'

'He says your family better pay for the funeral or he's going to sue. He wants you to pay for everything – out-of-town relatives' transportation, hotels, food, pastor's fee.'

75

I couldn't think of anything to say. My mother's code of manners didn't run to who pays for the funeral of your brother-in-law, dead by your sister's hand. I did know which knife or fork to use on any given occasion, and I knew to always stand when someone older than myself entered the room.

'He told me to tell your family that if they think they and their rich doctor friends are going to get Claire off, they'd better think again. In the next breath, he makes it clear they want money.'

'Figures,' I said, remembering the bitter disagreements over who would pay for what at Claire's wedding. According to my mother, the groom's family pays for the rehearsal dinner. Wilson and Rilla Brown thought otherwise and Wilson had thrown a fit when the Waterton Country Club presented him with the bill.

'Might be a good idea to go to the funeral,' said Boyce. 'I'm going to be painting their boy just as big and bad as I can. It would be good to know how much trouble we'll be looking at from that quarter. Old Wilson sounded serious about avenging his only son's death. You might want to take your checkbook along. Tomorrow morning, 11 a.m. is the funeral service.'

I nodded, feeling Munsy's goose doing a veritable tap dance on my grave. I couldn't imagine how I would feel seeing Wilson Brown again, and I couldn't think how he'd feel seeing me at his son's funeral. Nothing boded well for tomorrow.

Thump, thump

Telling Boyce and the disapproving Edna stories of drunken teenage revelry and green pudding flying across our kitchen did nothing to dispel my feeling of impending doom.

Anything might happen

When Edna began packing up her recording device, Boyce put a hand on my arm. 'Wait a minute,' he said. 'Let's go into my office. We need to talk.'

Great. A tête-à-tête with Boyce. I couldn't wait. But,

76

actually, I had to. His secretary stopped him with several messages, and he gestured to me to wait in the reception area. For the first time I noticed a picture on the wall, a picture of a dark-haired woman, thirty, maybe thirty-one with a baby on her lap. I spoke up this time. 'Is that Boyce's wife?' I asked the secretary.

'Yes.' Just yes, no elaboration.

'His baby?'

'Yes.' This time, she leaned toward me and whispered, 'Don't say anything about the baby to Boyce. It's his wife who wants that picture up.'

I had no idea what that was all about, so I nodded okay.

I picked up a magazine, laid it back down. I couldn't concentrate. What else could Boyce have to say to me today? We'd been through the fucking pervert scene, Wilson Brown's blackmail routine, the prosecution chew up and spit out scenario. What was left?

'Richard?' Boyce poked his head out the office door. 'C'mon in.'

Thump

Jesus. Okay. I settled into the leather armchair. He sat across from me. Why did I feel as if an important client was about to tell me he no longer required my services? My hands slid on the leather armrests.

'What is it? Claire? Is she all right?'

'Claire's fine,' said Boyce quietly. 'It's the DA. She called about the gun.'

'The gun?'

'They found the gun. Outside on the ground. Behind a trash can in the courtyard beneath John and Claire's window.' Boyce paused. 'It's your gun, Richard. A .38 Smith and Wesson.'

'What?'

'It's your gun. Registered to one Richard Cory Hayes.'

'My gun? I thought it had to be John's. How'd she get my gun?'

'That's what the DA's asking. She says they're going to run you.'

'Run me? What are you talking about?'

'A background check. They're going to run a background check.'

'Why? What does that mean?' *How dare they* My heart started pounding. My deep, unreasonable fear of the law felt like a live force in the room.

'Oh, it means the DA's having a fit of melodrama, I guess. Looking for a twist where there isn't one. Not in the direction she's looking, anyway. At least, I hope not.' I saw Boyce take a deep breath. 'They're not going to find your fingerprints smeared all over that gun, are they, Richard? Or, worse, wiped clean?'

'Jesus Christ, Boyce!' I was on my feet, leaning across the desk, my face in his. 'I don't even know where she got that fucking gun. I had it at the farm when I was a kid.' I pushed my face even closer. 'I didn't kill John, if that's what you're asking me here. I probably should have, but I didn't.'

don't get angry

I sensed Boyce wanting to give me a good, hard shove out of his face. Instead, he pushed back his chair and stood. We faced each other across his desk. 'Are they going to find a sheet on you? Aggravated assault? Assault and battery? Anything?'

'I don't know,' I said slowly, feeling my way. 'I mean I've been stopped for speeding, three, four times.' I swallowed. 'I paid the fines on time. Never went to court. And I got busted for pot in college. The security police. Me and half the fraternity. They called our parents.'

'Richard, have you ever been fingerprinted, booked and jailed for anything?' Something in Boyce's voice had changed; I could swear I heard an undertone of laughter at this point.

'No, no. Of course not.' No way.

'Then sit down and relax.' He shook his head as if he couldn't believe I'd leaped up in the first place. He sat down and started thumbing through some papers on his desk.

I sat down.

He apparently found what he was looking for. He pulled out a single sheet and laid it in front of him. 'Well, there's no doubt that it's your gun that killed him,' he said. 'I've got a copy of the autopsy report right here. "Immediate cause of death: Blunt trauma to the head as a consequence of gunshot wound." They recovered a bullet traced to your gun. No question about it. Powder burns match, too.'

'It wasn't me,' I said.

'I know that, Richard,' said Boyce. 'The DA does, too. She's just being a prick.'

I almost crawled out of Boyce's, stopped at home only long enough to get into my sweats, and took off for the gym. Two hours later I emerged, my whole body worn out from punching the bag. Three people lined up behind me, waiting, but I refused to budge. Fuck pushy New Yorkers. I needed to slug that bag. Left, right, left, right, Boyce, Jack, Max, Claire, John, Bev, the DA, left, right, left, right. I could not believe the fucking DA had the balls to run a background check on me. I could not believe how terrifying that had felt to me – like a childhood nightmare come true. I could not believe what I'd learned about my father today. How could I have not known about those malpractice suits?

Afraid to know

I showered at the gym and again at home. I dressed in a T-shirt and an old pair of cut-off blue jean shorts.

They're not going to find your fingerprints smeared all over that gun, are they

I drank a beer. And another. I ate a can of green beans and a crunchy peanut butter and jelly sandwich.

I wondered whether Sam was just being polite when she said I could call. Was she really interested in me? With my luck, she was probably seeing somebody else.

I drank another beer.

Your father's a fucking pervert

79

I opened a third bottle of beer, sat down on my sofa bed, and dialed my parents' phone number.

My dad answered on the first ring, 'This is Dr Hayes.'

It pissed me off for some reason. 'You're not even practicing medicine anymore, Dad. Why answer the phone that way?' I said.

'Get to the point, Richard. What did you say in your statement yesterday and today?' So my mother had been listening when I told her I'd be talking to Boyce.

Two could play his game.

'Wilson Brown is demanding you pay the funeral expenses. He wants you to pay hotel bills for out-of-town relatives, too.'

My father said they'd send flowers or make a memorial donation. He and my mother would not be attending the funeral. They hadn't seen the Browns since Claire and John's ill-fated wedding and they didn't especially care to see them now.

Especially under the circumstances.

'I think it's a good idea for you to go, Richard,' he told me.

For a second I heard Max's voice in my ear: *He hasn't got the balls, big bro. He's afraid.* 'Shut the fuck up, Max,' I said out loud, before understanding it was my father at whom I was angry. Why *did* I have to do his dirty work? Why did I have to take another day off from work? He's the one who was retired. I gulped some beer.

'What? What are you saying?' shouted my father.

I started to yell back at him, but stopped, my hand clammy on the beer bottle, my heart starting its fearful thump.

I am on watch

'What?'

I took a deep breath, trying to quiet my racing heart. 'Have you heard anything from Claire?' I asked. No way was I going to challenge him.

I am on watch the rest of my life

'No.' Righteous indignation crackled across the wire. 'I've

put in several calls to that Dr Glassman and he's not returned them.'

This news relaxed me a little. If she'd called them and not me, I would have been really pissed. My father'd always felt entitled to any medical information about us. I found myself starting to provide details about Claire's Psych Institute incarceration but stopped. I didn't need Max's voice for this one – seven, or was it eight, complaints to the state medical board? He wasn't the same man to me anymore.

We hung up.

I polished off the beer and drank another one. By the time I called Mary, I was pretty drunk. I told her I'd be off to Blueberry, Maryland, for John's funeral and not to expect me in the office. 'I'm sorry,' I said. 'Sorry, sorry, sorry. I know there's appointments I'll miss, but I've got to do this for my sister, for my whole family. Nobody else can do this.'

'Take all the time you need,' she said. 'And, Richard,' she added, 'it's time to cut back on the drinking alone. You ought to hop on the subway and come see me and Hal.'

'How'd you know I was drinking?'

'A little birdy told me, you idiot,' said Mary, and hung up the phone.

Before drifting into sodden, restless sleep, I once again wondered what it would have been like to have Mary as a mother. She would've known I was drunk that night in her bedroom, I thought. She even knew over the telephone.

Chapter Five

WHEN my alarm buzzed at six the next morning, I was barely able to get out of bed and stagger to the bathroom. Two aspirin helped, but not much. The Metamucil I'd taken two days earlier at the office hadn't done a damn thing for me so my stomach felt as heavy as my head.

Thursday. Only four days since the murder. A lifetime.

In a rainy fog, I boarded the train to Baltimore from New York's Penn Station, dressed in basic funeral attire, a Robert Parker detective mystery jammed into my pocket. My head felt foggy as the weather. I think that made it easier to push yesterday into the far recesses of my mind. I planned to rent a car in Baltimore and drive to Blueberry. I'd timed it so I'd arrive half an hour or so before the 11 a.m. service. I figured I'd get directions from a local gas station. How many funeral parlors can there be in a town called Blueberry?

I gave the bar on the edge of my seat a flip, reclining my seat. I shrugged out of my overcoat, pulled off my jacket, and prayed no one would sit down beside me. I closed my eyes, wished I had a beer, and thought back to the beginning of John and Claire's relationship . . .

They meet when she's at Parsons, a fourth-year graphic-design student, and John, who graduated from NYU's art program two years earlier, is teaching a class of hers. Claire says he's known from the time he was nine years old he wants to get out of Blueberry, away from his mother and a future in the Sears Catalog franchise store his parents own.

They marry in December, three months after they meet. I don't like her marrying some guy I don't know. None of us knows him.

At least I'd known Skip.

It had been a long time since I'd thought about Skip Mannis' romance with Claire. I introduced her to Skip one college weekend at Colgate.

The campus is maybe eighty miles or so north of Waterton. Sometimes my parents let Claire, who's still in high school, ride the bus to visit me for the weekend. Not all brothers would have liked that, but I do.

Skip's tall, easily six feet, a pre-med student with intimidating scholarly glasses and a faint tinge of Boston in his speech. We play jazz gigs together; he on the piano, me on my trumpet. Miles Davis, Thelonious Monk, and Charlie Parker are our heroes. We've made kind of a reputation for ourselves around the college town and the college, too. Skip's good, really good, and when Claire comes to hear us one Saturday night at a little bar called the Get Down, she's really taken by him. Skip and I join her after the show, and the three of us go back to the frat house, settling in the kitchen to drink beer. After a while I go to bed, and I find out later that Claire went with Skip to his room for the night.

For two months Claire visits Skip every weekend. She looks happier than I ever remember her looking. A burden seems to have lifted from her, so that her thin face looks lighter, brighter, almost a different face.

Claire's phone call about Skip comes on the upstairs hall telephone in the fraternity house on a Monday night and, by chance, I answer it. At first, I can hardly understand her, but after a bit, she calms down.

'He hit me last night,' she says. 'Punched me. I've got a black eye.'

'He hit you? Why? What happened?' I feel as if she's punched me. Skip, my friend, my fraternity brother, hit my sister? I am dazed. He's said nothing to me; I ate dinner with him not three hours earlier.

'I didn't do anything, Richard. We're in his room, the two of us after dinner. He's all dark and cloudy acting. He says I was flirting with one of the frat brothers, but I wasn't. I smiled at the guy, thanked him for getting my salad dressing.' My eighteen-year-old sister's voice trembles. 'I never felt this way about anybody before. I love him. He hasn't called me, Richard. He called me a slut.' Claire's voice whirls wildly over the wire. 'Just like Dad does.'

She sounds as if she's spinning out of control. 'What about Mom and Dad?' I say, thinking that if I can stick to the here and now, the concrete, I won't have to deal with my feelings or Claire's. I can take charge of the situation.

'They haven't said or done anything,' wails Claire.

'But your eye,' I say. 'Hasn't Dad done anything for your eye?'

'No,' she sobs.

I hate that my father hasn't done anything. I slam my fist against the wall. If she was my daughter, I'd beat the shit out of the guy. 'Look, Claire, I'll talk to Skip,' I say. 'The motherfucker. I'll tell him he can't hit you.' I slam the wall again.

'Don't, don't say anything, I love him, please, please.' She can't stop crying and her voice is getting higher and higher, piercing my heart.

don't get angry

'It's okay, Claire. I love you. It's okay.' It's five minutes before we hang up with me promising not to say anything to Skip, but I don't mean it. I want to kill him. How dare he hit my sister? Stomping to his room, I feel like a father looking out for his kid, the way I think my father should have felt when he saw Claire's black eye. I feel a rush of strength, knowing I am fulfilling a parental role that no one filled for me. When Chucky Mindeman, five years older than I, beat me up time after time, nobody defended me.

Nobody saved me from Dad's fists or the buggy whip

My hand shakes as I pound Skip's door. He stands in his doorway in faded red sweat pants, glasses clear as windexed glass. With a casual gesture, he scratches his dick.

He sees my face.

'I just got off the phone with my sister and she says you hit her,' I say, putting my face close to his and keeping my voice loud. He's got to look up to see my eyes. I can feel the vein beating in my forehead.

'Well, uh . . .' He takes a minuscule step back. 'Well, she provoked me. Did she tell you that? Did she tell you she gave the come-on to Mike Poke with me sitting right there? Did she tell you that?'

I step closer, close enough to hear the rapid flit-flutter of his heartbeat, close enough to steam his glasses when I speak: 'I don't care what she does, you don't hit my sister.' I don't want to get thrown out of the fraternity or, worse, arrested, but I want to hit him so badly my knuckles turn white with the effort not to. I wipe my sweaty brow. 'You got that? You don't hit my sister.'

'All right, I'm sorry, I didn't think it was that big of a deal.'

I get right in his face. He puts up his hands and backs off. 'Okay, okay. I said I was sorry.' His glasses glitter, reminding me of my father's. I back off, then, and go outside for a walk.

Without warning, I suddenly remembered a summer at Brookfield Court. For some reason we're not at the farm, we're in Waterton and it's May, maybe June, and Claire and I are maybe five and seven years old. We sit at the breakfast table surrounded by boxes of cold cereal – Frosted Flakes and Cheerios and Sugar Pops. Claire is at my mercy. I'm to think of a number between one and ten and she has to guess it; if she gets it wrong, she has to eat another bowl of cereal. She never gets it right, not ever, and she sits there, smiling at me, and eats bowl after bowl after bowl of cold cereal and I smile and keep her guessing. She smiles back, a breathtaking smile of trust and love, and still I keep pretending to think of a number and still she keeps guessing, never doubting my honesty.

Sitting on that train to Baltimore, I could see that trusting smile of hers. I could hear her screams the night she killed John, and more than anything I wanted to go back to that long ago summer and not make her eat those bowls of cereal. I wanted to go back in time and rewrite the ending to the Skip story . . .

I continue to play at the Get Down with Skip. We give the appearance of being friends. I don't want any of the fraternity brothers to know what has passed between the two of us. His and Claire's relationship straggles on for maybe another month, but not much more. I never tell her that I confronted Skip and she doesn't ask. She pulls away from me after that, though, and I know I've failed her once again. A kernel of shame begins growing deep within me. I'm not any better a father to her than our father. Fuck the fraternity. Fuck an arrest. I should have beat the shit out of him.

I straightened my seat with a jerk and stared out the window. The sky looked cold and gray. When I heard a rumble of thunder, I wasn't surprised. Figures, I thought, it'd rain on my way to John's funeral. He was the first boyfriend that Claire let me know anything about after Skip. And I didn't meet him until two nights before their December wedding in Waterton.

John and his parents drive up to Waterton from Blueberry for the wedding. They're due Thursday evening for a five o'clock dinner party but arrive at seven thirty. I hear John tell Claire they stopped at Muhammad Ali's training camp in Reading, Pennsylvania, to watch him train. I think, the son of a bitch. Isn't he anxious to be with his bride?

I sit across from John and Claire at the party. I feel as if I'm in the company of movie stars, maybe an Academy Awards reception for John's performance as Fiancé of the Bride. I don't like it. I'm her brother. She's been shadowing me for years. Transferred from RISD to Parsons because I'm in New York. Who the hell is this guy? He's one of the most handsome men I've ever seen and I'm not given to thinking that much about whether a guy is handsome or not. His good looks knock you over. Like a Kennedy's. When Bobby was running for Senator of New York, he came through Waterton on the back of a flatbed truck. I'm just a little guy, but I remember the excitement, the crowds in the front of City Hall, and I remember his wide, white smile. If I'd been able to vote, he'd have had mine. I like the way he's larger than life. Nothing invisible about him.

John has that same blinding charisma. No one else exists at that table, only John. His looks are better than Bobby's. Tall, maybe six three or four, streaky blond hair, a shade longer than anyone else's in Waterton, and a small gold hoop earring in one ear. Nothing faggy here. On him, it looks great. All the men in the room including me wear trousers and sport coats, nice quality, and dark ties with plain gold tie tacks. Except John. He sports an off-white Nehru shirt and heavy cotton double pleat khaki pants. His jacket's a soft powder blue. This guy makes conversation with everyone like the leading man in a movie or a politician. Claire sits beside him, frail, pale and beautiful in a skinny black tube dress designed to show off breasts and bare back. She puts her arm through his and every now and again he gives it a little shake as if to brush her off, but she holds on.

'I've never felt this way before,' she whispers to me. 'I love him so much.'

I feel a vague shadow of apprehension. Munsy's proverbial goose. Hasn't Claire said something very similar about Skip? But I ignore it. She's my sister, she's getting married, she's happy.

Still, she seems remote.

I think of an article I've read describing Jackie Onassis and her glazed smile – that's who Claire reminds me of: Jackie stepping from the limo into the glare of flash bulbs, a smile pasted on her face.

John's mother looks shrivelled, one of those women with that white, white skin that freckles easily and then one day crumples like tissue paper and there's not a thing they can do about it. Right in the middle of a story John's telling about his climb to success in New York, the Big Apple, as he puts it, he turns to her and says, 'I need another drink. Tell them Wild Turkey, two fingers,' and without a word, she sidles out from her place at the table, across the room to the bar. When she sets down his drink, it's with a tentative air as if she fears displeasing him. It creates an odd tension at the table that increases when he neither thanks her nor pulls out her chair. Claire says something to him that I don't catch, but he ignores her.

At some point during the meal, Mrs Brown leans across John and says to Claire, 'John tells me you're having someone sing the Ave Maria during the ceremony.'

There's a pause. 'That's right.' Claire's voice trembles. I know it's an effort for her to talk with someone she doesn't know that well. She pulls her chair closer to John, thus closer to her about-to-be mother-in-law as well. 'You know Jackie Kennedy had a singer sing that in her wedding,' she says softly, and I know from her voice she's sharing something important to her. 'Jackie's been my heroine ever since I was a little girl.'

John's mother's thin lips open and she says, 'Your family's just like Jackie's mother, that pushy Janet Auchincloss. Don't think I haven't read about her over the years. Money, money, money. That's all she was ever after.'

Later, Mrs Brown turns to me, putting a cold hand on my forearm. 'I think a son's wedding has to be the hardest thing in the world,' she says.

I hope Claire hasn't heard her.

'It's not as if he's ever spent much time with us anyway,' she continues. 'Not since high school, not since that girlfriend of his Raylene Little.'

The table is silent. John chews on his *filet mignon*. Claire twists her napkin.

'That girl was from one of those uppity families in Blueberry that think they're better than everyone else. Better than us, and John's father owning the Sears franchise,' she says. 'That girl pushed, pushed, pushed at John to get ahead and once he caught a glimpse of how the other half lived, that was it. Goodbye, Blueberry. Goodbye, Mom and Dad. Just like that.'

'Claire says he won scholarships to schools all over the country,' I offer, thinking I'll get her onto a new track.

'He got his talent from me,' she says.

I realize John got his gift of the gab from her, too. It seems, once started, Mrs Brown might not stop. 'Do you know he only came home once, freshman year? All because Suzanne Taylor had him in her clutches and she lived right there in Scarsdale, in a big fancy house just like your parents',' she says. 'Now it's Claire who's got him in her clutches.'

'Now, wait a minute,' I start.

'Let me tell you something, Mr La-di-da Hayes, I was never ashamed of where I came from. It was plenty good enough for us,' she says. 'I was born and raised in Blueberry and so was my mother and so was my father. Is it criminal that I wanted to see my grandchildren raised there, I wanted John to live next door to us? Was it too much to ask that John stay in Blueberry? He's our only child and that was never my fault, ask Wilson about his low sperm count.' She leans so close I can see tears glistening in her eyes. 'Hasn't your mother ever told you the old saying "A daughter's a daughter all her life, but a son's a son till he takes a wife"?' I wonder if she's had too much to drink, but only one empty vodka Collins glass sits on the table in front of her.

John says in a loud voice, 'That's enough, Mother,' and the tension, lurking at our table all evening, thickens. Claire wears her Jackie smile and all I can think about is how, no matter what the circumstances, I can't imagine my mother with tears in her eyes.

89

John launches into a story about his glory days as a Golden Gloves boxer when he was in college, wading into the tension as if it doesn't exist. 'I had the swiftest right hand of anyone in NYU's team,' he tells us. 'I use that speed in my painting,' he adds. 'I can paint five pictures for every one of Claire's.'

Glazed smiles from Claire.

'Claire won Parsons' award for student most likely to succeed,' I say, pissed that a jerk like him had been in the Golden Gloves. I'd never even come close, and I'd spent hours punching that heavy bag in our garage.

'Do you really think there's any comparison between NYU and Parsons?' John's whole demeanour irritates me. What does Claire see in him? Then I see him smile and give her a quick hug, his arm fully around her bare shoulders, his fingers pressing into her upper arm and I see her inadvertent shiver that I know isn't fear but delight.

Max flies in the day of the wedding. Instead of Saint James Episcopal Church, Claire and John are marrying in an elegant Victorian mansion called the Afternoon Tea Club. My mother thinks a Victorian mansion the perfect setting for Claire's dress, which long ago had been Munsy's. Max and I are the only groomsmen, and John has no best man. Elizabeth is maid-of-honor, Tina the flower girl. Like John, Claire has no friends in the wedding.

Down the aisle comes Claire, hand resting lightly on my father's stiff forearm. I feel the collective gasp of the guests as she floats down the aisle in Munsy's wedding gown, a froth of lace and folds of luxurious ivory satin. A heavy gauze veil hides Claire's face; a toothy grin cracks my father's. With a start, I realize he and John are the same height and breadth, their smiles similar. My sister marches down the aisle to the trill of Trumpet Voluntary, a huge bouquet of orange tiger lilies blooming in her hand – a breath of the farm in summertime right there in the Afternoon Tea Club. I stand near our minister, facing the bride in her glory, thinking she looks like a zombie bride. Max takes a good look at her and I wonder if he's thinking what I'm thinking. He, too, used to have that dazed look and he'd told me that Dad used to pay him to pop pills out of sample foil wrappers and into the glass jar he kept in his bedroom. 'I popped a fair amount straight into my mouth, big bro,' he said.

Claire sits alone at the bridal table during most of the reception, her tiger lilies a wilted tangle in front of her. John, spectacular in stroller suit and snow-white boutonnière, works the wedding guests, smile dazzling, charm misting the room like Tinkerbell's fairy dust. Champagne flows. My parents smile and shake hands and perform perfect introductions. Wilson and Rilla, John's parents, seem subdued. They sit together at a small table at the far end of the room.

I sit down beside Claire. She flinches, then smiles when she sees it's me. 'Hey, little sister,' I say, feeling inadequate. How is a big brother supposed to act at his sister's wedding? Is he supposed to be happy or do other brothers feel vaguely threatened the way I do? Relieved, too? I shut that thought down in a hurry. Claire's no burden to me.

She seems to know how I'm feeling and pats my hand. 'I'm crazy about him,' she says. 'I keep pinching myself.'

'His mom might be a bit of a problem,' I say.

She shrugs. 'I'm marrying him, not his family. I never felt this way before, Richard. I can't believe we're married.' I watch her look across the room at him, his back to us, his shoulders broad, the couple he's chatting with, laughing and gesticulating. It's with a start I realize that's my father, not John at all. I say nothing to Claire about her mistake.

John settles into the seat next to his bride, his arm around her shoulder, tangled in her veil, his fingers pressing into her arm. 'So what's going on over here?' he says. 'You two having a private talk?'

Something in the loud, possessive way he speaks, pisses me off. 'Yes,' I say.

We eye each other, Claire sandwiched between us, suddenly silent. To me it seems as if the whole room has gone silent.

'Take good care of my little sister,' I say at last.

'Don't worry,' he says. 'She's my wife now.'

They leave on their honeymoon not long after, and Max disappears in the same whoosh of air. He can't get out of Waterton quick enough. Refuses to stay for the post-wedding supper at 37 Brookfield Court. Tina and Elizabeth stick close together. I'm the outsider and I feel very alone.

I'm the Incredible Shrinking Boy

I gave an inadvertent shiver, one of those that shakes you from head to toe like a mini Tourette attack. Munsy's goose, I thought. A woman across the train aisle stared at me. I turned away and looked out the window. The mottled sky looked like Claire's bruises the day she'd killed John. Tenement slums seared the landscape. Tattered clothes flapped on ropes strung from porch to porch. Yellowed cloth diapers, overalls, gray T-shirts. I thought I saw a rat slither out from under a step, but maybe that was imagination. Baltimore looked uglier than New York. At least when you slid into New York's Penn Station, the last mile or so was tunnel. No bleak poverty slapping at your conscience.

Claire's bruises

'Penn Station, Baltimore,' called out the conductor as the train rattled to a halt. I hurried up the steps to the station. Compared to New York's Penn Station, the place was tiny. One shoeshine stand. One magazine shop. Thirty, maybe forty people, including two beggars. I saw the silvery shine of pay phones clustered against one wall. For a brief second I thought of calling Sam, but I pushed away the thought. This wasn't the time or place.

It was Max I wanted to call. I needed him. I needed to hear his voice:

Are you crazy? Why are you going to that asshole's funeral?

Dad wants me to go.

Fuck Dad. Fuck John. Fuck his family.

For Claire?

Forget the fucking funeral. Get out your trumpet, big bro.

What?

Your trumpet? Remember? Blast away the blues.

Max didn't understand the pressure I felt, couldn't know my need to protect the family, but maybe that's why I needed to talk to him. He'd always had a way of poking at my big-brother pretensions, and while he'd infuriated me many times, I'd counted on him, too. It's as if he kept me from going too far out on Dad's limb.

Honor thy father

Of course, I didn't have his phone number. Claire had it, but I didn't. Claire had called Max, not me. I'd tried the Psych Institute, but wasn't allowed to speak with her. I felt as if the well-being of the whole family somehow rested on my shoulders, that how I conducted myself at the funeral and with John's parents would determine Claire's fate and somehow the fate of the whole family. And I felt alone, on a mission without anyone to help me.

Whatever you say reflects on the whole family

Another mini Tourette shook me, and I moved to the circular information desk to find out about renting a car. Blueberry was less than an hour away by Budget Rent-A-Car.

Anything might happen

Chapter Six

I GOT to the outskirts of Blueberry at 10 a.m. Oddly enough, the only clear radio station I could get aired the same Gordon Lightfoot tape the fat man liked to play. I sang along, pressing my fingers against the steering wheel as if it were my trumpet.

Blueberry turned out to be a Southern picture-postcard town. The main street, called Market Street, ran about ten blocks. Three-story red-brick buildings lined either side. Very Williamsburg. Very clean and nice. Not a telephone wire in sight. Red-brick sidewalks, neatly trimmed with rounded curbs and carefully tended saplings. Potted flowers sat in front of stores. Street signs were big and blue with scripted letters, not small and green and hard to read. I saw a woman climb into her Jeep Cherokee, two stickers attached to its bumper: My Child Is An Honor Student At Blueberry Middle School and Save the Whales.

Max would have hated it. Middle America at its finest, he'd say. Anti-black, anti-Jew, anti-gay.

I parked my rented tan Buick Skylark in front of Ye Olde Coffee Shoppe and went inside. I sat on a stool at the counter and avoided thinking about John, his family, or his funeral, or the fact that my heart was beating too fast and my hands were damp. I focused on the farm. Pallstead had a luncheonette just like this one called Wally's.

'What'll it be?' A woman who looked about my age stood across the counter from me. She had brown hair twisted into a tight braid and her bangs were teased like a poodle's. The woman's sherbet-green uniform was short and tight, a splotch of ketchup over her right breast.

'Coffee,' I said. She slapped down a mug of coffee, no saucer, and pushed a creamer toward me.

'Where's the funeral parlor?' My voice squeaked. I think I was a lot more nervous than I'd let myself know.

I wiped my hands on a paper napkin and tried again: 'Where's the funeral parlor?'

'There's two,' the waitress said. 'Smith's is right here in town, and Garden of Memories is further out, toward Baltimore. The newcomers go there.'

'It's got to be Smith's,' I told her. 'It's a local family, been here for generations.'

The woman started to laugh. 'When my granddaddy was lying over at Alma's, I called down there to see when the body'd be ready, you know? And she tells me he'll be ready about dinnertime. Made him sound like a Thanksgiving turkey. Another time,' she continued, 'my mama called over on a weekend to see about getting into the cemetery and Alma says no visits, they're real busy and working with a skeleton crew. I kid you not.'

'Sounds like the funeral parlor this guy would be in,' I said. 'Who is it?'

'John Brown.' I wondered if in this Southern-style town she'd laugh at the name.

She didn't. She made a face. 'Oh. Of course. That's big news around here.' She looked at me. 'You gotta be from New York, huh?'

I nodded.

'You a friend of his?'

'Not exactly,' I said. 'Are you?'

'No way, Jose,' she said. 'I went to high school with him. He was a creep. Thought he was better than everybody else.'

She swiped at the counter top with her rag. 'He got what he deserved as far as I'm concerned. I say hurrah for his wife.'

I sipped my coffee, figuring she'd say more.

She did. 'That father of his, old Wilson Brown.' She dabbed at a crumb and swept on: 'Here he comes every day and he settles himself at the counter and stays an hour, maybe two. Drinks coffee, globs of cream and sugar and never, ever leaves me a tip. Not even when he orders a luncheon special and dessert as well. No tip, but he wants to chaw my ear off with tales of his wife.'

I looked up from my coffee. 'His wife?'

'Oh, yeah. I got to be honest, he's not making a pass. Nothing like that. But he goes on and on and I guess he's lonely but I couldn't care less. When they come in here together, which is about once a month for the Friday night dinner special which is a seafood platter, he's Mr Wimp hisself, but on his own, he can't badmouth her enough.'

'What's he say?' I asked, curious, and glad of any distractions.

'You know, I don't even listen, he reminds me of my ex-husband talking about his ex-wife. Same old stuff, but with Wilson, it's mostly about John. How he should have been more involved, how she always kept him out of the picture, wouldn't let him in on her and John's relationship, whatever that means. Sometimes when he's talking it sounds more like he's talking about his mother than his wife, yet I know it's Rilla all right that he's yapping about, even though he calls her Mother. I can tell you this, though,' and here the waitress looked straight at me, 'There's a lot of rage in that Brown family, maybe half buried, but it's there. I don't think Wilson likes women much. It's in his attitude, you know? Here in the restaurant and in the store, too. I'm a lot happier when I go in there and see Rilla behind the counter. That guy adds nothing to my day.'

The woman took a deep breath and kept talking. 'Sometimes John and his parents came in here, you know, long after he'd married some hoity-toity thinks-she's-better-than-everybody girl from New York, not that we ever laid eyes on her, mind you, that's just what we'd hear through the grapevine. Rilla did not like that wife, the wife's family either, but she'd say how John had made it big in New York, big as an artist, raking in the moola, you know, which makes it even more awful that when the three of them, John and his mother and father, came in here, he never, ever picked up the tab. Not once. He'd come in here like a movie star, flashing that million-volt smile, say hello to me but never by name, like he hadn't gone through twelve years of school with me, like he doesn't remember my name, give me a break, and he and Rilla'd sit on one side of a booth and Wilson on the other, and she'd be clutching him for dear life.

'Now me,' she said, 'I got a boy twelve and a girl ten. I'm hoping they'll look out for me, make sure I don't croak in the night and start stinking my place up. I'd say John wasn't a bit caretaking. Still, Wilson came in here yesterday and you'd a thought he'd lost his franchise.'

'He'd lost his son,' I said, and wondered what, if anything, my father would feel if I was dead. My mother had once told me she'd wished she never had any children.

'Oh, I know. I had a miscarriage four years ago, same time my mother died a cancer. I got some idea of loss, you know. But I was close to my mama. Not like John who showed up in town once or twice a year. Still, Wilson looked broken and for once he hardly had anything to say. Just that all he'd ever really wanted was a boy to take over his store. The one thing I've done in my life that I'm proud of, he told me and he meant the store. "Now I can't even dream," he said. He'd a been dreaming even if John wasn't dead, that's for sure.' She looked at me. 'If John's not a friend of yours or nothing, why are you going to the funeral?'

I shrugged. 'I knew him in New York.'

'So?' said the waitress. 'I knew him in Blueberry. Doesn't exactly send me over to Alma Smith's Funeral Home and set me down in a chair with tears in my eyes.'

I liked this woman. She reminded me of Max. 'My sister was married to him,' I said, and watched her process this information. It took a minute. Then she looked at me. 'I'm sorry,' she said.

'Me, too.' We were both quiet and then she started to laugh. 'If I'd a been her, I'd a done the same thing,' she said.

'It's kind of gotten her into a lot of trouble,' I said. 'I think maybe she should have just divorced him.'

That would have let me off the hook

'No offense,' said the waitress. 'I mean about your sister.'

'No offense taken,' I said.

She adjusted her uniform and told me Smith's was about half a mile down the street, big white building with pillars. Right-hand side, parking behind the building. I wondered if they'd be doing John's funeral with a skeleton crew.

I left her a two-dollar tip, grateful for her chatter. It was time to leave, though, and I was scared. Already the pounding of my heart had begun. I felt like Daniel entering the lion's den.

Anything might happen

And then, just as if he'd jetted into Blueberry, I heard the reassuring sound of Max's voice: *Cool it, big bro. It can't be as bad as what Dad did at the farm, can it?*

What do you mean?

You know

I was not going to listen to this. I left Ye Olde Coffee Shoppe.

Thump, thump

I headed on foot in the rain toward the funeral parlor, leaving my car parked in front of Ye Olde Coffee Shoppe. I had a curious feeling of being on a movie set, detached from where I was and where I was going. I'd had this peculiar sensation off and on throughout my life, but as I hurried down the Main Street of Blueberry toward my sister's husband's funeral, I remembered a time when Claire pointed out to me that our life was like being in a play. I stood still for a moment, recalling it . . .

It's wintertime at Brookfield Court, the sky outside the kitchen windows gray with snow clouds. It must be a Wednesday evening, hospital meeting night, because we're all at the dinner table except my dad. Buddy's yapping, Tina's hitting the high chair with her spoon, my mother's face is pink and she's laughing loudly at something Max has said. I'm watching Claire poke her fork into the macaroni and cheese. She hasn't looked at me once the whole meal. Elizabeth's got *Marjorie Morningstar* in front of her nose and my mother doesn't say anything. The phone rings a sharp blast and we all jump. My mother picks up, still laughing a high, fake kind of laugh.

She listens for a minute, laughs again. 'It's Herbie Levin,' she says, looking at Claire. 'Your little classmate Shelly's father. He says you've been beating up on poor Shelly. You talk to him, Claire.' With a mocking smile, she holds out the phone to Claire whose face has gone suddenly white. She takes the receiver. I see it slide in her hand and I hear her whisper, 'Hello?' Then I hear a peal of laughter. Is it my mother? No, it's Claire, sounding just like my mother. She hangs up the phone and sits back down. My mother puts her hand on Claire's shoulder. This is the only time I've ever seen my mother caress Claire. 'Those people had better not call again,' she says, sounding smug and in control. Claire is pale and she pushes her macaroni around on the plate, not eating and it's her favorite, and the only time my mother makes it is when Dad isn't home. I see Claire look around the table at all of us. We're all smiling and happy, glad my mother is so happy.

Later, Claire tugs at my arm and pulls me into her room.

'Boys aren't allowed in girls' rooms,' I say.

'He's not home, and she's loading the dishwasher,' Claire tells me, not letting go of her hold on me.

I step into her room and she shuts the door. 'It's like being in an inside-out play,' she says. 'Everything is backwards.'

'What do you mean?' I say, somehow threatened.

99

'You know,' she says.

'Tell me,' I say.

'I did the worst thing today. I was so mean. I pushed Shelly down in the snow. I washed her face in it. I got Libby and Pam to help me. We taunted her about being put back a grade. I didn't let up. I hurt her.'

'What are you saying?'

'Her father told Mom that, he told her all about it. She laughed.'

'So did you,' I say, defensive.

'It's because they're Jewish,' Claire says, and starts to cry. 'That's why she laughed and handed me the phone. That's why she didn't care that I laughed. She was proud of herself. You saw her.'

I just stand there, not wanting to look at what she's saying. I feel unreal, as if the bed and dresser in her room are props.

'The mother's supposed to teach the kids right from wrong,' she says. 'It's a backwards play. We're the stars.'

A sudden clap of thunder got me moving again and the memory faded, leaving me saddened. Claire's instincts had been right all along, but I hadn't wanted to listen. She'd made sure I'd hear her this time.

Smith's Funeral Home loomed large on the next block, a white mansion of a building with gothic pillars and a sweeping circular drive. A dark cloud behind the funeral structure made its paint gleam white and the long black hearse parked in front appeared shiny and slick as wet tar on a summer's day.

I edged into the building, feeling panicked. The waitress had taken the edge off my fear, but this place made me feel as trapped as I did on that long ago evening in Claire's room.

Piped-in music hummed in the air, and it was with gratitude I recognized a hymn we'd sung at Cranklin Hill, the farm church, making me feel a sense of familiarity:

I come to the garden alone, while the dew is still on the rose,
And the voice I hear falling on my ear . . .

100

And he walks with me and he talks with me, and he tells me I
am his own . . .

I headed straight for the room with the casket. Large women swathed in black and smelling of perfumed body lotions surged around me. 'It's just so terrible for Wilson and Rilla,' I heard one say.

'They'll face their old age alone,' said another.

They would have anyway, I told myself, and sat down in a seat about the tenth row back and looked around. The last funeral I'd been to was my sister Tina's, a mean, tight little ceremony, her ashes stuffed inside a vase on the altar of Saint James Episcopal Church. No music. No funeral home. No hearse. No feeling. Later, they'd shoved her vase into the family vault not far from Munsy's cubicle. I pushed away thoughts of Tina. Right now I could not afford to do anything but concentrate on the Browns and how I would handle the inevitable confrontation. I was afraid, afraid of their sorrow and anger, but I was angry, too. Angry they'd use their son's death as a way to get money out of my family.

Dad's using you, big bro, said Max's voice in my ear. *He's using you to do his dirty work.*

I shook my head, not wanting to examine what I was doing here any more closely than I already had. I looked around at the white walls and three cut-glass chandeliers hanging from the ceiling. Frosted window panes made it look cold outside but, if anything, the funeral parlor was too warm. Music was continually piped in and I recognized every song, all hymns we'd sung in the Cranklin Hill Church at the farm in the summertime.

On a hill far away stood an old rugged cross . . .

The casket was open from John's waist up. He lay on a creamy *écru* cushion, his head on what appeared to be a velvet pillow. They'd cleaned up whatever mess Claire had made of him when she shot him. From where I sat, his hair shone gold and his skin appeared pink and healthy. I saw the gleam of cherrywood under the soft lights and a huge spray of yellow mums lay at the foot of the casket. Could Bev and Jack have sent that?

They should be here

A dais stood behind the casket and so did numerous floral arrangements. A florist stand shaped like an easel had a Styrofoam Bible lying open across it. Its foam edges glittered with gold and the words Holy Bible were emblazoned across the top. In the lower right-hand corner was a blue phone, its receiver off the hook. A big banner stretched itself across the entire top of the easel proclaiming 'Jesus Called'. This was something I knew for certain Bev and Jack had not sent. I'd never seen anything like this before in my life.

They're John's in-laws

In the front family pews sat Rilla and Wilson. A man sat next to Rilla and two women beside him. That seemed to be it for family. I watched several groups of people troop in and sit ahead of me. The men had bad haircuts, the kind that look as if someone slapped a bowl on their heads and started snipping, and high-water pants and the sleeves of their jackets hung short as well.

I wondered if Alma Smith, the director of this funeral home, had an easy time skimming cash from the business. If Alma wanted to increase the bottom line, did she skimp on make-up and hair care? I wondered if any of the funeral parlor men were gay, reflecting on Max's comments about funeral directors' personal lives.

When the piped-in music turned to 'Amazing Grace', I pictured myself playing it on the trumpet and knew I'd jazz it up a little, play it faster and in a lower key.

The service was brief, led by Pastor Fred Tuttle. We all joined in a slow-moving rendition of 'Onward Christian Soldiers' and one of 'Tell My Mother I'll Be There In Answer To Her Prayer'. The man sitting next to Rilla identified himself as John's Uncle Joe and he said his wife, God Bless

Her Soul, had been an art teacher and it was at their farm that John had first developed his interest in drawing. 'We've still got a box full of his pencil sketches,' he said.

Pastor Fred, too, spoke briefly about John, saying he'd known Rilla and Wilson for nearly forty years, John since he was a baby and this was as near a tragedy as anything he had ever experienced. He led us in the twenty-third psalm, and added that all his life he'd believed in a divine plan and he still did.

The final hymn was 'God Moves In A Mysterious Way' and the last verse seemed to linger in the heavy air, thick with sadness:

> Blind unbelief is sure to err, and scan his work in vain;
> God is his own interpreter, and he will make it plain.

To the gentle motion of 'Eyes On the Sparrow', pallbearers moved to the front of the chapel in a sea of blue. When they passed my aisle carrying their heavy load, I saw their pinstripes were painted on and peeling, their suits faded, too, worn spots on the knees, elbows, seats of pants.

Folks began to rustle in their seats. Men leaned toward women to help with jackets. I remained in my seat. What was it Boyce had said? Wilson wanted the funeral paid for? I couldn't seem to remember anything. But I did know my sister Claire's future in some degree rested on how well I handled myself. Underneath the Browns' demand for money was a very real threat – Boyce did not want them in court as the bereaved parents of a dead only child.

I cleared my throat and stood.

Wilson saw me. Easily three to four inches taller than everyone else in the room, I was hard to miss. I saw in his reaction that he knew right off who I was. He looked again, but he didn't need to. He took Rilla by the arm, leaning toward her, whispering.

Together, they approached me. That sense of nonreality overwhelmed me once again. We stood in the center aisle.

John's Uncle Joe scurried up to Wilson and Rilla and said, 'Is everything okay?' He glared at me. Must have met me at the wedding. He looked exactly like Wilson. One of the undertakers slid to our sides and oozed understanding. Wilson did a lot of throat clearing before he said, 'It's fine, Joe. Don't worry. We've got some business to do.' Everyone looked at me, including the undertaker.

'Are you sure?' The concern in Joe's voice reminded me of Max and his concern for me. I swallowed, hands clenched at my sides.

'I'm sure.' Wilson gave Joe an impatient wave of the hand and Joe nodded, leaving the room, looking back over his shoulder not once, but twice. I knew he'd keep an eye on us, ready to come to his brother's rescue if necessary.

I wished Max was waiting in the wings for me.

Anything might happen

The Browns and the undertaker looked at me. I felt others pressing nearby. Rilla's eyes looked like the lower pond after a hard rainstorm – muddy, thick with God knew what. I shrugged. 'I think we ought to discuss this in private, Mr Brown.'

He stared at me from under his bushy brows. I noticed they weren't brows at all; they were a single thick brow. Was money something the Browns felt comfortable discussing in public? We Hayes would just as soon discuss our own excrement as money in front of outsiders.

'I think we ought to talk in private,' I repeated, feeling a flush spread from my neck to my face. I remembered this flush from when I was a kid and my father'd attack me unfairly, yet I knew I had to hold my tongue. 'Don't speak to me in that tone of voice,' he'd say. 'Take that expression off your face.' I'd learned to modulate my voice and my face. I did it right now in Blueberry, Maryland, while Wilson Brown got to the point with a swiftness that took me by surprise but shouldn't have. The guy was a successful businessman.

I saw his hand tighten on his wife's arm, his knuckles

whiten. 'I want a check for this funeral,' he said. 'I want a check for out-of-town relative hotel bills, dinners out, plane fares. I want a check for the coffin.' He turned toward the empty space in front, the place where John's casket had rested. Rilla's head sank to her chest, her shoulders bowed. She was crying, I knew it, I felt her misery, and I wanted this conversation stopped. I hated displays of emotion. Didn't they have to get to the cemetery? When Wilson failed to make any attempt to comfort her, I considered putting my arm around her. Anything to get the crying stopped. From what Claire had told me, her feelings about John's death had to be a great deal more complicated than the average mother's.

I touched her arm. 'He used to hit you, didn't he?' I said softly. I felt her go almost limp before she stiffened.

'How dare you?' she hissed. Those muddy eyes of hers were opaque and scary.

'What did you say?' demanded Wilson.

I spoke in a firm tone: 'I said, John used to hit her. I heard he used to punch her hard enough to blacken her eyes,' I said. 'He did the same thing to my sister.'

'Your sister deserved anything he gave her.'

Alma Smith was at our sides in an instant, wiping her brow with a limp handkerchief. 'This is not the time or the place for this discussion,' she said.

'I told him not to marry her.' Rilla's veil slipped down her forehead and covered her eyes.

'She was a slut,' rasped Wilson. 'He married a slut. Ask him. Ask John about the way she came on to anything in pants. He'll tell you.'

A loud silence filled the funeral parlor.

I should have slugged him, but I felt a wave of nausea. Not because of his talk of my consulting a dead man, but his words about Claire made me sick. They touched a place deep inside me that had been there for years, but I'd always refused to think about Claire's sexual habits. From the time Claire was eleven years old, my father'd said that she was a slut. The funny thing is, the way I remember it, Claire was shy with boys.

'I want the money,' said Wilson, 'or I'll go to her trial and tell the world what a slut she is.'

'I'm getting the pastor,' announced Alma, in a firm voice. 'You are holding up the procession. It's time to leave this alone.'

So here we were, back to the money. It was up to my father to decide, but I knew what I was going to recommend. Pay them off. Wilson's threats frightened me – not that he would show up at the trial, but that inner part of me that I wanted silenced.

'Fine,' I said, in a loud voice. 'Send my father the bill.'

'How do I know he'll pay it?' Wilson said.

I tried to force myself to stay calm the way I did with clients who sometimes got in my face when they fucked up and wanted me to bail them out, but this situation was tougher. 'Hey, look, Mr Brown,' I said, my voice louder still, and I bent down, putting my face close to his and ignoring the fact that Pastor Fred was hurrying our way. 'You can send a bill or would you rather hold up your son's funeral procession while I write out a check?'

Wilson took a step back, nodded to Pastor Fred. 'Well, I just wanted to make sure it would be taken care of,' he said.

I needed to leave, but my mother's admonitions since childhood of what constituted good manners swirled inside my head. Did I turn on my heel and leave swiftly and in silence? Did I back slowly from the room? Did I go to the cemetery with the family? Rilla lifted her head and I saw an expression I'd never seen on my own mother's face, not even when Tina killed herself. It was the same look that Vietnamese mothers had during the war when you saw them on television bending over a bloody child lying in the road. A look of pain and loss that went beyond tears.

'We'll be in touch with the Manhattan DA if your father doesn't send a check. Count on it.' There was a long pause in which it suddenly occurred to me that this business with the money was the only way Wilson knew how to cope with his grief. I heard him say in a trembling voice, 'You tell your father I want the money for the rehearsal dinner, too.'

Pastor Fred touched Rilla on the arm. 'Come, your family is waiting for you.'

'Family?' she said. 'What family?' Her voice cracked.

'I'm leaving, Mr and Mrs Brown,' I muttered. 'I'm sorry about John.' My eyes met Pastor Fred's and I could see that my sincerity was not lost on him. His warmth made me feel better even though I knew he couldn't realize that my sincerity came from my fear that, if it was I lying dead in that coffin, my parents might display no grief at all.

Etiquette be damned. I left Smith's Funeral Home. Looking back over my shoulder, I caught one last glimpse of Rilla and Wilson. Pastor Fred had his hand on Wilson's shoulder and Alma Smith stood beside them. She must have said something because I heard Wilson say, 'Can't you see we need to be alone?', all venom gone from his voice. Only pain remained.

I got in my rental car and left Blueberry, Maryland, fast. I'd done what I set out to do, but had no feeling of accomplishment the way I did after completing a particularly complicated tax return. I'd done everything in my power to eliminate chaos from my life and now, through no fault of my own, it was back.

I wanted a beer. When I saw a dilapidated barn at the side of the road with a neon sign blinking Billy Bud's Tavern, I pulled over.

Chapter Seven

As I stared through an alcoholic mist at the Baltimore slums outside my scummy window, the train stopped with a harsh, grinding halt that jerked cars front to back and front again. A repeated loud cracking noise snapped through the train and my heart raced. Gunfire?

A conductor entered the car. 'Remain in your seats, please,' he said, moving rapidly down the aisle and disappearing through the other door just before another loud explosion.

A woman stood up and screamed. The man beside her pulled her back down and told her to shut up.

I turned away, hearing gunfire in my mind, and suddenly, in the now motionless train, I floated down a dark passageway of memory . . .

I am on watch

I'm in my parents' bedroom at 37 Brookfield Court, furniture pressed against every wall. Two dressers, a vanity; an antique glass cabinet, once used as a breakfront now serves as a gun cabinet. Sunshine peeks in through the windows, casting glimmers against the cabinet's glass so the guns seem to glisten in a way they never did in my father's hands. Pistols lie on the shelves; shotguns and rifles line the rest. He must have twenty altogether.

I'm eight years old, a little boy. I'm wearing gray shorts, a T-shirt that says Grand Slam Baseball across the front in big red letters. My hair is a bristly crew-cut. I'm in that bedroom and my dad is sitting beside me on the bed. He's big, six feet tall, wearing L.L. Bean khaki pants and a red shirt open at the neck just like all the other dads in the neighborhood wear on weekends. I can see his dark chest hair squeezing out of his shirt. I can smell him. He smells of bay rum and something else, something slick and moldy, something horrible. I think if I licked him he'd taste like rotted woodchuck. I sit so still beside him I think maybe I'm invisible, but I'm not. He reaches forward and touches the cabinet's glass door. His fingers barely flick its surface – just light, airy, a butterfly. I see black hair on his fingers. I know the hair on his chest and back is so thick it could choke an infant pressed to him for warmth. The key is in the cabinet and he turns it. It makes a squeaky sound. The door swings open and the guns are freed.

A .357 Magnum lies in his hand. His hand is sweaty. I see the marks his fingers leave on the gun's surface. His forehead is sweaty, too. I see the shine. The rancid smell of his sweat mixes with the gun's oily odor. I can't remember when, but I know I've been here before with him – this place he goes when he's excited and nervous, hands shaky, mouth dry and sticky. I'm afraid to breathe, so I stop and just sit there feeling his rush. What is he going to do? It doesn't occur to me to run away from him, to run out of the bedroom and away. He's all powerful. I'm enveloped by him.

'Look, Richard,' he says, and I feel that damp, dank hand on my head. He's pointing the gun at me. 'It's only got one bullet in it. The other chambers are empty,' he tells me, and presses the gun into my hand. It's cold. He wraps his hand around mine and pushes the gun's nose under my chin. 'Pull the trigger,' he whispers, and I realize I'm wetting my pants. No longer am I a little boy. I am silent fear.

'Pull it.'

I sit there, frozen. His leg is next to mine on the bed, hard as a shotgun barrel.

'Pull it.' I hear the note in his voice that means he's losing control. I'm more afraid of him than pulling the trigger. The gun's barrel is a chilled circle under my chin. It sends a coldness through my body colder than any winter's night on the farm. I think if hell were cold instead of hot, it would be this cold. I pull the trigger. Click. Nothing else. Just a click. We sit on the edge of the bed together for a moment, breathing deeply. I sense someone else has entered the room. It's my mother. I feel her looking at us. The gun gleams in my hand. The trigger is ice against my finger. I look straight at her. I have this odd sense that there's no one there behind her pale blue eyes. Her eyes are marbles. She leaves the room without saying a word. I have a curious, deadened feeling as she pads so quickly and quietly out of that room.

The flash faded as quickly as it flared.

The train remained motionless.

I remembered a time when my dad and I went alone to the farm for the weekend. My dad makes blueberry pancakes that weekend with blueberries from our own bushes. I gather a bucketful from the bushes near the upper pond, and he shows me how to make the thinnest pancakes I've ever seen in my life, blueberries popping from the sizzling pancakes. And he douses them in maple syrup from our own trees. The two of us sit together at the kitchen table like old friends, chomping on crispy golden pancakes oozing the purple juice of big round blueberries.

'The train will resume its journey to New York via Wilmington, Trenton, and Newark. Thank you for your cooperation, ladies and gentlemen.'

The conductor's voice broke into my thoughts and I took a deep breath. No mention of the peculiar cracking sounds or forced stop was made. Typical. We'll all just pretend this never happened. Just like my family. I focused on getting my heart rate back to normal. If I wasn't a grown man, I'd say that what I wanted, more than anything else in the world, was someone to hold me close and say everything was going to be all right.

No one did. No one ever had.

I am on watch for the rest of my life

I got out my Robert Parker novel and tried immersing myself in the troubles of Spenser, a tough, sensitive thug who righted the world's wrongs in the name of honor, but instead I heard the steady beat of Boyce's voice: *Your father's a fucking pervert, your father's a fucking pervert, your father's a fucking pervert . . .*

The train rattled into Penn Station about 6 p.m. I'd slept maybe the last hour or so of the trip and had that dizzy feeling you get when you wake up from an unexpected nap. The beer had left an unpleasant taste in my mouth. The loud noises on the train seemed to have happened long ago and so did my trip down Memory Lane.

Maybe it was a dream

I stepped into the orangy light of the train station and headed for the main terminal. I hustled up the steps, still feeling dazed. Four tattered street people lay on the ground next to the escalators and the harsh voice of a conductor attempted to hustle them on their way.

Someone near me gave me a shove and I stepped over what appeared to be a breathing bundle of rags and tried to get my bearings. I checked for my wallet and looked around. A row of public telephones caught my eye. I saw that one actually had a telephone book still attached to it.

The funeral was behind me now.

I could call Sam Saunders.

I reached into my pocket, remembering I'd shoved a St Marks Place theater bulletin that showed old classics in it. *Marjorie Morningstar* was playing. Sam liked flowers. Maybe she'd want to see it with me. It had that great scene with Marjorie and Wally at the Cloisters.

And maybe she wouldn't be home and I could leave a message on her answering machine, which would be much safer. Calling on a Thursday evening like this was pretty dangerous. She might be insulted that I'd expect her to be home. She might not think we'd have much to say to each other. I wasn't sure myself.

I stepped toward the telephone. I felt it had to be now or never. If I waited until I got home, I might not have the courage.

It took me forever, but I found her – S. Saunders on Leroy. My finger shook as I dialed. I'd met my ex-wife Johanna at a party. She'd been the one to call me. Even in college, I'd had a policy of never calling a girl. If she wanted to go out with me, she had to do the calling. I didn't know if it was that inviting smell of azaleas that drifted around Sam or the way she'd managed to make Boyce look uncomfortable that attracted me to her. All I knew was that I wanted to talk with her.

A disembodied squawk announced a departure at gate fifteen.

My heart in my throat as I listened to her phone buzzing, I watched a panhandler unroll three tattered blankets and prepare to settle down for a rest.

Sam answered on the third ring.

I cleared my throat and wiped my free hand on my pant leg. 'It's Richard,' I said. 'Richard Hayes. I met you yesterday. In Boyce's lobby. Remember?'

'Of course. Hello.' I thought she sounded quizzical, as if she was thinking, What do you want? Why are you calling me so soon? We both knew I'd broken the unwritten protocol that said you waited at least a few days so as not to seem too eager. Tuesday night was a more accepted night to call for a first date.

'I'm at the train station,' I said. Brilliant, Richard. That kind of repartee will really impress her. You are one scintillating guy.

'Oh?'

I took a deep breath and plunged. 'I'm not that far from your place. I thought maybe you'd go to a movie with me or something. St Marks Place is showing *Marjorie Morningstar*.'

Sam sounded pleased. 'I love that book,' she said. 'I'd love to see the movie sometime, but tonight my sister and I are having a party.'

'You live with your sister?'

Sam laughed. 'Oh, no. Never that. We didn't get along as kids. No way I'd live with her now. She lives in Chicago, thank goodness. She's very didactic. Knows everything. No, we're having a party because she's leaving for a seminar in Europe, and she's spending a few days in New York with me before she goes.'

'Oh.' Not quite like the life and times of my sister, but I didn't think now was the time or place to tell Sam my sister was living in the Psych Institute and might well be on her way to prison. It didn't occur to me to mention Elizabeth or Tina. In a way, it felt as if ever since Claire's desperate phone call, nothing else did exist for me – only Claire and Max, our past a swampy quicksand, sucking me in. I saw that part of my motive in calling Sam was the hope that she could help me out of the mire. She appeared so very self-possessed.

'Why are you at the train station?' Sam's voice seemed far away.

'The train station?' I said.

'Yes, why are you there?'

'I went to a funeral near Baltimore,' I said, and was grateful she couldn't see my flush of embarrassment.

Silence from her end. I figured she wasn't sure what to say. It might have been my mother or father, someone near and dear.

'No one I was close to,' I added, and took a deep breath. 'But I thought it was politically correct to go.'

'One of those kinds of funerals,' said Sam.

'Yep,' I said. 'One of those.'

'Look, Richard,' Sam said suddenly. 'Would you like to come tonight? To the party?'

A full five seconds passed before I said, 'Sounds great.'

'People will probably start arriving in an hour or so,' she said.

I'd had the day from hell. I didn't want to go home, and I didn't want to eat dinner alone in some noisy place in the Village. Desperate, I did something entirely out of character. I asked Sam if I could come over now, straight from the train station. There was a small pause, and then she said, 'Okay. You can come now.'

She lived on Leroy just off Hudson in the Village.

Sam's place turned out to be pretty fancy, as far as Village apartments go. Off the street, its own brick alley, with a gate to keep out intruders. Sam said she'd been in her apartment six months and not one break-in.

'It's the gate,' she told me when she let me in. 'There's an alarm system and burglars know it. It's so much easier to just go around the corner and rob someone else. You know?' She looked up at me as if my opinion mattered. She wasn't annoyed I'd arrived before anyone else; in fact, she seemed pleased. 'I'm going to put you to work,' she said. 'I need green olives and ice. I think I'll send you out to the deli. There's one right around the corner. I thought my sister would be here, but she had errands of her own to run.'

'Okay,' I said, prepared to walk back out the door straight to the deli. She reminded me of Mary. She could tell me what to do, but somehow it wasn't a power thing; it was just life, like you do this and I'll do that and everything'll get done. Different than with my mother, who had a way of making me feel that if I didn't do her bidding, not only was I worthless as a human being but I was damaging her in some irreparable way as well.

Richard, you come with me to help

'Later'll be fine,' Sam said. She told me I looked nice, and I realized how dressy I was in my funeral suit for a casual evening get-together. I guessed I didn't appear as disheveled as I felt after my long day. I smiled and shrugged.

114

I leaned against the refrigerator door and watched her pour Mr T's Bloody Mary mix into a short fat glass. It was hard to believe I'd been at John's funeral earlier in the day. It felt like a long time ago. I said I'd take a Coke Classic and that's what she got me, no questions asked. She was either too classy to ask why I was abstaining from alcohol, maybe fearing another recovery tale, or she smelled the stale beer on my breath and figured I'd already had my share for one evening.

She looked beautiful, soft and cuddly in some kind of pink caftan over white tights. She wore her hair on top of her head in a precarious bun with a pink satin ribbon wrapped around it. Silver earrings dangled from her ears almost to her shoulders. She wasn't all hyper and snippy the way my mother was before a party; Sam seemed to be enjoying herself.

While she mixed dip and lit candles, I had a chance to observe her apartment. Lush green plants everywhere. I began to relax. I breathed in its spaciousness, enjoyed the fact that I could stand in the kitchen and see into a living room, a bedroom, a third room, which appeared to be a study. A tiny staircase curved upwards.

'Nice place,' I said, wondering how she afforded it. It had to run her 2000–2500 dollars a month. I doubted I could afford it. Did her ex pay for it?

Sam must have read my mind. 'Phil – my ex – pays me eight thousand a month alimony for two more years; then it ends. At least, according to our most recent agreement.'

'What is he? A gangster?'

'He and Michael Milken,' said Sam. 'He's on Wall Street. A manager for Legg Mason.'

'Oh,' I said, and stepped into the living room, which gleamed with hardwood floors and dusted surfaces. A black ivory studio piano sat against one wall, a tall, slim bookcase against another. A couch, a rocking chair, a comfortable chair covered in blue print fabric, and a couple of occasional tables were grouped around an Oriental rug not unlike the one in Boyce's office. Books and magazines lay scattered. I left the kitchen and took a closer look at titles: *Cosmo*, *Mademoiselle*, *People*, *Teachers Today*, *New York Times Book Review*. Robertson Davies' trilogy sat on a separate pile on her bookcase. So did a stack of Agatha Christie and biographies of Nicholas II and Harry Truman.

'Are you reading all these books?' I asked.

She laughed. 'Sort of. I get started on Harry and need a break, so I race through a Robertson Davies, then go back to Harry. When I need another break I go for Nicholas and sometimes I'll read five Agatha Christies in a row.'

I watched her move to the stereo and slip in a disk.

Thelonious Monk.

A woman after my own heart.

I peeked into the study. More plants. Textbooks, maps, laminated letters lay scattered across a big pine work table and a bulletin board held pictures of children. 'You teach? In the city?' I was astounded. She didn't look tough enough to teach inner city New York kids. I didn't know anyone who was that tough.

'I teach right around the corner,' she said. 'At St Mark's Washington Place School. It's not the same as public school teaching. It's like parochial school anywhere. That's why I don't like it. It's the kids in the public school system who need me.'

'You're being naïve.'

'I don't think so.' There was an edge to her voice – not the kind of edge Johanna's voice had, the kind that felt like an attack, but an edge that said, Look, it's my life, I know what I'm doing. 'I've been in the Peace Corps,' she said. 'I've taught school where there's no electricity, no running water, no textbooks, no paper. I've taught school where the kids don't speak English.'

'It's not inner city New York,' I said, following her into the kitchen. 'The kids probably weren't carrying knives or guns. They couldn't say fuck you.' I would never have dared behave the way kids in New York do. The kids I read about in the *Times* feel a freedom I never had and it made me angry. Every time I read a *Newsweek* article about student rights, I wanted to lash out at those snotnosed kids. 'You ought to stay where you are.'

'It's not like you know me,' said Sam.

'Yet,' I said, and felt debonair.

She walked to the living room and got some earthenware dishes from beneath the couch. I noticed a series of three oil paintings on the wall above the couch. The first was a still life. An unusual still, both because of the bright colors and the fact that the artist had drawn a Matisse in the background. The other two paintings were variations of the first, but bolder and brighter. Original and alive. Very different from Claire's work, nowhere near as sophisticated, but these paintings had something that many I'd seen in shows didn't have. They were better than anything Johanna'd ever done.

'Are these yours?' I hoped they weren't. I'd had enough artists in my life.

'One of my students did these.'

'I thought you taught little kids.'

'I do, but I teach English as a second language at the New School, too, and that's where I met Bernice.'

'Bernice?'

'She's Haitian, arrived in New York four years ago, speaking no English, living in a Brooklyn slum. It took her two years to learn English, another two to make a friend.' Sam put down the dishes and looked at me. 'She's what makes teaching worthwhile. I love the way she thinks and strives and keeps on going. Nothing's stopped her. She went to James Madison High School. I've put in an application for next year.'

'Still the Peace Corps worker.'

'You bet.' She didn't sound angry, but she did sound firm and she didn't appear to need my good opinion. Johanna had always turned to me for decision-making; so had Claire. And my mother's lack of respect for me made me try all the harder to attain it. But I was never good enough.

I had a feeling Sam was different. More like Mary. Her self-assurance made me feel different, too. I didn't feel the weight of responsibility I was used to feeling around women. I wiggled my shoulders: burdenless.

I followed her back into her nice big kitchen, a kitchen nothing like mine. Blooming flower plants stood against one wall. A bowl resplendent with green and red apples and a clump of bananas sat in the center of a round table. A far cry from a cornucopia of pills.

'They're not fake, are they?'

Sam laughed as she opened a can of black olives. 'Of course not. Why would I have a bowl of fake fruit on my table?'

'I don't know. I guess you don't like dried flowers, either.'

'I like the real thing,' she told me. 'I told you, when I was growing up, my parents had a huge yard with a sunken garden.'

'That's right,' I said. 'You told me orange tiger lilies and lilies of the valley and daffodils are your favorite flowers.' I looked at her. 'Mine, too. Orange tiger lilies.'

Sam poured the olive juice down the drain and pulled a crystal bowl from her freezer. I watched her slide the olives into it. 'To keep them cold,' she said. 'I loved my mother's wild-flower section in the garden. I always pictured heaven looking like that.' She smiled at me.

'And now, Richard,' said Sam, 'it's fifteen after seven, and you need to run out to the deli.' She jammed a twenty-dollar bill into my hand and almost pushed me out the door. 'Olives, green olives, and ice, lots of ice. You better get paper towels, too. White.'

The deli she'd sent me to didn't have green olives, but I happily trudged another few blocks; all I could think about was that she loved tiger lilies. Johanna didn't know the difference between a tiger lily and a dandelion. My mother'd spent years at the farm and I doubt she knew the difference, either. I was smiling for the first time that day as I returned to the market to pick up the ice, then realized I'd forgotten the paper towels.

I didn't care. Sam and her party were helping me forget Boyce, Claire, my parents, Johanna, the Browns.

By the time I got back to her apartment, fifteen or twenty people had arrived and were milling around acting familiar with her cupboards and refrigerator. I plunked down my purchases and searched for her. Sam stood at the piano next to a guy seated on the bench. He looked affected to me, with a long ponytail and one gold earring. Next thing I knew, the guy was playing jazz like he was born to it. Like English was his second language, jazz being his first. He was better than Skip.

I walked over to Sam.

'This is Barry Benner. He's played the Blue Note,' she said. The Blue Note was the Village's answer to New Orleans. I knew how tough it was to get a gig there. Big fucking deal for Barry.

A skinny woman in a sheared hairdo and blast of red lipstick dashed up to us. She grasped Barry's arm. 'You have to meet Max,' she gushed. Bony arms, the kind with loose skin around the elbows, clutched Barry, but he ignored her. Turned out she was Sam's sister, but I took a step back, startled by hearing my brother's name. I craned my neck, looking, hoping Max was right here in New York. But the man Sam's sister introduced was not my brother Max. Some of that good feeling I'd had when Sam and I had been alone together evaporated.

'Are you okay?' Sam touched my hand. I looked at her, wondering for a moment what I was doing with a stranger in a crowd of people I didn't know, listening to jazz played by a man who had played the Blue Note, a place that had turned me down at least twelve times when I'd gone begging, years ago, trumpet in one hand, demo tape in the other. All the stress from the day came rushing back. I found myself longing with all my heart for Max, his warmth and honesty, his familiarity, wishing for those long ago nights in our shared bedroom at the farm. I wanted to hear piss splashing down the tin roof. To my horror, tears welled in my eyes.

Sam tried guiding me to the couch, but I detoured to the kitchen and plucked a beer from the cooler first. I think I just wanted its reassuring coldness in my hand. We sat and I sipped. Sam touched my hand again and I saw that her nails weren't just pink tipped, but manicured to perfection, pale pink with white tips. From the piano came the jazz standard 'Blue Monk', Thelonious Monk's original bebop.

I set down the beer can on top of *Mademoiselle* and looked at Sam. 'Look at my nails,' I found myself saying. 'My mother did them until I was fourteen.'

'Until you were fourteen?'

'Yep. She had her Saturday night nail routine for us five kids. She lined us up in front of the kitchen sink.' I paused to sip more beer. Sam looked confused, but she stayed with me, didn't leap up to play the hostess, didn't get that glazed look in her eyes that Johanna used to get when I tried talking about my family to her.

'She'd grip our hands and clip our nails over the kitchen sink. Sometimes there were bits of food in the sink. Shreds of carrot, rotted potato parts, mushy brown banana stubs. She combed our hair, too.' No one else at that party existed for me. Only Sam and Thelonious. Barry had switched to 'Straight No Chaser'. 'Used a metal comb and Waveset. I was a stinging fingernail, an aching scalp all through church. I was the Incredible Shrinking Boy.'

I took a deep breath and looked at her. 'Did you go to church when you were a kid?' I said.

She looked surprised. 'Every week.'

'Did you ever wonder about the fifth commandment? Honor thy father and thy mother?'

She looked across the room at her sister. 'My sister says if there'd been an honor thy children commandment, that would have been the only commandment needed. The rest would take care of itself.'

'What do you think?'

'I wonder who wrote them. Probably a control freak.'

I leaned over and kissed her on the cheek, surprising us both. Sam moved a fraction of an inch closer to me, her thigh a tender, tentative kiss all its own.

The music stopped. Barry Benner drifted over to the couch and sat down on Sam's other side. She turned to him, the warmth of her thigh vanishing. It felt as if she'd pulled herself away from me, leaving me alone. All that remained for me was a hint of her perfume. A well of hurt opened inside me.

I stood, feeling panicked. The Incredible Shrinking Boy was no longer in the past, but right there in Sam's living room. I had to get out. I couldn't risk anyone seeing how fragile I felt. 'Look,' I said, interrupting her and Barry, 'I've got to go. It's late. Tell your sister it was nice meeting her. Thanks for having me.'

I moved swiftly to the door and she followed me, perplexed. 'What are you? The local quick-exit artist?'

'I'll call you if that's okay,' I said.

She nodded, and I slipped outside to her carefully guarded alley, my heart pounding. It was almost as if her kindness was what hurt so much. Or was it my own sudden willingness to confide secrets from the past? Had the day from hell caught up with me? All I knew was that I'd never let Johanna catch even the slightest glimpse of the Incredible Shrinking Boy. She'd been married to the King of the Mountain.

The gates clanged shut behind me and I faced the bustle of Greenwich Village at night. I began walking up Hudson toward Christopher, to Sheridan Square. I moved fast, hands shoved in my topcoat pockets, head up. I felt an unexpected exhilaration from the chilly air and the beat of a live blues band drifting out from one of the many restaurants I'd passed. Men in leather jackets seemed to spill from the bars, holding hands or arm in arm. As I crossed Seventh Avenue South, I saw the Lion's Head and smiled. Claire and I had met there more than once for a quick drink and sometimes Mary and Hal and I stopped in for a beer.

I headed toward Sixth Avenue and kept going. Something about the neon lights and a young-looking crowd bopping in and out of pubs cheered me up. A regular hodgepodge of people filled the street. Tattooed women, men sporting three or four earrings, a girl with three rings through her eyebrow and one in her nose. What seemed to be an entire Asian family scurried past. A few older folks were out, too, walking dogs or strolling hand in hand. I liked the smell of fresh flowers and produce sitting outside the delis. Only a few aluminum awnings were pulled down over entire store fronts.

By now I'd reached West 57th and started cross town. It must have been close to midnight. Despite that painful sense of abandonment I'd experienced on Sam's couch, I knew in my heart that talking to her that night had been one of the highlights of my life. I'd caught a glimpse of a side of myself that I'd never met before. When I saw a pay phone on the corner, I thought it might be a sign that I should call her and say I was sorry for rushing out that way. I got to the corner and discovered the receiver had been yanked from the box.

What did that mean? That I shouldn't call her?

I kept walking.

Another pay phone loomed on the next corner. I stood in front of it for at least a minute before grabbing the phone book from its chain. Half the pages were missing.

Another sign? I should have memorized her number at the train station.

With a trembling hand, I dialed information and got it.

She answered on the third ring. I heard the party rustling in the background.

'It's Richard Hayes.' My voice sounded odd in my own ears. Like someone else's. Like someone who was not in control, someone who was vulnerable. 'I'm at a call box on the way home. I wanted to say thanks for the nice time.'

'Honor thy party givers,' said Sam.

An inner knot of fear relaxed. 'Could I take you to dinner this weekend? You and your sister?' Old impetuous me. I

glanced at myself in the metal phone box. This was a Richard
I didn't know.

'This weekend is bad, Richard. Maybe next week?'

'I'll call you,' I said. 'We'll make a plan.'

'I'd like that,' said Sam.

I hung up the phone, smiling like a goon, and started
running toward home. I veered onto First Avenue, part of
the marathon route, but I quit running pretty quickly. Winged
tips are not the ideal running shoe, and my thin dress socks
slid from my ankle inside the shoe.

By now East 88th was no more than a mile away.

Cab drivers kept honking, street people kept pissing, and I
kept on moving. For the first time in my life I had a glimmer
of what it might be like to run toward something instead of
away.

I'd like that, she'd said

Chapter Eight

THE steps to my apartment felt like nothing. I took them two at a time and wasn't even breathing hard. I stood in my doorway for a moment, staring in the darkness, and feeling a little bit like King of the Mountain. A man's home is his castle, right? And I'd just been to a party at the princess's.

I'd like that

I snapped on the lights. After the coziness of Sam's, my place came as a shock – cramped, dirty, neglected, the papers to my auditing book scattered like trash on a New York highway. It was the first time I'd really noticed how I'd let it fall apart after Johanna left. It gave me a funny let-down kind of feeling like the feeling you get sometimes on Christmas morning. You've waited and waited, thinking this year things will be different – only this year comes and you don't see the dump truck or electric trains or BB gun, so you just feel empty inside. I had a swift memory of Elizabeth pulling me aside one year, yanking me into the closet off the family room and telling me that Tina had had the worst Christmas of all. 'She wanted twin dolls,' she'd told me. 'Twin boys to keep her doll Holly Bell company. And she wanted twin cribs for the dolls, too. She's only five, Richard,' she said. 'They should have gotten her what she wanted.' I thought, I never got anything I wanted, why should anyone else? I guess Elizabeth knew what I was thinking because she'd said in a low urgent voice, 'It's worse for her, Richard. You pretend you don't care. You go out to the garage and smash that heavy bag. That's okay for you. Tina thinks she has to comfort Mom and Dad because Santa made a mistake. She's worried about their feelings. She doesn't have any of her own. It's like they're making her into a nonperson.'

These were not thoughts I wanted to be having just then. In fact, I did my best to avoid thinking about Tina at any time. All I wanted to do was relax. I didn't want to think about my family at all. I wanted to enjoy the idea of getting to know Sam better.

I closed and locked the door behind me and took a deep breath. I tossed my coat onto the sofa bed and reached for the refrigerator. It was then I noticed the light on my answering machine, and the old adrenalin started rushing. Claire? Max? Mary? Wilson Brown? The pleasure of Sam disappeared and all I felt was a sudden exhaustion. What now? I was so tired of the memories, of trying to protect my family, of my own need to keep a lid on the past. Maybe Claire had called to say the whole thing had been a big mistake.

I pressed the button on the answering machine.

'Richard? It's Mom. Let us know what happened at John's funeral.'

Click.

'It's Mary. Hope everything went okay.'

Click.

'Richard? It's me.' My heart pounded. 'Johanna. I got a phone call from Boyce Regner today. Wanted to know what I knew about you and Claire. Thanks for letting me know about John. If my friend Charlotte hadn't called me, I wouldn't have had a clue.'

Boyce Regner. The son of a bitch.

Johanna had nothing to do with any of this. Our relationship was private, off limits.

How dare Boyce Regner call her

I didn't discuss Johanna with anyone – not with Claire, or Max, or Mary. No one.

Thump, thump

What had Johanna told Boyce

I snatched up the phone and called Mary's and my answering service. I told them I wouldn't be in tomorrow and to let Mary know. I riffled through the Manhattan directory until I found Boyce's home phone number. My fingers snapped against the digits. When Boyce answered on the third ring, I told him I'd be in first thing in the morning. 'We're going to talk,' I said, and hung up. I realized that my hands were black from the telephone pages and I wiped them off on a napkin before trying Johanna's number. My heart beat fast.

No answer.

I let it ring ten times before I hung up and tried again. This time her answering machine picked up on the second ring. She had to be there. She had to have been there talking the first time, my call clicking away on call waiting. As soon as she hung up, she must have switched on the answering machine. She had to have known I'd call. Bitch. She could still hurt me.

'Meet me tomorrow for lunch,' I told the machine. I didn't leave my name. Let her figure it out. 'High noon. Cottonwood Café.' I knew she'd know I picked the Cottonwood because we'd courted there and I knew her well enough to know she'd show up.

I yanked out my sofa bed, snapped off my light, and collapsed on my bed, still clothed. I felt incredible pressure from Boyce, my parents, John's parents, Claire, and I wasn't certain I could live up to everyone's expectations. I felt as if I'd been trying all my life and now I wasn't even holding up my end at work. It seemed unlikely that Sam would find me very appealing once she got to know me.

The phone blared, jarring me, but I didn't answer.

My mother again: 'Call us when you get in. It doesn't

matter how late.' As soon as she'd hung up, I took the phone off the hook.

Fuck you, I thought, feeling Max inside my head.

I pulled off a shoe and slammed it against the wall.

Fuck you.

The other shoe followed.

Why hadn't Claire called me?

I tossed and turned all night, buzzing like an electronic keyboard. Beneath the reggae beat throbbed the low steady hum of anger.

How dare Boyce call Johanna

And underneath:

What had Johanna told Boyce

I marched down the hall to Boyce's office at eight sharp the next morning. Friday. Five days since the murder. That buzzing electronic force from last night still surged through me, and I felt strong, ready for battle.

The door was ajar, so I walked into the reception area without knocking. No secretary, just an odd silence met me – a silence that felt uncomfortable. The kind of silence that settled around our dinner table at 37 Brookfield Court after one of the kids spilled his milk. I wondered if Boyce was here yet. Had I walked into an empty office? A burglarized office? An office with a burglar?

I hesitated for a minute. The door to Boyce's inner sanctum was open, too. Just a crack. I thought I heard movement, the rustle of clothing, but I wasn't sure. It was then I heard a woman's voice, a whimper, but clearly a woman's whimper. Then I heard Boyce: 'No, Sarah. I don't think it's a good idea.' There was an edge to his voice. Something else was in his voice, too, but I couldn't identify it. Pain?

I felt like barging straight into the room with them, turning to the woman and saying, 'So he's fucking with your life, too? I know how it feels, believe me!'

At that moment, his door swung open and he and a small,

127

dark-haired woman emerged. She appeared to be about thirty-five or -six, no older, maybe younger. She came up to his shoulder and she held his hand. Tears dripped down her face. The outer door opened, too, and Boyce's secretary came in. He and she exchanged a look; the woman with Boyce attempted a smile. Everyone ignored me. Boyce walked the woman out of the office, and I heard them head down the hall.

His secretary settled herself firmly in place. She offered me coffee, but I shook my head. 'Is Boyce going to be back?' I demanded.

'He'll be back.' Her voice was abrupt, not its usual friendly chirp.

I paced back and forth.

A full five minutes passed before Boyce walked back through the reception area and into his inner office. I felt angrier than before the time lapse. How dare he just walk out like that?

Without waiting for a welcoming gesture, I stalked into his office. He stood by his bookcase, looking out the window.

'What'd you do to that client, Boyce?' I said. 'Call her ex-husband? Mind her fucking business?'

Pause.

Then: 'That was my wife.' Still looking out the window.

'Your wife?' I said. 'Your wife?' Oh, yes. The dark-haired woman in the picture with the baby.

'My wife.'

'You must be a great husband. You've made her real happy. I can see that.' And then I said, 'How about your baby? Is your baby a happy one? One big happy family?'

Boyce turned to face me. For a minute he just looked at me, but I had the feeling it wasn't me he was seeing. 'My baby's dead,' he said. 'A Sudden Infant Death Syndrome baby. Two years ago. My wife's had three miscarriages since then. She's determined to keep trying.'

I remembered, then, the secretary telling me not to mention the baby to Boyce. I felt awful. I wanted to say how sorry I was, but first I needed to tell him how I felt about his contacting Johanna.

After an awkward pause, I demanded, 'What's the big idea calling Johanna? She's none of your business.'

'Why don't you sit down, Richard?' Boyce sat down himself behind his big desk.

I stayed on my feet. 'I'm sorry about your baby,' I said, 'but that doesn't change anything between you and me. You had no right to call Johanna.' To my horror, I realized my voice had a tremor.

Boyce remained calm. He looked tired, his face drawn. He gestured toward the leather armchair facing his desk.

I had this horrible feeling that I might start crying. I didn't think it was my error about the baby. No, it was more as if my anger hid a well of sadness so great that it seeped through the anger like liquid through a sump pump. I swallowed hard, wanting to maintain my anger. My heart raced. I realized I was a person used to being angry and afraid: it was the daring to be sad that felt threatening.

'You had no business calling her.'

Boyce shrugged. 'I'm representing Claire.' He didn't turn red in the face and pop veins, but I saw a pulse beat in his jaw. 'We've been over this before, Richard. I'll do whatever it takes to help Claire.'

His words struck my heart. Wasn't it my job to help Claire? It seemed to me as if, from my earliest memories, there was Claire, looking up at me, pleading for my help, but I hadn't known where to start. I never had. I knew that now. I sensed Boyce knew it, too.

I panicked. 'You think I don't have what it takes to help her? Is that it? You waltz into our lives a week ago and you know it all.'

'Not yet,' said Boyce. 'But I'm going to. It's my job.' He didn't stand and he didn't raise his voice. 'I entered a plea of not criminally responsible by reason of insanity.'

'It's my job!' I shouted, barely registering what he'd said

about a plea. 'I'm her brother, not you. You don't know what it was like in my family having all those younger siblings to protect. Butting into my business isn't going to prove a thing, not one fucking thing.' I leaned forward, my hands on his desk, my face inches from his.

don't get angry

Boyce stood. I could feel his breath on my face and smell the mint of his toothpaste. 'You came in here uninvited. You shot off your mouth. Now sit down in that chair and listen to me or get out. You've got thirty seconds to decide.' He looked at his watch and I took a deep breath.

'You've got ten seconds.'

I sat down, but this thing between me and Boyce wasn't over.

Boyce, still standing, looked down at me. 'I got another phone call from Wilson Brown late yesterday afternoon. Says he and the family have talked it over and they're going to need more than funeral expenses. Says they're going to need compensation for John's not providing for them during their old age.'

Jesus, what next? My voice was loud, angry. 'John wouldn't have looked out for them. What are they talking about?' My heart still raced.

Boyce sat down. 'Scratching the golden goose, that's all. In court, I'll use what they've done to defame John.' He shrugged. 'It might be a good idea to buy them off, though. Get them out of the picture. Use 'em, but don't let them smear Claire in court or get sympathy for John.' He pushed a sheet of paper toward me. 'I worked out some numbers based on funeral expenses and stuff.'

I shoved the paper back toward Boyce. My hand shook. I'd made up my mind in Blueberry that I'd recommend to my parents that they pay the Browns' demands. Boyce didn't have to convince me. 'How do we keep them from increasing their blackmail?' I demanded.

'Let's let time take care of that.' Boyce leaned back in

his chair, hooking his arms behind it. 'This business with Claire and the trial will get settled and then the Browns can do whatever they like and it won't make a particle of difference. I'd say, pay now and see what develops. It's worth a few thousand to keep the grieving mother out of court.'

'He beat up Rilla, you know,' I said, feeling the heat in my face. 'If you had her under oath, she'd have to admit to it. She could grieve all she wanted, but it wouldn't change the fact that her son was a creep.'

'Don't be naïve, Richard. Even if she told the truth, which she wouldn't, a jury'd want to help her, not let off her son's murderer.'

'You listen to me, Boyce,' I said, thinking this time, this time I had him, 'I'll talk to my parents, get the money for the Browns, whatever, but you leave Johanna out of this. Leave my private life alone.'

'I'm going to tell you this one more time. I'm representing Claire. I'm going to do whatever it takes, talk to whomever I please, say whatever I want if it will help her. Do you get it? Johanna might be able to support some of Claire's allegations against your family. She and Claire were friends. You're not giving me much, Richard.'

'Jesus Christ. What the fuck do you want from me?' I was on my feet again.

'The truth.' Boyce stood, too. 'All you've given me is a bunch of bullshit about chainsaws and hunting. That sure as shit isn't where Claire went with your dad on that farm.'

'I'm not Claire.' My fist clenched.

'But you were there, Richard. You lived in that war zone your parents called home. Do you know your sister has flash-backs? Like a POW? Did you know that?'

'Shut up.' I felt the power in my clenched fist.

'Denial's a pretty thin protection from reality. She's walking down Memory Lane and she's got no one's hand to hold and no one to validate her so far. Looks like she's got more guts than either of her two brothers.'

I drew back my fist.

'Claire's out there on a limb clinging for dear life and it sure doesn't look to me as if her brothers are going to catch her.' Boyce put his face in mine. I could see the pores in his skin. 'And now,' he said, 'you can take your clenched fist and get out of my office. One more wrong move and I'll call the cops. I like protecting victims, ol' buddy, but believe me, I'm not one.'

'Big man,' I found myself sneering. 'Why not pull out a gun? Why not point it at my head? Convince me what a big guy you are. C'mon, show me.'

'Take a hike, Richard.'

'Big man.'

Boyce left his desk, moved swiftly across the room to the door. 'Time to go. We'll talk another day.' I saw him press a button on the wall.

The door was open, Boyce's secretary at her desk, two people sitting on the couch. The secretary looked up and, at Boyce's look, nodded. 'Lieutenant Nunez will be on the line in a minute,' she said.

'You don't have to call the cops, Boyce. I'm leaving. But you better leave Johanna out of this,' I hollered, and slammed from the office.

Outside, the October wind blew cold, mean, and relentless as if it were January.

I marched toward my office ten blocks away on Lexington. Every step was a smash to Boyce's face. A left, a right, a left, and a right hook to the jaw. Five long blocks later, I was pretty tired.

I did not want to think about what an ass I'd made of myself, I did not want to think about what Johanna might have told Boyce, and I did not want to think about Claire and whatever the hell she was spilling to Boyce. And I did not want to think about insanity. All my life I'd worked so hard to keep things under control, in compartments, manageable. Boyce wanted everything in the same fucking pot.

What happened to Claire on the farm

Something pelted me in the face and at first I thought it was a violent bystander, but within seconds I saw it was hail. All around me, people continued bustling as if hail were an ordinary October occurrence, but a few, like me, stopped and looked upward at the sky. No clouds, no gray skies. Only wind and hail.

What had Johanna told Boyce

I could remember only one other storm like this in my life and that had been at the farm. A weekend only my dad and I are there. We're outside the horse barn. A light dusting of snow lies on the ground and mists bare tree limbs. Snow sprinkles the rocks like powdered sugar on gingersnaps. The cloudless sky shines blue. And then, out of nowhere, a blast of hail. Big, round balls of ice that hurt when they strike you. My father shares my sense of wonder. He tells me he and his dad once experienced the same phenomenon. In their own backyard, he says, and it was sudden and swiftly over. Just like the one at the farm.

Just like the one in New York City twenty-five years later.

What happened to me on the farm

When I arrived at my office ten minutes later, Mary started off on a tangent about a hailstorm she'd barely survived as a girl, then stopped abruptly. 'I thought you weren't coming in today,' she said.

'I changed my mind,' I told her. I hung up my coat and headed down the hallway to my office. No way was I in the mood for questions. I slumped into the chair behind my desk. I took several deep breaths, trying to relax. It wouldn't be long before I'd have to leave to meet Johanna, and I didn't want to be more stressed out than I already was. Mary stuck her head in the door and said we had no clients coming in until after lunch. Without an invitation, she came in and sat

across from me. She lit up a cigarette and said, 'Boyce telephoned me yesterday.'

I jerked open a desk drawer and slammed it shut. 'What is
it with that guy? I just came from his office. He's determined
to ferret into my life. What is his fucking problem?' I wanted
to break something. I jumped up from my desk, moved to
the door and shut it. 'What did he want from you? What secrets
of mine did he want to know?'

Mary glanced at me. I looked away. Had she told him that
I was afraid to be in our office alone at night? That once I'd
thought I heard someone and become so frightened I couldn't
move, couldn't call for help, couldn't do anything? I'd thought
it was a man with a gun. Did she tell him she'd found me the
next morning practically catatonic with fear? Had she told
him my stomach gave me so much trouble I had to take
Metamucil every day to keep it regulated? Worse, had she
told him that I'd once confessed I envied Max his lifestyle?
Did she suggest to Boyce that Claire killed John because I
wasn't man enough to protect her?

Mary's voice was calm. 'Quiet down, boy. We talked about
old times. You know, Murders in the Rue Café 57.'

'What else?'

'He wanted to know more about you.'

'He won't leave me be,' I said. 'You'd think I murdered
John. He suggested it, even. He's fucked up.'

In a characteristic gesture, Mary ran her fingers through
her hair. She'd drive my mother crazy. 'When we were going
through that other trial and depositions and stuff, it was the
same way. Don't you remember?'

'No,' I said. Then it clicked. I'd been in Las Vegas, ostensibly
for an accounting seminar but also to get away from the
problems with Johanna. I counted it as time at the office,
though, because I had spent hours every day listening to some
guy from Atlanta drawl on and on about tax reform.

'You can't imagine the prying he did into my life. Surprises
me now that he didn't fly out to Vegas and sift through your

life, too, but he was on a tight time frame. Said he had to make sure I would survive the witness stand, that he couldn't have somebody appear out of nowhere that the DA dredged up and destroy my character. So he raked through my life with twelve-foot prongs. Talked to my cleaning lady. My hairdresser. Checked out Hal and tenants in our condo building. I'm telling you, Richard, the guy is a winner. He's doing his job.' She dragged on her cigarette. 'You're being a jerk.'

'Is that what you told him? Claire's busy shooting off her mouth, too. She's got time for Max and blabbing to Boyce, but she sure hasn't had time for me.'

'You sound like a whiny little brat. Claire is sick, she's in the nut-house, she needs your help. I'll damn well tell Boyce anything I think will help her and you need to do the same.'

'So now I've got you breathing down my neck, too,' I said.

Mary didn't say anything. I could see where her make-up ended and her make-upless neck began. She peered at me through the haze of her cigarette smoke. Her eyeliner was black and thick and her fingernails long and red as fresh strawberries. The tip of her cigarette was white ash. 'This isn't about you,' she said. 'It's about Claire.'

'Yeah, well, why doesn't she call me, then?'

'She will. Give her time.'

'You and Boyce,' I said. 'You're so sure of everything. Tell him anything you want, Mary. There's the phone.' I pointed to the sleek black phone on my desk. 'Tell him all about me. That I'm a constipated coward, an insomniac, a faggot. Go on.'

Mary ground out her cigarette in the ashtray I kept on the left-hand corner of my desk.

'Did he ever tell you he had a dead baby?' I demanded.

Mary shook her head.

'He called Johanna, too, you know. Why so surprised, Mary? My life is fair game. He gets to have his dead-baby secrets. I don't get to have any.' I grabbed my coat. 'You just go ahead and talk to Boyce. I'm just your partner, what difference does it make what I want?'

Mary said nothing.

I pushed my arms into my coat and left my office, hurrying out into the hall to the stairs, too angry to wait for the elevator.

I guess I thought if I ran fast enough, I could get away.

Sam's party seemed a lifetime ago.

Chapter Nine

AFTER stomping around town awhile in the cold, I scrunched into a seat on the crowded subway heading downtown between a fat lady and a skinny black kid with three earrings looped through each ear and a diamond piercing his nose. The train felt sticky and hot after the chill outside, oily somehow. Three panhandlers sidled through, each one's hard-luck story a marvel of misfortune. Vietnam. Abusive husband. Mental illness. I thought about joining them: psycho sister, partner's betrayal, battering attorney, tell-all ex-wife.

What had Johanna told Boyce

I was nervous about seeing Johanna. I hadn't seen her in months, not since the divorce was finalized. I wanted to hate her, but the truth is, I missed her. I'd never really understood why she'd left me, but maybe that was because I hadn't wanted to.

Three more stops and I'd be at Astor Place. Fifteen, maybe twenty minutes from the Cottonwood Café. My heart did a sickening flip-flop. I loved the way she looked in her skinny black tops and skirts. Her skin was so white, she never sunned, and her long, shiny black hair disappeared against the blackness of her blouses.

'I want to show Charlotte my new work,' she'd say, standing back to look at a drawing. 'Let's invite her and Aaron over.' But I hadn't wanted her friends invading our tiny space. I didn't want them calling or coming over. I didn't want her to have any friends.

The subway train clattered along its tracks, people jostling in and out, but I was lost in memory. Johanna and her friends were in their early twenties. Six of them rented a studio loft on Bleecker, using the space to paint and give private lessons to kids whose Upper West Side parents thought it gave them status.

Oddly enough, she and her friends admired me at first. 'I flounder,' she told me once, as we struggled to push the sofa bed back into a sofa so there'd be room to sit at the table for breakfast. 'But you,' she said, and I remembered how her voice tickled my ear as we pushed at the sofa, 'you know exactly who you are. You're an accountant. You work with numbers that don't change. People will always come to you begging for ways to lower their taxes or straighten jumbles in their checkbooks.' I had laughed but felt superior to her and her friends. I'd accepted that you had to toe the line to get anywhere. Most of her friends waited tables or bartended to make ends meet, and I figured it was just a question of time before they'd have to enter the real world. More than once I'd pointed out to Johanna that I'd had to give up the trumpet. Now, as I hurtled toward Astor Place in a dirty subway car amidst NYU and Cooper Union students with purple hair, linty black coats and cheap dangling earrings, I saw that maybe I'd sensed her ambivalence about the marriage from the beginning and thought I had her where I wanted her because she didn't make enough money to survive in New York without me.

I was so angry when she left I wanted to smash everything or anything at all. Mostly I wanted to smash her. How dare she leave me for somebody else? Maybe I'd made mistakes, maybe I hadn't paid her enough attention, but she was my wife. I had loved our life together. I couldn't get enough of her. Being inside her felt like coming home. I finally had a place I belonged. The feeling of safety I had when I was with her made me try sexual feats that still arouse me in the remembering. She was so slight I could flip her like a pancake.

I needed to change the direction of my thoughts.

The train jerked to a halt at Astor Place and I leaped off and marched past the Astor Place barber shop, past the NYU dorms, and through Washington Square Park. Someone jostled hard against me and I did a quick wallet check. I faced the wind and headed toward Bleecker to meet Johanna.

I got to the Cottonwood ten minutes before noon. I knew from experience she'd be late, but I didn't want even the slimmest chance that she'd get there first. I wanted to see her before she saw me. I stood outside and froze.

At exactly fifteen past twelve, she hurried up Bleecker, and I swallowed my irritation at her lateness. My heart surprised me by not doing anything more than one roll-over play-dead flip-flop.

I saw at once that she was nervous. She didn't look at me, just said an abrupt hello, brushed past me and swished inside the door. We settled into seats. A waiter took our order. Within minutes, Johanna swirled a Texan Hot Bloody Mary swizzle stick and I sipped draft beer.

The Cottonwood looked the same as it had in our courting days with its down-home Texan decor, rustic tables, scratched wooden floors. Johanna looked the same, too. Pale, dressed in black, long hair swept into a bun with a dark green knitting needle thrust through it. She wore black boots and a black coat, black turtleneck, and a long pleated black skirt. When we sat down and she pulled off her gloves, I saw her fingernails were short and grimy, green and yellow paint staining her fingers. She saw me looking. 'Still from different worlds, Richard,' she said.

'Maybe,' I said, and thought of Sam's pink nails with their white tips.

'Did you think I'd be here?' She tilted her head to one side in the way that always made me think of a puppy. I noticed she wore only one earring. A big silver one with turquoise stones. It dangled against her shoulder.

'I knew you'd come.'

'You knew more than I did, then. I wasn't sure at all. I didn't like that you hadn't told me about Claire. And I didn't like the tone of your message.'

'You're here, aren't you?'

'I was really hurt to hear it from Charlotte.' She had that snippy edge to her voice.

'I was really hurt when you left me.' I took a slug of beer and hoped my shaking hand didn't slosh it over the edge of the glass. The odd thing was that I was speaking the truth to her, probably for the first time since she'd left. My anger had hidden the pain.

Silence. Clink of ice. More slurps of beer.

I watched her take a deep breath. 'You sure never told me that at the time,' she said. 'You dumped all over me. You acted like you owned me. You tried to sue me for adultery. You called Charlotte and tried to set her against me.'

'You fucked around on me,' I said.

Johanna stood, grabbing her gloves and trying to shove her hands into them. Her face looked white as whipped cream against her turtleneck. 'I'm not listening to this shit from you. I only came here today because I felt bad about Claire. You can forget my sympathy.'

First Boyce, then Mary, now Johanna.

'Sit down,' I said. 'I'm sorry. I'll watch what I say. I want to help Claire, you know that.'

She looked at me. 'Not one more word about Ed. Understood?'

I nodded. She yanked off those gloves. She sat down.

The waiter slapped down enormous plates of food. A chicken-fried steak with mashed potatoes and golden gravy and mounds of coleslaw for me; fried chicken and fries smothered in gravy for Johanna. I pushed aside my plate and ordered another beer.

'I thought you weren't going to drink anymore,' Johanna said.

'What?'

'Claire told me with your family being the way it was, you thought you ought to quit drinking. She says you told her you were going to quit.'

'Did you ever know me to drink too much?'

'No.'

'Then, what is this bullshit about my drinking?'

'Because of your father.'

My beer arrived and I took a gulp. 'My father?'

She gave me her look, the one that once had filled me with guilt and a searing need to do her bidding. 'It's not like I don't know he's got a drinking problem.'

'What are you talking about?'

'Earth to Richard,' said Johanna. 'Like Claire hasn't told me? Like I haven't spent enough time at that blasted farm to know your father's whole personality changes after one of those giant Scotches of his? I've seen him turn from Raging Bull into Mr Happy Face, all friendly and affectionate like he's my best friend. You know that. C'mon.'

I felt angrier with her then than I had when she left me. I wanted to leap up, grab her Bloody Mary and smash it into her face. Maybe break a tooth or two. Mar that white face.

don't get angry

'Look at you and that Bloody Mary,' I said. 'How many'd you drink that night with Charlotte? Four? Five? How much vodka did you go through that last month we lived together? Two bottles? Three? Maybe you ought to think about quitting.'

'I am not here to talk about me. Whom are you protecting?' Johanna's voice grated. 'It's certainly too late for Claire.'

'He didn't drink in Waterton.' I enunciated each word.

'Wow,' she said. 'From what Claire tells me, it's your mother who was swigging away in Waterton. Quite the wine addict. Queen of the back-porch winos.'

I took my hand off my beer glass, afraid I'd break it. 'When are you and Claire doing all this talking?'

'She called me yesterday,' said Johanna quietly.

'She called you yesterday,' I repeated, feeling stupid. 'What did she want? Why did she call you?'

How dare she

'I think she wanted to talk about you.' My ex-wife tilted her head to the side and her earring brushed her shoulder. 'We didn't get that far, though. She wasn't quite focused.'

I waited for her to go on.

'I thought she was talking about John, but I'm not sure. She talked about him sexually abusing her. She said he'd forced her and that he made her do things she didn't want to do, but mostly she talked smells and darkness and his oozy rank sweat.' She stopped and looked at me. 'It didn't sound like husband stuff to me. She sounded like a child.'

The gravy congealed atop my mashed potatoes.

'So,' I said, 'what did you tell Boyce?'

'About the drinking. About Claire's phone call.'

'Well, aren't you Miss Helpful Fucking Hannah,' I said.

'What is the matter with you? This is Claire's life, her future, her mental health. What else matters?'

'My privacy,' I blurted. 'My family's privacy.'

'God, you remind me of your mother and all that crap at our divorce about the family's right to privacy, blah, blah, blah. She was always going on about the family like it was some sacred cow to be worshipped. She always acted as if your family was better than mine.' She jabbed at a piece of chicken-fried steak, but I could see her hand was shaking.

'What else did you tell Boyce?'

'I told him you hit me.'

I felt the heat in my face. 'I hit you one time, Johanna. One time.'

'With your fist.'

'You told Boyce I hit you with my fist? Did you tell him that you nagged, nagged, nagged? Did you tell him all I did was notice a new painting of yours and ask about the colors? Did you tell him you called me a pompous bastard? Did you tell him you had a fucking boyfriend?'

Johanna stood up again. 'This is why we're divorced, you asshole. Nothing's your fault, is it? I sounded too much like your mother to suit you, right? You weren't noticing my painting, you were making fun of me, but I wasn't ever supposed to say anything that rocked your boat, was I? Couldn't mention that you never touched that trumpet, could I? Couldn't mention the way you stayed at that damn office morning, noon and night, could I? You and your family are perfect, right? That's why your sister Tina blew her brains out in your parents' bedroom and your sister Elizabeth's hidden herself in obscure books for years and Max ran all the way to San Francisco to be himself. All this because Bev and Jack are so fucking perfect, right? That's why Claire's locked in the nut-house and you're running from reality as fast as you can go. What do you suppose happened to Claire at that farm that's making her crazy as a bedbug twenty years later? You think she turned crazy one day with the flick of a switch? I've known her since college days and she's always been weird. And you're a tightassed controlling son of a bitch. Fuck you, Richard. Fuck your family.' She grabbed her coat.

I stood, too, towering over her. 'What else did you tell Boyce Regner?' Three waiters appeared from nowhere and hovered close by.

For a minute she said nothing, as if considering her words or getting control of her anger. She gave a yank on her gloves and with a jerk fastened the top button on her coat. Then she looked straight at me. 'I told him about the gash on Claire's forehead,' she said, and left the restaurant without so much as one backward glance.

Chapter Ten

I ORDERED another beer. The waiters disappeared, but someone I took to be the manager now appeared at the table. 'We don't want any trouble,' he said.

'I don't, either,' I said.

'I think, after this one, you've had enough beer.'

'Okay, fine,' I told him, embarrassed. Never in my life had I been in a situation where the restaurant manager had to reprimand me. I had to calm down. I could not allow Johanna to make me that angry. What was the point? She was nothing to me. I was caught in a mess over which I had no control and I hated it.

Oddly enough, I had a sudden sense of finality about my relationship with Johanna and it felt okay, as if it was complete. I saw that signing the divorce papers hadn't brought an end to my involvement with Johanna, but that somehow this lunch meeting had. I almost smiled when I realized it was a feeling not unlike the feeling I had each year on April 16, the day after tax returns are due to the IRS – exhaustion, relief, and a certain emptiness.

Instead of gulping down my beer and hurrying from the Cottonwood, I let myself feel the emptiness. Beneath it lay sadness and the recognition of loss. Johanna's angry words about me and my family forced me to acknowledge that it wasn't just chance she'd gotten involved with someone else.

At the time we'd divorced, I'd been too angry to admit any responsibility for our marriage's failure. But I had neglected her; I'd patronized her talent, too. We did love each other, I thought. Johanna had obviously lost her belief in me, and I, I now saw, had lost the ideal that what took place in a marriage and a family was private.

I told him about the gash on Claire's forehead

My anger surged back. I sat in the Cottonwood for at least an hour, until my heart rate resembled that of a normal person, and then I paid the bill, being careful to avoid the waiter's eye. Normally I tipped exactly fifteen percent; today, I tipped twenty, hoping to appease the Cottonwood and show them I was a gentleman, after all.

I headed outside and wandered through SoHo and Chinatown, not feeling the cold but my past. No amount of beer could keep out Johanna's accusations about my parents' drinking. Nothing could erase her grating voice: *I told Boyce you hit me*, or my own vicious response: *Did you tell him you had a fucking boyfriend?* And Johanna: *Nothing's your fault, is it?* I'd never known how to tell her I was sorry. I'd pretended it never happened, but the shame of hitting my wife was as great as the shame I felt at my failure to protect Claire long ago at 37 Brookfield Court . . .

What else did you tell Boyce Regner
I told him about the gash on Claire's forehead

I supposed she still had the thin white scar, although I never noticed it, not even when we'd sat facing each other over one of the tiny round tables at the Village Patisserie. Now, as I hurried across narrow streets and down the crowded sidewalks of lower Manhattan, I recalled her telling me how Skip didn't like her scar. 'You ought to have plastic surgery,' she told me he said to her one night in his room. 'He needs a nose job,' I remembered telling Claire. She'd smiled, but smiles don't erase unkind words. They don't erase memories like ours any better than beer.

I kept on walking, but I wasn't thirty-five years old anymore, and I wasn't on Canal Street. Lunch with Johanna had pushed me back to 37 Brookfield Court and I'm nothing but a kid and my heart is thump, thump, thumping . . .

My mother's prepared supper – some kind of chicken casserole and a tossed salad. She's mixed Russian salad dressing out of ketchup and mayonnaise and all us kids hate the speckles of unmixed ketchup looking like blood. We sit in our assigned seats around the table, my father at the head, my mother to his right. Claire sits to her right, then me, opposite my father with Elizabeth, Tina, Max lining the other side. My father's home from his rounds at the hospital and wearing his black suit, starched white shirt, skinny dark tie. His hair is slicked back and his skin has the fresh scrubbed look of a newly washed little boy. Mother's wearing her red and white checked wraparound house dress.

I can feel the tension. We're all waiting to see what mood he's in. We're wondering which child he'll focus on tonight. Not me, I'm hoping. There's a buzz of fear inside me and my heart beats fast. Beside me, I see Claire picking mushrooms out of her casserole. 'They're squishy,' she whispers to me, 'like slugs.'

Then it happens. He sees her. I touch Claire's leg under the table. She looks at me. He's out of his seat and she doesn't realize it yet. I stop breathing. Elizabeth, Tina, and Max sit in silence, unmoving. He comes up behind her and cups her head in his hand. He smashes her face into her plate. I see the prongs of the fork press her forehead. I see the veins in his hand. I peek at his face. Elizabeth and I exchange a look, and I see her glance toward our mother. No help there. He's got the look that means he's out of control. His face is red and there's spittle in the corners of his mouth. A vein throbs dead center in his forehead. I wonder if his patients would recognize him or the helpful nurses hovering in the operating room.

Fear is in our dining room, familiar and palpable as a family member.

He grabs her hair and pulls back her head. I catch a glimpse of her face. It's expressionless, like the corpse of our grandfather resting in his coffin last summer. Crack! Her face hits the plate again. 'Eat them.' His voice is loud. Claire ignores him. He yanks back her head. This time I see four red marks from the fork lining her cheek. She reaches for the fork, but he's quicker. 'Here, Bev,' he says, shoving the plate toward our mother. 'You feed her.'

Mom's quick. She's got the fork rammed down Claire's throat in no time. My sister chokes and the mushrooms go flying. One hits Elizabeth smack on the forehead. One lands on my plate. One plops on the linen tablecloth, a mushy brown blob. I think I might vomit.

He's got Claire's chair pulled back from the table now. His hand's on the back of her head again, and *bam*! He smashes her forehead against the edge of the table. He does it again. Again. There's blood. I stop breathing. I don't look at Elizabeth or Max or Tina. What if he kills her, I think, but I'm immobile with fear. I can't do anything for my sister.

I hear Mom's voice, then. A low whiny noise that's speeding up and getting louder. 'Jack, Jack, Jack.' I see her snake out a hand and lay it on his arm. 'Jack,' she says, and this time her voice gets through to him, and he drops his hand. Claire's plate is full of mushrooms swimming in blood. The flower pattern on the china looks forgotten. The place where Claire's hair meets her forehead is matted with blood.

Now there's another feeling around our dining-room table. I can sense it, but I don't know what it is. It makes me think of two animals who've been on the hunt and succeeded. It's a tired feeling, but there's triumph in it, and a certain pulsing excitement. I feel the adrenalin. I smell my sister's blood. I see my father wipe the back of his hand across his forehead, sweat drops zinging through the air. My mother's face gleams, too. My father returns to his place at the head of the table. He and my mother exchange a glance. They look at Claire's head resting in her mushrooms. Her hair has become the same color as the bloody gravy. She doesn't move. There'll be no signal from me that everything's all right.

My father looks around the table at his other children. We pick up our forks and push tasteless bits of casserole into our mouths. I lift my fork, I put it into my mouth; I lift my fork, I put it into my mouth; I lift my fork, I put it into my mouth.

Claire remains unmoving. The bloody gravy on her plate overflows onto the white linen tablecloth. I don't let myself think about my mother's reaction to the stain. Who will clean up the mess?

The atmosphere in the room is changing. I know my mother's revving up to take charge. I see her glance at him. His face is still red, so she knows anything can still set him off. She says, 'Claire must have hurt herself when she fell against the table. I think we better take her to the emergency room.' Her voice is bright, almost cheery. 'Richard,' she adds, 'you come with me to help. They all know your father at the hospital, so we'll get the best of service.' Some small mean part of me is glad she didn't pick Max.

I hold Claire against me in the back seat on the way to the hospital. She opens her eyes. We both see our mother's marble eyes in the rear-view mirror. We hear her say, 'You slipped and fell, Claire. That's how you hurt yourself,' and there's such menace in that voice and so many years of knowledge that we say, 'I know.' It doesn't occur to me that I have any choice at all.

Richard, you come with me to help

And there it was, the memory I'd been shoving away.

Richard, you come with me to help, come with me to help

The flashback vanished and I found myself hurrying along Mercer Street. I kept on moving, not stopping until I reached the South Street Seaport and one step further would have put me into freezing water. I had a crazy thought: Could playing my trumpet blow away my memories? Could a wild rendition of 'Round Midnight' explain a father who made me pancakes thick with blueberries and love, and bloodied my sister over uneaten mushrooms?

Couldn't mention that you never touched that trumpet, could I

I don't remember how I got home that evening. I know I stopped at the coffee shop on the corner of 75th and Second for supper before heading to my apartment. I remember Lucy made me smile once or twice and that I mentioned meeting Sam to her, but I also remember I couldn't shake the sense of doom hanging over me or the rapid beat of my heart.

Richard, you come with me to help

I climbed the steps to my apartment, afraid. Of what, I don't know. Maybe the bogeyman.

I stepped inside my door and, as if to confirm my fears, the first thing I noticed was the light flashing on my answering machine. Claire? Max? Boyce? I peered at the machine. Two messages. I took a breath, trying to still my rapid heartbeat. It was then, as I slowly counted to ten, that I remembered that, as a kid, sitting at Bev and Jack's six o'clock dinner table, my heart had done this same wild dance. Not just the night of Claire's gash. Every night. It was as if I was at their table now, every muscle tensed, awaiting developments. A blast of the phone at supper time could set Jack off on a rampage. I remembered Tina turning to me, after he'd spit at her that she was 'a pitiful excuse for a human being', and saying, 'Poor Daddy, having to go to the hospital in the rain.'

Tonight, a simple flash of the answering machine was enough to put my body on watch.

You are on watch for the rest of your life

Who could be calling me? The Browns? Johanna? Boyce? My parents?

I pressed the play button.

'Richard? It's Mom. Call me back tonight. No matter how late. We have to have your help with this Brown situation.'

Richard, you come with me to help

149

'I don't want to help,' I said, and my voice seemed to fill the room.

Now Claire's voice skittered around the room. 'I've talked to Max. And Johanna,' she said. 'Don't be mad.' A pause. Then, 'Call me tomorrow. I can only take calls between eight thirty and nine thirty in the morning on Saturday. I miss you, Richard.' She gave me her number at the hospital and hung up.

I got a beer from the refrigerator, ripped off my tie, and flung myself down on the couch, crushing my coat. I was afraid of what Claire might tell me and what response she might expect from me, but my mother's call was a different story. Like the Pied Piper of Hamelin, her haunting voice lured the Incredible Shrinking Boy forth to follow her.

I took another swig of beer. The can felt slick and cold in my hand. I pressed it against my hot cheek. Here's the thing: Old habits die hard.

Honor thy father and thy mother

I picked up the phone and dialed the Waterton number. I could feel the knot in my stomach tighten and my heart rate pick up. I looked at my hand and it appeared smaller. My whole body looked smaller to me.

A loud click, then my father's commanding voice came over the wire. 'What's going on down there, Richard? That lawyer of Claire's hasn't been very forthcoming.'

I could picture him in bed in that scratchy wool maroon bathrobe of his, every hair slicked into place, some religious book like *The Jesus Party* in his hand. My mother'd be lying next to him looking like death.

The better to see you, my dear

'I went to the funeral,' I said. 'Let's just pay and get them out of the picture.'

'I don't think it's necessary to put it quite like that, Richard,' said my father. 'If we pay, it'll be because it's the right thing to do. They've lost a son. Claire is somehow involved.'

I pulled the phone away from my ear for a minute and

stared at it in amazement. Claire is somehow involved? I found myself almost shouting: 'Dad, she's not somehow involved. She shot him dead in their apartment. Her involvement is clear. It's her responsibility and motivation that's at question. We don't need the Browns muddying the waters. Pay them.' Even as I spoke, I knew this was not the way to handle my father. Euphemisms were the big thing. Never, ever say what you really think or feel. But I realized I was sick of the shit. I had the strongest sense of Max being in the room with me.

'Dad,' I said loudly, 'do you remember all the drugs we used to have around the house? The Miltown in the kitchen, that cupboard in your bedroom filled with the jar of a thousand pills?'

'What are you talking about?' My father's voice was thin, but its edges were thick and spongy.

'The drugs, Dad.'

'We didn't have drugs in this house.' The thin part of his voice became a wire, but the thick spongy part grew thicker and spongier.

'Yes, we did. I'm not accusing. I'm just wondering about them, that's all.' Already he had me backing off.

'You're as crazy as your sister, Richard.' Now my father laughed. 'They'll lock you up next.'

I don't know why, but his words almost made me sick with a sudden dizzying fear. My ears plugged, my heart raced. I thought I might throw up.

thump, thump

And then Max's voice came to me, loud and clear and reassuring: *Look out, big bro. Black is white, Richard. Up is down. Claire is crazy; your mother and I are normal. Now you see the pills, now you don't. The better to eat you with, my dear.*

I cleared my throat, swallowed. 'Dad,' I said, my voice shaking, hand slick on the phone, 'I'll send you a breakdown of the funeral costs and stuff. Mail them a check. Don't write anything that can be used against Claire in court.'

He acted as if he knew what I meant, and after a bit we

hung up. No more mention was made of the drugs, and I realized no more would be. Boyce might think denial's a pretty thin protection from reality, but my parents' denial seemed tough as a New York streetwalker to me.

this never happened, never happened, never happened

I finally pulled out the sofa bed, but I couldn't sleep. I kept seeing the mirage of my life as a child – the doctor father, the homemaker mother, the five children impeccably groomed, nails clipped, hair combed, clothes ordered from Best & Company. We all dressed alike when we trundled off to church with Jack and Bev. Max and I wore plaid shorts with bibs and Claire and Elizabeth matching plaid jumpers. Our shirts were starched white with Peter Pan collars. Claire and Elizabeth had blue wool coats with two rows of round brass buttons and blue velveteen collars. Max and I had plain double-breasted camel's hair coats with matching caps. Marching into church each week, I felt proud. Sometimes Jack was there, sometimes not, due to hospital emergencies which we considered very important. In fact, I'd always registered Jack's work more important than God's. Nothing in my life ever led me to believe otherwise. But my mother went to church each Sunday and she led the way for us children and she smelled wonderful and rustled. It was a lovely sound of slips and petticoats and silken stockings swooshing against each other as she swayed down the church aisle. We followed the seams in her stockings, Claire in the middle. I'd see the envious glances of not-so-fine churchgoers and be proud. Especially because I was the eldest and the tallest.

Honor thy father, honor thy father, honor thy father . . .

Could Max and I have been mistaken about the drugs? I knew I didn't want to give up those blueberry pancakes thick with butter and warm maple syrup nor the feel of my .22 rifle, slick and powerful beneath my hand, nor the chainsaw rife with the sounds of manhood. I needed *Uncle Wiggily and Curley and Floppy and Twistytail* in the hammock and I needed the farm to stay green and lush and I needed the great horned eagle to swoop down from its nest in the Blue Ridge Mountains each and every summer. The way I saw it, that's all I really had.

I tossed and turned all night.

Is white black

What had happened to me on that farm

Chapter Eleven

I DRAGGED out of bed Saturday morning feeling as if I'd been on a major drunk the night before. I had that thick-mouthed feeling I remembered from high school and college and my head felt heavy. As I put the tea kettle on my big burner, the sounds of Gordon Lightfoot drifted over from the fat man's apartment, a song filled with heartache about a woman named Lavender. I thought it was the right tone for my day.

The weather looked right, too. Cloudy, sky gray and tinged with yellow. Pollution or an ugly storm on its way.

I glanced at the clock. Another hour and I could call Claire. Even though I knew it was childish, a part of me resented being dictated the terms of the call. In my accounting practice, I returned calls between two and three every afternoon, and my clients soon learned that about me.

I fried myself a sorry little egg and tried eating it. It was supposed to be sunny side up but had managed to break and ooze all over the pan. As I dumped salt and pepper on my Egg MacMuffin, I remembered mornings at 37 Brookfield Court. Bev had a routine she followed as surely as if we were in the army.

Sunday mornings we sat down to scrambled eggs, bacon, and warm bakery cinnamon buns. Every single Sunday. The thing that always struck me odd about the buns was that she knew Claire and I loved them, yet she always bought four, never more. They were big, so there was enough to go around, but why four? Why not half a dozen? Why not a dozen if you get right down to it? No matter how much we fussed, her number remained the same. As did her breakfast routine.

Mondays we had boiled eggs, toast, orange juice and milk. Max, Claire, Elizabeth, and I each had to have a tall glass of orange juice and a tall glass of milk along with our eggs and toast. Tina had milk in a pink plastic bottle. My mother always toasted white bread and buttered it while hot, so the butter melted into the bread and made it soggy. I liked it that way, but Max didn't. Max and I liked the eggs, but Claire didn't. If it wasn't boiled hard enough, she'd make terrible faces at me and Max and sweep it into her napkin.

Tuesdays were Wheatena days served piping hot without milk. Sometimes, my father swirled honey onto our cereal. Elizabeth and I liked that, but Max and Claire both thought he ought to ask first. Plus he had a very nasty habit of rolling boiled kidneys onto our hot cereal. They were reddish brown and smelled rank, the way dead animals at the farm smelled. I shuddered, remembering. It always made me mad that my mother helped cover for Max as he slid them into his napkin, but I had to swallow them down like a man.

Wednesdays were scrambled eggs again, but no bacon or cinnamon buns, and Thursday was hot cereal again, usually Cream of Wheat but sometimes oatmeal. Friday we had fried eggs, bacon and toast, and every morning we had those tall glasses of orange juice and milk.

Nobody else I'd ever known had a breakfast routine like ours and as I sat at my tiny table in my studio apartment in New York swallowing a semi-scrambled egg, I wondered exactly how that routine fit into our childhood. At the time, I'd given it little thought. It was great to have a mother who got up every morning and had breakfast ready, no question there. We ate at the exact same time every day, too, 7.15 a.m., no surprises. Max and Claire hated the routine. Even on

Saturdays, they determined the type of cold cereal we could eat: Cheerios, Shredded Wheat, and every other week, she bought Frosted Flakes or Sugar Pops. No wonder I remembered my dad's blueberry pancakes with such fondness.

I pushed away my egg and poured a glass of orange juice.

What was in it for my mother, I wondered. I don't think she was someone who enjoyed cooking or planning an aesthetic table. Again, I thought of that tray with its Miltown, Excedrin, the variety bottle, the Darvon, Librax, multi-vitamins.

I remembered her looking pinched and efficient on those long-ago mornings, her Sunday-siren persona gone, her death-in-bed role vanquished by morning. Mornings she'd bustle downstairs, a slash of pink across her mouth, hair still in criss-crossed bobby pins, wearing Bermuda shorts and a matching shell, and she'd make all our breakfasts. I don't remember her sitting down with us. I think she must have eaten as soon as we left for school.

I sipped my orange juice, remembering how pressured I'd felt by our morning schedule and the efficient bustling mother persona. I guess there was what Johanna would call a subtext present in that kitchen. I recalled a time in the college frat house when Skip had offered to cook me an omelette. Go for it, I'd said. And he had and it had been great and I'd done my dishes and his as well, yet that omelette lingered in the air between us. Later in the day, he asked me to pick him up a *Times* when I was at the student union and I said sure, but I forgot. You know what Skip said? He said as if it was a joke, 'Give me back my omelette, then.' I think he meant it. A subtext, I thought. My mother's subtext was, now you owe me your life.

I tossed the rest of my juice down the sink and plopped my egg plate down, too. I didn't feel like eating anymore.

Maybe my mother longed for a different kind of life.

Maybe none of the roles she played fit her.

Maybe she hated us for ruining her chances.

Nobody tied her down and forced her to make babies

I yanked my gray sweats from the floor of my closet and pulled them on. I felt chilled.

The first three times I tried my office to tell Mary I'd be late getting in once again, the line was busy. Even though it was Saturday, I knew she'd be working on final extension tax returns and a divorce valuation due at the end of the month. By the time I reached her, my hands were damp with nervous sweat, my heart racing rat-like around an experimental wheel. Not only did I owe her an apology for yesterday's behavior and for leaving her alone at the office yet again, I wanted her to calm my fears about talking to Claire. Her own brothers and sisters called her at least once a day about calamities in their lives; her sister with the varicose veins was getting a divorce; her professional basketball-playing brother had been busted for drugs; her youngest stepsister wanted to know if she was supposed to save her paycheck stubs. The funny thing was that Mary professed not to be all that fond of any of them, and I, who claimed to be close to Max and Claire, scarcely ever talked with them. Somehow, I'd managed to convince myself that my way, the Hayes way, was superior. Reserved and dignified. We didn't intrude on each other's lives. Right now I envied Mary her easy camaraderie and the way she'd holler at Kerry or Brian or Robin and, in the next breath, laugh.

Fourth time I tried, Mary picked up on the first ring. 'Hayes and Lintini. How may I help you?'

'Mary? It's me.'

'I'm here, big boy.'

'I'm sorry about yesterday.' It was really hard for me to say that, but I meant it, and I felt less nervous the moment I'd spit out those words.

'You should be.'

'I know, you're right.' Telling Mary she was right didn't feel like losing. In my family, admitting someone else was right was the same as confessing your total inadequacy as a person. Jack and Bev were never wrong.

'So what else is on your mind? You could have marched your butt in here and told me that.'

All nervousness disappeared. 'Claire called me,' I said. 'She left a message on the answering machine. I'm supposed to call her this morning at eight thirty.'

'Hallelujah,' said Mary.

A silence fell between us, and then she said, 'I'm glad Claire got in touch, Richard. I hope the call goes well.'

'I know. I am sorry, you know, about yesterday and all.' I felt a lot better. The thing about Mary, I'd learned, was that I could make mistakes, and she'd still be there the next day. I didn't have to be perfect. I didn't have the feeling she was keeping a tally sheet the way I'd always felt my sister Elizabeth did. Judging from Max's calls, maybe some of the other sibs did, too.

'Hey,' I said. 'I went to a party Thursday night. Sam Saunders, a woman, a client of Boyce's, invited me.'

Mary let out a whoop my neighbor across the way probably heard. It drowned out Gordon, that's for sure. And for a moment, I wished I was her brother Brian or Joey, instead of her senior partner at Hayes and Lintini.

'She says it's okay to call her, and you know what?' I confided, surprising myself. 'I think the timing may be exactly right. It's really over with Johanna. I see that now.'

'Just a few other minor complications,' said Mary.

'Thanks for the vote of confidence,' I said, but I was smiling. 'Just pile returns on my desk. Don't try to do it all. I'll be in sometime today.'

'Don't worry,' said Mary. 'I'll struggle on without you, believe it or not.'

I still had a smile on my face when we hung up.

Eight thirty. My smile was gone. Nervous anticipation replaced it.

I sat at my table. I picked up the phone. It felt as if it weighed ten pounds. If it had been later in the day, I know I would have gotten a beer from the frig. Until that moment, it had not once occurred to me to not return Claire's call, but as I sat at my kitchen table I considered it. Here she was blabbing away to Boyce, to Max, to Johanna, and she clearly felt entitled to contact me in her own sweet time and didn't doubt that I'd jump when she snapped her fingers.

I wished I could block out thoughts like that. I was her elder brother. I felt as if I'd been father to Max and Claire all my life and only realizing now how exhausting it was. Elizabeth may have fought me for top-dog position in the family, but I was the one who'd taken Tina on her first city bus ride when she was four years old and she'd clung to my hand as tight as any little girl ever held her daddy's. I was the first one Max saw in the hospital after his emergency appendectomy. I'm the one Claire shadowed throughout our childhood. I'd carried the burden of them needing me all my life. I had yet to have any kids of my own and I was already worn out from childrearing.

I wished none of this was happening. Why couldn't things be the way they were before she'd killed John?

You ain't kidding nobody but yourself, big bro, if you think those were the halcyon days

I dialed the number Claire gave me, and after one ring, she picked up. 'I knew it would be you.' Her voice sounded like a little girl's voice, thin and high like Minnie Mouse. There was a tremble in it that was so much like my little sister of the farm and Brookfield Court that my eyes welled with tears before she said another word.

'I get to talk for fifteen minutes this morning.' She lowered her voice. 'I'm locked in, but that's okay.'

'You're locked in?' Why did those words frighten me so much?

'It's to make me feel safe,' she said.

'Do you?' My voice squeaked.

Silence.

'Claire?'

'I'm trying to find the right words,' she said, and I remembered the pauses in our conversations growing up when she'd say, 'I'm trying to find the words in my heart,' and I'd picture her inside her heart searching through trees and brambles for words. Sometimes she'd telephone me at a friend's house or at Munsy's, but when I'd come to the phone, she wouldn't say anything at all. There'd be the sound of her breathing and that's it. I'd know it was Claire and that she wanted me to come home, and I'd go.

'They're still here with me,' she said at last.

'Who?' I said, but, of course, I knew whom she'd say before she squeaked out her confession.

'Mom and Dad.' Now she was whispering and I pressed the phone so hard to my ear I thought I might damage it.

'What about John?' I asked.

'Who?' she said.

What happened to me and Claire on the farm

When I didn't respond, she said, 'Remember the drugs on the kitchen table?' Then she laughed, sounding exactly like herself, not a crazy person at all, and said, 'And the secret jar he kept hidden in his dresser in the bedroom at Brookfield Court?' Again the laugh. 'Remember?'

We didn't have drugs in this house

'I think it's the money that I remember best,' I said. 'All those coins wrapped and labeled like precious treasure.' Why didn't I confirm her memories of the drugs?

Honor thy father and thy mother

'Max remembers the drugs,' said Claire. 'He says when he was in high school he used to grab a handful from the secret jar and sell them. He says everybody liked Darvon in those days. Max says Dad kept pills all over the house. He says he liked to go through Dad's coat pockets and find drugs for the day. He says they were in the glove box in his Land Rover, too. Max says the reason Dad ate dog biscuits was because drug users' taste buds aren't like other people's.'

You're as crazy as your sister, Richard

This whole conversation made me crazy. My doctor father tells me we had no drugs. My sister in the nut-house says we did. My memory says we did. I felt mired in quicksand and struggled to get out. 'The dog biscuits have nothing to do with drugs,' I said, in my best authoritative big-brother voice. 'He chawed those to show us what a man he was.'

'It's those drugs that nearly killed me.' Claire was back to her whispering voice. 'I'm about eleven years old and inside I'm a mess. I see how Mom'll take one or two pills and she'll get bouncy and happy, flying high, and I think, Wow! Pills can do that? Whoopee!'

Munsy's goose was damn near stomping me to death.

I tried to break in and halt revelations I didn't want to hear, saying, 'Mom took pills? What are you saying, Claire?' For a moment, I let myself believe that Claire was crazy. It would be so much easier if that was true.

Afraid of what she might say

'But I don't want to fly,' she said. 'I want to be the woman under the gravestone at the farm. Emma? Remember Emma? I snuck up to her grave at night when you and Max were sleeping and I'd lie down so my tombstone was right above me. Emma, Emma, Emma.'

'Claire,' I said, wanting her to stop, knowing in my heart that every word she spoke was the truth. I had that urge to tell her to shut up, to be her silent shadow self and to stop rocking the boat. It all happened a long time ago.

'I want to be like Emma,' Claire said. 'I want all the ugliness over, the chaos inside me peaceful. You know what I mean?'

'I know,' I said, my mouth so dry my lips were sticking.

'I get the giant jar from his cabinet,' she continued, 'and carry it downstairs to the kitchen. Mom is reading Frances Parkinson Keyes at the table and she's wearing those turquoise Bermuda shorts and a white shell. She's got the blue mules on her feet and her fingers look puffy, maybe the heat. There's a familiar tomatoey odor in the kitchen and I think she's making those meatballs in rice she likes to make and I peek into a pot on the stove and there's those meatballs, sure enough, rice sticking to them like maggots.

'I jiggle the jar and pick out the big red one that I think does the trick and I put it in my hand in front of her face. "Hey, Mom," I say, "does this pill make you sleep?"

'She looks at me, and she says, "Yes, that's a sleeping pill." She gets up and gives those dried-up meatballs a vigorous scrape and returns to her book.'

I looked at my watch. Eight minutes left. I can't believe this is my silent shadow talk, talk, talking after all these years. It made me feel crazy.

don't lock me in a mental institution

'I go upstairs and swallow four big red pills and a fifth to grow on. I don't know what I'm doing, I'm so miserable I want to die . . .'

'Claire,' I said, and my voice broke. 'I love you.'

'I make myself very sick,' said Claire. 'Unable to wake up or throw up or eat or do anything but flop around the house like a dying fish. Here's the thing that comes to me in the dark of night at PI: Why did Mom want me dead?'

'Maybe she didn't know,' I said, wondering even as I said it what horrible darkness of soul makes me run to my parents' defense when who and what they are is indefensible. Do concentration-camp victims say, 'Oh, well, the Nazis fed me while I was incarcerated, I shouldn't feel too bitter?' Or do they think, Well I survived, I ought to be grateful for that. They had the power to gas me but didn't? Wouldn't there be some truth in those thoughts? As I defended my mother, I realized I was defending myself as well: Hadn't it been my job to protect Claire? Was she pointing the finger at me? Is that what she told Max and Boyce and Johanna? That it was my fault?

Honor thy father and thy mother

'She knew, Richard. I saw her eyes.' Claire's voice was loud, no longer a whisper.

162

Because I felt attacked, I couldn't keep the edge from my voice. 'I don't know what you want me to say,' I told her. 'I did the best I could to protect you.'

'You're not listening to what I'm saying,' she said. 'You're just like Dad.'

I felt pressured. I could feel the beat of my parents' blood within me, the pulsating pump of defensiveness, the surge of anger to defend myself against Claire's reality. At the same time, I knew that I needed to support her – it was my job. I was so tired.

Get off the fence, big bro, came Max's voice, loud in my ear.

'I'm here for you, Claire,' I said, at last. 'You know that.'

Silence. This was more like the Claire I knew.

'Are you there?' I said, after forty seconds of nothing had passed.

'I can't have visitors yet,' she said, and clicked the phone.

Our fifteen minutes were up.

My hand felt in slow motion as I returned my phone to its cradle. I seemed to be losing my touch. There was a time when Claire thought I could do no wrong, and I suppose I'd accepted that notion of myself at least as far as she was concerned. Now her words kept repeating themselves in my brain with the slow, steady rhythm of John's funeral dirges: *You sound just like Dad, I come to the garden alone, You sound just like Dad, On a hill far away stood an old rugged cross, You sound just like Dad*

I laid my head down on the table not even cradling it in my arms, the same way I had as a little boy in first grade when Miss Bartlett yelled at me for whispering to Tommy Conroy and all I was doing was helping him find the page in our math book. I felt so misjudged by Miss Bartlett, and that's the way I was feeling about Claire.

Here's the worst part about what Claire had said: I thought she could be right.

Chapter Twelve

I SAT at my kitchen table for a long time. Gray skies turned grayer and I heard rain splatter sidewalks and windows drowning out Gordon Lightfoot. Or maybe my neighbor had left for work.

I had the strongest urge to push a chair against the door. I wished I had one of my father's guns. Childhood gremlins threatened to storm my carefully constructed house. Unwillingly, I admitted to myself that the only place I had felt safe from the past was in this tiny apartment, its four walls always in sight, no surprises. New York City was such a nice big place to hide. I'd always thought that was what Claire was doing here, too, although we never, ever talked about it. I wondered if she longed for those summer days on the farm with the tiger lilies blooming and the nose-tingling smell of fresh-cut hay wiping out the eye-watering stench of manure spreaders.

I plucked a paper napkin from its basket on my table and began tearing teeny tiny strips, one at a time. For a moment I pictured Claire's fingers the night of the murder as they plucked at the pillow's fringe and I saw her childhood fingers twisting her dinner napkin into slivers of paper. I thought back through Claire's and my conversation, trying to find a way to think about it that didn't make me feel so bad. I'd always been able to find the good in my father, plenty of good;

now I needed to find something good about Claire's Emma, Emma, Emma.

Her words about the graveyard frightened me more than anything else she'd said. To me, it was as if she was deliberately putting a twist on the truth to confuse me. How could we have had the same experience and remember it so differently?

Outside my apartment, the wind whistled and something cracked against my window.

All I could think about was the graves.

I'd never had a single nightmare about the graves on our property that ran alongside Old Man Pott's. Once long ago, I remembered Claire telling me she dreamed about the graves. 'Every night,' she'd said, 'I go to sleep wondering about the graves.' I didn't pay much attention. I wondered now if I'd listened would she still have sneaked out in the dead of night to lie beneath a cold gray tombstone?

I left my shredded napkin on the table and got up to turn on my tea kettle. I could feel that black cloud of depression that had overwhelmed me after Johanna's departure right up until the night of John's murder, menacing me again. I hadn't felt this way on those trips to the farm, Old Man Pott's shack a landmark announcing that the farm was only a sweep of the Steam Hollow away. I hadn't felt that way the day Claire and I found those graves. I'd felt only the magic of summertime . . .

My dad's in Waterton, Mom's at the farmhouse reading *Modern Screen*'s version of Barbara Parkins' tortured love life and sipping Carlo Rossi. Tina's napping in the kiddie-koop, a crib with a screened lid that snapped over the top. Elizabeth is reading, maybe in the hammock, maybe on the couch in the living room. Max is up at the pond by himself, paddling around on a raft I'd nailed together for him out of boards left from a fence I'd built at the horse barn. Claire and I are on an adventure. I'm Robin Hood, she's Maid Marian, draped in my mother's old maroon and white striped bathrobe, and we're hiking the property lines. I want to know them in my heart the way my dad does. He knows every rock in the streams, every tree in the woods. He knows where the giant frogs live and I know, too – in the pond above the horse barn, the one choked with algae and lily pads, its edges thick mud that try to suck you down. We kids have a secret pool, too, off the towpath on the way to the cow barn, and for a moment I wonder if my dad knows about it. He must. He knows and loves every other inch of his land. I don't know that he loves it with the innocent abandon of us children, though. I think he loves it with a sense of ownership. Kind of like the way he feels about us.

So I'm leading Maid Marian around the farm and we find the graves. They're pretty close to the road, across from Old Man Pott's house, hidden beneath a cluster of half a dozen pine trees. Dead leaves from nearby birch and poplar trees and sticky pinecones and needles coat the ground. A thicket of blueberries and a heavy undergrowth of ferns shroud the place from daylight, making it creepy and dark.

Claire's always on the lookout for the bogeyman, so it comes as no surprise to her when the tombstone appears. She pulls my mother's old bathrobe around her and takes a closer look. It's old. Gray and slanted. And it says Emma on it.

Claire kneels down in the gluey needles right away and says a prayer, crossing herself at least five times. We're not Catholic, of course, the Catholics are all immigrants, according to my parents, we're Episcopalians come over, no doubt, in 1607 to the Jamestown Colony, and no one in our family crosses themselves, but Jackie Kennedy does and Claire brings her into all our activities. Like Jackie at JFK's gravesite, Claire puts a knee to the ground, bows her head and crosses herself. If she'd had a veil, it would be hiding her face.

There are no dates on the gravestone, and we don't know what to think. I'm loving the mystery, the idea of making a discovery, the idea that I know something my father doesn't. He's never mentioned these graves. I'm feeling strong and confident.

I'm King of the Mountain.

Maid Marian's on her knees.

And then Claire says, 'He did it, Richard. Maybe he killed some Pallstead girl. Or maybe it's a sister of ours they haven't told us about.'

I tell her to shut up about the dead sister. She's had a dead-sister fantasy forever and seems to spend half her time in search of her. I tell her Dad would never kill anybody. 'He's a doctor,' I say.

Now, standing in my tiny apartment, tea kettle whistling in my ears, I wondered how it was that we considered the possibility that our father was a murderer. Sure, I told her to shut up about it, but the fact is, I responded as if it was a legitimate possibility.

Father Almighty, Maker of Heaven and Earth

I thought about the dead dogs scattered across the farm's backyard. Maybe their bodies were the clue to thinking our father a killer. If you went out the farmhouse back door, you ran into a dog graveyard. Did other families have ten or twelve dead dogs lying around like compost in the backyard? Max conducted funerals for one and all, even poor Helga whom my father said was killed in a hunting accident, and Duke the Second who died of a stomach obstruction while alone at the farm with my dad. Or maybe it was just the dead coons and woodchucks and deer and beavers that clotted the landscape of our childhood that made me and Claire think about my dad as Emma's destructor.

The tea kettle's whistles seemed less a song now and more a shriek. I yanked an iced-mint herbal tea bag from the cupboard – leftover from the days of Johanna – and slapped it into a mug with a wild swish of water.

I remembered how Claire discovered another grave that same long ago afternoon. I'd left Emma and started to scout around.

'Richard!' I hear her call and hurry to her side. She's on both knees scraping moss from a stone. 'It's another grave,' she says, and something in her voice makes me kneel beside her and reach for her hand. She holds on tight.

Baby Pott.

That's all the tombstone says, but it's clear to us now that Emma was the mom. Claire crosses herself and I almost do, too.

Outside our dark shady grove of trees it's hot, but I shiver. My heart feels cold with premonition, but I don't have words for the feeling. We stay on our knees a long time. Claire's hand grows damp and cold in mine, and my teeth start to chatter. It's damp enough under those trees to smell of pond water and mold.

I'm afraid, but I don't want Claire to know. She remains silent, letting go my hand and crossing herself again. 'I think Old Man Pott loved her,' she says. 'I think he loved her so much he couldn't let her go away from him. He buried her here so he could touch her tombstone every day and carry valley flowers to her.' In springtime, a spray of tiger lilies grows up in the midst of thistles around his shack, so maybe she's right. Maybe he lays bursts of lilies on her grave. I don't point out that the tombstones appear abandoned. He's old now and maybe can't climb the hill.

'Let's not tell anyone,' she says.

I use my jackknife to sliver our fingers. We mingle blood in a pact agreeing to never tell, not even Max.

I remembered the good feeling in my heart about that day. I'd felt proud, as if I'd handled it well. Robin Hood protects Maid Marian. No nightmares, no aftermath. Two secret graves nestled in the pines not so different from eggs in a nest.

And now I discovered I hadn't protected her at all.

My tea grew cold in its mug and I didn't care.

No wonder Boyce was freaking out. Did he know about the drugs? Had Claire told him about the graves? With a source like Claire, he was bound to know a good many family secrets.

I hated outsiders knowing about my family.

I hated knowing about my family.

I had this sense of struggling on the bloody fields of Gettysburg. Maybe I was suffering battle fatigue.

Suddenly, I stood up. I refused to wallow in emotion, as my mother would have said. No way was I going to let the black cloud get me. Fuck it. I'd stop by Boyce's and ask him outright what he knew. This was my business, too. I'd stop by Boyce's and then head to the gym. I didn't bother dressing up. I shoved my feet into sneakers, grabbed a jacket and headed to Boyce's.

Left, right, left, right, left, right, a jab to the jaw, to the gut, to the jaw . . . I would fight to the finish, damn it.

What are you fighting, big bro

I walked into Boyce's outer office at ten forty-five. It hadn't crossed my mind that he wouldn't be there on a Saturday, and he was. In fact, no sooner had I told the secretary I needed to talk to Boyce and settled myself in a far corner chair to wait than his office door opened, and he and an attractive woman dressed for success in a severe navy-blue suit stood in the doorway.

Neither was aware of my presence.

'I think you're making a mistake, Boyce,' the woman was saying. 'I'm not going to offer this deal again.'

Boyce shrugged. 'She's not guilty.' While there was no question the woman looked the consummate professional, she also looked pale, her face a bit taut and strained. Her white silk blouse made her look thin, almost sickly, instead of slender like Sam Saunders. The hand holding her briefcase showed blue veins. I recognized for the first time how handsome Boyce was. Next to this woman, he appeared tall, dark, glowing with health, and supremely confident.

'You're obliged to present the deal to her. It's her right.'

'She may be deemed incompetent. Remember?'

'Talk to her next of kin. Talk to her brother.'

'I don't get it, Eleanor. Why the big push for a deal? If your case is so great . . .'

'It is great, you know it's great. She's admitted it, for God's sake. We've got her hand prints on the gun, we know he beat her up, we know she had ample cause to get rid of him. It's open and shut.'

'She's not guilty.'

'Please. No judge today is going to buy that bullshit.' The pale, thin woman seemed to be getting rosier and fatter by the minute.

Boyce didn't bat an eyelash. He laughed. He put his hands casually in his pants pockets, as if he was making small talk at a cocktail party. 'Eleanor, Eleanor, Eleanor. It's me you're talking to, good old Boyce from law school. Remember? You're not going to pull this over on me. What's up? Who wants this settled? Come on, come clean.'

For a second, something flashed between them like a shared intimate memory and I wondered if, indeed, they did share a couple of old memories. Of course, I realized this was Claire they were discussing and I gathered Eleanor was the DA or assistant DA or whatever, but I had no intention of drawing their attention to me. Boyce's secretary had vanished, maybe to the restroom or on an errand, so she wasn't about to interfere, either.

'I don't see any point in wasting the state's money on a trial.'

Boyce laughed again. 'Some things never change, do they?' he said, and she surprised me by blushing, a deep pink becoming blush.

She made a sound that was probably meant to be a laugh, but it didn't sound entirely mirthful to me. 'No, they don't,' she said. She walked across the outer office, still unaware of me, I think because she was overly aware of him.

I glanced at the wall where the picture of Boyce's wife and baby had been. It was gone.

'I'll be talking to you, Boyce,' Eleanor said, and left the office.

She must have come damn close to running smack into Boyce's secretary because within a second of her departure, the secretary was back in the office. Boyce still stood in his doorway, and she nodded in my direction. He jumped. I swear, he actually jumped. I think that's the only time I ever saw him disconcerted.

'You should have told me you were here, Richard.' He motioned me into his office. 'That's the DA,' he said, standing behind his desk. 'Eleanor Banning. Came to offer me a deal. Somebody somewhere is putting the pressure on. I don't know why. She wants Claire to plead guilty to first-degree manslaughter. Save everybody the cost of a trial. Says she'll recommend leniency in sentencing to the judge. Mitigating circumstances.'

I looked at him. I wasn't thinking about the cost of a trial; I was thinking about the revelations of a trial. 'What does that mean to Claire?' *What does it mean to me?*

'Prison.'

'Claire? In prison?'

'Exactly, Richard.'

'You should have discussed it with me.'

'I just did.'

'Before you told her no.'

'What are you saying?'

'I'm saying you should have discussed it with me. That's it. That's what I'm saying.' I'm not sure what I was saying. Maybe I was asking him to acknowledge my position as elder brother. Maybe I was asking him to give me the opportunity to put an end to the pressure. But I wouldn't have done that to Claire. *Would I?*

'Bullshit. I'm Claire's attorney, not yours.'

We looked at each other across his desk. I no longer remembered why I was in his office in the first place. I just knew I felt worse than when I'd arrived. I needed to get away from him. I needed to get to the gym. Like Eleanor, I said, 'I'll be talking to you, Boyce,' and left the office.

Nobody'd said anything about the way I'd slammed from the office the day before.

I walked through the lobby of Boyce's building, head down, hands in my jacket pockets.

'Richard?' I heard my name as if from a distance and it took me a minute to look up and focus.

Sam Saunders stood right in front of me, a smile on her face. 'That bad, huh?' she said.

'Yeah.' I nodded, but seeing her smile helped me block out Boyce. If someone like Sam could find me likeable, I'd be all right, wouldn't I? I felt embarrassed, but she didn't seem to mind that I was in gray sweats and sneakers. She looked so pretty in a long, flowered dress, a jean jacket, cowboy boots, and her hair loose on her shoulders. I realized how much I'd like to spend time with her, but I also knew that once she found out why I was spending so many hours in Boyce's office, she'd probably take off and I'd never see her again. Well, I told myself, maybe pursuing her right now isn't a good idea, anyway. It's not like I don't have enough to deal with. Maybe Mary wasn't joking.

'You just coming from Boyce's?'

'Yeah.' Another brilliant example of my repartee.

She tapped a folder in her hand. 'I'm on my way to see him. I see him more than I see my friends.' She laughed, not a particularly happy laugh, and tapped the folder again. 'Every time I think everything with my settlement agreement is done once and for all, my ex files some new document that demands a response. Boyce thinks it's Phil's way of maintaining some kind of contact with me.' She shrugged.

I remembered the way I'd bombarded Johanna with legal procedures when she'd wanted to divorce me. I looked at her. 'Maybe he's having a hard time accepting you're gone,' I said.

'Is that how you feel about your ex-wife?'

'No, not anymore,' I told her, and knew with relief I was telling the truth. That sense of finality I'd felt after lunching with Johanna had been accurate. I was ready to leave that relationship behind.

Several people brushed past us and I touched her arm. 'Let's move over to the side.' We moved to a corner of the lobby. I wanted to get a bit out of the public eye because I wanted to ask her out again and I didn't want anyone to overhear. What if she said no? In the past, I'd been careful to never appear impulsive or anxious. In college, I had roommates take messages for me and I'd wait a day or two to return girls' calls. I didn't dare risk looking too eager; I wanted to be careful that the relationship started off on my terms. When Johanna left, it didn't occur to me to tell her I loved her or that I wanted her to stay with me. I feared appearing vulnerable.

I swallowed. I didn't know if it was Sam or if I had somehow changed, I just knew I wanted to get to know her. 'Look,' I said, ignoring my own earlier decision to not pursue her, 'I'd really like to see you before next week. Haven't you got any time before then? Like tonight?' All I could think of was a song my mother used to sing 'Where Fools Rush In'. I could feel nervous sweat in my armpits.

When she didn't answer, I rushed in with: 'Your sister can come, too. That's fine. We'll all three go somewhere. Anywhere you like.' I couldn't seem to stop talking. 'White Horse Tavern,' I said. 'Pete's Tavern. I don't care. Let's go to the Rainbow Room. I'll pay, no problem.' Good grief, had I really said that?

Sam laughed. 'I would love to go to dinner with you tonight. My sister's made plans with a cousin of ours. I see him twice a month for a movie, I don't need to see him tonight.' She laughed again as if she was in on a private joke and I wasn't.

I didn't care.

'I'll pick you up about seven?' I said. This was going to be a bona fide Saturday-night date, my first in months, and I

173

didn't want to meet her somewhere. I hated that meeting someone somewhere business everyone does in New York.

'That would be terrific, Richard,' said Sam. 'I'll see you then.' She left me to go up to Boyce's office, but she turned around when she reached the elevator and gave me a little wave.

It took me two seconds after she disappeared to call Mary and tell her I was on my way. No clients on Saturday so my clothes wouldn't matter. 'Big news, too, Mary,' I said.

'Claire?'

Even a reminder of the murder couldn't dim my excitement at the prospect of seeing Sam tonight. 'Well,' I said. 'There is Claire news. I'll save that for when I see you. But here's some news that can't wait.' I paused for extra anticipation value, then blurted, 'I've got a date with Sam Saunders tonight.'

Mary's screech of excitement blasted through the phone.

'Calm down,' I told her. 'It's just a date.'

'Right, and the Pope's Jewish,' said Mary.

I'd no sooner stepped back inside my apartment at about 5 p.m., feeling pretty good about myself because I'd finished the returns on my desk and checked one of Mary's as well, when Boyce's secretary called to set an appointment for the next day. She didn't mention I'd shown up at the office without one two days' running, but she didn't hesitate to mention she'd called my office first. Like I should feel guilty for playing hooky. Or maybe for mentioning Boyce's baby.

'Tomorrow's Sunday,' I said.

'Boyce wants you here first thing tomorrow morning,' she said, quite definite.

'I'll be there.' I had no choice, especially after yesterday and today's fiascos, but I tried to sound as if I was doing her and Boyce a big favor. I couldn't help it: I didn't like people telling me what to do. Boyce's expectations felt not unlike the kind of pressure I'd had as a kid.

Do what I say or bang! You're dead!

All my pleasure in the day's accomplishments vanished and my anticipation at seeing Sam as well, and I remembered a time out at the farm when Max and I had spent hours and hours stacking hay bales in the horse barn . . .

It's in the days before we had a baler that tossed bales onto the wagon, so before we even start stacking, Max drives the tractor, a David Brown, white with a yellow scoop on the front, and a big seat that's red with holes in it almost like a colander, with our rickety wagon hooked behind, and I run alongside, picking up hay bales and tossing them into the wagon. It's hot and sunny and I like the feel of the sweat running down my back.

Claire's sitting in the shade of the barn, waiting for us to finish stacking the wagon so we can unload in the barn. I can't hear the radio she's got going, but I know it's the local country and western station and the DJ's probably playing 'I'm Crazy' or maybe 'Sweet Dreams'. Claire loves country and western, she likes the singers' heartache. When I get to the barn, I'll make her change to a jazz station out of Waterton that we can get at the farm on a clear day.

Tina's down at the house with my mother, and Elizabeth's in Waterton. Now that she's a teenager, she doesn't come out to the farm much; she stays in Waterton with our grandparents. My dad has bought a bulldozer and he's up at the upper creek, bulldozing the rocks and mud around. Says he's rerouting the water.

It takes me and Max over two hours to clear the meadow of hay bales. I'm beat, but my dad said we have to get the hay into the barn before supper, so we hustle on up to the barn. I'm driving the tractor now, Max is riding beside me. I can smell the heat coming off him. It's that warm odor of lightly burned skin. I press my own arm to my nose and I've got the same sun-baked smell. On the fifth try, I manage to get the wagon backed into the barn.

Sure enough, Patsy Cline's wailing away and I can see

Claire's lips moving. I leap down from my perch on the tractor and turn the radio dials.

'Richard,' cries Claire, but that's all she says, and she makes no move to change it back to her station. I know she won't. I'm the big brother. I'm doing more work than anyone else.

Another two hours, and Max and Claire and I have that hay piled neat as you please in twenty rows, ten bales each. We stand in the doorway, admire our handiwork. The smell now is more than fodder and sunburned skin, it's that bitter oniony smell of sweaty boys. I lift my arm and sniff my pit. Whoo – almost knocks me over and I grin at Max and Claire. We're pleased with ourselves. It's almost six o'clock and we're done in time for supper. Mom's doing hot dogs and hamburgers on the grill and she's even bought potato chips which she hardly ever does. Hurrah! She makes this great dip – sour cream mixed with Lipton's onion soup mix.

A shadow appears near the doorway, a long dark shadow, and we exchange looks. It's my dad, wearing nothing but a pair of khakis, large straw hat, and L. L. Bean muck lucks. The hair on his chest glistens. Claire steps behind me.

For a moment there is silence. I'm waiting for the hearty words of praise he sometimes bestows on me. I'll do just about anything to see a smile on his face and hear the words, 'You've done a good job here, Richard. I don't think I could do it better myself.' He'd said those very words once when I'd cleaned the tack, another time when I'd built a split-rail fence for the horse pasture.

I look at him, watching his face. I see him look around, slowly. He opens his mouth. Here's what comes out. 'You silly little horse's ass. You've stacked the wrong barn.' And he laughs. 'You'll have to start all over again. I told you to take the towpath to the cow barn.'

'No, you didn't,' I surprise myself by saying. I feel Claire stiffen behind me. Max doesn't move at all.

'What did you say?'

'No, you didn't,' I whisper, looking right at him.

Anything might happen

'Don't talk back to me,' he says.

The only sound in the barn is the hum of crickets.

I bite my lip and I have to fight tears, too. We've worked hard.

'Get started. I want it finished tonight.' With that, my dad spins around and leaves. I hear Max and Claire exhale. I go to the barn door and watch him disappear over the meadow ridge leading to the house.

Do what I say or bang! You're dead!

'You fucking bastard,' I say. 'I hate you.' I smash my fist against the barn wall, once, then twice. I stop abruptly, stare at my skinned knuckles. I keep my face to the wall so Max and Claire can't see it. It takes me a while to get there, but I tell myself that maybe my dad was right, maybe he did say the cow barn, maybe I didn't hear him because I wanted it to be the horse barn, it's so much closer.

don't get angry

Here's the thing: I have to set a good example for the sibs.

I turn slowly and face them. 'Okay, guys,' I say, 'let's get unstacking.' I grin and shrug my shoulders to show I'm on their side.

Max gets right in my face and says, 'Go ahead and be angry, bro. You've a right to be angry.'

His long ago words rang in my ears some twenty years later as I yanked off my sweats and headed for the shower. I pretended the shower sponge was my trumpet and blasted out a new song called 'Go Ahead And Be Angry'.

Chapter Thirteen

I PICKED up Sam at her apartment right on time.

I thought I looked pretty sharp. I wore my favorite blue jeans and a red L. L. Bean shirt that Johanna had told me brought out the blue in my eyes and the gold in my hair. You can't beat that combination. Plus I wore my leather bomber jacket and leather gloves.

She looked terrific in black tights and a black turtleneck with a green, button-down sweater. The sweater had a hood that she pulled over her hair when she went outside. She didn't seem worried about messing it up, either. I couldn't imagine Bev not worrying. She's a woman who gets her hair permed, and on drizzly days she wears a plastic rain bonnet, and moans, 'My perm, my perm.' A gold cross earring dangled from Sam's right ear. A tiny gold hoop pierced her left.

She told me she loved Italian, so we went to this little place near John and Claire's that I'd been to a million times and knew was good. It was in the basement of an old building, and dark and musty and candlelit and she'd never been there, which made me feel terrific.

Like I was in charge. This was not a bad feeling, considering the turmoil following John's murder and how unrestful this woman made me feel.

We sipped wine, and she ate linguini with clam sauce and lettuce drenched in oil and vinegar and chunks of bread thick with butter and garlic while I could do no more than nibble. She told me more about her marriage and said she thought she'd married because her family expected her to and that it hadn't occurred to her until after the fact to wonder if that's what she really wanted. I told her I thought maybe Johanna and I had married for the same reasons.

'She left me,' I said, 'after fourteen months.'

'Don't give me that hangdog look,' said Sam. 'You won't get any sympathy from me.'

'Hangdog?' I said, after recovering myself.

'Hangdog,' she said.

For dessert she wanted a hot brownie with fudge sauce and she knew a tavern a few blocks away where we could get that very thing. I realized I wanted to determine where we would eat and so I suggested a ride uptown to the Broadway Diner that also served up a mean hot brownie.

Sam looked at me. 'Why would we trek to the subway, clatter our way uptown amidst drunks and dirt, walk another six blocks cross town to get a brownie when we can slip right on down around the corner?'

'I don't know,' I said, stumped.

'I don't either,' said Sam.

At her insistence, we split the dinner bill and marched around the corner.

The brownies were thick and chocolatey and wonderful. I ordered an Amaretto coffee and then another. I felt expansive, defenses relaxed.

'Better than the Broadway Diner?' she said.

I grinned. 'What is this? A contest?'

'I don't know yet,' she said.

'Has Boyce told you anything about me?' I was glad the bar was dark and smoky. I could feel my face growing red and didn't want her to see.

'No,' said Sam.

For the first time in my life, I had this wild urge to spill out everything to another person. I felt as if Boyce and Claire and my parents and the Browns had been push, push, pushing at me and now the hatches were bursting. Oh, I'd confessed my mother's Saturday night nail clipping ritual and the hair slicking and how I'd felt being at her mercy, but this was different. This was glimpsing an open door and instead of slamming it shut, I wanted to rip it right off its hinges as I ran inside. I wanted to tell Sam about Claire and John and the Psych Institute. I wanted to tell her how afraid I was. I wanted to ask her what I should do.

I pushed aside my brownie plate and told her about Old Man Pott's graves.

'I think you should be a writer,' she said. 'Not an account-ant.' She laughed. 'The graves are only whipped cream, froth. It's you and Claire who are the story. Does she live in New York?'

Show her your stuff, big bro. Go for it. Here's the brass ring, buddy.

'She's in New York.' My voice was high. 'She's in the Manhattan Psychiatric Institute.' I grabbed my napkin and started shredding.

At first Sam said nothing. She didn't look away from me, though. After a bit, she said, 'I'm sorry.' Her voice was quiet, but it didn't hold pity. I didn't sense judgment, either, or backing away from me which I guess is what I really feared. She didn't ask questions. She sat quietly. She didn't seem tense or anxious or like she had to leap in and fill the silence. Bev would have jumped in with a million platitudes and under-neath she'd be my judge and jury finding the defendant guilty, guilty, guilty.

I blurted, 'Boyce is Claire's lawyer, not mine. She shot her husband last Sunday night.' Six days ago, I thought. I'd seen Sam for the first time five days ago. I heard my voice go from high to a squeak. 'She killed him.' I watched her face take on that pained I-can't-believe-I've-hooked-up-with-another-weirdo look. That look divorced dating people get that says, 'Does New York have anything but jerks in it?' I almost reached out my hand to reassure her that I wasn't a jerk, just a guy trying to find his way through the labyrinth of life. A guy whose labyrinth was maybe a little more complicated than most, that's all.

Sam pushed aside her dishes with sharp jabbing motions. They ended up in the middle of the table beneath the flickering candle. Wax would drip onto them in a minute. 'What are you telling me? Your sister's a murderer? Like Lizzie Borden or something?' Her one dangling earring jangled back and forth.

I tossed my shredded napkin onto her plate. A blob of bright red candle wax splatted onto it. I felt the heat in my face but it wasn't from the candlelight. 'I can see sensitivity's your strong suit,' I said, pleased my voice was almost down to its normal tone. 'That'll be a big help when you're helping all those inner-city kids.'

The look on her face was less that of the disappointed divorcée and more of confusion. 'You took me by surprise. Give me a minute to digest this.'

'Yeah, well, while you're digesting, I'll tell you this: Claire thought she had to do it; she didn't think she had a choice. I know her, Sam. I know her almost as well as I know myself and she's gentle and she's fragile and I'm worried sick about her.' I stopped, hearing my voice begin to break. My anger was no more than the thinnest defense against a great well of sadness. Why was it that when I was with Sam the Incredible Shrinking Boy lurked in the shadows?

Sam remained silent. I knew she was thinking about my sister, maybe deciding whether to get up and leave. I wondered if she'd been on dates with other guys who told her their sisters were murderers. I wondered if the stories I'd told her about my mother had turned her off. I wondered if she thought I was a wimp. I felt vulnerable as only an Incredible Shrinking Boy can.

I waited in silence for the jury's verdict. I could hear my heartbeat. I reached across the table for Sam's napkin and began tearing it into tiny white slivers.

181

'I'm sorry,' she said at last. She looked right at me. 'I'd like to hear about it, if you'd like to tell me. If you don't, that's okay, too.'

The thing was, I did want to talk about it. I wanted very much to talk about it. What was it about Sam Saunders that made me drop my guard? I'd tuned Johanna out and her nagging. Why did I care so much what Sam thought? For some funny reason, Sam reminded me of Boyce. They both had an aura of compassion. And there was something in Sam's eyes that made her different from anyone I'd ever known. My mother's eyes are marbles, lifeless, cold, my father's, the pathway to rage. Claire's eyes hold wariness and mistrust. But Sam's were different. Like the secret pool at the farm, they were peaceful, but I saw she'd experienced pain, too. They weren't the eyes of an innocent.

'I'm afraid she'll break,' I said.

Sam remained silent, listening. She pulled her chair closer to the table.

'I'm her big brother,' I said, keeping my eyes on the table. 'She looks up to me.' I'd abandoned the napkin and clasped my hands in front of me. I felt, rather than saw, Sam's hand come across the table and rest on top of mine.

I met Sam's eyes. I told her how after all these years I'd found out that Claire had sneaked out nights to lie on top of Emma's grave and I'd never known. 'I thought we'd shared the same experience,' I said, and I know the pain was clear in my voice and I know she knew that tears were close to the surface. I think she also sensed that I was terrified by our sudden closeness.

It was a long time before she spoke. The waiter had come and snatched away our brownie plates. He'd set two mints in front of us and left the check. He'd been back a time or two but had had the good sense to vanish again. 'I think that's what's so scary about life,' she said at last. 'We can't know another's experience. We can think we know, but we can't. Nobody can.'

'You don't think it's my fault?'

'You'll have to find your own absolution, Richard. I don't begin to know the circumstances of her life or yours, but she's an adult just like you.' Sam tilted her head to the side, but the tilt didn't have that puppy-dog effect Johanna's tilt did. There wasn't a childlike quality to it at all.

'She needs me,' I said.

'Yes,' said Sam. 'Is there anyone else?'

I shook my head.

'Your parents?'

Again, I shook my head no.

'Brothers and sisters?'

'Not really,' I said.

'It's all up to you?'

I nodded yes.

'What will it cost you to help her?' Sam's voice was quiet.

'It's the cost if I don't help her that's tearing me up,' I said. 'It's my parents or Claire.' I paused, then added, 'Boyce has pretty much made that clear.'

'Tell me.'

'Boyce feels my parents did some pretty awful things to Claire as a kid. He's planning to use that in her defense and he wants me to validate her.'

'Well – did they?'

Here it was, the two-million-dollar question. Sam made it seem so simple. No fancy law-office setting, no legalities, no Edna tapping away. Just me and a beautiful woman asking, 'Well, did they?'

'I guess.' It took me a long time to answer and I didn't meet her eyes.

'You sound like my students,' she said, 'when I ask them if they know they should have studied for the test. They know the answer is yes, but all they can spit out is an "I guess".'

She took me by surprise. I think I expected a more sympathetic response. I met her eyes. 'Easy for you to say.'

'My family is complicated, too,' she said.

183

'Complicated?' I said. 'Interesting word choice.'

'Look, Richard, everyone past the age of thirty has family stuff to resolve. Claire is in a bind, and that puts you in a bind. Knowing Boyce, he's putting the screws to you.' Again, that tilt of the head. 'Bottom line, it's up to you. Do what he wants or don't. Live with your decision and be done with it.'

'Just like that?'

'Either Claire's telling the truth or she's not. You can answer that. I can't.'

I sensed impatience. The impatience that came with having solved a few of life's problems yourself and the unwillingness to put up with a lot of nonsense from someone else. The thing was, I liked this woman and I wanted to see her again. I respected her saying what she thought. At the same time, her attitude felt like one more shove against the wall.

'Boyce has me scheduled to continue my statement tomorrow.'

'There's your chance.'

I nodded, knowing the subject was closed at least for the time being. When the waiter checked on us yet again, we ordered two more Amaretto coffees, causing him to snatch up our check and make furious additions. When he brought the coffee, steaming hot and topped with great swirls of whipped cream, we sipped in silence. A compatible silence, yet on my part at least, it had an edge to it. Damn it, I wanted to say, I have the balls to take care of this. Give me a chance. It made me feel defensive, so I told her a little about my accounting practice. I mentioned that I'd worked on lots of divorce settlements. I offered to help her with taxes.

She looked at me with a smile. 'I have an accountant, Richard.'

I walked her to her apartment door. She didn't invite me in, but she didn't turn her head when I kissed her lightly on the lips.

'I will take care of this business with Claire,' I said, against her ear.

'Good.' Sam's voice was firm, not soft at all.

'Can I still call you next week?'

'Yes,' she said. A good solid yes, nothing iffy about it. 'My sister says she'll pass on dinner, though.'

'Good,' I said, a trace of defiance in my voice. 'It'll save me having both of you ganged up on me.'

'Is that how it feels to you?'

'A little, I guess.' A lot.

Sam gave me a look. 'You guess?'

Here's something that registered through my defensiveness: Her demeanor wasn't like Johanna's. She wasn't like my mother. She kept reminding me of Boyce, and Mary, too, for that matter.

'Boyce is pressuring me. My parents are pressuring me. I feel pushed at from every direction, and I just want things to be the way they were before Claire killed John.' I paused, then said, 'So, yes, I guess, you make me feel pushed, too.'

'Everybody's got to grow up some day,' said Sam.

You know what? If Max or Claire or Elizabeth had said something like that to me, I would have been furious. I would have wanted to pound them, force them to take it back. But Sam? I felt she'd tossed me a challenge, and I intended to do whatever it took to meet it.

Before John's murder, I would have arrived home and worked on my auditing book. The last few days, though, I couldn't even pick up its papers, strewn confetti-like about the apartment. My concentration was at an all-time low. Instead, I thought about calling Sam when I got home, verify that I'd call next week. I knew I was being ridiculous, but there was something about Sam that was different from anything or anyone I'd known before. While I knew my life was shifting wildly all around me, waters muddied and wild and heading out to sea, my thoughts about Sam were solid ground. I remembered the smile she gave me when she told me she already had an accountant. I decided it meant here's a woman who stands on her own. She's not in need of a protector. What does this mean for me? I asked myself.

Here's what it means for me: Freedom.

Oddly enough, it didn't occur to me to get a beer. This was one feeling I had no inclination to anesthetize.

'She's losing it, big bro,' said Max, awakening me with the blast of a telephone call. 'She thinks the car wreck really happened.' His voice was trembling and I thought, This can't be the Belle Dame Sans Merci.

'What car wreck?' I said, groggy.

'You know. At the farm on the way to Malificent's Castle.'

On the way to the Castle? It took me a minute, and then I remembered as if from another life that Max and Claire called the mountain behind the farmhouse Malificent's Castle. While I'd be baling hay with Dad, they'd be hiking the creek bed to the Castle, picnicking, building dams, searching through the dump for green jars for the cider mill they'd built in the old barn.

'Don't you remember the rusted hulk of car to the side of the creek bed?' Max was crying and I could barely understand him. 'It was just past the bend in the creek, in the cove of trees beyond the dump,' he said. 'It looks as if it had wrecked, rolled over the embankment, years ago, killing its occupants.'

'I don't remember it,' I said, and sat up in my bed. My apartment was dark, darker than it had ever been, street lamps murky in the mist. I felt myself getting defensive, ready to ward off whatever accusations he might be getting ready to make. Max had always been swift to tell me what I ought to do.

'Claire and I pretended it was Mom and Dad in the car,' said Max. 'We played it over and over again. We'd be the kids and come upon the car wreck and it would be our parents and we'd bury them. She'd be Jackie Kennedy and I'd be the gravedigger. A favorite game. She thinks they're dead and buried at the farm. She thinks they're in the graveyard we built.'

'Graveyard?'

'I built a white picket fence like the one they first had around JFK's grave, just a little fence with a hinged gate so it'd swing open. She wants it just like the president's, so that's what I build. And she wants mounds in that graveyard. She tells me his dead babies are buried next to him at Arlington and she has to have dead babies so we jam two of her stuffed animals into those green jars and bury them alongside our parents. Don't you remember?'

'No, I don't remember,' I said, and wondered how I could have forgotten. I snapped on my bedside lamp, hoping to feel some control over my situation.

'You knew about it, Richard,' said Max. 'You knew because Claire and I hiked you up there one day and showed you the graveyard and the picket fence and you ran back to the house and got your trumpet and ran back.'

'What?' I could hardly breathe.

'Oh, yes,' said the Belle Dame Sans Merci. 'You swing open the fence and stand right on top of the parents' mound and pull out all the stops on that trumpet. "Hail Thee Festival Day", that's what you play and when Claire and I beg for more, you blast "Praise, My Soul, the King of Heaven". I dance around those pickets, singing, and Claire wraps herself in the black veil she's made from hair nets and stays on her knees swaying to the beat.'

'You wanted them dead, Richard,' said Max.

'Stop it!' I put one free hand over my ear.

'She's going fucking crazy. I'm losing another sister.'

He was crying and the phone line went dead.

I sat on the edge of the sofa bed for a long time. More than anything, Max's last words etched a feeling of unbearable loss in my heart. Poor baby Tina. That's how I always thought of her. Even when she was twenty years old she was baby Tina to me. I'd never been able to cry about her death, not at the funeral and not in these three years afterwards. Now I recollected a chilly Saturday morning at the farm with her, and my heart began to ache. It's one of those winter weekends when we cruise out to the farm after school on Friday, and the house is damp and cold until my father or I warm it with fires.

I'm fifteen and Tina's maybe four, and sometimes if she awakes early on a Saturday morning, she and I cuddle up together in one of Munsy's old blue wicker rockers in front of the fire. I know this time it's really early because the sun is no more than a blush in the sky. Tina's wearing one of those sleeper suits, the kind that zip from her toes clear to her neck. It's pink and fluffy and her cheeks are pink and flushed from the fire's glow. I love the feel of her cheek against mine and I love the smell of her neck, kind of warm and powdery with the spice of baby sweat thrown in. Her hair is as gold as mine, but thinner. I can see her scalp through the curls and I rub her head gently with my hand.

Tina's dozing a bit by now and I must be, too, because out of the blue she slips from my lap, smashing her face against the stone hearth.

Not my baby Tina. Oh, no.

'I didn't mean it,' I say, reaching for her. 'Please be okay. I love you.'

She's white, as if someone had pulled the plug on her blood, draining it out. I stare at the hearth. Two bright red droplets. I keep Tina pressed against me with one arm; with the other, I use the sleeve of my long johns to wipe up the blood. It's instinctive. What if my mother should appear?

Now I settle back in the rocker and take a good look at my baby sister. Her color's coming back, two small rosebuds bloom on her cheeks. It's her lip that's cut, a small gash that I clean with my sleeve.

'There, there,' I say. 'Don't cry, cupcake,' and she doesn't. Nary a whimper. I hug her so tight I fear I've squashed her. She giggles. 'I won't tell,' she says, and she doesn't. Her morning upset is our secret until she dies.

I snapped off my light. Tomorrow was another Sunday morning in my life. A Sunday morning with Boyce. How odd that it is Claire's crisis which brings up the pain of Tina's death for me. How odd it is Max's phone call that brings back that long-suppressed memory. I wasn't mistaken, after all. My siblings and I are close – just in a different way than Mary and hers.

You wanted them dead, Richard

I doubt I slept more than three hours.

Honor thy father and thy mother, honor thy father and thy mother, honor thy father and thy mother

I awoke at seven o'clock with a start, thinking I smelled crispy blueberry pancakes. Still half asleep, I thought a pitcher of thick, sugary maple syrup fresh from the sugaring house sat on my kitchen table. Disoriented, I peered about the room, expecting to see my dad at the stove, hair tousled from bed, wearing L. L. Bean khakis and a plaid shirt, flipping pancakes on a sizzling hot griddle.

The room was empty except for me. I had a funny empty feeling inside, then, as if I'd lost something important. I felt as close to crying as I had Thursday night at Sam's.

I took a deep breath and headed for the shower. I could not afford to indulge in feeling sorry for myself. I'd be facing Boyce in two hours.

Chapter Fourteen

Boyce's waiting room felt like a dentist's office. It smelled like one, sterile and fearful, filled with cleanliness. I half expected him to come out from his inner sanctum dressed in white with a mask and rubber gloves. I glanced at his secretary, wondering if Boyce made her work every Sunday. She looked extremely sanitary. I was sure she'd flossed. I ran my tongue over my teeth, worried I'd brushed the wrong direction that morning. She did not say a word to me about the way I'd departed the office two days ago or her own phone call to the police. Nor did she mention yesterday's visit. I could feel the flush of embarrassment on my cheeks.

The picture of Boyce's wife was still missing.

It was a relief to see Boyce emerge, dressed in jeans and an open-necked blue broadcloth shirt. I wanted to get the discomfort of our immediate confrontation over with fast. Like Boyce, I was dressed in jeans.

We went into his office and he closed the door. We looked at each other. Boyce nodded at me. I nodded back. Neither of us extended an apology. The tension felt thick as steam rising from Steam Hollow Road after a rainstorm.

'Lots of phone calls after you left yesterday, Richard. Eleanor Banning called to see if there'd been any change in my position. I said no.' Boyce looked straight at me. 'Our case is really shaping up. Dr Glassman telephoned yesterday.' Boyce plunged right into Claire's situation. 'He called again this morning. Depending on how you look at it, things for your sister are going okay.'

'I talked with her yesterday,' I said. 'Max talked to her last night.'

Boyce and I exchanged a glance. 'And?' he said.

'She's not okay at all. To quote Max, she's going fucking crazy.' I was stiff, in control. I didn't want Boyce to see me the way I was at home – unable to sleep, to eat, to concentrate.

'I'll get some coffee.' Boyce left the room, returning with a tray, two coffees, two sugar packets, and a pitcher of cream. He set this on a table behind his desk and mixed us two sweet, milky coffees. He offered me one and I took it.

We sat and sipped for a bit in silence.

'I'm looking at it from a legal standpoint.' Boyce set down his cup on his desk, careful to put a napkin beneath it. 'I want her actions the night of John's death vindicated, and I think I can pull it off.' He looked at me. 'That family of yours is the lock. You're the key, buddy.'

I set my cup on his desk, too, but I didn't put a napkin beneath it. 'I don't want her used to further your career,' I said.

The look on Boyce's face wasn't much different from my Sunday school teacher's the time I threw Billy Williams' Bible on the floor. 'You know what, Richard? You're not the only guy in the world with problems. Later this week I've got meetings with a ten-year-old kid who wants to divorce his parents. His mother has abandoned him for up to three weeks at a stretch; his father has used him as an ashtray and a sperm receptacle.

'Next week I'm meeting with a woman claiming to have been abused by her employer over an extended period of time. She says the guy weighs in at three hundred pounds and managed to convince her that if she didn't let him fuck her in the ass, he'd see to it that she'd never, ever find another job. And this woman supports her mother. The victim is just that, a victim. And you know what, Richard? I believe their stories.'

He looked right at me.

'I'll tell you something else, buddy boy. I believe Claire's story, and you do, too. All this fancy stepping around the real issues is your problem and all you're doing is making her life harder. Glassman tells me nobody reaches the point she's reached unless something from the past traumatized her, something beyond her conscious grasp that she's still running from. Glassman needs your help and so do I.' Boyce snatched up my cup and set it down on top of a yellow legal pad. 'Don't make this adversarial, Richard. That's not what it's about. And we've got more problems now, too.'

'Like what?' I felt defensive as hell. I felt as if here is this guy I like and respect and he knows I hit my wife and he knows I haven't looked out for my sister and he knows I'm a fucking wimp when it comes to my father and now he wants more and more and more. He'll be calling Sam next, for Christ's sake.

Everybody has to grow up some day

'Glassman contacted your parents.'

'And?'

'He wants them to come up here and begin family therapy. He thinks it's essential for Claire to confront them in a safe setting. He thinks it's possible her memories will continue to surface. He wants her to see that she's safe from them now. They can't hurt her anymore.' He paused. 'That's the therapy point of view. From a legal standpoint, some tangible memories would be great, details and specifics, with you to validate them.'

'How's all this really going to help her in court?' I demanded. 'She didn't murder our father, she murdered her husband.'

'I'll tell you something, Richard. You never know with a jury. There was a case last year in Wyoming where a woman murdered her sister, thinking she was her stepmother who had spent years abusing her, and the jury let her off. There was even some talk of indicting the stepmother for child abuse. It got as far as the grand jury. In another case, a jury convicted a guy of murdering a little girl and the only evidence was his own daughter's flashbacks. That guy's in prison.'

'So what was my parents' response to Glassman?'

'He talked to your mother first. She told him the family had no problems. She was upset, he tells me, hostile. He asked her how come her daughter was in the Psych Institute if the family had no problems and she said Claire's situation had nothing to do with them, that they were going on vacation, she had to get away from all the stress.'

'She didn't complain that Claire's situation disturbed her sleep or that she just didn't understand how Claire could have done this to her?'

Boyce gave me a smile of appreciation. 'Actually, I think something like that was said.'

'What about my father?' I tensed, dreading Boyce's response. Jack could be so convincing. Nobody knew that better than I did.

'Glassman and I talked to him yesterday. He's a strange duck, Richard.'

Like I didn't know this?

'Glassman says your father sounded discombobulated. That he went into some long rambling speech about how sensitive Claire is, even as a little girl she had a wild imagination. He babbled something about the Hayes men, that that was part of being a Hayes man. Sounded like a little kid when he said it. Glassman didn't know what he meant. He confirmed, though, that some graves she's been talking about do exist. Glassman didn't pressure him, just listened. The main bent was that Claire fantasized a lot. Implication: Don't believe a word she says.'

'That's a bunch of shit.'

'Here's the clincher, Richard. Your dad called Glassman back late last night and told him they wanted Claire removed from his care and from the Psych Institute. They want to move her to a place near Waterton. He says he knows the people there and Claire will be better off. He's planning to petition the court first for legal guardianship, then for removal to Waterton.'

'The motherfucking son of a bitch.' My stomach was a knot.

'I thought he was such a great guy. Taught you to run that farm and all.'

'Shut up, Boyce.' Take Claire to Waterton? Then what? Lock her up and throw away the key? Tell everyone she's crazy? Finish stealing her life? At least if she went to prison, she'd be released one day.

Honor thy father

'Oh, God, Boyce, he's my father.' The knot in my stomach tightened. I refused to meet Boyce's eyes. I don't know which I feared more – condemnation or pity.

Boyce shrugged. 'Yeah, well, big deal.' He stretched his arm toward his bookcase, pointing straight at Joe McGinnis' books *Fatal Vision* and *Blind Faith*. 'Those assholes were fathers, too.' He got up from his desk and picked up *Affliction*. 'Ever read this? This guy loves his father. But you know what? He kills him in the end and guess what? I'd defend the guy in a heartbeat. That guy's father needed killing.'

'Parricide your specialty or something?' I said.

'I'd hate to have you on a jury, Richard. You've got cement for a brain. Nothing alters your mindset, does it?' He rested both hands on the desk top and leaned toward me.

'Save the theatrics for the courtroom.'

'I just want to tell you something, buddy. When I was nine years old my mother left my father because he beat her up once or twice a week. In those days there wasn't much in the way of shelters or protection for women. Lucky for her, my grandparents took us in. Lucky for us, my grandfather was a successful businessman. But I never forgot hiding in dark hallways listening to my mother's moans as my father hit her, nor did I forget my grandfather's lectures to my mother about a woman's place and duty in life. According to him, she'd failed her husband. She died of cancer when she was fifty-one years old and I think she figured she was well rid of this life. I don't suppose I've ever forgotten that I didn't protect her from my father.'

We looked at each other across the desk top.

'Why'd you defend that college thug?' I asked. 'The one who killed the girl at the Green Garden?'

'Don't be naïve. I made a lot of money from that and got my name in the news and raised my fees all the way around. Thanks to that college kid, I can represent the kid who wants to divorce his parents and do it as my *pro bono* case for the year.'

'So you're going to avenge your mother?'

'Yeah, something like that.'

'I'm supposed to avenge your mother, too.'

'Avenge your own goddamn mother or sister or self, Richard. You've got a chance. Do it.'

I took a deep breath. 'Look,' I said, not knowing if Boyce had any control over this or not, 'I don't want Claire near them. Keep her in New York.'

'There's more.' Boyce stood and turned to look out his window. 'Your father says he's not paying the bills. He says he doesn't feel what I'm doing is going to prove helpful to Claire. I'm wondering if somehow he's not behind this deal of the DA's. He really wants Claire silenced. Didn't you tell me your mother's family knew a lot of judges?'

'Yes,' I said. 'Some of them are judges.' My hands were clammy against the leather arms of Boyce's chair. 'Did he fire you?'

'He can't. I'm not his attorney. But I have a feeling he's going to make trouble. If he gets legal guardianship, we're up Shit Creek.'

'My father can't afford to quit paying you.'

'You're going to tell him that?'

195

Confront God? At that moment I realized how large he still loomed on my horizon. New York had put no distance. Fifteen years had put no distance. Jack was still the dad who was way bigger than I was. I knew he was sixty-five years old and retired, but I didn't think of him that way. In my mind he was forty years old and master of a thirty-piece gun collection, any one of which could kill me in an instant.

Back talk me? Bang! You're dead

Disagree with me? Bang! You're dead

Tell anybody on me ever? Bang! You're dead

'I guess I'll have to.' Even I heard what sounded like a lack of conviction, but I don't think that's what it was. It was lingering fear of a man who'd had complete power over my existence. When I thought of my father, I pictured myself small and defenseless. The passage of time had altered that imprint very little.

'You'll need to do it soon, Richard.'

Honor thy father and thy mother

Up against the wall.

Once I started adding to my statement, it went quickly, a kind of singing of time with notes zooming past in high C. Edna's fingers went wild and when I'd look over at her, she wouldn't meet my eye. I had to pay her time and a half since it was Sunday, so I shouldn't have let her bother me, but she did. 'C'mon, Richard, keep going, there's more to the story, more to the story, the story,' pressed Boyce, and with every word I spoke, her features grew colder. She knew I was betraying my own family. By late afternoon she was a granite slab at the far end of the table. Boyce and I were hot and sweaty and wired. I'd told him about the graves and the guns. Hating myself and him, I told him about the drugs and the alcohol and Claire's thought that my mother wanted her dead. I told him about dog biscuits and dead dogs, and I told him my version of the gash on Claire's forehead.

'Because of a mushroom?' asked Boyce.

'That's the way I remember it.'

'Maybe the wrong combination of drugs and lack of sleep,' said Boyce. 'That's McGinnis' theory on Jeffrey MacDonald, the Green Beret doctor who killed his pregnant wife and two little girls.'

'Maybe.'

By four o'clock, my high C song had dropped to an A minor. My voice was hoarse and I smelled bad. We'd decided to do my statement in Boyce's office instead of the conference room and the air had grown close and sweaty with our intensity. Boyce had his sleeves rolled high and sweat circles under his arms. My shirt was unbuttoned clear to my waist. Only my white T-shirt saved Edna from complaining, I'm sure. If this had been a gig, my trumpet would be spit-filled and gross, and that's sort of the way I felt.

After Edna packed up her machine and left, Boyce said, 'I like the gash, I like it a lot. There ought to be hospital records stashed in a basement file on that one. Maybe a nurse with a good memory.'

Honor thy father and thy mother

'You're just scratching the surface, Richard.'

'What's that supposed to mean?'

He shrugged. 'Your sister's a lot more honest than you.'

'Back off.'

'No.'

I took a step toward him.

'Look,' Boyce said, his face reddening. 'Keep your family secrets, let Claire bear all the heat, but you've got to put your father out of the picture.' He put his face in mine. 'All you've got to do is pull his chain a little. Let him know you know about him. Tell him his kids are in charge now. Tell him to forget legal guardianship. Before it's too late.'

'Big man,' I said, 'but your dad left, he didn't stick around to fuck with you. You don't know what it was like for me. Or Claire.'

'I'm trying, you asshole.'
We looked at each other.
I turned on my heel and left the office.
Keep your family secrets

Chapter Fifteen

I PUT on my running clothes straight away when I got home. I couldn't get out of the apartment into the streets fast enough. The cold and dreary weather didn't matter. I was anger in human form, slap-slap-slapping the sidewalk with my thick-soled sneakers. Rat-ta-tat, rat-ta-tat, rat-ta-tat.

Why did Claire have to kill John?

What happened at the farm

Why couldn't Boyce leave me alone?

There'd been a phone message from my parents when I'd returned from Boyce's. Both of them on the line, an out of sync duet.

'We'll be out of town for the next few weeks, Richard. We're leaving in ten days. Reservations are all set.' Deep, authoritative, spoken as if this was the definitive statement of all time. 'Your mother needs a break.'

A break? From what?

'We're going on a cruise, off the coast of Scotland and Wales,' my mother's voice piped in.

'I've decided not to pay this Boyce Regner. He's not what Claire needs. I don't like this Dr Glassman, either. I've gotten in touch with my friend Tom Buckley. He's at the psychiatric hospital outside Waterton.'

It's like they're in outer space, I thought, pounding the

pavement. He still thinks he can control Claire's life. He thinks this is the dinner table, he thinks it's the farm.

'It's too late, Dad!' I screamed out loud. 'It's spun out of control. She's killed John! Get it, Dad? She's killed him!'

Rat-ta-tat-tat.

I hate them

By now I'd wound my way around town until I was back at my favorite coffee shop on 75th. As soon as I panted my way inside and collapsed on a chair, Lucy waved and came over. Her beehive was high and in place, her lipstick thick as Mary's.

'Hey,' she said.

'Hey, yourself.' Even in times of stress, I was ever ready with the banter.

'Coffee?'

It wasn't until she said that that I realized there was only one thing I wanted to do and it wasn't drink coffee and it couldn't wait. 'No,' I told her, 'I don't want anything except some quarters.' I held out a dollar and she gave me change. I was up and out of the booth and in the back of the diner in seconds. I called information and got the number for the Manhattan Psych Institute. I called and asked for Claire. She was in group, they said, but they would take a message. I told them to tell her I was going to confront Dad for her. I thought announcing this intention would make me feel better. I thought telling Claire would make it real. I thought I'd be able to face Boyce. I thought I'd feel proud, as if I could call Sam, too, and let her know I was growing up, taking care of business, I'd be a good risk.

The thing is, I felt sick after hanging up.

I went into the bathroom and locked the door. I got down on my knees, hung my head over the toilet bowl. Nothing happened but a few dry heaves. It had been years since I'd been on my knees. I had a curious sense of praying or at least that God was somehow involved.

I emerged pale and shaky from the bathroom. Lucy took me by the arm and sat me back down in the booth. She vanished for a moment and returned with a Coke and one of those straws shaped like a pretzel.

'Drink,' she said.

I did and felt better. I sat for a bit, watching her scurry back and forth from the counter to her tables. I thought she might take a minute to sit down and chat, but she didn't. I liked her all the better for keeping her distance.

I finished my Coke and left a five-dollar bill on the table before heading outside to run the last few blocks to my apartment.

Rat–a–tat–tat.

It was dark by the time I got home, the sky starless, First Avenue's yellow and blue Blockbuster sign bright against the night's blackness. I showered and changed into clean sweats. The anger I'd felt at Boyce's office was still with me, making me nervous, agitated.

I knew I should call my parents, but I couldn't get myself to do it. If I showed up unexpectedly, my mother would go into a conniption fit about fresh sheets and towels and oh! the guest bathroom isn't clean and she's only got two lamb chops defrosted. Calling ahead ensured clean bed sheets and a third chop, but it also entailed knowing how many engagements they'd had to reschedule due to your presence. Her response to a visit had a way of making you feel guilty before you even got there.

I thought about drinking a beer, but instead I opened the door to my jumbled closet and stared at my trumpet. I pulled out the case and sat with it in my lap. My hands left fingerprints in the thick dust. I put it back again.

I wanted to call Sam, but didn't. I had an alarming insight as I reached for the phone. I saw a picture of that same hand resting on the phone, reaching into the refrigerator for a beer.

It stopped me dead from picking up the receiver. Was I reaching out to Sam the same way I did for a beer?

I thought you weren't going to drink anymore

I remembered how angry Johanna's words had made me, how I wanted to smash her for saying it. Now I wondered if maybe I myself wasn't worried a bit about my drinking. I certainly knew I'd substituted beer for Johanna's company after she left. I also knew that I wasn't a drunk, but maybe I was a person who used other people or beer or work as a way to avoid thinking about who I was and where I might be headed. And I realized I had no intention of using Sam that way. She'd never allow it, anyway, but I didn't want her to have to call me on it.

I wandered about my postage-stamp apartment, opening a can of Spaghettios, heating them up. I ate them at the stove right out of the pan. The meatballs tasted like rubber. I sat on my sofa bed and flipped channels on my television. The phone rang and my heart jumped. Sam? I snatched it up.

'Yo, bro,' Max's voice sloshed over the wire. 'I been thinking about ol' Bev, ol' bee-u-tiful Beverrly, Mama on the make . . .'

'What are you talking about?' Jesus Christ. First he doesn't call me for two years, then he calls me every night like I'm his goddamn mother. 'Why don't you call me when you're sober?'

'What about you? Have you quit? Claire says you were going to. It's not all right to get a little drunk, big bro, ease my pain, as they say?'

'Take it easy, Belle.' Another voice bringing up my drinking. An unexpected one. I thought it far more likely that Max was the one in the family with the drinking problem, not me. Outside my window, a street light flickered twice, then stopped shining altogether.

'Why'd she have to be so beautiful?'

'Who?'

'Beverly. Our mother. Our lady of dogshit.'

Max had to be more than drunk. It didn't matter how many beers I drank, thinking Bev beautiful never infiltrated my mind. I didn't say anything. I thought I'd see where he was going. I wondered if he remembered his tirade from the night before.

'I was her best girlfriend, big bro, for years. We'd watch the soaps, talk about Dad. I'm just a little boy and she's got me in hair nets and petticoats and we laugh and giggle and it's fun and I love the attention and she's getting off on letting the good times roll . . .'

'What are you saying?'

'She talked to me, Richard.' When he called me by my given name I knew how desperate he was. 'She'd tell me things about her and Dad, how he didn't love her, she'd tell me about their love life, she'd say he didn't want her. She told me one time she dressed in a see-through gown, white, diaphanous, and she'd powdered and puffed herself, shaved her legs, smoothed on pink lotion and she was a flower, Richard, she told me she was a flower, ready to open, and he turned away, called the hospital, left the bed, took off in the Land Rover.'

'Oh, Max.' Those oily Spaghettios wanted to come back up. I had to swallow hard. I could take our parents' make-believe funerals better than this.

'She did love me, you know.'

'I know,' I told him. 'I was jealous.' I said that to make him feel better, but I realized I spoke from the heart. There'd been times when I'd see the two of them exchange a look and I'd wondered what it would have been like to have my mother exchange a look like that with me.

'The teen years changed everything,' he said, after a while.

'Our budding sexuality triggered something in them,' I said, as if I was joking.

What happened to me on that farm

'It's when she turned full force on Claire,' said Max, and his voice was clear and sharp, every trace of alcohol seemingly vanquished. I heard the Belle Dame Sans Merci when he added, 'It's when she severed me and honed in on Claire. Remember the chip-chip-chippy song?'

I did, but I didn't want to. When we were growing up together, none of us talked about this stuff. We baled hay together, played at the secret pool together, helped each other with homework, but we never discussed how we felt about Mom and Dad. Elizabeth has said that it's because of my parents' divide-and-conquer strategy, but I think maybe it was too scary to break implicit family rules: Hayes don't cry; Hayes show no feelings; Hayes honor thy father and thy mother.

'Boyce says Dad and Mom won't pay for Claire,' I said. 'He says they're petitioning the court for legal guardianship and then to have Claire committed to that hospital outside Waterton. I'd like to kill them.'

'It wouldn't be the first time, big bro,' said Max.

'What?'

'Don't you remember that afternoon in the Brookfield Court house when you were sixteen or so? I was on the back stairs. You never saw me. Neither did she.'

'Are you still guzzling wine or what?' I was angry. He's going where he doesn't belong, I thought. 'I've got to go,' I said.

'Always the coward,' sneered the Belle Dame Sans Merci. 'Even now when your fucking balls are on the line. Hang up, run away. Leave me hanging. Fuck you.'

I felt as if the last week of my life had been nothing but fuck-yous and run-away scenes. I was tired of it.

'Shut up, Belle,' I said. 'I remember.'

And I did. It happened and it had lived alongside me for a long time, never quite integrated into the Richard I thought I was. The Richard who walked that tightrope between being the son my father wanted me to be and the brother my siblings needed.

Like Max said, I'm sixteen at the time, Elizabeth fifteen, Claire fourteen, Max, thirteen. I've come home from school to find my mother laughing at a picture Claire has drawn, one she's worked hard on, one with lots of creative daring. It's of the farm and the creek and the dog graveyard, but that's not what you see on the canvas. The canvas is splotches of dripping color but there's a rhyme and reason to it.

I understand because I've been working on a trumpet composition and I know the way your mind can go off on a wild tangent. I know Claire's work is her heart splattered for all to see and showing our mother takes great courage, greater than drawing it in the first place because she's your mother, yet you know there's a twist inside her and so you risk yourself – hoping that this time she'll hug you and tell you how beautiful your work is, and maybe, maybe she'll tell you a little bit about her own dreams of becoming a famous pianist.

Maybe this will be the time she'll take your hand and pull you down beside her on the couch and put her arm around you. I think there might be room for me and my trumpet, too.

Maybe today is that day.

But the day Claire shows her farm abstract is not the day.

That day the kitchen is cluttered. The drug-filled lazy Susan sits dead center on the kitchen table hidden by piles of folded laundry. Plus, she's been cleaning out cupboards, so boxes of Betty Crocker cakes and date bars, brownies and square boxes of Jello criss-cross the table like a crazed grocery-store shelf. And here's Claire, holding up her painting, face shiny with pleasure and hesitancy, and then my mother starts laughing an out of control laugh that embodies mockery and a certain evil intent. I sense destruction.

'So this is what your father spends his money on,' she says. 'Art lessons for you. Looks as if you need a few more.'

She's wearing that dress again, that red and white checked thing, and she's gotten her hair permed recently because it looks like an SOS pad. Her lips are bare of lipstick and the blue mules are on her feet.

I hate her.

205

I don't know where Claire goes or what she does, she fades from the room like a shut-off television screen and just my mother and I are left. She leaves, too, says she's got to go to the grocery store and tells me to clean up the mess and I do. I clean up everything. I put boxed food away. I stuff dog pellets back into the smelly bag and wipe down the counter. I take every drug from that lazy Susan, wash the lazy Susan and put all the drugs back. It's Claire's job to set the table, so I go ahead and do that, too. My heart is pounding with hate and love and a sense of it's now or never. My trumpet lies in its opened case on the counter next to the stove, reminding me of my grandfather in his coffin.

Up the back stairs I go. I don't think about Max or Claire, where they are, what they're doing. I think only about my mother and how ugly she is and how she's a destroyer of hopes and dreams and I want her dead.

I slip into my parents' bedroom. All the shades are down, the draperies pulled. Dark, spooky, uninviting.

The gun cabinet sits against the wall, gloomy and dark. I take the key from my father's top drawer, unlock it, remove a 12-gauge shotgun. It feels familiar, cool, empowering. A shotgun holds few surprises for me. I've been shooting since I was seven years old. I get the shells from my father's drawer, load it up, head back downstairs. I enter the spotless kitchen and sit down to wait.

I feel strong and sure about protecting my sister. I want to set her free from my mother and the undercurrents I sense between her and my father. Every part of my body is tensed and ready. The veins in my neck are tight and my heart a beat away from explosion. But I sit unmoving, awaiting my mother's return.

With a snap and crack of the kitchen door, she's home, a brown paper sack in her hands. I look at her, shotgun aimed. She looks at me. We look at the truth. She backs out the door, silent, still clutching that bag, a sunshine-yellow box of Cheerios peeking over the rim.

I don't know how long I sit there in my assigned seat at the kitchen table. It might have been a minute; it might have been half an hour. I sit there, numb with my own self-loathing.

And my shame.

Honor thy father and thy mother

Nothing was ever said. She didn't say anything to me. As far as I know, she didn't say anything to my father. I doubt very much she acknowledged the nuances of this particular afternoon at 37 Brookfield Court to herself. I never mentioned it, either. Just as if it had never been.

Now I knew that Max had seen.

Max knew.

'I'm going to Waterton,' I said.

'What else is new? You've spent your entire adulthood trotting off to Waterton to pay homage.'

'I'm going to make them pay Boyce's bill,' I said. 'I'm going to make them back off. I'm going soon.'

'When?'

Why did Max have to pressure me? 'I've already planned to go next Sunday,' I said. 'One week from today.' That was true, too. I knew their Sunday schedule. I knew they'd be home.

'I hope that's not too late, Richard.'

'Get off my back,' I said.

'Why didn't you kill her, Richard?'

'There's no point talking to you when you're like this,' I said.

'You wanted her dead for yourself, but you can't deal with that, can you? Can't deal with the truth, but I can't figure out why you couldn't have killed her and told yourself you were doing it for Claire. Why didn't you kill her?' Max's voice felt like my mother's voice shrieking in my ear.

'I don't know,' I told him, and pressed my finger on the button to disconnect us. I held my finger there a long time.

I'd told Max I didn't know why I hadn't killed her, but in a way, I did know. I don't think I understood at the time, but now I could see that it was in part because of my need to keep the family balanced. I wanted everybody to get along and I saw my role as eldest son as one of compromise. If I killed her, I'd upset the balance. I'd be taking sides. I think I thought it was enough to put her on notice.

For a brief moment, I became sixteen-year-old Richard. I'm sitting in that kitchen chair once again, shotgun in hand. My mother appears in the doorway. She sees the pointed gun. We look at each other and this time I see in her eyes a flash of scorn. She doesn't have to say a word; I know what she's thinking: *You won't shoot me, Richard. You're a coward. You're afraid of what your father'd do to you if you did.* Her thoughts are no more than the faintest sneer on her face, but I know she's right and shut the knowledge right out of my brain.

And there's something else shut out of my brain, something that's always there and out of reach, something more terrifying than my father, something no boy in his right mind would risk . . .

What happened on the farm

Here's the thing: I didn't want to know. Not even now; not even twenty-odd years later.

I didn't pull out the sofa bed. I sat upright most of the night, my heart racing, my hands damp with fear. Was it Claire's bogeyman? It wasn't until dawn erased the orange blur of the street light that I stretched out full length and dozed.

I hope it's not too late

Chapter Sixteen

I WENT to work Monday and Tuesday and stayed late, accomplishing nothing. I couldn't concentrate. The Internal Revenue Code might as well have been braille.

I didn't hear from Boyce. Claire didn't call. My parents didn't call. Max left me alone. Almost as if the murder hadn't happened. Almost as if my parents' legal actions and cruise didn't loom large.

See, Max, this coming Sunday is plenty of time

I couldn't eat. I couldn't sleep. I felt agitated, in a state of constant upheaval.

And I was afraid of the upcoming confrontation in Waterton.

I talked to Sam Monday evening from the office. She said she could have dinner with me Saturday but not Friday. 'Friday's my sister's last day here. I guess I better spend the evening with her.'

'You guess?' I said.

I told her more about Max. About his being gay and a former funeral director. That since he was a kid, we'd called him the Belle Dame Sans Merci.

'Why?' said Sam.

'Because he always says what he thinks,' I told her.

Tuesday evening I called Sam from the office about six, and she agreed to meet me for a drink.

'Can we make it my neighborhood?' she asked. 'I've got papers to grade and a parent conference at the crack of dawn tomorrow.'

I stepped into the smoky gloom of a place called Firebrand's on Sixth around the corner from Sheridan Square at exactly 6.01. Sam waved to me from a booth.

I slid in across from her.

She looked as beautiful as ever, hair swept back from her face in some kind of ponytail thing, no earrings, and she wore a deep blue turtleneck.

She sipped a Coke. 'Papers to grade,' she said, with a smile. I ordered the same.

'So,' she said. 'How are things with Claire going?'

'Fine,' I said.

'What about your statement for Boyce?'

'What about it?'

'You don't have to snap at me,' said Sam.

'Well, what about it?' Even as I answered with an edge to my voice, I knew I had been waiting for her to ask. I had been disappointed that she hadn't asked the day before when we spoke on the telephone.

'Look, I just wondered if you'd gotten things resolved in your own mind. You said Boyce was pushing you to support Claire. So, did you or didn't you?'

'He doesn't have to push me. She's my sister.'

'So, how'd things go?' Push, push.

Johanna'd back off if she sensed my anger. This woman did not quit. I was smart enough to realize that I had nothing to gain from yelling at Sam. She owed me nothing. She'd get up and leave, refuse to go out with me, tell me what a child I was. I took a deep breath. 'Lousy,' I said.

Silence stretched between us. She swirled her straw and her ice cubes clanked.

'The fat lady hasn't sung yet,' I said at last.

'Oh,' said Sam. 'I guess that means you're going to what? Talk to Boyce again? Decide if your sister's telling the truth?'

'My father's working against Claire. Wants to lock her up in a nut-house for life. Boyce wants me to tell the old man to mind his own business. I'm going to see him on Sunday.'

'Mmm,' said Sam.

'What's that supposed to mean?'

'I'm just thinking. This reminds me of my divorce. When I first told my parents I wanted a divorce, they said I was their daughter, of course they'd be supportive, but all their sympathy lay with my husband. My mother'd call and write him these empathetic little notes. I had to get really blunt and tell them it was a contested divorce and they couldn't have it both ways.'

'So what are you saying?'

'It doesn't take a rocket scientist, Richard. You can't have it both ways. It's Claire or your dad. Simple.'

Push, push, push. 'You don't understand,' I said. 'It's not that easy.'

She shrugged and we began to speak of other matters, students and lesson plans, but I knew beneath the chatter lay her gauntlet: *It's Claire or your dad, it's Claire or your dad, it's Claire or your dad.*

There was more at stake than just my family.

On Wednesday Boyce called.

Bright and early. At the office. 'Meet me at Verymore's,' he said. 'Twelve thirty.' Neither of us mentioned our last meeting.

I got there at twelve twenty and he was already seated at a booth. The same booth Mary and I had been in when he'd come blundering over. Was that only a week ago?

We ordered iced tea and burgers, medium rare, two garden salads, and an order of onion rings to share.

'I feel as if we're married,' I said, trying to be funny. I felt the sweat in my armpits, that plugged feeling in my ears.

Boyce attempted a smile, but he didn't look happy. He didn't bring up anything about the case. Maybe law school etiquette demands you wait until after eating before plunging the knife into a client. I know when I take a client to lunch, we never talk business until dessert. Of course Claire was the client, not me. We certainly had that straight.

Boyce surprised me by saying, 'Being married's tough, isn't it?'

'I didn't think so,' I said, 'but I guess Johanna did.' I took a deep breath, then, and added, 'Yeah, being married was tough.'

Silence.

'How'd you meet your wife?' I asked, uncomfortable.

'Sarah,' said Boyce, 'her name's Sarah. I met her in law school. Fell in love with her the first time I saw her. During a mock trial. She's a tax attorney. Works for the Bank of New York.'

I didn't know what to say so I said nothing.

Our burgers arrived in the midst of another uncomfortable silence.

After a bit, Boyce said, 'My wife is pregnant again. I'm really worried about her. It's dangerous for her to be pregnant. I thought she was on the pill.'

I'd listened to Mary's feminine observations about people enough to understand that Boyce might not be really talking to me, but just talking, trying to make sense out of things. Maybe, in my own way, I felt safe to him.

He'd get to me and Claire soon enough. I didn't doubt that for a minute.

'Before I went into criminal law, I worked mostly with divorces. I never understood why people got divorced.' He looked at me, bemused. He shrugged. 'It's always a trust issue. I see that now.'

'Right,' I said.

Back to the burgers.

We finished lunch.

Boyce cleared his throat. 'What are you waiting for, Richard?'

That's all he said, but I knew exactly what he was talking about.

'I'm going on Sunday.'

'I talked to you last Sunday. It's now Wednesday. If your fucking father gets that petition for guardianship filed before Sunday and there's an emergency hearing, that could be the end of Claire. It could fuck her forever.'

'I told you I'm going on Sunday.' I could feel the vein beating in my forehead. Maybe he told me that shit about his marriage to soften me up. It didn't work. I didn't like being pressured.

'Sunday? This Sunday or next Sunday? Or maybe you're referring to Sunday three weeks from now?'

'Four days,' I said, vein thumping. I wanted to tell him it was none of his damn business, but, of course, it was. 'I've decided to take him by surprise. They'll be there on a Sunday.'

'It better not be too late, Richard.'

This time it was Boyce who slammed out the door.

Thursday: No phone calls from Boyce or Sam or my parents or Max or Claire.

Friday morning I awoke with a bolt at 5.36, as if something or someone had deliberately awakened me. But there was nothing, not daylight, not cars in the street, not Gordon Lightfoot bleating from across the street.

I felt like a big lump of run-over dead meat. I'd hardly slept. Sam's words from Tuesday night went through my mind: *You can't have it both ways, it's Claire or your dad, you can't have it both ways, it's Claire or your dad* . . . In between the drumbeat of Sam's voice, was my own inner voice: *Waterton, Waterton, Waterton* . . .

I felt a pulse beginning to beat in my forehead. Boyce, Jack, Bev, Claire, Max, Sam. It felt just like the pressure of being a kid with everyone pushing and pulling at me, trying to make

213

me into the son or brother he wanted, instead of me being who I was.

I showered, dressed, ate a bowl of Shredded Wheat. Outside, it looked raw and cloudy as February on the farm. I buttoned my overcoat and snapped shut my briefcase, relieved that I had a busy day planned at the office. My hand was on the doorknob when the phone rang.

I waited for the answering machine to click on. I continued to stand motionless, listening.

'Pick up, Richard, pick up.' Claire's voice was high, that voice of hers from the dead of night when she came creeping into my room, frightened by the bogeyman.

I picked up. How could I not?

'There's this guy here at the Institute,' she said. 'He's like sixty years old. He sits next to me at every meal. Why?'

I realized after a silence that she expected an answer. 'I don't know.' I kept my voice calm.

Claire's voice came at me over the wire, clear and sharp. 'He's out to get me.'

'What do you mean?' I set down my briefcase on the sofa bed. I unbuttoned my coat. I sat down beside the briefcase.

'It's John. He's having me followed.'

'John's dead,' I said, with a sinking heart.

'What do you know? You weren't here last night.'

'Tell me,' I said, but I didn't want to hear. Maybe a doctor or nurse would pass by the phone booth and help her. I thought I better speak to Dr Glassman. Have her phone privileges rescinded. Anything to stop the pressure.

It's Claire or your dad, it's Claire or your dad, it's Claire or your dad . . . Waterton, Waterton, Waterton

'The same old thing, Richard,' she said. 'We're in the room with that table. His plants are hanging on hooks over every window opening. He says he's got to use the table to do some replanting. He pushes my art stuff off the table, caps tubes of paint, shoves paintbrushes to one side.'

I realized she was speaking of her and John's Village apartment.

'It's pitch black outside,' she said. 'Nothing but a solid sheet of blackness. John's yanking flower pots from windows, spreading out newspapers across the table, whirling around the room. My art things are shunted aside. Pigments I've been working on for months.'

'Claire,' I said. 'Are there any nurses around?'

She kept right on: 'He's getting sweaty. I can smell him – bitter as dried sperm, pungent as woodchuck. It's a wet smell, damp, like the pond, and one in the woods filled with algae. I need him to leave my things alone, to stop smelling. "Stop," I say, but he won't. He says it's his apartment, he pays the rent, my art isn't enough to pay my share of the groceries, so what he says goes. But, Richard, I sold a painting the other day. Did I tell you that?' All the wild agitation faded from her voice and I heard the shy pride. 'It's the picture of the farm-house in winter. The one with the lone tiger lily. John says three hundred dollars doesn't amount to a hill of beans.'

'It doesn't matter what he says,' I said and, with pain, remembered my attitude toward Johanna's art.

I yanked a blanket from my sofa bed and wrapped it over my suit and unbuttoned overcoat. If the man across the street saw me, he could laugh; I didn't care.

'Oh, Richard,' and now Claire's voice was thin, a little girl's voice and I could picture her as seven, eight years old as easily as I could see her as a grown woman, 'she's there, too, hovering. I'm on that table, I'm wearing my red corduroy zip-up suit. I don't dare move, I lie on my back. They're nervous. I smell his hospital smell, the one where I can tell he's scrubbed his hands in liquid disinfectant, his skin is so pink, so wrinkled. Her lipstick's worn off, bits left in the corners and it doesn't match the red of her checks, she's tired and tangled, but she's excited, too. It's in the air . . .'

Her words felt like a pistol to my head. 'John's dead,' I said, knowing full well it wasn't John she was talking about.

215

Claire lowered her voice as if to share a secret. 'It's dark outside, Richard. I think about eight or nine o'clock. I'm still in my play clothes, so maybe no bath that night, maybe they kept me at the kitchen table since dinner, maybe it took me that long to swallow those mushy sour Brussels sprouts, maybe, maybe, but I'm there, all right. I lie on my back in my zip-up suit. I lie there quiet as an unborn baby, fear surrounding me like mist and I can't think or breathe or talk or cry. I just am.'

I clutched my blanket closer. All week long I'd managed to escape the pain of the past and now I felt as if I was an unhealed sore, a place that needed a stitch and didn't get one, and here was Claire poking a hot fork into it, dabbing it once, twice, three times. What was I doing while my little sister lay like a sacrifice on the kitchen table?

Her voice grew louder as if she'd put her mouth tight enough against the receiver that there'd be no room for interference. 'Remember pills splashed from that lazy Susan? Bottles, bottles, everywhere. Acromycin, pink and gooey. There's a funny half-hospital smell, a musty, sore throat, kitcheny smell and it's sweeping wide around me and I'm trying to hang on to it because there's another odor, too. It's him, no her, him, I don't know who, but it's there and I've smelled it before but I don't know when or where, but it has to do with them and what they're going to do to me . . .'

Claire stopped. Was she finished? Had a nurse come by? I didn't know. I'd stopped wanting to hold or comfort her. I wanted to get away from her. I didn't want to journey to 37 Brookfield Court. What was the point? It wouldn't change anything.

'He darts to the windows. A star or two and a half-moon are out there peeking in, no one else, no neighbors can see through our kitchen windows, we're too far away, but he pulls shut the curtains. They're pleated, lined and pleated and plaid, remember? Remember, Richard? Remember?' Her words were the beat of a drum in my ears, pounding harder and harder. I pulled my blanket over my head. If I'd had a pacifier to suck, I would have sucked it hard enough to rip off the nipple.

'It's that corduroy suit, Richard, you know the one? It snaps up the crotch like a baby's, as if I was still wearing diapers, but I know, I know I'm five, maybe six.' She paused, but swirled back in seconds. 'So now the curtains are drawn, he's sweating with excitement, she's whimpering, "Jack, Jack, Jack," but it's the whimper of a kid who wants to do something naughty, desperate to do something forbidden and doesn't want to get caught. It's a doctor and a nurse, it's a patient and an operating table, but it's skewed, like you're looking at the wrong end of it. What's wrong with this picture? Remember that, Richard? Remember *Highlights for Children*? Remember "What's Wrong With This Picture"?'

'Yes,' I hissed at her.

'I see his bridgework,' said Claire. 'I see the gleam of gold in his mouth. His tongue, his gums are pink and wet and slick, juicy like fresh bubble gum. Against the back of my head this table is as hard as steel pipe. Hard as those steel rods he's got running from the upper pond spring to the lower pond out at the farm.'

'Forget it,' I said, an edge to my voice.

'They've got the snaps unsnapped, my underpants lie white beside me like used Kleenex and I grasp them, balling my fist around them for comfort. I feel my fingers pressing against my palm, no sharp nails to make this real, just fingers and the only other thing I feel is fear, so intense I think I'm dying and I'm only a little girl lying on my parents' kitchen table, legs spreadeagled and they're coming at me now. He's got a thin sharp instrument, she's got her fingers and those gleaming marble eyes. Leaning forward, he whispers into my ear, "If you move, I'll kill you." I don't doubt him for a moment. I've seen raccoons drop at fifty feet from the blast of his gun, I've seen woodchucks splat at sixty. Remember the blood in the kitchen the day he shot Misty? The pools, the red round pools that Mom said she wouldn't clean up, but she did?

217

Remember? And she vomited straight into one, and we giggled at the stench of wine mixed with vomit and death and we started to laugh and laugh until Elizabeth took us by the hands and dragged us upstairs and locked us in her room like prisoners of war. Remember?'

'Misty was a dog. A sick dog.' I couldn't stand the pressure.

'He knows I'll lie there and never say a word, just like I never say a word when he slithers into the living room after dinner and sidles next to me on the couch, the only time he ever has time for me, the only time he's ever nice to me and he whispers, "What book shall we read?" and I slip off the couch and into his den and grab a book, any book at all, *The Secret Garden*, *Beautiful Joe*, it doesn't matter, and I sit close beside him and he lowers his voice until it's just a warm hum in my ear, making me warm and snuggly and happy that my daddy loves me and then his hand slips inside my pants and he's touch-touch-touching me and, Richard, I like it, it feels nice, he's so gentle and I never stop him and afterwards he looks at me and I know he thinks I'm disgusting for letting him do that, so he knows I'll never say anything, I'll never say anything at all. And I never did, did I, Richard?'

My mouth felt stuck together, my lips gooey with spit and shame. I thought the trips to the living room with him were only between him and me. Just the two of us. Special. That's what he'd told me. Until now, with Claire dragging me through the mire with her, I'd forgotten even that.

the afternoon at the farm did not happen

'Stop it.' Beneath my blanket and clothes, I was freezing. My teeth chattered, my stomach churned. 'Can't you see all you've done stirring up the past is make trouble?'

'Trouble for whom? I'm the one in the Psych Institute.' Claire's voice was as loud as I remembered our mother's being when she was angry.

Voice shaking, finger slick with sweat against the release button, I found myself saying, 'If you scream at me, I'll hang up,' as if I was actually confronting Bev, not Claire. The pressure was so great, I couldn't breathe. I threw off the blanket.

Silence from her end. I took deep breaths. I counted to ten. I stared out my window straight into my neighbor's. He was home, light on, shades up. I watched him scratch his belly.

'When are you confronting Dad?' Claire said at last. Her voice told me she expected me to cop out, to leave her flapping high and dry in the wind like the clothes Mom hung on the line at the farm.

'I'm going on Sunday,' I whispered. 'I'm going to Waterton on Sunday.'

'Honest to God? Two days from now?'

'I'd sliver our fingers and mingle our blood if I could, Claire.'

'John was making me crazy.' Claire's voice was quiet. 'He was blending into the past. He was Mom, he was Dad, he was fear and violence.'

'You're safe now,' I said, through stiff, cold lips.

She continued as if I hadn't said anything. 'Sometimes Dad appears in my room wearing that black suit, that starchy white shirt, that thin dark tie.'

'What do you mean, Dad appears in your room? He's been to the hospital?' Jack in New York? He hadn't called me to say he was in town. My blanket fell from my lap to the floor as I sat up straight.

'He's in my head, Richard. Don't you get it? He's in my head. I can't get him out. He arrives like a ghost to torment me. He arrives whenever John hits me. He arrives when I'm upset. He brings fear with him. Jiggly, dark fear. Barbed-wire fear. It's all around me.'

'Draw it,' I said. 'Put it on paper, Claire.' I felt inspired. I'd given her an answer.

'There's a picture inside me right now,' she said, 'struggling to find shape. The farm's part of it, but I haven't figured it out yet. Those are the drawings John swept from the table that last night.' She paused, then added, 'The farm was always beauty, Richard, but something's in the new pictures, something that's off, something that makes the farm a mirage. I don't know what it is.'

She sounded calm now, but this business of my father appearing as a phantom bothered me. This seemed like something beyond imagination. Something dangerous.

'Claire,' I said. 'You know John's dead?'

'Yes,' she said. 'I killed him.'

'Dad can't hurt you anymore,' I said. 'Don't let him appear. Push him away when he shows up. I won't let him get you.'

'I didn't mind that Skip hit me, you know,' she said suddenly. 'At least he held me in his arms, at least he cuddled me.'

I couldn't speak.

'Our time's up, Richard,' she said, and then all I heard was the bleak sound of a dial tone.

I sat and watched the man across the street get ready for work. He didn't play his Gordon Lightfoot record. Or, if he did, its sad strains were too low for me to hear over the pain beating in my heart.

it did not happen

I called Mary, said I'd be in late, maybe not at all. 'I'm sorry, Mary,' I said. 'It's Claire.'

I heard her take a drag on her cigarette, pictured her sipping black coffee, a big red blot rimming the mug.

'Can I help?'

I felt so weary and confused, I almost said, Yes, let me cry on your shoulder. 'I'll let you know, Mary,' I said. 'Thanks.'

'Do what you have to do. I've got everything under control.'

Control.

Aha.

The key word. Mary had things under control, but did I? My life seemed to be zooming so far out of control I could barely think anymore. Max had once said that living in our family was like living in the state fair's House of Mirrors. I finally understood what he meant.

I sat on my sofa bed, still in my suit and tie, and swallowed again and again, trying to erase the picture of my parents as sicko Nazi tyrannizers of my sister. If I believed her, I'd have to kill him. It'd be back to the kitchen, shotgun aimed at their hearts and when they walked in, I'd blast them away. No turning back, no big eye-contact thing and no action, no more secret knowledge of rage, but a big blast of reality.

I did not want to believe her. I did not want to assimilate this knowledge. If I did, my life as I knew it would change. Although I didn't like visiting my parents, I did it. I had to admit that part of me got off on being the dutiful child, the one who carried out the family rules, the one who didn't turn gay and flit to California, the one who didn't hightail it to Europe and never return, the one who didn't kill himself, the one who didn't go crazy and kill her husband.

I was the good son.

I called Sam and got her answering machine. I considered hanging up but didn't. She was at work, but maybe she'd check her messages. I said: 'Sam, it's Richard. Here's something I want you to know. Claire is telling the truth. My parents did do bad things to her. There's no guesswork involved.'

Claire is telling the truth

Fifteen minutes later my phone rang. My heart pounded in fear. I felt that, in announcing the truth to Sam, I'd opened a door to my inner self that had never before been opened.

It wasn't Sam; it was Boyce. First time I'd heard from him since our Wednesday lunch.

'Three hospitals confirmed Claire's story.' Boyce's voice was firm, loud, upbeat, a courtroom voice.

'Claire's story?'

'About the beatings.' Not only because I expected Sam on

the phone, but because I didn't know what he was talking about. The gash in her forehead?

'Her husband John beat her up badly. On more than one occasion. She says he beat his mother, too, and we're working on following that up. Mrs Brown hung up on us, but Blueberry, Maryland, can't have many hospitals and Claire says she had to go at least twice.'

'He beat her up badly enough that she had to go to the hospital?' I could barely get words to spit from my mouth. Claire told me he hit her, I knew that, but somehow, after our childhood, a beating here or there didn't seem like that big a deal to me. I had pictured him slapping her face or knocking her down, maybe kicking her, but I hadn't pictured blood or trips to the emergency room. Why hadn't she told me?

'This is going to help us a lot.' Boyce's voice boomed into my ear. 'So far, you've validated some of Claire's accusations, but there's a lot you haven't said. I have no statement from Max yet. Claire hints at something behind your younger sister's suicide, but then she floats off somewhere. Get hold of that other sister of yours. Claire says Elizabeth has Tina's suicide note. I can't keep her focused long enough to get Elizabeth's number or address or anything concrete at all. I'm not even sure she's really talked to Elizabeth, but I can tell you that all five of you telling the same story will help persuade the judge that Claire acted in the only way she could. I think I can get her off. The *Times*'ll go nuts. We'll make the cover of *People* magazine with this case. Fuck Eleanor's plea bargain.'

'I could try,' I said.

'I don't want to hear you'll fucking try. Get the note. Get it before you leave for Waterton.'

Chapter Seventeen

B Y now it was close to noon.
I took off my suit and put on sweats.

I ran down the three flights of stairs to the outside door.

The sky looked even less promising than yesterday. Dull gray. Wind rustled telephone lines. I faced the bleak afternoon on a dead run.

Get the note! Get the note!

Rat-ta-tat, rat-ta-tat!

Waterton, Waterton!

I hadn't heard from my sister Elizabeth in years. She left for Europe her sophomore year in college. She made a few forays back to the homestead, but they were couched in secrecy, she and my parents having discussions none of the rest of us were in on. After Tina died, she left for good. As far as I knew she lived in Norwich, England, and taught at the university there. She'd wanted to be an Episcopalian priest, but my father didn't believe in women priests, wouldn't pay her way, not even undergraduate school unless she agreed to not study religion. Now she taught women's studies and was working on her PhD thesis, a treatise on autocratic fathers and their daughters, Lizzie Borden and Emily Dickinson her focus. I was ambivalent about her refusal to take part in family matters; on the one hand, I thought, as eldest daughter, the parents were in part her responsibility;

on the other hand, I felt powerful being the one dutiful child.

So when and why did she take that note

She must have gone snooping, I thought. She must have bided her time, pouncing on my mother's dresser drawers the minute the coast was clear. Or under the mattress or in the pocket of that dreadful red and white checked house dress. She'd found it and read it and kept it.

Why?

Revenge? Blackmail?

Who, I thought, is Elizabeth?

Who am I

Raindrops splatted onto my sweatshirt, but I kept on running.

Rat-ta-tat.

I don't want to hear you'll fucking try. Get the note!

It was two hours before I returned, a sodden puddle of sweat clothes.

Boyce had called in my absence.

Twice.

'A couple of monkey wrenches got tossed into Claire's case since I talked to you,' his voice boomed on my answering machine. 'Don't put off calling me, Richard.'

My heart started beating fast with fear of what I'd be hearing, so I did a few routine tasks to calm down. I stepped into the bathtub and removed my wet clothes. I opened my closet door to get jeans and a sweater and my trumpet case got in the way of closing the door. In a fit of pique, I jerked it out and set it on the table. Dust poofed into the air.

I considered washing the dishes in the sink, but cleaned off my trumpet case instead. When I got done, it looked as good as it used to look when I was lugging it from gig to gig with Skip.

I went to the refrigerator for a beer.

I thought you weren't going to drink anymore

I stared, unfocused, at a six-pack of Cokes, and then slowly closed the refrigerator door. I wasn't going to call Boyce – I would go to his office.

Grabbing an umbrella, I headed for First Avenue and hailed a taxi.

After a long wait in the reception room, Boyce motioned me inside his office. He wore a neat gray suit, blue shirt, a thin red tie. We sat down across from each other.

'My secretary's out all day,' he told me. 'The girl I've got in here is screwing up messages left and right, but it seems your parents called while I was in court and are saying they're Claire's legal guardians at this point. They've fired me and hired Wade Rockwell to represent her. They're pushing for a plea bargain that commits her to a private hospital in Waterton. They've got John's parents behind them, too.'

I couldn't identify which voice this was: Lawyer, comrade, authority? He sounded unlike he ever had before. Defeated?

'Claire says I'm her attorney and at this point I still am her attorney of record. No papers otherwise are on file yet. But it's been a fight. The judge had Dr Glassman in chambers this morning. Of course Eleanor was there, but I'm not convinced at this point she cares much one way or the other. What's the difference to her? Prison for maybe eight to ten or the nut-house for the rest of her life? I still think your parents were behind her original offer.

'Your father's pressing to wrap this up in the next week. Says he's got to get your mother away, Claire's situation is destroying her health. She's hell bent on this cruise. Judge Barrett is a friend of the family. His father knew your mother's father or some such shit. I don't know whether to request a change there or not. It might make for more trouble.' I sensed Boyce wanted to say more but wasn't sure how to phrase it. 'I've never had a case quite like this,' he said, in that same low tone. 'Usually the parents of someone in a situation like this will say anything to protect their child. They'll tell me black is white and white is black. They'll lie and lie and lie.'

'I don't think my parents are any different,' I said.

'Except they're working against their child,' said Boyce.

I said nothing. He was right. I probably felt as sick as I'd ever felt in my life.

'The way I see it, if you don't get off your ass and tell the old man to butt out, you're not a whole hell of a lot different than he is. In fact, I'd say you're a chip off the old block.' The defeated note had disappeared, replaced with cold, calculated scorn.

'I'm going to Waterton on Sunday,' I said.

'Let him know the consequences if he doesn't butt out of Claire's life.'

'Consequences?'

'Yeah, you tell the motherfucker you know about the malpractice. Tell him you'll contact the local newspapers. Tell him you know what he did to Claire and Tina and, by God, you let me know what's in that suicide note before you go. You understand?'

'Yeah,' I said.

'You got the picture here? You got what's at stake?'

'I got the picture.' I enunciated each word. I wanted to tell him that it was he who didn't realize what was at stake, not me. I got the picture all right.

'By the way,' said Boyce, 'Blueberry Hospital has no records of Rilla Brown seeking treatment. But Shenandoah Hospital, in the next town over, does. She checked in on three different dates within the last two years, but they've got records that date back to when John was fifteen years old.' Boyce had that strong, self-assured lawyer tone in his voice again. 'I got some chatty Kathy nurse on the line who bent my ear for forty-five minutes. Said she'd never heard of a family like the Browns. She says the father knew all about the beatings from the time John was a kid. Never sought police intervention or counseling. Nothing. One of the doctors told her he thinks

226

John was just acting out Wilson's secret desires. Nurse says John brought her to the hospital himself two years ago and acted like a sulky kid and him a grown man. They had to keep the old lady a day or two because he'd damaged her eye so badly. Black and blue and purple and pink, says the nurse, a rainbow of destruction he wrought on his own mother.'

I wanted something cold to drink badly. I thought of myself sitting in the kitchen at 37 Brookfield Court, a gun clutched in my hand.

'I subpoenaed the records, and when the time comes, I'll subpoena the nurses and doctor. Of course, it's just to send the Browns scurrying for cover, but it'll still give them something to think about. There's no reciprocity between New York and Maryland with subpoenas.' My head was spinning. 'I dug up two old girlfriends, too,' he said. 'Figuratively speaking.'

I couldn't laugh. It was all I could do not to throw up.

'Both say he was abusive. One took a trip to Albert Einstein Hospital right here in New York.'

'Bingo,' I managed to say.

'It's good news,' said Boyce. 'According to the girlfriend, she was in the hospital for over a week. Broken rib, black eye, busted jaw. She's willing to testify. I thought I might send a letter to the Browns. Nothing fancy, nothing threatening. Just mention a couple of these facts. Keep them up to date on the case. Maybe one to your parents, too. Except they already know all this. I told them quite clearly.'

And they still wanted to put Claire away.

'Call me the minute you know what's in that suicide note, Richard. Call me at home tonight.' Boyce stood up.

Our meeting was over.

Do what I say or bang! You're dead!

Home again, I sat motionless on the sofa bed and stared at my trumpet case. The phone rang and I didn't pick up, not even when I heard Sam's voice say, 'Hey! I got your message. Great.

Not great that it's true, but you know what I mean. Now what?'

Now what, indeed. I could hear Max. He might just as well have been in the room with me: *Listen, bro, we're lined up waiting for you to pull the trigger this time. You're the big brother, you're the protector, do your stuff. Jack's pulling strings left and right and he might succeed. He's trying to put our sister away for good. No more silent pissing, bro. Splash that bastard, you're King of the Mountain, do it, do it, do it!*

Chapter Eighteen

I DIDN'T want to call Elizabeth.

I didn't want to ask her for that note.

I don't think I liked her that much. My relationship with her was different from mine with Max and Claire.

I pulled a Coke from the six in my refrigerator and set it on the table beside the phone.

Reaching her wasn't going to be easy. I spent a frenzied twenty minutes rooting through drawers, under cushions, behind the couch in a wild search for my address book. Halfway through a stack of old magazines, I thought to look in my briefcase. It stood by the door where I'd dropped it when Claire called that morning. Clean, smelling of expensive leather, files labeled, pencils snug in a leather compartment, my briefcase was in perfect order. The address book was in a file folder neatly labeled ADDRESS BOOK.

Elizabeth's phone number was harder to track down. She moved every couple years, so there were many Elizabeth addresses and phone numbers crossed out or smudged over. As I paged through the Es – I did sibs by their first names – I wondered if I'd know her if I passed her on the street. I hadn't seen her since Tina's funeral, and I'd barely recognized her then. She made a few hurried trips back to Waterton, never to the farm, point-blank refused to set foot on the property, no reasons, just refusal and she'd have hurried, muddled sweaty conferences with my parents and fly back to England and that would be that. I remember her at that time as longhaired and earthbound, a little heavy but not fat. Slung low, is what my friends would have said if I wasn't around. Dresses long and flowery, always the white T-shirt underneath, sandals with white ankle socks and she liked thick woolen cardigan sweaters.

I didn't see her from the time she was twenty-one years old to the time she flew back for Tina's funeral three years ago. I picked her up at JFK. When she stepped off the landing ramp and into the waiting area, all I could think of was how she looked just like my father. My sister Elizabeth had vanished. I don't mean that she resembled him in that way that family members resemble each other — Oh! she's got his eyes, or Look at her jaw — she's her father all over. Her hair was short, clipped close to her head and a pair of wire frames not unlike the pair my father had taken to wearing in recent years perched on her nose. I remembered how thin they were, almost indistinguishable at first, not hiding those blue eyes a bit. A statement, I realized, that said, 'I will not lower myself to such vanities as contact lenses.' She wore an outfit identical to what my dad sported on his weekends at the farm. L. L. Bean khaki-style pants with a thin brown leather belt. A white T-shirt, crew-neck, and a bright red Viyella shirt, hiking boots on her feet.

I was freaked out.

On the long ride from New York to Waterton, I ventured a remark about her similarity to Dad. Nothing offensive, just one of those comments like Isn't it weird, you're the one who turned out to look like Dad, and I, the son, look so different.

She went wild. Denied any resemblance. Denied Dad's wearing clothes like her own. Said she dressed the way she saw fit and it had nothing to do with anyone else. Certainly not Dad. Certainly not the farm.

When I saw the vein in her forehead pop, I backed off fast. It wasn't until then that I remembered her curious dislike of the farm. While the rest of us were climbing Malificent's

Castle and discovering graves on the far side of the property, Elizabeth sat on the couch in the living room and read. At least, I supposed that was what she was doing. She wasn't helping Dad. You never saw her in the fields, and I'd never sensed her being close to Mom the way Max was. As soon as she was old enough to stay in Waterton on farm weekends, she did. She stayed with friends or our grandparents. I don't remember it as being a big deal, either. Elizabeth simply didn't come to the farm much after the age of thirteen. The odd thing, in retrospect, is that my parents allowed her that freedom.

As I flipped through my address book with nervous fingers, I remembered wondering on that long ride from JFK to Waterton for our sister's funeral if I dared ask Elizabeth about that curious freedom. I had glanced over at her and decided to keep on wondering. For a time we rode in silence. After fifty miles or so had passed from the time I'd said I thought she looked like Dad, she turned to me and said, straight-faced, 'When I walked into that waiting room and saw you standing there, I thought you were Dad.' There was a real undertone of getback in her voice, as if she wanted to punish me for saying she looked like Dad. At the same time, I sensed she was telling the truth. To her, I looked like Dad.

As my finger settled on what I hoped was her current number, I realized why I didn't like her all that much. That memory of the ride to Waterton with her and her complete lack of fear of me, she hadn't been intimidated at all, pinpointed it for me. She hadn't needed my protection the way the others had. I realized now I'd always resented that.

I looked at the alarm clock on the table beside the sofa bed. Although the sky had grown almost dark, the hands on the clock read 4.20. I hated the idea of calling during prime phone-rate time, but feared if I put it off I might not do it. I tried to figure out what time it would be in Norwich, England, but couldn't and I didn't feel like calling some operator to find out. I dialed Elizabeth's number, and after a great deal of fizzle and fuzzle was rewarded with her voice, which sounded like my father's to me. Deep and authoritative. Maybe she'd decided to quit researching Edward Dickinson and become him, I thought.

'It's me,' I said.

In the dead silence that followed, I realized what a gulf existed between us. My own sister didn't know my voice. How could it be that we shared a childhood unlike anyone else's I'd ever encountered and now, fifteen years later, my sister didn't know my voice?

'Richard,' I said.

'Oh,' and Elizabeth's voice got no less authoritative. 'I figured I'd hear from you. Claire said she'd told Boyce Regner about Tina's note.'

Right then and there it dawned on me that all these siblings that I had thought were so close to me, seemed closer to each other. Claire called Max and Elizabeth and chatted up a storm. No one told me.

'I didn't even know you and Claire spoke,' I said.

'She's part of my thesis,' Elizabeth countered.

'What? Lizzie Borden, 1990s style?'

'Shut up, Richard. She's the product of an autocratic father. She's an artist and a survivor. Not unlike Emily Dickinson or Charlotte Brontë or Virginia Woolf for that matter.'

'Sorry.' Unlike when we were kids, I realized I was genuinely sorry. But my sorriness went a lot deeper than the remark about her thesis. My sorriness was sorrow and pain and a longing that our lives could have been different. Max and Elizabeth and Claire and I were all alone in this world, our connections to each other not what I'd thought and thus my connection to myself wasn't what I'd thought.

My sister's deep voice came to me over the miles. 'I took the note from Mom,' she said. 'She'd hidden it out on the back porch in that secret cubby.'

'Secret cubby?'

'You know, the one under the back staircase.'

I didn't know, but it didn't matter. 'Does she know you've got it?'

'No,' said Elizabeth, and I heard the thrill of power in her voice. 'I knew she had to have it somewhere. Tina would never not leave a note. She wrote everything down from the time she was eight years old.'

'She did?' One more fact unearthed by John's death.

'Of course she did. Don't you remember that red leather diary of hers? She wrote poems and stories and daily happenings. Mom stole that, too.'

'She did?' Was I a broken record? I settled back farther on the couch, phone hot in my hand. My sweater itched.

'Tina told me Mom visited her at college freshman year when she was having all those problems, and before Mom's visit the diary was in her bureau drawer and when Mom left, the diary was gone. We searched high and low through all Mom's things once when we were both home, but it never turned up. Tina thought she burned it. Too incriminating.'

'What do you mean?'

'Don't be such an ostrich. You know what I mean.'

For someone who looked like a man and dressed exactly like my father and then had the gall to deny it, I thought Elizabeth was pretty ballsy telling me not to be an ostrich. My head was further out of the sand than it had ever been and, in calling her, it was getting higher every second.

'Did you read the note?' I said.

'Yes.' Elizabeth's voice softened and I heard the ghost of my *Little Colonel*-reading sister.

'I have to know what it says,' I said.

Silence.

'Is there anything in the note I can use to force Dad's hand?' I heard the tremor in my voice. 'He's trying to put her away for good.'

'I know,' said Elizabeth. 'I know about those malpractice suits, too.'

'What?'

233

'I knew about them when they were happening. Mom kept the documents in the secret cubby. She might have had it built for that purpose. I don't know and I don't care.'

'Do they know you know?' I was having difficulty breathing.

'Yes.' I heard a sound that could have been a laugh. 'That's how I got to go away to school in Europe and never return. I made Xerox copies and threatened to show Munsy.'

'Jesus.' This woman was blowing my mind. I'd spent my whole life trying to protect the family, and Elizabeth dances out of the country looking out only for herself. It pissed me off.

'Why not go the whole hog and force him to pay for seminary, too?' I said. 'Nothing like starting off on the road to the ministry on the right foot.' I watched the Coke can slide of its own accord an inch or so across the table.

'You self-righteous prick. I don't need you sitting in judgment.' Elizabeth's voice shook with a fine edge of superiority. 'Look at you. Richard the Lionhearted, Richard the great Protector. That's you, isn't it? Big man. King of the Mountain. Great job you did. Tina's dead. Claire's in the nut-house. Max is drinking his way through life. You want to judge me, go ahead. But I got out and I got out on my own terms. It's more than any of the rest of you did.'

'You're the ostrich,' I said. 'The runaway ostrich.'

She hung up on me.

You're doing a great job helping Claire, I told myself. Knowing Elizabeth, she'd call me back. That religious streak of hers that wanted to be good, and that believed she was a little better than the rest of us because of it, would make her call back. She had the note, and from what little she'd said there was no doubt in my mind it was the club I needed. Tina had been too much younger than I to exist other than as a flush of shy smiles in a rocking chair, a hand clutching mine on the bus. I didn't remember her keeping a diary or writing poetry.

I didn't remember my own sister.

I lay back on the couch, bewildered and unhappy. What I liked was to know the answer, to fill in the blank, sign on the dotted line. I liked things to be what they were. A tax question with an answer to be found on page 158 of the *Accounting Code of New York*. I think that's one more reason I didn't like Elizabeth – I'd never been able to define her. Claire was always the silent shadow, Max the Belle Dame Sans Merci, Tina the baby. But Elizabeth? Sometimes she was one of us kids, sometimes not. I remembered a time when we were playing hide 'n' seek at the farm. It was summertime, after dinner. Sky still blue, sun a ball of pink hanging low over the mountains. We kids are still young, not teenagers yet but almost. Claire and I cart the paper trash to the incinerator near the machinery barn and Max lights the fire. The three of us admire the blaze for a bit and feel its heat in our faces.

'Now what?' says Max. 'Want to play Robin Hood?'

Claire shrugs, but there's no smile on her face, so I guess that's not what she wants to do.

'What about hide 'n' seek?' I say, and at that very moment, Elizabeth appears. The rest of us turn to her in excitement; she rarely joins us for outdoor games after dinner.

'Are you playing?' I ask.

'Maybe,' Elizabeth says, putting a hand on her hip. She's wearing an 'outfit' – a madras skirt and matching halter. I can tell she thinks she looks hot. I think Claire in an old pair of my shorts and a torn T-shirt is prettier.

'We're playing hide 'n' seek,' I say. Somehow, I feel she's arrived on the scene to challenge me. It's in that hand on the hip, the one foot jutted out in front of the other. Trouble is, I know the other kids are going to want to do what she says because they're so thrilled she's decided to join us.

'You can hide first,' I say to Elizabeth. 'You, too, Max, and you, Claire. I'll be It. The barn door's home free. You can't cross the Steam Hollow. You can't go past the upper pond. Everybody got it?'

At first, I think Elizabeth will try to wrest control. She looks at me, that same cold look my mother gives me when she's mad. 'How about it, Lizzie Tish?' I say, calling her an old, old nickname, but one I know she likes. It's a nickname only I've ever called her, just like she's the only one who's ever called me Hayseed. It's a bond between us. I smile at her. 'C'mon,' I say. 'Let's play.'

We two exchange a long look, and then she says, 'Okay. You have to count to one hundred, Richard, and you have to turn around and close your eyes. No peeking.' She smiles and adds, 'Hayseed.'

'Right,' I say, and turn around and close my eyes and put my hands over them as well. 'One, two, three, four, five, six, seven,' I count all the way to one hundred. I've closed my eyes so tightly, I've got black dots swimming around for a minute or two while I orient myself. I look around. The pink ball of sun is disappearing fast and I can just make out the croquet mallets flung here and there on the lawn beside the farmhouse, vague bands of orange and red and blue and green. Shit, I think. Somebody's going to catch hell if those aren't put away before we go in, but I don't want to bother right now. I want to find Max and Claire and, most of all, Elizabeth. I want to win. I want to be King of the Mountain.

I'm all over that farm. At the upper pond. At the lower pond. Searching the treehouse. The maple tree. I shimmy the rope to the oak-tree branch. I'm in the cellar and there's Max scrunched behind the water cistern.

One down, two to go.

I crash through tiger lilies lining the stone wall in front of the house. Just as I round the corner of the house toward the barn, I hear a wild 'Ole, ole oomp free!'

Is it Elizabeth? My heart is pounding. Please, no. And it's not. It's Claire, the silent shadow, hollering at the top of her lungs. I can see her hopping up and down in triumph clear across the yard.

'Yeah, yeah,' I say. 'I let you get home free.' I say it loud in case Elizabeth is close enough to hear. Claire's shoulders droop, but I can't help that. I'll talk to her later. Right now, I've got to get to Elizabeth before she makes it home. Max and Claire settle on the front stoop of the barn, and I'm aware that it's getting darker and darker.

Where is she?

I refuse to give up. I tell Max and Claire to put away the croquet game, but I never cease my search for Elizabeth. I go clear to the horse barn at the top of the meadow, I hike the towpath toward the cow barn. It's pitch dark by the time I get back. Max is at home base and so is Claire. My mother has turned on the outside spotlights. The maple tree looms large under the light. The oak tree fades into blackness where the light drops off.

'Where is she?' I say. I'm hot and sweaty and afraid that somehow Elizabeth is going to make me look like a fool in front of the other kids. Has she sworn them to silence? Is it a conspiracy? Where is she?

'Richard!' It's my mother. 'Time to come in!' She knows the others are with me. Well, I decide, it's Elizabeth's funeral if she doesn't come now.

'It's over!' I scream. 'The game's over. No winner.' There, that ought to bring her out of hiding. I'm not saying I won. I think I did, though. I think she should have made a dash for home base. That's the way the game's played.

Nothing.

No streak of Elizabeth across the dusky yard toward the barn door.

Oh, well.

The other kids and I trudge inside, worn out. 'I don't know where Elizabeth is,' I say to my mother. 'She's still hiding.'

My mother stares at me as if I'm an idiot. 'Elizabeth is in the living room,' she says. 'She's been in there reading for at least a half hour.'

I race to the living room. Sure enough, Elizabeth is rocking in one of Munsy's wicker chairs, a Nancy Drew mystery clutched in her hands. She grins up at me. 'I came in when it got dark,' she says. 'It's stupid to play when it's dark.'

'I won, then,' I say, angry, forgetting Claire's ole ole oomp free. I hate that Elizabeth's all smug and calm.

Elizabeth smiles, a superior smile that says, 'Boys will be boys,' and it dares me to start something. I know better. My mother always sides with Elizabeth. We both know that. She's managed to triumph over me. Claire and Max stand in my shadow, watching me lose. I want to kill her.

How dare she

The phone blasted and I jumped. This is now, I told myself, not fifteen or twenty years ago. She can't get to me now.

I picked up. 'Yes?'

'It's me,' Elizabeth said, and her voice had lost most of its authority, sounding blurry at the edges as if she were melting. Good, I thought. No more of that superiority crap. 'The note was addressed to me. Mom had no business reading it, no business not giving it to me.'

'Is that why you took it?'

'No. I didn't know she'd written it to me until I found it.' She paused, and all the way across the Atlantic Ocean I heard the tremble in her voice. 'But as soon as I heard what Tina'd done, I knew in my heart she'd have written something to me.'

It had never occurred to me that Tina might have written to me. I did wonder at the time if she'd left a note, but no one mentioned it and I didn't bring it up. I didn't want to know.

What if it pointed the finger at me

'It was in a sealed envelope with my name on it. Mom had ripped the seal.'

'No surprise there.' It was time for me to know what had happened to Tina. This was one note that had been signed on the dotted line in blood and, like it or not, I damn well better hear it.

'Read it, Lizzie Tish,' I told her softly.

There was a Claire-type silence.

I waited, thinking maybe she was crying or maybe getting it from wherever she kept it. I'd learned, though, that it was best to say nothing when somebody on the other end of a phone wire went silent on you. Sooner or later, that person would have to say something and you wouldn't have rushed into the void, thereby losing control of the conversation.

I waited some more.

At last Elizabeth said, 'I don't have it.'

All that waiting for nothing.

I don't want to hear you'll fucking try. Get the note!

I lost control. 'What do you mean, you don't have it?' I shouted. 'That's just like you. Just like the way you played hide 'n' seek at the farm. You're all show, no follow through.'

'The farm, the farm, the farm,' said Elizabeth. 'It always comes back to the farm for you, doesn't it, Richard?'

the afternoon at the farm didn't happen

'Shut up,' I said. 'You don't know what you're talking about.'

'I might know more than you think.'

'You cheated at hide 'n' seek.' I had to stop her. 'It was all of us and you cheated and made me look like a fool.'

'You don't change, do you, Richard? Everything has to be about you.'

'Nothing happened at the farm.' My voice was loud but controlled. 'Nothing.'

'You're crazy, Richard. We're talking about Tina's note. I don't know what you're babbling about. Do you want to know where the note is?'

'What'd you do? Tear it up? Burn it? Throw it away?'

'If you'll shut up and listen, I'll tell you. Are you going to listen or keep yelling?'

She made me mad. No wonder she wasn't married. No wonder she lived alone. If somebody had to live with her, she'd probably be deader than John by now. 'I'm listening,' I said.

'You've got the note, Richard,' said Elizabeth, very slowly as if she were talking to an imbecile. 'After I read it, I put it in your trumpet case.'

'What?'

'Remember you brought it home for the funeral? You thought you might play at the service as a tribute, but Mom and Dad nixed the idea. Well, I read the note and I don't know, I wasn't really thinking, I just decided to put it in the lining of your case. You'd left it in the front vestibule. I took the case upstairs and locked my door, ripped open the lining, stuffed in the note and sewed it back up.'

'That's crazy,' I said. 'What if I'd sold it? Thrown it out? Given it away?'

'You'd never do that.'

Silence. I stared at my trumpet case sitting on the table not five yards away from me.

The Atlantic felt deep and black between us.

'Look,' I said. 'I don't want to fight with you. I didn't call you to make trouble. I called to help Claire. I'm heading to Waterton on Sunday,' I said. 'Two days from now. They're supposed to leave on some damn cruise Tuesday or Wednesday and Dad's trying to tie things up before they leave.'

'You know the papers I Xeroxed? My ticket out?'

'Yeah.'

'One of them was about a death.'

'A death?'

'Some woman died on the operating table. Old Jack baby was the doctor. Her husband filed suit. The evidence was pretty damning.'

'What happened?'

'They settled out of court, I guess. All I remember is thinking, So the old fart's a murderer.'

'You've still got the papers?'

'Somewhere.'

'I don't think Boyce has anything on that. Send them to him.'

240

'I will.'

Another silence.

'Honor thy father and thy mother,' I said.

'The note's in the lining at the top of the case,' said Elizabeth, and hung up. I knew this time she wasn't going to call me back.

I sat on the couch for a long time. Outside, the sky darkened and the street lamp came on. I'd sat at the kitchen table at the farm many times in this same position, the outside lighting casting the same yellow-orange blush inside the room.

I didn't want to think about the farm and I didn't want to read the note. There was something about the tone of Elizabeth's voice when she'd said that maybe she knew more than I thought she did that made me want to throw away that note, unread. To tell Boyce Elizabeth didn't have it, after all, that she'd destroyed it long ago.

Afraid of what she might say

Still, Tina was so much younger than I. What could she know? It was all so long ago. I wanted to leave the past behind me and forge into my future. I wanted to get to know Sam better.

Everybody has to grow up some day

All right. I'll read it and get it over with, I thought. I stared at my trumpet case, half expecting that note to burn through the lining, smoking its way over to me. It was weird Elizabeth had hidden it in my trumpet case without my knowledge. It felt kind of like the Pott graves to me – secretive, illicit, and a little scary.

I sipped my Coke, but it was warm from the heat of my hand. I walked to the sink and poured what remained down the drain. If Elizabeth had read the note to me, no matter what it said it wouldn't be as bad as reading it to myself.

I wanted the distance of that ocean between me and Tina. Elizabeth had whammied me one more time.

I marched to the trumpet case with a knife and slit the lining. A long yellowed envelope with Elizabeth's name fell out onto my trumpet. I shoved aside the trumpet and its case, snapped on the table lamp, sat down.

I opened the envelope with sweaty fingers.

Thump, thump

The note was on typewriter paper, but handwritten.

I am on watch

I left the letter on the table and walked to the refrigerator for a beer. Three six-packs sat on the second shelf. I thought of Max and his drunken phone calls and I remembered my mother's trips to the back porch and my father's empty bourbon glasses at the farm. One, two, three, sometimes four.

nothing happened at the farm

I slammed shut the refrigerator door and returned to the table, empty-handed. It was time to read the letter. Like going to Waterton on Sunday, this was something I had to do. I told myself that I was doing it for Claire. With trembling hands, I unfolded its pages. I swallowed hard and began reading.

Dear Elizabeth,
I can't take the crazy think any longer.
I've never told anyone this before. It's my crazy-think story.

I set the letter down. Crazy think. I knew what she meant; I'd just never had a term for it. It's the old black-is-white think. The we-don't-have-drugs-in-this-house think. The I-broke-this-lamp,-didn't-I? think. Here was my baby sister with a name for that kind of think. I relaxed a little. Maybe this wouldn't be so bad. I already knew about crazy think. It wouldn't be anything I didn't already know. I took a deep breath and returned to Tina's letter:

I'm eleven. You're gone. Richard's gone. Claire's gone. Max is around but he's in high school and working at that funeral parlor and driving a hearse. Mom and Dad are different from when you older kids lived at home. She's guzzling sherry or wine and then she lies around

242

on the couch and watches soap operas she doesn't move and she's mean and whiny and she'll want me to start dinner and then Dad comes home with his hospital smell drinks nothing at all because of the patients.

And they pick at each other. On and on and the sound sings in my ears and I'll do anything for quiet and so one day I go to the farm with him all alone. After you guys left, the farm was shut up for a while.

It's there on the way to the farm that it starts.

The farm again. I turned the letter over so I couldn't see the words. It always came back to the farm. Something felt so wrong. I'd read some book a long time ago, a true-crime book where a member of the family comes home and walks inside and the mood of the house's silence tells him something is wrong and he begins to walk hesitantly through the foyer, through the living room, down the hall to the kitchen, calling out, 'Mom? Dad? Charlie?' No answer. He reaches the dining room. His mother, father, and brother are dead and bloody on the floor. That's what this letter felt like and I sensed I'd only reached the foyer.

I turned it back over and continued reading.

It's a sunny March day. We're riding along in his green Chevy Blazer on old Route 9 instead of 81. I'm afraid of him and wondering how it happens I agreed to take a run out to the farm but I think I thought it would stop the fighting and I didn't want him to be as lonely as I am so he says, 'Look at that cow over there, Tina,' and points.

'I don't see any cow,' I venture, my voice a thin teardrop.

His arm zings across the seats and lashes me in the head. He's so fast, the sound of him sweeping his arm across the jeep is a song.

Song of death.

243

I felt as if I needed air. I kept reading.

I say, 'I see a cow, okay?' He clips me a few more for good measure and my head is tingling and something inside my brain is gray dots buzzing together like a bunch of bees on an old cartoon.

'Look over there, Tina,' and his voice is soft and fuzzy hanging over my head and fading in and out. I think when he hit me this time something came unglued.

'Look over there, Tina. See the sheep?' And I look and there's a sheep farm and they're shearing two of them.

Here's what's weird, Elizabeth. There isn't any sheep farm on the way to the farm. Not on the old road. Not on the new interstate. Not anywhere.

'Yes,' I say.

The green jeep swishes around and around and then we're onto the Steam Hollow Road and it looks different. It's been a long time since I've been to the farm.

And then we arrive in a screech of rubber and the farmhouse sits in front of us and looks abandoned.

Old, grayed white like an old person.

The farm is a frown with drool.

There's no let-up on the farm. Maybe Elizabeth did know more than I thought. She'd known enough to get herself to Europe, she'd known enough to find this note. What else did she know?

He unlocks the door and into the kitchen we go.

The farm smells of death.

Is it the dead mice on the walls from D-con?

Has a raccoon croaked in the cellar?

I say I want to go up to the woodpile at the barn and start dragging down wood so we can build a fire. I want to get away from him.

It's him who smells bad.

He says, 'We've got an hour before your mother'll be here.'

Why am I wet with fear and instinctive disgust? Has this happened before? Or has our time together been building *to this, to this?*

There is no cow. Yes there is. No, yes, no yes, yes, yes YES.

We go into Mom and Dad's bedroom. He's already shut Buddy outside. Guns are everywhere. He's got the curtain to the tack room open and the door to the bathroom. The pump's not primed yet and there's no hum, hum, hum of the pipes. That's what I can remember.

Here's what I can't remember. What happened next.

Oh, I didn't want to read anymore. This was my sister talking, the same sister who cried when Max flushed her Bubblecut Barbie's head down the toilet and I'd ridden my bike to the store to get her a new one. The same sister who named every dog in her china dog collection: Tanya, Marybeth, Sonny, Lou Lou, Frizzelle, Bunny Hug, and Tuna. And she was talking about Dad, her dad – my dad.

What happened between the time we two are dressed all snug in our jackets and the time I find myself naked in the bathroom on my knees, head over the toilet bowl.

The pages shook in my hands as I continued to read.

He's dressed, I know that much, and he's on one knee beside me and I smell the wool of his shirt and I smell anger that smells like the inside of a pill capsule. He dunks my head in the toilet bowl and holds it down, down, down . . .

is he going to flush me away like so much shit
am I shit?

'This never happened,' he tells me.

I felt the vein in my forehead throbbing. I couldn't stop reading. It was as if a force greater than myself kept my eyes riveted to the page.

My own hand comes in contact with the smooth cold porcelain of the toilet bowl. I know I am in the bathroom. I know this is happening.

My father is holding a gun to my head as he holds my head under water.

'Aarrgh,' I say.

Down into the water I go again.

'This never happened,' he says.

I hear the click of the gun, and I know I have ceased to exist. 'This never happened,' I say, and he releases my head and I fall on my back onto the bath mat.

I lie there for a bit and here's what's odd, Elizabeth: I'm lying on the rug and I'm watching myself from somewhere far away at the same time. I see Tina lying naked on the bath mat. She is the ugliest person I have ever seen in my life.

I hate her.

I want to die.

Your sister, Tina

I felt the rush of heat in my face, the throb of my forehead vein. No wonder Elizabeth felt so smug talking to me. I hadn't protected anyone and she knew it. I'd let that bastard kill Tina.

it happened at the farm, at the farm

'Shut up!' I screamed, and jumped up from the table. I crumpled the note into a ball and flung it across the room. I felt like such an idiot. All these years I'd spent talking the old guy up to the sibs, protecting him, telling them he wasn't such a bad guy. Claire, Max, Elizabeth must all think I'm the biggest asshole on the face of the earth. This felt worse than being cuckolded by my wife; this was betrayal by my own father.

I hate him

Why'd he have to trick me? Who'd he have clutching

246

that fucking chainsaw? Gobbling up motherfucking blueberry pancakes? Me, the biggest fool in the family. Why was it so important to me that he think well of me? That I fool myself into thinking I could have it both ways?

because you're like him, big bro

'The fuck I am!' I hollered. 'I gotta get out of here,' and what I needed before I left was something to drink. Not beer, a real drink: Jack Daniel's. I gave the closet door a jerk, knowing I'd stashed a full bottle on the shelf. When it didn't open, I yanked the door hard enough to rip it off its hinges. I shoved it aside and grabbed the bottle. I felt my face getting hotter, the rush of heat spreading throughout my whole body. I knew I was losing control, but I wouldn't let myself.

I will maintain, I will maintain, I will maintain.

I felt the threat of tears. 'No way,' I said, through clenched teeth. 'You won't get to me, fucker. I'm getting out of here.'

I slammed out the door, down the four flights of stairs and on out to 88th Street, Jack Daniel's tight in my hand.

Thump, thump

I stopped, tipped up the bottle and drank. From the gut up I felt its heat, and it burned my throat.

I started jogging, clutching the bottle by its neck with my right hand. I felt a rage inside me hotter than any drink could ever be. I jogged with my head down, feeling my feet pound the pavement hard enough to go through it.

I will maintain, I will maintain, I will maintain.

nothing happened to me at the farm to me to me

I will maintain, I will maintain, I will maintain.

How could he have done that to Tina? How could I have let him?

I crossed Lexington, Park, Madison, and Fifth. I jogged straight into Central Park and kept on going, feet pounding, harder and harder.

I hate you

Out of nowhere a black-leather-jacketed, greasy-haired boy appeared and blocked my path. He couldn't have been more than fifteen or sixteen, maybe five seven, 130 pounds.

247

'Hey, look what we got here,' he sneered. 'A drinkin' jogger. Now what do you make of that?' He lunged for my Jack Daniel's, reminding me of the way my father would leap up at the dinner table to smack one of us.

I tossed the bottle over his head. Whiskey and glass sprayed me, him, the sidewalk, grass, and the fallen, crushed leaves all around us. He swung out wildly at me, catching me in the stomach. I hit him with my left fist, catching him hard against the jaw. The heat in my face was burning me.

'You want to keep fighting?' I said. 'You want me to beat the crap out of you?' I knew the kid had had enough, I knew he didn't want to fight, but I knew he was afraid to say so. I saw it in his face. I don't know what he saw in mine, but he started running. I started after him, but this kid was quick, a blurry dash into the dark. I kept after him, *Marathon Man* once again, but my lungs were starting to hurt with the effort.

He was way ahead of me. I lost him in the dark. An incredible rage shook me and I found myself screaming, 'I hate you! I hate you! I hate you!' at him and my voice was echoing through Central Park like an owl's cry run amuck. I heard a crash ahead of me. The kid had fallen on the pathway. Within seconds I stood over him. 'I hate you,' I said, and the kid looked up at me in the dim park lighting as if I was his dad smashing his world and I half expected the sidewalk to crack and crumble and him to fall beneath its depths, only that didn't happen. I peered down at him and I hissed, 'I'd like to kill you,' and he said nothing, he was a sphinx, and all I could think is, How dare he punch me?

How dare he

I had the wildest urge to kick him, kick him over and over and over again. I felt that flush in my face and the vein in my forehead throbbing. I felt a surge of power.

I am King of the Mountain

I stared down at him, breathing hard, seeing only him, not the sky, not the trees and bushes, or the chipped gravel pathway, not the zoo entrance, or the thick clouds shutting starlight from the night. Just the kid, his eyes wide with fear. 'Why not pick on someone your own size? Why beat up on a kid?' The kid's voice broke.

I kept staring down, unseeing this time. Something in the kid's voice, in the trembling arm held up for protection hurtled me down the dark tunnel of my past. Somehow he was an echo of some long-forgotten piece of my life, a piece I'd taken great care to disengage from my concept of who I was.

what happened to me on the farm

'No!' I shouted. 'Shut up!' I whirled around and headed out of the park, out of my past and into the bright lights of Fifth Avenue. I knew I was far more frightened than that kid would probably ever be.

By the time I got to my apartment, it was all I could do to manage the steps. I felt very old and out on a limb and like I'd like to be anybody but who I was.

I realized the knuckles on my left hand were bleeding. Feeling numb, I rinsed it off with cold water and wrapped a paper towel around it. I felt no pain. I felt nothing. I saw Tina's wadded-up note lying in the far corner of my apartment. I didn't have to reread it. Her words were engraved on my heart: *I can't take the crazy think any longer . . . I smell the wool of his shirt . . . I smell anger . . . one of his hands is on the back of my head . . . He dunks my head in the toilet bowl and holds it down, down, down . . . I hear the click of a gun and I know I have ceased to exist . . . 'This never happened,' he tells me.* In slow motion, I leaned down and picked it up. I got an envelope from a stack on the table, stuffed it inside and put Boyce's name on it.

My numbness was wearing off and my heart hurt so much I thought I might be having a heart attack. I sat on the couch, my head in my hands. I couldn't stop the tears this time and I didn't try. I wept like an exhausted little boy, like the little boy I had never been allowed to be.

★

Later, much later, I called Boyce at home. I told him what was in the note and said I'd bring it to him. I told him about the death on the operating table.

'This case will make College Boy in the Rue Café look like peanuts.' His voice trumpeted a blast of triumph. 'Now get your ass to Waterton. Call me when you get back.'

'Sunday's D-Day,' I said, and meant it from the bottom of my heart.

At ten o'clock I called Sam. Maybe she'd be sick of her sister by now.

No answer.

I didn't leave a message.

I called back. This time I said I'd be by at seven the next evening to pick her up. I told her to call if that was a problem.

It was still only Friday.

Two days to go.

Chapter Nineteen

S LEEP eluded me. I tossed and turned. First I was too hot
and I flung off my covers; then, I was too cold and my
teeth chattered. I hauled the blankets back over me. The
night smelled damp to me and I thought I heard cockroaches
scudding up and down the walls.

I couldn't keep all the voices I'd been hearing over the last
couple weeks out of my head. I'd try to think about the farm
in summertime, tiger lilies blooming all over the front yard,
but instead what would come to me was Johanna, Sam,
Elizabeth, Tina, Boyce, Max, the Browns, Claire: *it always
comes back to the farm with you . . . I told him not to marry her . . .
your father's a fucking pervert . . . I thought you weren't going to
drink anymore . . . I want a check for this funeral . . . you're a
tightassed, controlling son of a bitch . . . everybody's got to grow up
someday . . .*

Underneath was a steady rumble of *Waterton, Waterton,
Waterton.*

Somewhere around six or seven o'clock, I dozed off, awakening at one thirty that afternoon, feeling incredibly dazed
and stupid. My mouth was cottony and my eyes burned.

A cold shower helped, and so did a dose of Metamucil and
a cup of instant coffee.

I sat at my table sipping coffee and staring at my cleaned
trumpet case and at my dirty apartment. I wondered what

251

Sam would think about a guy who lived the way I'd been living. My broken closet door slanted against one wall. Piles of unread magazines cluttered the table and paperback books were stacked in corners of the room the way Sam had plants.

A sudden blast of the telephone made me jump.

'Listen, Richard,' Boyce said when I picked up, 'Judge Barrett scheduled the hearing for Wednesday. Four days from now. A definite. No time to request a change of judge or venue or anything. Everyone's going to be there. Claire, Dr Glassman, me, the DA. This is it. What happens at that hearing will affect everything that follows. Get your parents to call the judge. They've got to change their big plan for Claire's commitment to Waterton. I should have Max's statement by then and you'll bring me Tina's suicide note. I'll have the old records against your father and the hospital records for John's girlfriends and mother. Can I count on you?'

'I'll be there.' I took a deep breath and let it out. It whirled around my apartment with an unpleasant smell.

'Claire's calling you today at four p.m. She's telling you what she told me today. It changes everything. I'm thinking about a plea bargain. Be home. It's important.'

A plea bargain? *A plea bargain?*

do what I say! Or bang! You're dead.

'Okay,' I said, and hung up.

what had Claire told Boyce

I looked at my watch: 3.15. Forty-five minutes to go.

as if I didn't know

Forty-two minutes to go.

thump, thump

I opened my trumpet case and stared at my trumpet. It looked moldy. The mouthpiece hadn't been changed in fifteen years, the slides would stick, the valves would need oil. Slowly, I opened a small velveteen kit tucked inside the case and with shaking hands began to clean it.

Three fifty-five.

anything might happen

I grabbed my now shining trumpet and set it down on the sofa bed beside me. I felt fear in my heartbeat, in my clogged ears, in my slick, sliding hands.

Three fifty-nine.

The phone blasted and I jumped about a foot. I laid my slippery hand on top of my trumpet for comfort.

It was Claire, as Boyce had promised, as I'd known it would be, as I'd feared.

No time for amenities.

No time to switch gears or take a deep breath.

no time to run

Her voice through the phone wires was one of her wild, abstract paintings sprung to life, swirling inside my ear, oil paint bleeding onto my heart. She didn't greet me, she didn't say anything about PI or phone restrictions, she swept into her story as if we were sitting side by side on the couch at the farm, a roaring fire heating our cheeks, Buddy curled on the hearth.

'Richard,' she cried, her words loud and big, inescapable as my mother, nothing like the silent shadow of yesteryear. 'Boyce told me to tell you what happened the night I killed John. He says you'll do whatever it takes to help me.'

I said nothing, unable to do anything but hold the phone. I kept hearing Tina's deathcry, a sound far more piercing than any rabbit's after Buddy caught it at the farm: *after that afternoon at the farm . . . I want to die . . .* I couldn't bear listening to another sister's pain. Another failure on my part.

'Will you help me, Richard?' she said at last. 'Please?'

I took a deep breath. 'Yes,' I said. 'Yes.'

Claire's voice spiralled high the same way it had one afternoon at the farm when she'd slipped and gotten tangled in barbed wire: 'The night I killed John we had a fight. A typical fight. He's been working on a design project for a long time with a fellow named Ralph. He's riding John's coattails, but John can't see it.

'In storms John that evening, filling the whole apartment. His big project with Ralph fizzled. For him. Not for Ralph. Ralph slipped into the project boss's office with the designs a day earlier than he'd told John. Took all the credit, got his name in highlights with the boss. And John goes to the boss, too, and gets the door slammed in his face and he goes over to Ralph's and Ralph oozes around him a bit and wants no hard feelings and John wants to believe in him. Underneath he knows he's been set up and he's angry. But he can't admit he's angry. He can't admit he made a mistake. Here's what he can do. Hit me. Call his mother, scream at her. Hit me some more. Run away, clattering down our steps and into the streets and I can watch him from the window and see him kick a puddle of huddled rags and I can see him hesitating on the corner of Sixth and Washington Place. Where to go? What to do? Which bar?'

I could scarcely breathe. I thought about the night before when I'd wanted to kick the kid in the park over and over and over again, only that flash of kid's vulnerability and something dark from long ago keeping me from it. Something having to do with the law. What could it be? My hand ached from its grasp on the trumpet, but I didn't let go. I wanted to get under my sofa bed and hide.

Claire didn't stop. I had no choice but to listen, doing my best not to hear where she was going with her story: 'After he leaves, I huddle under the covers and clutch my Holly Bear as close to me as I can. No sleep comes. It's the bogeyman who comes, thick and sweaty and oozy and hard. And now I hear someone on the steps.'

'Stop,' I said.

afraid of what she might say

'Up those stairs John creeps and sidles into the bedroom to make up. He settles in my old pink easy chair from the farm and wants me to sit in his lap. "I'm sorry," he says, and hangs his head low on his chest. "I love you, Claire."'

Maybe this wouldn't be as bad as Tina.

'And now he's curled around me like spoons, naked except for an undershirt. My pink pajama bottoms are bikini panties and he brushes past the elastic waist with his penis and lies it between my legs. A thick warm cuddly sausage. Then that thick sausage finds its way inside me and he's on top of me and he's warm and hairy all over and he's rough and pushy and he's not going to take no for an answer even as I say, "No, No, No!"'

Oh, no

'I smell Death on his breath. It's in the rigid pose of his body. He weighs a hundred pounds more than I do. He's going to kill me.

'I reach for the gun in the table drawer next to the bed. His gun. Loaded. And I know how to shoot it. Haven't we spent Sundays shooting out at the farm? Don't I know how to kill as well as you do, Dad?' Claire's voice faded, a thin trickle of pain.

please make her stop

I slid my hand back and forth, back and forth on my trumpet. So many years with no tears. Now I felt them dripping down my face.

please

'Do you get it, Richard?' Claire's voice now was nothing but a whisper.

I could scarcely speak, but I choked out, 'Yes.' My knuckles were white against the gold of my trumpet.

'He did it to me at the farm,' she whispered. 'Over and over and over again. He says he loves me. He's so gentle, so loving, it doesn't hurt, not really and it's because he loves me, I'm so beautiful and it's our secret and somehow I know if I tell, he'll kill me.'

it always comes back to the farm

I no longer felt tears, only sweat, as if I'd climbed the highest mountain in the world.

'Claire?' I said. 'I'm sorry. I'm so sorry.'

'I got them mixed up,' she said, and started to cry.

'I tried to help you when you were a kid. I just didn't try hard enough.' This time it was my voice breaking. 'I won't let you down this time. I promise.'

Silence.

'Claire? I'm going to Waterton. I'm going tomorrow.'

A strange voice came over the wire. 'Hello? Who's this?'

'It's Richard Hayes. My sister is Claire. Where is she?'

'She'll be fine, Mr Hayes. She's perfectly safe here.'

Safe? Had she ever been safe? I'd failed her every step of the way. Elizabeth was right about me. What kind of protector had I been that my sisters were raped at the place I loved best in the world, the only place I'd ever been happy, the only place where I could believe my father loved me?

I hung up the phone, feeling wrung out and sick.

I'd known all along what had happened the night she killed John, but I hadn't wanted to know, and if she hadn't put her life into words for me I never would have asked for them. I'd have done all I could to help her as long as I didn't have to take a good long look at the truth.

I was exhausted. I'd take baling hay day after day after day before I'd opt for this kind of fatigue. This felt more like I imagined death would feel.

I lay under the covers for a while too tired to move. The stories my brother and sisters had been telling me drifted in and out of my consciousness. Max and his Malificent's Castle. Elizabeth and her blackmail. Tina lost in crazy think. Claire, well on her way. But here was the rub: Claire survived. She killed him, not herself.

Suddenly I remembered that long ago trip to the hospital with Claire bleeding against my shoulder. The day Dad had smashed her face into her plate and Mom had manufactured the lie I carried out at the hospital.

What have we here, Mrs Hayes?

Oh, poor Claire fell. She slipped from her chair and hit the corner of the table. Jack wasn't home. I didn't know what to do, so Richard – loving glance in my direction – and I hurried right over. Elizabeth stayed with the others. I didn't think the children would do well at the hospital. But I can always count on Richard.

I was that teenaged boy again, the one who failed to protect his sister, the one who sat back and watched as his father crushed her face, the one who'd felt pride in his mother's dependency on him. She'd turned to me, not Max. I began to feel the feeling I'd been afraid to feel then . . .

I see my mother's eyes gleaming in the rear-view mirror. I pulled my pillow close, sheltering it in my armpit. 'Don't you touch her,' I found myself whispering. 'Don't you touch her.'

And then I was saying it louder and louder, I was sitting up, I was shouting at the top of my lungs: 'Don't you dare touch her, motherfuckers!'

In a surge of energy, I leaped from the bed, grabbed a broom from the closet and beat the mattress with its handle.

It's my mother I'm pounding; it's my father; it's Skip; it's John.

'Don't touch her!' I yell. 'Don't you touch her!'

No one in nearby apartments seemed disturbed. No one pounded my door.

I slammed the broom handle to the bed until my hands were raw. My throat hurts. My ears ache.

But – I am KING OF THE MOUNTAIN.

Aren't I?

Waterton, Waterton, Waterton

I wanted to kill that motherfucker. I wanted to go to the gym and punch the heavy bag. I didn't care that my knuckles still hurt from last night; I didn't care that I had a date with Sam in less than an hour; I had to take care of this business with my father before anything else.

I would have to call her and explain.

For a split second, I considered not calling her. I'd done that to plenty of other women in the past. I didn't owe anyone explanations. I'd hated my mother always butting into my business. I'd hated Johanna demanding I call her if I'd be home late.

everybody has to grow up some day

I reached for the phone.

She answered on the first ring.

'It's me.' My voice sounded squeaky. I felt brave and grown-up calling her, yet foolish for feeling that way. On some level, though, I was aware that I was changing, something inside me was different. I cleared my throat. 'Look,' I said, and now my words tumbled out swift as bullets, 'Claire told me what happened the night she killed John. She thought he was my father. She thought he was raping her.'

Silence. Had I taken a foolhardy risk?

thump, thump

How could risking a telephone call to a woman I cared about and telling her the truth feel as frightening as going to Waterton?

Waterton, Waterton, Waterton

I wiped damp hands on my sheets. 'Don't forget I'm going to Waterton tomorrow,' I said. My ears clogged. 'Look, I think we should put off tonight, Sam. I've got to go to Waterton first.'

Silence.

'Say something. Are you mad at me or what?'

'Mad at you?' I heard Sam from a distance. 'I'm disappointed, but you've got to do what you've got to do. Your father sounds like a bastard. What he did is sick. How dare he?' Sam's voice seemed to get louder, reaching right through the fog in my ears. 'When you're up there tomorrow, remember that you have all the power. Threaten them with Waterton newspaper exposure: LOCAL DOCTOR'S CHILDREN CLAIM SEXUAL ABUSE.'

Sam was right. Boyce had said the same thing.

'Thanks, Sam,' I said quietly.

I hung up knowing that being able to tell her that I didn't

feel like being with her that night made us closer than ever before. Closer than I'd ever been to anyone.

I was out the door, on my way to the gym within thirty seconds.

kill the motherfucker

Chapter Twenty

I STOOD on the empty train platform at Waterton. A bulletin board with an army officer pointing at me, an empty bench, and me and my trumpet. That's all there was.

I took a deep breath.

Nothing had changed.

Waterton remained a tired industrial town. Gray buildings blended with the gray sky. In the distance I could see the gold dome of St Cyril's church tower.

Two blocks from where I stood was River Front Street which ran the whole length of Waterton's downtown. Unlike New York, Waterton didn't have an uptown and a midtown and downtown, only a downtown. Saint James Episcopal Church, the church of my childhood, was only three blocks away.

I glanced at my watch: 10.53. I'd planned to call a cab and head straight to 37 Brookfield Court, but instead I turned toward Saint James. My parents would have gone to the early morning service. I felt a powerful urge to see and feel the place that had played such a part in shaping my perceptions of life.

I Am the Lord Thy God; Thou Shalt Have No Other Gods Before Me.

With my trumpet case sliding against my damp hands and a rapid heartbeat, I headed toward Saint James Episcopal

Church, hoping the dress code had relaxed enough over the years that khaki pants and a crisp L.L. Bean shirt and jacket would be suitable.

I hesitated on the stone steps.

Church bells jangled, jarring memories.

I trembled hearing 'The Church's One Foundation', but there it was, a voice from the past, belted from the belfry of Saint James. I crept inside, late, after everyone else was seated, and hovered in the vestibule, breathing it in: a seemingly violent organist hurled high notes and low, swelling, soaring, swirling through people-packed pews, surging past stained-glass windows, past Virgins holding sweet baby Jesuses, yellow-haired, blue-eyed. Like me. I touched my trumpet case the way someone else might take hold of a friend's hand.

Thou Shalt Not Take Unto Thyself Any Graven Images.

A golden cross, smaller than the way I'd remembered it, sat dead center on the altar, draped in crushed green brocade, trimmed with thick gold rope, tassels tapping the altar railing. Lighting was dim and distant. Only the candles on either side of the cross fluttered, sending a glitter of light across the bowed heads of all those worshipping Episcopalians.

No one looked familiar.

I looked around at different windows and remembered staring at them as a kid. I'd always liked the way the morning sunshine brought the colors alive.

Today no sunshine glinted through stained glass.

I heard a sudden spatter of rain and shivered.

As I faltered in the back of the church, a man dressed in a neat dark suit and white shirt hurried toward me, program jutting from his outstretched hand. His skin was paper-thin-looking, his eyes the pale blue of fresh trout. When he smiled, a flicker of gold gleamed.

I felt a prickling of fear.

'What's that in the case, sonny?'

'My trumpet.'

'I'll have to take a look-see,' he told me. So Waterton

261

wasn't so different from New York. I showed him my trumpet, but closed the case fast.

I slunk away from him and into the nearest pew. The rituals came back. It was automatic for me to reach for the kneeling cushion and kneel. I knew it didn't matter that the others were standing and singing, tradition demanded I enter the church, get a cushion, kneel and pray. All around me, Episcopalians rose tall and dignified. Their words eddied around me. I knew if I looked up, I would see everyone holding his hymnal the same way: high, at face level, mouths opening wide to shape the words. My mother taught me that was the way to hold a hymnal, not down around the waist, and whatever else I did, I was not to mumble the hymns. Sing out!

honor thy father and thy mother

Saint James smelled cold. Not the fresh biting cold of a frosty January morning, but the dank, moldy cold of a mausoleum. I let the air settle around me and pictured mold growing on me and everyone around me. When the woman next to me opened her mouth declaring, 'And with Thy Spirit', I thought I saw her breath floating in the air like rainy morning fog. For one terrible minute, I felt as if I was locked in a freezer and everyone around me was dead – frozen zombies that walked and talked but were dead.

I grabbed my trumpet case and walked out of Saint James and into sleeting rain. It felt like a nice warm shower after the Episcopal church. I walked across the street to a phone booth and called a taxi. Ten minutes later I climbed into one of the old yellow cabs I remembered from when I was a kid, complete with jump seat in back.

'Thirty-seven Brookfield Court,' I told the driver, and we were off in a splash of rain.

I watched the cab drive off before turning to look at the house. Against the gray morning, the cab stood out yellow and bright as a buttercup in a field of dead grass.

Nothing stirred on Brookfield Court. Houses appeared abandoned, giving me the feeling I'd entered an empty movie set. I hadn't been for a visit since Tina's funeral, and I hadn't noticed then if the neighborhood had let itself run down. Now I noticed cracks in sidewalks and chipped driveways, the concrete a grayish yellow. Without the lush green of springtime, none of the houses could hide their peeling paint or faded bricks.

The rain had stopped, leaving an icy sheen on the sidewalk. Even though I had a key, I headed for the front door and knocked.

thump, thump

No one answered.

I knocked again.

anything might happen

Nothing.

I pulled out my key and went inside. The door made a hollow sound as it shut behind me.

Everything was exactly as I'd remembered it. Same Oriental rugs, same upright Steinway piano, same Waterford sherry decanter sitting on the coffee table. From the vestibule I could see straight into the dining room. A dusty film coated the empty mahogany table.

The place seemed lifeless.

I'm dead inside

I set down my trumpet on the piano stool. I moved toward the dining room, pausing to look into my father's den.

Fusty. My eyes watered.

Papers scattered everywhere. Books piled high on the floor, on the desk, on the couch. A desk drawer hanging open. Bookcases crushed against every wall. I stepped into the room.

Diseases of the Breast.

Herpes: A New Venereal Infection.

Menopause: A Breakthrough Study.

The same books that had lined the shelves when I was a kid. I'd spent so many hours poring over that breast book,

I'm amazed I ever brought myself to touch an undiseased breast. One woman had had three breasts, another, no breasts at all.

His chair was pushed back from the littered desk as if he'd stepped away for only a moment or two. The bottom drawer of the desk hung open. This was the drawer he kept locked when we were kids because he kept our bank books in it. Each one of us kids had a file folder with our name on it. Each folder had our tax returns, our financial statements, and a little red bank book that held our savings for college.

No one was allowed to touch those books except my father.

Each time we received birthday money, half went straight into the little red book. Each time we received an A on our report cards, my father put a dollar into our little red book. Half of our allowances went into the red books. After we started working, half of each pay check went directly into our red books.

I stepped closer, barely breathing. Was I actually going to see one of those red books? Touch it? Hold it in my hand? I started to laugh, the sound an eerie ripple in the silence. Max had found the key in Dad's top desk drawer and drained his account by the time he was seventeen. I still couldn't believe he'd had the balls to do that.

Either could Dad, big bro. Here's the thing, though. It was my money.

It Was My Money

IT WAS MY MONEY

I touched the opened drawer. His .357 Magnum lay in front. The file folders were still there, though, in the back, labeled in his scrawling handwriting. Richard, Elizabeth, Claire, Max, Tina.

I looked over my shoulder.

No one.

I reached for my bulging folder. Jammed full of yellowed bank statements and notices from the brokerage firm of Doctrow, Smith and Wesley. I pulled out the sacred little red book. The edges were frayed as if he'd had to read it again and again. The entries began on the first page and continued straight through to the thirtieth page and onto the back cover as well. Funds in; funds out. Notations as to college payments. Several scribbles that I couldn't make out. According to the last note, though, there was still thirty-eight thousand dollars in the account. The date was over twelve years ago.

You wanted to make it as a musician. Why didn't he tell you you had money? Why didn't he help you?

A baby spider edged out between two pages.

I threw my folder onto the desk and grabbed Tina's. Twenty-three thousand dollars in the account. Elizabeth – forty-two thousand. Claire – fifty-three thousand. Max's book was missing.

I sat down in his desk chair, glancing toward the hallway again and through the window to the backyard.

I am on watch

No one.

The amount of money in the books didn't jibe with the amount of money I'd earned as a kid – either doing odd jobs or as an A student. Where had the money come from? I didn't think he'd put funds earned in stocks and bonds in a savings pass book. It didn't make sense. Max never said anything about there being a lot of money in his book, and he sure as shit would have.

I looked in the open drawer again. This time I noticed a folder marked Munsy. My heart gave a curious thud as if that goose of hers had plopped down dead.

I opened the folder, half expecting to find a hand or some other body part. Numerous yellowed papers met my eye, and I riffled through them. The last papers were a Xerox copy of something, something that had been printed originally on lined legal paper, folded not once, but over and over again. The creases were frayed and I feared the papers might crumble if I tried opening them.

I opened them anyway.

It was her will, handwritten, witnessed by Spink and Sally, her two maids. It was short and sweet, and it left everything to us five children, not a dime to my mother or her mother.

Interesting.

As an accountant, I'd handled enough estates to have an idea just how interesting it was when someone cut out her only child and grandchild. Trouble always ensued in one form or another. I'd seen families who divided, the two sides never speaking to one another again, and I'd seen folks march straight to court in attempts to break wills.

I sat back, reflecting, remembering Boyce's comments about Munsy's money. So Elizabeth had been right. Of course, I'd known my great-grandmother had a lot of money. Money she'd inherited. Money she'd made with wise investments. I'd never really thought about it. I guess I'd never wanted to.

This explained my mother's tight silence at her death, both parents' inscrutability and vague, hovering bitterness. A mystery resolved. Munsy's money the answer.

None of us kids had ever heard about our inheritance. Had he kept it? Most likely, we'd all paid for our own college educations. Maybe what the red bank books held was the leftovers. Or maybe there were still stock certificates in our names as well. Boyce was probably right on track when he suggested the estate might have not been settled until after Max drained his red book funds. My father had probably destroyed his book and stolen his share of the inheritance. I'd have to go back and read through all those damn bank statements and stock reports to figure out what the hell my father had done, but it didn't matter.

it was our money

I thought about my dreams of becoming a trumpet player. I remembered the nights I'd trudged the streets of Greenwich Village knocking on doors, pleading with managers to give me a chance. I remembered the demo tapes I'd put together and my acceptance at Juilliard, and I remembered not having the money to go.

It's a nice hobby, Richard. It's not something a grown man does for a living. Accounting, that's the way to go, Richard. I paid your way.

I thought about that fifty-odd thousand dollars of Claire's, and I thought about my father saying he wasn't going to pay Boyce's bill. Shit, Claire and I could pay a large portion of her bill ourselves. She didn't need Dad. I wondered if our lives and our money mattered so little to him that he'd forgotten what he'd hidden in his drawer.

I tossed the folder across his desk. The will spilled out. 'You goddamn motherfucking son of a bitch,' I said.

He stole our money, he took what was ours. He stole my dream.

he stole our lives, big bro

'Not any longer, Max,' I said. 'He'll pay Claire's fucking bill, I'll tell you that.' I stuffed the bank books into my pocket. I jerked open his top desk drawer. Sure enough, the extra set of keys to the house, the farm, the cars – all were there just as they'd been when we were kids. I snatched them up and headed through the empty house to the garage. The Blazer was missing, but my mother's paneled Buick station wagon was there.

where were they

Then I realized the date. It was the third Sunday of the month.

They were at the farm. Every third Sunday in October, from the beginning of my memories, there had been an old fashioned ice-cream social at Cranklin Hill Church, our farm church. A time-honored tradition, it didn't matter that it was late in the year for such an event. Munsy had taught my mother to churn homemade ice-cream and my mother donated both Munsy's ice-cream maker and her own knowledge to Cranklin Hill. They would have gone to church this morning and she would have stayed to set up for the evening's festivities.

My father was at the farm for the weekend.

it always comes back to the farm

267

My finger hit the electric buzzer to the garage door. I was in the car and splashing through the rain in less than a minute, my trumpet on the seat beside me. Brookfield Court flashed past and I was on the interstate, headed toward the farm before my finger had time to snap on the radio. When I did finally turn it on several hours later, lo and behold, the same religious station she'd insisted on when we were kids blared: '. . . and remember, all you Christian brothers and sisters out there in our listening audience, Jesus died for you so that you could be saved . . .'

I didn't shut it off. I needed to remember. The time had come.

The Blue Ridge foothills edged closer to the highway. In the rain, they appeared forlorn and gray, leaves dead and fallen to the ground. The sky, too, was nothing but gray. Not a hint of white cloud, not a speck of blue sky. Gray, only gray.

> *Gray, gray*
> *Time to pray*
> *Make the H-Man go away*

Max's old H-man story came back to me in a splatter of rain on the windshield. He'd told it to me long ago, eyes wide. He'd told me that Dad told it to him and that it was true and that we'd better be on the lookout from the moment the car turned onto the Steam Hollow Road.

He's still alive, Richard, and haunting the Steam Hollow Valley. Dad says all the old-timers in the valley know about the H-Man, that Boots Lindsey warned him, Eddie Wells, even Old Man Pott.

He says it all happened before our farmhouse was built, back in the early eighteen-hundreds. The house was a log cabin built on a solid stone foundation and the cellar had bars for windows. The foundation's still there set back a ways from the Steam Hollow Road. Dad doesn't post the land because he knows no one in this valley will set foot within a hundred yards of it.

The H-man lived in this house with his wife and three children, a boy and two girls all under the age of five. The little boy's still a baby, but wild, never stops crying.

One night a fire breaks out in that cabin. The whole place is engulfed. Shooting flames, orange and blue and red and yellow, blast across the dark night sky. The wife gets out with two of the children. The older ones, not the baby.

According to the story, the family's out in the yard, sparks flashing, sending signals to all the neighbors. Horses start flying through the night down the Steam Hollow Road. Mama realizes her baby's missing and starts screaming and Dad creeps back into the flaming house, vanishing into the blue-orange blur. The squawk of a baby reaches the ears of those outside. Everyone's waiting for Dad and his baby to emerge.

But they don't.

In a rushing roar of heat and flame, the house collapses.

Even the basement seems to melt, bars on the window oozing in upon themselves. The wife topples to the ground, the children lie beside her, eyes open and staring and frightened.

And then the crowd sees him.

In one of the windows, bars pressed to his chest, hair aflame, mouth one round circle of pain. At that point no one's too sure what happened, but Eddie Wells says his great-great-grandfather swore on a stack of Bibles that he saw him emerge through the melting basement bars, an H emblazoned on his chest.

no baby

Out into the cold dark night goes the H-Man. Seems he's got a fort all set up, high in the mountains, stacks of firewood, water jugs, gun collection.

Wife and two kids never see him again, they're taken in by the neighbors, kids raised by her sister, she goes crazy, nobody can help her.

The H-Man roams the Steam Hollow Valley.

Haunting men with children, whispering words of hate in their ears, whispering words of look at me, free, free, free

no wife, no kids

So when later that year Eddie Wells' great-grandfather slaughtered his wife like a pig one afternoon while the kids were at school, the whole valley breathed – H-Man, H-Man, H-Man.

And, maybe, just maybe that's what happened to Old Man Pott's family.

Maybe that's what happened to our family, big bro –

The H-Man . . .

The H-Man, my ass.

I pressed my foot harder to the pedal.

I glanced at my watch: 3.40. She was likely to still be at church setting up for the social, but he'd be at the farm.

Outside, the sky remained dark. No clouds, no rain, but gray. I remembered how Claire sometimes began a painting that way. Covering the canvas in gray before beginning her picture. 'I want the gray to seep into the painting,' she'd told me. She could paint a hell of a picture today.

It was odd being behind the wheel of my mother's station wagon. I knew it wasn't the same station wagon she'd had years ago for those weekend jaunts to the farm, but it felt the same. I half expected to see my younger brothers and sisters cavorting in the back seat, Buddy dashing side to side, pressing his nose to the window. Spooked, I glanced over my shoulder. No one here but me and the dulcet sounds of what had to be Pallstead's Presbyterian Choir:

> *A mighty fortress is our God,*
> *A bulwark never failing.*
> *Our shelter He amidst the flood . . .*

I swerved onto the Steam Hollow Road. I gripped the wheel tighter to wind around the five miles of curves leading to the farmhouse. It was getting darker outside, almost as dark as it used to be on our trips to the farm on Friday afternoons. White knobs showed up against the brush, but the electric wire was invisible. I could barely make out the reservoir. From the road, it was no more than a black blot.

Thump! I hit a pothole. Thump, thump. Another and another. Old Man Pott's shack appeared. I couldn't believe it was still standing, but there it was, the pine trees nearly hiding it from view. The old man failed to wave and I realized he must be long dead.

It was dark enough outside now that I saw only the shapes of bushes and trees outlined against the gray sky. I edged around the giant curve in the road, drove swiftly to the hill. From its peak, I looked straight down at the farmhouse. Its chimneys smoked, the outside lights glowed.

Swish! I was down that hill and parked in the driveway.

I stepped out of my mother's station wagon, clutching my trumpet case. His Blazer wasn't in the driveway. The doors to the cellar hung open, padlock hanging unhooked. I moved to the cellar and peered inside. It was completely dark and smelled cold, stale, forgotten. Inside, its chill enveloped me. I heard the drip of water and smelled the odd fusty odor of coal, a smell not unlike the musty decaying wood of the ceiling beams. I automatically reached for the light switch where it dangled on an extension cord to the left of the doorway. I knew, if it worked, I'd see glints of reflecting light on shiny chunks of coal.

It didn't work.

But I knew he'd been in that cellar that day. I felt it in my bones, in the chilly air, in the damp hand on my heart.

The steps to the first floor were slick with damp and mold. I slipped once, putting out my free hand to catch myself. My hand went nowhere, grasping at empty space, and I realized the railing was gone. The door at the top of the steps was ajar. I stepped into the house, straight into my parents' bedroom. The bed was made, shades pulled down, curtains drawn. The lamp next to my mother's side of the bed gleamed and a stack of magazines lay in a haphazard pile. A pair of wellies poked out from under the bed, along with a pair of moccasins and two sets of two-toned pumps. I could smell damp horse hair.

A pistol lay on his bedside table. I picked it up and shoved it inside my pocket.

I left their room and moved into the kitchen.

Some remodeling had gone on here.

The flooring was new. Gray and white patterned linoleum replaced the old scraped-away wood floor. They'd installed a dishwasher and the stove was clearly new, sporting that red handle that proclaimed a self-cleaning oven. I wished they'd left the place alone. I would have liked the farm to remain forever unchanging, a safe spot in my memory bank.

maybe they used Tina's inheritance money, big bro — maybe they used mine

An empty glass sat on the table. I sniffed it. Bourbon. Only four in the afternoon. I wondered if he'd had two or three or four glasses. I tiptoed through the rest of the house, peeking around the corner of the living room to see if he was working on the fire.

He wasn't.

I moved back through the kitchen and stepped outside the back door, setting my trumpet on the stoop. I stood still. Off in the distance, there was a grinding noise. It got louder, then softer, then stopped altogether.

I knew where he was.

I pulled my L. L. Bean jacket closer around me and headed across the meadow. Still no rain, just leaden skies. My red jacket must have stood out like a beacon and I wondered if he saw me coming.

you motherfucking son of a bitch

I knew then that I no longer cared about building barbed-wire fences or gutting a deer or priming a pump. I cared about Tina and Claire. I cared about Max and Elizabeth.

I cared about me.

honor thy father and thy mother

'You motherfucker.' My voice seemed to rise high as the mountains, blue-black and jagged against the muddy sky.

I was scared.

All my life I'd been scared of him. He was bigger and stronger and more powerful.

My father was God.

Well, here I was, going to meet him at the mountain top, my heart nothing but a loud beat in my ears. With each football, the beat got louder. I could feel the dank air in my lungs, but I kept moving across the meadow. I stopped once and stared back at the farmhouse, allowing myself for just one moment to think this was all a dream. I guess I wanted to be like Tina and Claire and move right outside my body and stare at everything as an outsider. Then maybe I wouldn't have to admit this was my life.

He was my father.

I had wanted him to be the all powerful father. I'd needed to believe in him and to defend him and to somehow convince the other kids that he was a good father. With every fiber of my being I hated to admit that I was wrong.

your father's a fucking pervert

I stopped in the middle of the meadow and closed my eyes. I took a deep breath. Boyce was right. My need to have him be different wasn't going to change the facts. He might as well have put the gun to Tina's head. He might as well have pulled the trigger on the gun Claire used to kill John.

I opened my eyes and looked toward heaven. 'I hate you!' I shouted at the top of my lungs. 'I hate you, motherfucker!' The Steam Hollow Valley filled with echoing trills: *hate, hate, hate, hate.*

Thunder cracked and I started to run. A gust of wind blew up from the south, setting tree limbs to rattling and my hair blowing in my face. Thump, thump went my heart.

I heard a dog bark, a series of short yelps. The chainsaw shrieked. It wiped out the labored sound of my own breathing. Its fumes leaked across the meadow. My nose twitched at its familiar odor of burning gas and oil.

And then I saw him. His red jacket opened, his red and black checkered shirt blazed against the sky. Sixty-five years old. I saw the blaze of a fire and I knew he hadn't changed a bit. He'd be using the same sawhorse, the same giant chainsaw. Old Jack didn't change. I let my fingers run back and forth over the gun in my pocket. My damp fingers were slick on its barrel.

I crossed the road and stood not twenty yards from where he held the saw. The heat from the fire blazed hot in my face. I saw that his own face was red and sweaty and his hair damp with sweat. The crisp dry smell of sawdust was everywhere, blotting out the damp smell of a rainstorm on its way, blotting out the dank smell of my fear. Rivulets of perspiration ran from my armpits to my waist. He'd shrugged off his jacket and I saw our shirts were identical and our khaki pants, too. I glimpsed the V of his white T, and I acknowledged for the first time that his eyes were the exact same shade of blue as mine.

up against the wall

The saw sputtered and died.

We stared at each other across the fire.

He never let go of the saw, but kept both hands on it, a giant blade between us.

'So, the prodigal returns home.' His voice was loud in the silent valley, but thin, as if it came from his mouth and not from his heart.

I said nothing. The gun was smooth to my touch.

I waited.

'I'm not paying that charlatan lawyer,' he said. 'Claire's coming to Waterton. She's not going to sing her sad lying blues in court.'

it's not over till the fat lady sings

He knew what he was doing. He knew what he'd done. There wasn't any out. It wasn't a misunderstanding. He wanted to protect his own ass. The son of a bitch. That's it. That last vestige of hope I'd been nursing somewhere deep in my heart crumpled.

I took a step closer. I had no intention of mentioning Claire's money from Munsy. My father would pay. I felt the hard outline of those little red bank books against my leg.

The fire flickered bright, casting shadows behind him. He

274

looked enormous against the dark sky. I saw his hands tighten on the saw.

For a moment we stood our ground. All around was our farmland, all one thousand acres of hills and trees, meadows and hayfields, ponds and creeks and secret pools. It was the strip of blue mountains behind him and the hardened meadowground behind me. It was the black-as-pitch barn and the blueing fire sizzling in jagged flames of orange and yellow. It was everything I'd ever loved as a child. It was the only joyous memories I had. It was Max. It was Claire. It was me.

He took a step toward me. He kept hold of the saw with one hand and flung the other arm out wide. 'I'm selling it,' he said.

His threat was clear: Back off and the farm is safe. Max would have seen it coming. It hit me like a blow out of nowhere. My hand left the gun and went straight to my heart.

I didn't know if that vein in his forehead was throbbing or if I just thought it was. I knew he was gripping that saw and I knew he was moving toward me. Twenty yards had narrowed to ten.

The pounding in my ears was so loud, no other sounds reached me. No flutter of birds before a storm. No scuttle of woodchuck or rabbit. No whistle of the wind through the evergreens. Just the pounding. The tingle of fear reaching from my sweaty hands to my heart to my ears and shaking legs.

He stepped closer.

A streak of lightning raced across the sky.

My hand left my heart, returning to the gun. In my fear, my fingers did a rat-ta-tat-tat against its barrel.

He had both hands on the saw. I realized it was not the same one we'd had when I was a kid. This was brand new, its yellow brighter than the flames spurting behind him.

His smell was all around him like a shield. A dank, rank odor, not unlike a dead deer's. A smell like day-old vomit.

I heard my heartbeat slashing against my chest and in my

ears. Fear rose in my mouth and I wanted to spit, get rid of its foul matted aftertaste. Like the rotted carcass of a cow Max and I had found on Malificent's Castle.

I spat a gross glob of gook onto the ground between us. I looked up and found myself staring straight into his eyes. They were my eyes, but they weren't. They were my father's eyes, but they weren't. These were an old person's eyes, not the eyes of an all powerful father, not the eyes of God at all. These were the eyes of a frightened old man. This man looked like someone backed against a wall with no way out. His manner reminded me of a woodchuck I'd captured in a garden trap not that many summers ago. I half expected to see him cringe, and all my years of training as the son/brother who protected the family surged through me as fierce as the lightning bolts in the gray sky overhead.

I wanted to reach out my hand.

In a fierce flash of memory I recalled that when I'd held bread out to my trapped woodchuck he'd bitten me. A vicious deep bite that had gotten infected. It had happened so fast that there was no way I could have protected myself.

I backed away from my father.

'Get off my property.'

I saw the triumph in his eyes.

'Dad.'

'She's coming to Waterton.'

'No.'

'You're in over your head, Richard.'

'I've got Tina's suicide note.' My voice was the kind of whisper that floated thick, staying in the air like New York's smog.

He was breathing hard. 'Don't you threaten me. Without me, you'd be nothing. Nothing, Richard, you hear me? Nothing.'

'I know all about those malpractice suits, Dad.'

I saw his hand move on the saw.

I knew now that this was the moment we'd been moving

toward all my life. He was top gorilla. Nervous sweat broke out on my forehead. Lightning raced through the sky again with a wild crack of thunder. We were in a place that was neither night nor day. I felt inside the heart of the farm, as if my childhood surrounded me in the blue-black of the mountains, the hiss of the fire, the dark splotch of barn behind my father. It was a timeless moment as if I'd stepped into a chapter of Revelation where nothing exists but a realm of the nether world. He raised the saw.

Its shrieking grind groaned between us, yellow and blood red and blazing blue.

He stepped toward me.

I pulled the gun from my pocket and aimed for his heart. 'Put it down,' I said. The saw's roar drowned out my words. This time, it was I who stepped closer. 'Put it down,' I mouthed.

My father moved closer still. That vein in his forehead beat steadily. Sweat dripped down his face. As the saw veered ever closer to me, I realized he was shaking.

It didn't stop his approach.

He'd claim self-defense.

I could do the same.

I cocked the trigger, moved the point of the gun from his heart to within a half-inch from his foot and pulled the trigger. Dirt spritzed the air.

The chainsaw seemed to fly across the sky, a harsh streak of brilliant yellow. When it hit the ground, its roar ceased and oil spurted in a lethargic ooze.

My father kept moving toward me.

He stopped, no more than two feet away.

I thought about killing him. He must have seen it in my eyes. He put his hands up over his head, a gesture managing to both mock me and admit defeat.

'So you've got balls after all, Richard,' he said. He let his hands drop to his sides. I thought of all the years of my and my siblings' childhoods stretched between us. I thought about my trumpet in its case on the back porch of the farmhouse and all the years I'd locked music right out of my heart.

'Your mother's expecting me.' His voice was soft. 'She'll be angry if I'm not there.'

'She'll have to wait.' His response was a way to blow me off. Like, this whole scene with you, Richard, is so unimportant that I've got to get to an ice-cream social right away.

your mother will be angry

He shrugged.

More than anything in the world, I wanted to punch him for that. I wanted to haul off and nail his ass. I wanted to feel my fist crushing his jaw. I wanted him writhing at my feet, begging.

I spat on the ground between us. I put the gun back into my pocket. 'Don't interfere with Boyce,' I said. 'Don't fuck with his bill.'

He shrugged again.

'Forget this Waterton loony-bin idea,' I said. 'You call Judge Barrett and you tell him you and Mom support whatever Boyce recommends. Send him a check tomorrow.'

'And if I don't?'

'I'll go to the Waterton papers. I'll publish Tina's letter. I'll tell our story. I'll publish the malpractice suits.' I sensed Sam right there beside me.

'Who's to say you're not as crazy as Claire?' My father's tongue slid out like a lizard's as he licked his lips.

'Elizabeth and Max and Tina. It's all of us, Dad.'

Silence. The pulse rattled against his forehead.

More silence, only now the storm that had held off all morning seemed to be pushing up from behind the mountains like the evil thirteenth fairy Malificent. Gusts of wind sent dead and tattered branches swirling through the air, and big droplets of rain began to fall. The sky was a curious mixture of flat gray with streaks of orange that looked like overcooked pumpkin pie.

'I don't think Mom would want to be in the newspaper,' I said.

'We'll leave your mother out of this.'

'You're not going to tell her?'

'No, and neither are you. That's the deal, Richard. I'll do what you want about the judge and Boyce. You keep your mouth shut when it comes to your mother. Take it or leave it.'

Same old, same old, big bro. He's got to save face with his mommy. Got to make it look like he's calling the shots. Tell him to go to hell.

We each stood our ground for what seemed like a long time. The droplets of rain stayed droplets, never gathering force into a downpour. Just a steady blob coming down on my shoulders, splashing my cheeks. The burned-pumpkin color crept across the sky until no gray remained.

Max's voice was loud in my head and my hand was hot on the gun. I pictured Tina dead and Claire huddled terrified in her apartment and almost wrenched the weapon from my pocket. But I listened to my own inner voice, a soft insistent whisper: You're not Max, it said, you're Richard. Do this your way. Sure Max is tough, but you're the one with the guts to be here. You, Richard Cory Hayes, eldest son. You're the one who faced off with him.

honor thy father and thy mother

The voice kept talking and it made sense to me: Use your head, Richard, don't strip him of his dignity. You've got a long way to go until Claire is home free. You've done what you had to do, you've confronted him. For the first time in your life, you stood up to your father. Now let it be.

'You got your deal, Dad,' I said. 'I'll tell Boyce.'

I started to stick out my hand, a reflex action, but pulled it back. A crack of thunder crashed around us, but he didn't flinch. He looked me straight in the eye, his eyes blue and cold and dead as one of the dogs he'd shot and buried in the backyard at the farm.

'This property will never be yours,' he said. 'Never. You'll

279

never walk the towpath again or see the pool or swim in the ponds.'

This time it was I who shrugged. He could huff and he could puff, but he couldn't take away what lived in my heart.

The farmhouse was cold and dank. I wandered around it aimlessly, touching cluttered dresser tops, skimming the top of the sink, the toilet basin, the tub with my fingertips. They felt damp with cold. He'd roared off up the old road to Upsomville, a back way to the church and I'd walked down the meadow to the house. The storm burst just as I got to the back door and headed inside with my trumpet, laying it on my parents' bed. Now I heard rain pelting the tin roof over the kitchen hard enough to scare off Max's H-Man. I figured the rain pissed its way down the drainage pipe same as Max's pee used to. Splitter-splatter.

I walked all over the house, upstairs and down. I poked my head into the old tunnels and the secret closet behind the cellar steps. I sat down at the organ and pumped the pedals. Dust flew from the organ in swirls that made me cough.

I went back into my parents' bedroom and opened my trumpet case. My trumpet gleamed gold. It seemed the only shiny thing in the whole place. I picked it up and cradled it in my arms like a baby. I touched my cheek to its smooth cool surface. I should have wanted to play a song, shouldn't I? I should have wanted to blast the roof right off the house.

I lifted its mouthpiece to my mouth.

And set it back down.

Again I tried, waiting for the soaring excitement I'd once felt, the tug at my heart, my mind, my fingers to play, play, play.

The feeling wasn't there.

If only Max had been there to dance, maybe it would have been different.

A dull tune played inside my brain that wouldn't go away, and it wasn't Max's voice, it was my own. Something was trying to push its way into my consciousness, something I did not want to know.

what happened to me on that farm

Chapter Twenty-One

'THERE'S no way I'm going to settle for some chicken-shit plea bargain,' I told Boyce the next afternoon.

I'd gotten home from Waterton close to one in the morning. After tossing and turning on my sofa bed for a while, I'd gone into the office. When Mary arrived, she sent me back home. I felt guilty about dumping such a load on her, but she assured me most matters could wait until I got myself situated with my family, so I'd spent the rest of the morning pacing my tiny apartment. I felt the breath of my demons hot on my back.

'I got a check Fed-Ex'd from your father today,' said Boyce. 'He faxed a note, too. Said he'd spoken to Judge Barrett yesterday after you left.'

'What's that got to do with a plea bargain?' I felt as if my trip to Waterton should have established something here in this office but hadn't. It should have established something in my heart but hadn't. I stalked to the window. I heard the tick-tock of his desk clock. I heard the muffled noises of his secretary closing up shop for the night. I turned away from the late-afternoon city lights. 'What happened to getting her off, Boyce?'

He leaned forward, hands on the desk. 'Claire, that's what happened. Didn't you hear one word she said to you on Saturday?'

'Spare me the bullshit.'

'It's not bullshit, you selfish bastard. A trial could shatter her into pieces that would scatter her from Manhattan to that farm of yours. She needs an extended stay in that Psych Institute with Dr Glassman, and I intend to see that's what she gets. I'll agree to her pleading guilty if I can work out a deal that says she stays there.'

'What about that case a few years ago?' I demanded. 'The one you told me about where a jury sent some old fart to prison for murdering a little girl? The one where his own daughter's flashbacks convicted him?'

'Richard,' Boyce got up from his desk and moved toward me, 'it's not your father who's on trial here.'

'If you won,' I said, 'you'd be splashed all over the *Times*. You'd be the next F. Lee Bailey, the next Alan Dershowitz. Boyce A. Regner, top billing. Tom Cruise could play you in a made-for-TV movie.'

'That's right,' said Boyce.

'You don't have the balls, do you?' I said. 'You're willing to take our money and talk a lot of legal mumbo-jumbo and hire detectives to tear through my family's guts, but when it gets right down to it, you don't have what it takes.' A vein pulsed in my forehead. 'You're afraid of my father.' I spit out those last words. In that moment I realized how angry I was that Boyce wasn't shaking my hand, telling me what a great job I'd done in going to Waterton, getting my father to send a check, to call Judge Barrett. 'You're afraid,' I repeated.

'Richard, I'm doing my job. Don't you get it? I'd love to go into court, make the papers, the cover of *People*. I'd love to get your father on the stand and tear into him. But my client is Claire. Her mental health cannot withstand a trial. What if we lost? Have you thought about Claire in the prison system? Have you thought about what would happen to your fragile little sister there? You're the one who's got unfinished business with your father,' said Boyce. 'Not me.' He put his face close to mine. 'You know what I think? I think you're using Claire to fight your battle with him, that's what I think.'

'Fuck you,' I said.

'You're a broken record. Like it or not, the hearing's Wednesday and I'm going to hammer out a plea bargain with Eleanor on my terms. Barrett was the judge a couple years ago for a sixteen-year-old girl who killed her father. Kid said he'd abused her for years. She pled guilty to manslaughter and he sentenced her to seventy-three days in jail, time she'd already served. I've got a chance here to do what's best for Claire. Be there.'

I slammed from his office and headed out into the street. I heard the clatter and clang of Manhattan, and I heard the pounding of my heart high and wild in my ears. I should have felt silly and melodramatic attacking Boyce, but for that one moment in time I felt like a hero, the hero my brothers and sisters had long been awaiting. The hero I had wanted to feel like at the farm the day before.

The feeling faded fast.

what the fuck happened to me at that farm

Chapter Twenty-Two

S AM and I sat at a sleek Formica table that night at Aggie's in the Village. The noise level was high, and waiters darted here and there with piled plates clittering against each other.

My hands found their way across the table to Sam's. Johanna had always wanted to hold my hand in public, but I never would. I held tightly to Sam's hands. When she suggested we leave Aggie's and go to her place for dinner, I agreed. I didn't stop and wonder if she was trying to control me or be in charge of our evening. I allowed her to fix me a quiet meal surrounded by the springtime odor of her pansy plants and the soft sounds of Thelonious.

I told her how much I liked her profusion of plants and that tiger lilies were my favorite flowers. I described the front yard at the farm with its profusion of tiger lilies. I told her how much I loved the place, that it was the happiest part of my childhood. Of my entire life, I told her. 'It's a place I can visit and revisit in my mind,' I said. 'It's part of me, a part of who I am.' I felt as if I was setting my heart on the table alongside her Greek chicken dish.

She waited until we'd cleared the supper dishes and sat back down at the table with coffee, to say, 'How did it go?' She looked right at me when she said it.

no time to hide

I didn't know how to tell her that I'd confronted him, but

that his foul odor still choked me. I'd scarcely been able to acknowledge it to myself. Instead, heart pounding, I looked at her and said, 'All the time I was growing up, my mother had a way of making me feel like the Incredible Shrinking Boy. I've done a lot of stupid things as a grown-up to avoid feeling exposed in that way.'

She kept looking at me as she said, 'You mentioned the Incredible Shrinking Boy at my party.'

'I wanted to be King of the Mountain,' I said. 'I wanted to be someone who couldn't be hurt.' I took a deep breath and added, 'When I'm with you, I can feel the Incredible Shrinking Boy lurking nearby.' My heart pounded. I felt as if my vulnerabilities sat on the table between us like a plate of gelatin dessert. Would she stick a fork in it?

whatever you say, reflects on the whole family

For a long time Sam sat, sipped coffee, smoothed the skin on the back of my hand. After a bit, she said that all her life she'd been told she was just like her mother by family, friends, their minister, and the thing was, she was smart enough to realize her mother was an unhappy, desperate, grasping kind of person, someone who fed off other people.

'I always thought of her as a praying mantis,' she said. 'An ugly, groping insect feeding off her own mate and children. Especially me. When I grew up, I thought I was she, that the only way I could live was to repeat her life, marry, be dependent. I never thought about what I might want. I didn't know who I was.'

She continued to caress my hand, but I knew she wasn't aware of what she was doing. 'I always felt as if my only worth came from pleasing my family,' she told me. 'They wanted me to marry Phil, to have grandchildren for them, to validate their lives, I guess.' She looked at me. 'You've got a lot of courage, Richard. I was in therapy two years before I could hold my parents accountable for their parenting or hold myself accountable for becoming a person.' She smiled at me, a funny quizzical smile, as if to say, *Now what?*

We moved to the living room. We sat side by side on the couch. Every now and again, her thigh touched mine and I felt the same thrill I'd felt as a teenager when a girl let me touch her breast.

'Boyce says he's going to agree to a plea bargain. No trial.' I pulled away so I could see her face. 'I wanted my father fried. I wanted him torn to shreds in front of a jury. I wanted to get up there on the stand and crucify him.'

She touched my cheek.

'I held a gun on him. I held a gun on my father.'

Sam didn't pull away. I wiped sweat from my forehead. My ears clogged. My next words came through thickness: 'Boyce thinks I want to use Claire for my own vindication.'

'What do you think?'

'I think I need to go back to Waterton. Tomorrow.'

'Go,' said Sam. 'Take my car.'

I leaned over and kissed her. Not a tentative kiss, nor a loving kiss, but hungry and passionate and demanding, as if I thought I'd find my salvation that way. I wanted sex, mind-numbing sex. I thought I could drown in her and get through the night.

She moved back and caught her breath, her cheek hot against mine. 'I think you need to confront those demons of yours before we get involved. I don't want to get caught in the middle.' Her voice was shaky but sure. Thelonious was on his third time through with 'Blue Monk'.

Sam stood, swallowing hard. Through the soft cotton shirt she wore, I saw the rapid beat of her heart. 'You'll have to go now, Richard,' she said, a catch in her voice. She walked me to the door, pressing her car keys into my hand. 'This isn't for Max or Claire or me either,' she said.

And then she sent me out into the cold October night toward the garage where she kept her car, to fight my own battles.

★

I couldn't sleep. I'd stripped to shorts, and still I was hot, nervous, restless.

Three a.m.

Sam's dinner sat inside my stomach like one of my father's dead woodchucks.

I poured every beer down the drain.

I collapsed on my sofa bed.

Deep inside me I'd known what Tina's note would say. Easier to let it stay buried right alongside her.

Easier to let Johanna walk out than deal with her.

Easier to quit playing the trumpet than to struggle with failure.

From my perch on the sofa bed, I saw my trumpet case lying on the floor beneath the table. For a long time, I sat staring at it, thinking about the way I'd allowed my father to steal its joy from me. I thought about Sam's saying she held her parents accountable for their parenting, but that she'd learned to hold herself accountable, too.

Five a.m.

It was a risk, but I yanked the case from under the table and pulled out my trumpet. I managed to link enough notes together to play some of Skip's and my favorite blues: W. C. Handy's 'Memphis Blues', Mamie Smith's 'Crazy Blues'.

I paused. Listened. No complaints from other tenants.

I looked across the street. Lights brightened my neighbor's window. He stood in its frame, clean-shaven, wearing a green plaid shirt, ready for work. He lifted his arm and waved to me. With a start, I realized that for him I was the half-naked man in the window.

I put my trumpet back to my lips. As if of its own volition, it began to play a hymn I knew from listening to that religious station of my mother's as a kid, 'Faith of our Fathers, holy faith! We will be true to thee till death.' It felt like more of a lament than a song, a hopeless dirge chanted at a child's wake.

I am on watch

It was then, when I'd played that song through once, only

once, that the memory came back to me as clearly as if it had happened yesterday. It assaulted me with its sights of brown fur and soft pinkness and sounds of crackling flames, its chill winter wind sifting through window cracks, and its sickening smooth smell of Scotch laced with love.

with fear

I set down my trumpet on the table. I huddled, fetal position, next to the pillows on my sofa bed, clutching the biggest one to my chest.

I knew what had happened to me on that farm

Chapter Twenty-Three

By the time I reached Waterton, my hands were damp on the steering wheel. I don't remember seeing any scenery. I don't remember if I called Mary. I don't remember if I locked my apartment. My adrenalin pumped so hard I felt drumbeats in my ears.

anything might happen

I swung into the Waterton house driveway.

No one came to the door or peered from the front window. No neighbors appeared to ask me my business.

It was now about twelve noon. A blank kind of day, the sky a cloudless dull blue. The sun seemed to have slipped behind a layer of sky. A thin layer of snow lay on the ground, but it had reached the point of grayness with edges trimmed black as if a charcoal grill had emptied its ashes.

Not even the sound of a dog's whining broke the dead calm.

I rang the bell.

thump, thump

I rang it again, keeping my finger pressed to its cold black button.

Nothing.

I walked over to the garage and peered through windows. Both cars were in there, all right. I knew they would be.

I pounded on the door. My nervous sweat turned to hard-work sweat and I thought, This is their first mistake. They should have answered the door.

My already bruised fists ached. I pressed the doorbell. I'd use my key in a minute.

My mother answered the door on the third ring.

We stared at each other through the cloudy storm door.

She didn't have on her red and white checked dress but corduroy pants, the kind with a zillion pleats around the waist, and a white blouse with a pastel flower design. She wore a pair of thick white socks and the usual array of diamonds glittered from her fingers. I let myself look at her face.

Dead.

That's all that came to my mind as I looked at her permed fried hair and white skin and the slash of red lipstick across her thin mouth. But it was the eyes that gave her away. Marble eyes. Pale blue glass.

'Are you going to let me in?' My voice seemed to come from my throat instead of my chest.

'Haven't you done enough damage to this family?' She hissed the words. I half expected to see the window crack.

I cleared my throat, a deep wild growl. I wanted to punch her. 'I haven't done anything to this family. You did. You and Dad.'

She started to close the inside door, but I was too quick. I snapped open the storm door and pushed against the heavy walnut inside door. For a moment in time she was my mother of yesteryear. Huge, demanding, thick with power, and I, a defenseless little boy. Little Richard who tried to save everyone and failed. More than anything in the world I wanted to turn tail and run away.

It was then I smelled her breath.

'The booze isn't going to help, Mom,' I said.

I pushed the door harder and stepped into the vestibule of 37 Brookfield Court. Emptiness spread across my gut like rattlesnake poison. The piano sat huge and inanimate in the hallway. No sheet music lay spread across it. The hymnal wasn't there. The chintz on the chairs appeared yellowed, the once blue drapes, gray with time and neglect. The black and white table-top family pictures appeared misty with dust. Empty cardboard cartons lay strewn about the room. Clothes covered the couch and an opened wine bottle sat beside a half-filled glass on an end table, its pungent fruity odor a sultry haze. I didn't see any opened whiskey or bourbon. Robert Goulet whined from a cassette player on top of the piano. I jerked its plug from the wall.

We stared at each other, my mother and I. It was easy to see in the daylight drifting in from the windows that I was taller than she by maybe six inches and had at least fifty pounds on her.

'Where is he?'

She took a step backwards, away from me. 'He's in his den.'

'You're my mother.' I felt the pain of a lifetime in those words. 'You need to hear what I'm going to say. We're going to the den.'

She didn't move. She was afraid. I saw it in her glassy eyes, in the way her age freckles stood out brown against her white skin. I felt it in her sidling movements.

'You need your drink, is that it?' I snatched the wine glass from the table and shoved it into her hand. I pushed past her to the den.

The door was locked. I wrenched the knob, started to kick in the door. I stopped, caught my breath, felt my heart pounding in my ears and left the hallway instead, shoving past my silent mother and up the front stairs to my old bedroom. A faint film coated all the surfaces. I could see the grayness of dust long left unattended.

I went straight to the picture window overlooking Brook-field Court. Using the desk chair, I climbed up so I could reach the top of the pleated drapes. Long ago, I'd put a replica Max had had made of my father's den key inside the third pleat over from the end of the left-hand drape.

My fingers slipped inside the pleat. For a moment I thought the key was gone, but then its smooth surface slid right into my hand.

Back down the stairs, two at a time.

do it, do it, do it, do it, do it

My mother sat on the piano stool, both hands pressed to her glass. She trembled so badly, I snatched the wine from her hand and set it on top of the piano so hard it splashed onto the ivory finish. I yanked her by the arm to the den. I inserted the key in the lock and swung open the door, my mother tight beside me.

The room appeared smaller and darker than two days ago. No daylight filtered through the draperies, only the dim bulb of a desk lamp and a dimmer floor lamp lighted the room. An odd oily odor of wine and death and dust and fur combined to make my eyes water. Guns lined every wall except one. His precious three-barrel shotgun had a place of honor over the couch. One wall had nothing but stuffed heads protruding heavily into the small space. Deer with eyes more alive than my mother's.

He was seated behind his littered desk, facing me, a pink sheen to his skin. No farm L. L. Bean open-necked shirt today. He had on one of those dark suits with the starchy white shirt and thin maroon tie of my childhood. I half expected to see a stethoscope around his neck. I smelled a mediciny odor now, too, a smell that made me think of the night I'd taken Claire to the Psych Institute and the smell of mental illness had drifted around me.

The pounding in my ears increased.

No bourbon glass sat by his elbow.

Of course. He'd always regulated the drinking to the farm. I guess in retirement he clung to that rule as well. Maybe that way he could lie to himself that he wasn't an alcoholic.

or worse

I walked through the doorway. That ruttish odor of his fanned around him. I thought of a gun to my sister's head, the smash of my sister's face against the dinner table, the hiss of *this never happened, never happened, never happened.*

Nervous sweat broke out under my arms, beneath my waistband, across my brow. I smelled myself now and recognized the sickening odor of my own fear, and the smell of a little boy's hopeless rage against an overpowering father.

I stepped into the room, closer to him. The ceiling was lower than I remembered.

I knew the surprise on his face was pretense. He knew I was in the house. He'd heard me come in, he'd heard me talking to my mother, he'd heard me try the door handle and he'd heard me thump up those stairs to my room.

I could hardly breathe. Silence clogged the den, thick and dark. My mother's arm felt lifeless, the limb of a corpse. It was hot and close in that room.

My father spoke genially, that friendly down-home doctor voice. 'I called Boyce. I'll mail him a substantial check today. I chatted with Judge Barrett, too. Claire will be fine. I've taken care of everything.'

I kept looking at him. His checkbook sat opened in front of him.

'We're leaving on vacation tomorrow.' As soon as he said that in a voice designed to put me right back at the bottom of the mountain, I realized that the house felt empty not only because we children were gone but because they'd been packing. That was the explanation for the empty cartons, the piles of clothing on the couch in the living room. It occurred to me that they might be planning a permanent vacation.

I stared steadily at him sitting behind his desk, ready to end the untidy chapter of Claire's situation with the flourish of his name on a check. I think for the first time I was letting myself see what Boyce had seen all along.

'Your father's done everything for you.' My mother's voice was thin, gray, a mist of threatening guilt. Her words sucked oxygen from the room.

My father and I remained still. For me, the past entered the present, left and came back and left again. Its presence lurked in the room with us and I knew he felt it, too.

'This isn't about Claire.'

He said nothing, waiting.

'I know what happened to me on that farm.'

I saw that vein on his forehead begin to throb. I saw his hand move on the desk and I remembered the gun in his top drawer. My hands grew damper and I felt the beating of my heart and the red in my face.

do it, do it, do it, do it, do it

Fear roared in my ears, but it couldn't compare to the fear I'd felt on that long ago afternoon at the farm.

My mother edged from my side to the couch behind my father's desk. I didn't stop her and I didn't stop watching his hand and I didn't stop the words that must have been building in me ever since that afternoon. I stood not more than five yards from where he sat behind that huge desk of his and I said: 'It's wintertime at the farm, Dad, and you and I are in the living room near the big stone fireplace. I'm just a little fellow and so proud to be with you. Your breath smells of Scotch, a smell I think is manly.'

'We made a deal,' said my father, his hand edging closer to the drawer.

I stepped closer, narrowed our distance to four yards. 'Mom and the other kids are on a run to Pallstead, maybe for milk or hamburgers or maybe popcorn to pop over the fire. You and me, Dad, we're kneeling in front of the fire, warming our hands, and you turn to me and say, "You know my brother died in a mental institution."'

'We made a deal to leave your mother out of this.' My father's face is red, his forehead vein beating. His voice is thin and cruel as taut barbed wire.

'"Your brother?" I say. "What brother?"'

'Get out, Bev.'

My mother went to the cabinet beside the couch and took out a bottle of wine. I watched her pull a corkscrew from a drawer and sit back on the couch. She thinks he's going to beat me up, I realized. She's staying for the fun.

like Claire's gash

'You tell me his name is Scott,' I said. 'You tell me he had problems from the time he was a little kid. You tell me by the time he's ten, he spends his time locked in the bathroom.'

'You can't remember this,' said my father, his voice loud, commanding. 'You're making this up.'

'I remember what happened next, too, Dad.' The hand near his gun drawer was sweaty, nearly as sweaty as his face.

'Get out of my house.'

'No.' I looked straight at him. 'You started grinning at me, Dad, grinning and you scared me. I thought you might get a gun and force me to shoot it like that time in your bedroom in Waterton. I don't know what's going to happen. You get up and leave and then you're back with a three-quarters empty bottle of Scotch and your shirt's off and you know what, Dad? All I can think about is your brother locked in the bathroom and that's where I want to be, anywhere but with you.'

I stared at him, seeing only him, not the deer and moose, not my mother, nor the thick draperies shutting daylight from the room. Just my father with his blue eyes so like my own. 'Why would you frighten your own child so badly?' My voice broke. I suppose at that point I was still naïve enough to think he'd feel remorse. I saw him see my weakness and relax.

He laughed. 'Is that it? Is that the big revelation? I scared you? You always were a wimp, Richard.'

'If I'm a wimp, Dad, you're a bigger one. I haven't finished.' I saw wariness return to his eyes. I stepped close to his desk. 'You turn on the radio, Dad, and you know what's playing? 'Faith of Our Fathers'. And you ask me if I want some Scotch but I shake my head, and I'm damp with fear and say I think I'll go check on Buddy and you say, no, you won't, you're going to learn how to be a man in the Hayes family, and your long arm snakes across the room, snapping out lights, and you know what I say, Dad? I say, "What about the blueberry pancakes, Daddy?" I'm trying to pull you back from wherever it is you're headed, but I can't and all I can think about is the pancakes you taught me to make, pancakes smothered in blueberries, please God . . .'

My father was on his feet in one swift motion, face red and sweaty, vein throbbing. We faced each other across the desk.

I watched him go for the edge of the desk. I thought he was going for his gun, but he grabbed the desk's ledge and heaved violently, sending the desk lunging toward me. I moved, avoiding its crash. Papers, books, pens, the lamp smashed heavily to the floor. The bulb hissed and blew out.

Nothing stood between us but the hulk of desk.

I stepped out from behind it. I put my face not six inches from his. For the first time in my life I realized I was taller than he. 'Sit down,' I said.

'What do you want?'

'I said sit down.' My voice filled the room. I didn't step back. I was bigger than he, younger than he, more powerful. 'Sit down.'

My father sat. I saw how thin his hair was on top. The bare pink of his scalp showed through. I saw a hearing aid fastened behind one ear.

'Turn up the hearing aid and listen, old man,' I said. 'I'm not done.' I peered over at my mother. 'Spoiled all your fun, didn't I? This time he doesn't get to beat me up.' I turned back to Jack. 'You had no mercy, Jack,' I said, 'no mercy for poor little Richard on that long ago afternoon. You pulled me beneath you, curled around me, held me close, so close, you know you confused me, I thought my fear was a fluke, but no, the next thing you do is unzip my pants and yours, too, and I feel your penis against my rear end and I whimper and you put your hand over my mouth.

'Look at me when I talk to you,' I said, and my father looked at me, the pulsing red sheen of his face turned to oatmeal. 'You were all warm and furry, Jack, warm and furry and loving and tender and gentle and your voice was against my ear saying, this is how the Hayes men become men, the Hayes men, the Hayes men, and your voice felt like a kiss and I love you and I want to throw up all at the same time but I have no words to know what's happening to me. It hurts, it hurts so much, but I feel wonderful and oozy and smooshy and loved.

'And then there's your hand on the back of my head and I know my face is near the fire and I'm hot and I think you're going to burn me and my face is an inch from the flame and now your voice licks me with words that say this never happened, never happened, never happened, and the Scotch smell is so strong I think we'll explode in the flames.'

His face was gray, blue eyes bleary behind his wire-frame glasses. His hands rested in his lap lifeless as empty gloves.

'But you weren't done, Dad, not yet,' I said. 'You tell me there's a law against little boys doing what I've done and you tell me that there's a special sheriff whose job it is to spy on little boys like me and if this sheriff ever finds out what I've done, the same thing will happen to me that happened to my Uncle Scott. You tell me Uncle Scott was arrested and locked away in a mental institution by the special sheriff because he got caught naked with your father. The trick, you tell me, of being a successful Hayes man is to never tell, never tell, never tell, never tell. Or the special sheriff will get me. And then you laugh, Dad, and you add in a voice soft as summer wind across the pond, "You know why Scott was never let out? You know why? Because he got angry, that's why. You can't ever do that, Richard, or you'll end up like Scott." And you laughed again.'

I put my face close enough to him he had to have felt the heat of my breath. 'That night the others come to the farm and, sure enough, we pop corn and you grill steaks over the fireplace just the way we love them, medium rare and juicy and for fun you let us eat on TV trays in the living room and even Mom looks pretty to me in the firelight. I think maybe that afternoon never happened, but I know I take care not to get caught alone in that room with you on a wintry afternoon ever again. I know I'm on watch.'

'What do you want?' His voice was thin, cracked, an old man's voice.

I looked down at him. 'You fucking pervert. You understand me, Jack? You're a pervert.' I spit onto the papers lying between us.

'Is it the farm?'

'You don't get it, do you? What I want, you can't give me. I want my life. I want my childhood. I want my brother and sisters. I want the energy it took to suppress that memory, you bastard.' I looked over at my mother, her face slack, her hand an iron claw on the wine bottle. 'I don't want either of you in my life. Don't write me. Don't call me. Don't visit me.' I looked back at him. I heard the sonorous sound of his hearing aid whistling in the dim dark den.

I spat once more, turned on my heel and left the room.

I went out to Sam's car. I got my trumpet from the back seat and marched back into the house. I set the case down and found myself kneeling to get at it, and I couldn't prevent excitement from surging through me. I found myself calling to my trumpet, 'C'mon out of there! C'mon out of hiding! C'mon, bird!' I sang out. 'Let's hear you soar!' I could hear the high notes I'd once played at college gigs inside my soul, music I thought I'd never hear again, and as I sang out, 'Soar!', I realized I was talking to myself as much as to my trumpet. As if on wings to heaven, I played 'Hail Thee Festival Day', and 'Jesus Christ is Risen Today' and 'Come Thou Almighty King', I played until my lips ached.

Not one sound from the den.

I blew the spit from my horn one last time, used my silver rag to polish it, touched it to my cheek, removed the mouthpiece, and carefully set my beloved trumpet back in its case.

I took a last look around the living room, slammed shut the door on 37 Brookfield Court, and started the long trip back to New York.

Chapter Twenty-Four

NO JAIL FOR HUSBAND KILLER

That's the headline the *New York Times* printed after Claire's hearing. I keep the story taped to my East 88th Street refrigerator door, a reminder of those troubled weeks five years ago.

The article goes on to say that a thirty-two-year-old woman accused of killing her husband, whom she said had abused her for years, will serve no prison time. It says Claire Hayes Brown admitted shooting her husband. Relatives and expert witnesses testified that John Brown physically and emotionally abused his wife. Judge Channing Barrett ruled that Ms Brown was in a psychotic delusional state when she murdered her husband and not criminally responsible for her actions, and, therefore, would remain at the Manhattan Psychiatric Institute where she is currently receiving psychological treatment. Defense attorney Boyce Regner said Ms Brown will receive treatment until hospital officials determine she should be released into society. Ms Brown's release from the psychiatric facility must be approved by either a New York County Circuit Court judge or a jury, according to New York District Attorney Eleanor Banning, who said the state would not appeal Judge Barrett's decision.

I'm not sure why I keep the article. In no way does it point the finger at my father. No one suggests that Jack ought to be indicted for Tina's suicide, John's murder, child molestation, or any other crime. I suppose I keep the article because Claire's killing John served as the catalyst for the changes I've been making in my life. Every time I open the refrigerator, I'm forced to think about Claire – and the farm.

Claire's story, like my own, begins and ends at the farm.

Oddly enough, my parents are now living full time at the farm. I only know this because their attorney Brad Patterson approached me through Boyce (who's kept in touch with both me and Sam) over a year ago. I told Boyce to tell him it was okay to contact me. So Mr Patterson called and informed me that Jack and Bev had sold the Waterton house and moved to the farm. Too much publicity in Waterton, he'd said. I imagine my parents put Mr Patterson up to this phone call, that it was a plea for sympathy, a desperate bid on their part to rekindle some contact with at least one of their children. As the former 'good son', they probably hedged their bets that I'd be the most likely to come running.

They'd guessed wrong. There'd be no more honor thy father and thy mother for me.

After politely thanking Mr Patterson for calling, I sat on my sofa bed for more than fifteen minutes waiting for my heart to resume its normal beat and for my hands to quit sweating. At the time of this phone call, I'd been in therapy twice a week for four years and could now resist the lure of my father, but it cost me. I might never have gone into therapy on my own, but soon after Claire's hearing, Mary had announced that either I got help or she was gone.

'Goodbye, Hayes and Lintini,' she'd said. 'Hello, Lintini. Because you know, Richard, the way you're going, that's exactly what's going to happen.'

Sam had been equally insistent: 'I want to be your companion, Richard, a partner, not your mother, not your therapist, not some whiny girlfriend who's intimidated by your anger. I refuse. Get help or it's over.'

Within the first couple weeks of therapy, I had faced a scary realization. I'd spent several sessions explaining how so much of the disintegration of the family was my fault; I hadn't protected my sisters or Max; I'd failed to see my father as he really was; I tried balancing the family to save it and instead, I'd toppled from the tightrope bringing the rest of the family with me.

'Wait a minute, Richard,' said the therapist. 'Who made you God?'

my father was God – not me

By the time my parents' attorney called, I knew that neither my father nor I were God, but I still hated having to feel the overwhelming sorrow of my past and the knowledge that Jack was still willing to trade on my misplaced loyalty as eldest son. After hanging up the phone, I wanted a drink more than anything. My therapist has told me he doesn't think I need to stop drinking altogether, but I have anyway. Something about the warm, bitter smell of alcohol brings back that chilly afternoon at the farm with my father.

it always comes back to the farm

I remember the feel of the land beneath my feet. I could walk blindfolded from the house to the cow barn across the creek and the meadow and the blueberry patch and the upper meadow to the horse barn. I could draw an accurate map of all one thousand acres and identify each beloved haunt of my childhood. I could sketch a topographical survey with no mistakes. I know the layout of that farm better than I know my own heart.

Just ask Sam.

She's stuck with me over the last five years and listened to all the farm stories. I don't know why she kept seeing me; I was depressed and angry and having a hard time digging out of the morass of swampland that was my past. Although I'd told off my father, he continued to hold sway over my emotions. My triumph faded, and I felt guilty about the pathetic silence coming from his shuttered den after I stomped from the room. It's hard to let go, to cut your losses and move on. Especially when your losses include a fantasy of who your parents are and that fantasy seems integral to your definition of self.

The day I began to accept my past was not unlike others at that phase of my life. I got up, showered, ate a bowl of cereal, swallowed a tablespoon of Metamucil mixed with warm water, and left for work by 7.30 a.m. It was December and I worked hard all day on preliminary audits and tax planning for the Flaherty Corporation, not returning to my apartment until after ten that evening. I came home to realize what a mess the apartment was, a real disaster area. It'd been in bad shape ever since Johanna left, but since Claire's hearing it had taken on a new dimension of sordidness. For a moment I had this irrational rage toward Claire for killing John and causing this clutter. But then I heard a little voice whisper, 'Welcome to the rest of your life, big bro. If you want a clean apartment, get busy with the mop. If you want your auditing practices book written, pick up the pages from the floor and get writing. If you want clean dishes in the morning, wash the scummy ones.'

That moment was a turning point for me. I picked up the phone and called Sam for the first time in a week. That same evening I picked up the scattered pages of my audit-practices-made-more-profitable book and set to work on a new chapter.

Day by day the book grows. Week by week, I begin to feel a greater sense of order in my life.

Sam's and my relationship is working, too, in bits and pieces.

She keeps her apartment; I keep mine. We've discussed living together but not acted on the notion. I steer completely clear of marriage conversations though I suspect that that is what Sam ultimately wants. I think she wants a family.

Oddly enough in this small town of New York City, it turns out Boyce and his wife have been seeing my therapist, too. Boyce told me that the whole pregnancy issue nearly destroyed their marriage. Sarah's pregnancy ended in another miscarriage, and two years ago they adopted a baby. His name is Boyce, Jr, but they're calling him Reggie.

I have had no contact with my parents. I think you could safely say that we are in a state of elected noncommunication.

Max calls me once or twice a year. He seems to be sober now when he calls. We don't discuss our parents. We brush over Claire and Elizabeth with quick glossy strokes, careful not to smudge ourselves with murky emotions. What we do talk about is his friend Todd, and we talk about his successful dance career and we talk about Sam and we talk about my accounting firm. I've made some changes of which I'm proud. Mary is now an equal partner and we've expanded our practice. We've got three new accountants, a receptionist and what I think of as a para-accountant. Instead of dragging home between eight and nine o'clock each evening, I'm climbing the stairs, unlocking the three locks and stepping into my apartment no later than six. That's each and every night. Even during tax season.

My stomach gives me little trouble these days.

I tell Max how I've got time to play my trumpet.

Since the hearing, it's almost as hard to talk about my trumpet as the farm. I think it's because I shut off the side of me that wailed with the best for so long that when I finally allowed myself to pull my trumpet out of storage, it hurt someplace deep inside me. Not unlike the way I felt when I'd let Tina fall from my lap against the hearth.

During the last five years, the sibling I remain closest to is Claire. I visit her every week. Dr Glassman tells me that learning to trust is her major issue and that the consistency of my visits is very important. I make my calls Sunday afternoons. I arrive at exactly 1 p.m. each and every visit.

There's a million-dollar question Claire likes to ask me when I visit her in the halfway house that she moved to three months ago. It's in a small town a couple hours' train ride from the city. Claire likes to pretend the town is Pallstead. When I visit, she likes to take me by the hand and lead me on walks in the countryside. Intertwining paths lace the mountain across the road from her house and that's where we walk. 'Isn't this like Malificent's Castle?' she'll say. 'Don't these mountains remind you of the Blue Ridge?' And then comes the million-dollar question: 'If you had a choice, Richard, between having our family and the farm, or having a loving family and no farm, which would you choose?'

She used to ask me that in the Psych Institute, but I avoided answering her. But she asks me again last Sunday. Sam and I have both come to see her, but Sam remains at the house to chat with the caretaker (she tells me she might get some behavior management ideas for her students from her) while Claire and I go for a hike.

It's late spring, the first week of June, and Claire and I are both dressed in raggedy jeans and white T-shirts and sweatshirts tied around our waists because the woods can get chilly even in summer. Her house is set back from a dirt road not unlike the Steam Hollow and we cross it to get to the mountain paths. We walk a path that winds up a hill dense with foliage. There's dead leaves from nearby birch and poplar trees, and sticky pinecones and needles coat the ground beneath the grove of trees we've entered. A thicket of blueberries and a heavy undergrowth of ferns shroud the place from daylight, making it creepy and dark. It smells moldy, the way the abandoned house foundation does, the one across the Steam Hollow Road from our farmhouse.

There's a clearing and we stare out across the dirt road to her halfway house. From where we stand it looks small, kind of ramshackle. Claire pulls on her sweatshirt and takes a closer look. I'm remembering how cold it was in the shady grove of trees where we found the Pott graves so many years ago. I remember the damp and a sense of foreboding. That sense of foreboding is with me again, and my heart beats fast.

'Looks kind of like Old Man Pott's, doesn't it?' says Claire, stepping up behind me, placing her hand on my shoulder. 'I wonder if the tombstones are still on that hillside.'

I feel the strength of those fingers, remembering with a shudder, This woman is a murderer. It doesn't matter whether she is criminally responsible or not: She's shot a man to death. I remember how her fingers looked the night of the killing as they ripped and tore at her pillow's fringe. I remember the thrill of fear that chilled me. I feel it now as she tightens her grip on my shoulder and I go rigid.

I am on watch

I'm afraid, but I don't want Claire to know. I remember how she said the graves haunted her, giving her nightmares. I fear that knowing my sister has killed someone is going to haunt me.

for the rest of my life

Claire drops her hand. It takes me a minute to get control of myself, to turn and face her. She's put her head in her hands. I want to comfort her, but there's nothing for me to say.

She lifts her head, blue eyes watery. 'Do you think I ever forget what I did?' she says. 'Do you think I can ever forgive myself?'

I look at her, I don't turn away, but still I say nothing. I've become the silent shadow.

'I miss him, you know,' she says.

I wonder if she's talking about John or our father, who has not once visited her.

'I miss him most on holidays,' Claire tells me. Something in her voice makes me relax and reach for her hand. She holds on tightly. 'He'd bring home wine and make up stories and sing them to me as if he were a one-man show. He made me laugh.'

I know it's John. Jack is not a song-and-dance man, now or ever.

'I loved him,' Claire says, and puts her hands over her face.

'He beat you. He beat his mother. He terrorized you.' I can't bear to see her weeping.

We are both silent shadows.

I wonder what she's thinking but don't ask.

'I thought he was Dad, you know,' she whispers. 'He raped me over and over and over again. When I was in the Psych Institute that first night, I remember thinking, I am safe for the first time in my life. He can't hurt me anymore.'

I don't know what to say. I am consumed by guilt. Why hadn't I saved her? And then I hear my therapist's voice loud and clear in my ear: *Who made you God?*

'There's no bogeyman, Claire,' I say, and put my arms around her. I feel her tense, her muscles tighten, ready to defend. 'I won't hurt you,' I say softly. I feel her take a deep breath and let it out slowly, then another and another. My therapist has taught me to de-stress by breathing slowly – in through the nose, out through the mouth. I feel her body begin to untighten.

Silence.

'I won't hurt you, either,' she says at last, and smiles. We smile at each other, and we might well have been that long ago Robin Hood and Maid Marian at the farm. Then she asks that million-dollar question again: 'If you had a choice between having our family and the farm, or having a loving family and no farm, which one would you choose?'

Without hesitation I say, 'I'd take the loving family any day of the week.'

Claire looks at me, confused. 'But you love the farm. It's everything that ever meant anything to us. It's the ponds, the graves, the car wreck. It's the pool and ice-skating and Malificent's Castle. I want the farm, Richard. I want to be back there. I want to be swimming and playing King of the Mountain with you. I want to see those sunsets. I want to listen to Patsy Cline in the barn. I want you and Max beside me.'

'It's where Dad drank,' I say, my voice little more than a whisper. 'It's where he raped you.'

Claire acts as if she hasn't heard me. 'You always said the farm was in your soul. You said it was in both our souls. You said the farm gave us a common soul. How can you give it up?'

I don't even have to think. 'But don't you see, Claire,' I say, my voice gentle as a ripple on the upper pond, 'with a loving family, we wouldn't have needed the farm?'

She gives me a blank look, her eyes glassy, and for a moment I see her resemblance to Bev. I pull her close, cradling her head against my chest. I don't want to look at those marble eyes. I pat her hair, wondering if any of us Hayes children can escape our heritage. I look out over her head at the blue-black mountains and in the distance see what I think is a great blue heron's nest. I see Claire's halfway house that resembles Old Man Pott's place and I watch as Sam opens the door and comes outside. She stands, looking toward us, a hand shading her eyes. I don't think she can see us, but it doesn't matter. Listening to Claire has made me realize something important: I know I have the greatest courage of the siblings. I see that Elizabeth will keep hiding. She'll never hook up with a guy and have a family; Max will talk big but stay far away; and Claire, poor Claire, thinks you can substitute a cherished place for familial love. I know better, and I will find a way to survive intact.

No more running.

Once committed to the truth, I will meet it head on.

I am King of the Mountain.

That night I stay at Sam's apartment.

Usually Sunday evenings we spend apart, each preparing for the week. I do my dishes and scrub the bathroom; Sam works on lesson plans. Sometimes she watches the Sunday-night movie and stays up late reading. Sometimes I play my trumpet at one of the neighborhood bars. A friend of mine plays the piano; another friend sings. Sometimes I work on my book.

That night, the night after the afternoon on the mountainside with Claire, I want to be with Sam. I don't want to be separated. I want to make supper for her, rub her feet, brush her hair, make love to her.

It's early when we go to bed.

When I wake up, Sam sits in an armchair across the room from me. A curtain in one of the windows is open and I see it is dark outside, and I guess it to be two, maybe three in the morning. Sam wears a long white robe, belted around the waist, and she's reading. Her head bends over the book and hair hides her face. I move a bit in the bed and the sweet sour smell of sex envelops me. The last few hours have been a sad sweet dream of touching and kissing and warmth and wild, wet desire and I am afraid the dream will vanish now that I've awakened. For a long time I lie there, awake and unmoving, watching Sam read her book. I barely dare blink for fear I will disturb her.

I want to get up, gather her in my arms and bring her back to me. I want to be inside her; I want that sense of coming home that being inside her gives me; I want her arms tight around me. I want to feel the softness of her skin under my hand. I know, as I lie there watching her, that this longing is different from anything I've experienced before.

I am different.

'Sam?' I whisper.

She looks up and smiles. She sets down the book on the floor and comes to the bed. She settles on its edge and holds my hand.

'You're trembling,' she says. 'What is it?'

I look at her. Her eyes don't glitter like marbles, there's a depth to them. My hand may be trembling, but hers feels warm and strong and solid.

I take a deep breath in, then slowly exhale. I hear my therapist's voice saying, *'Take in the love and kindness; let out the pain and anger.'* I take another breath, let it out. Sam smooths back my hair. 'What is it, Richard?' she says.

One more deep breath and I say what's on my mind: 'Sam,' I say, 'will you marry me?' I close my eyes; I've risked as much as I dare risk – my heart. It's a lot scarier than risking failure in barrel-jumping contests with Claire or a chainsaw massacre with my father. It's scarier than sitting in the Waterton kitchen, shotgun clutched in my hands, awaiting my mother. It is the scariest thing I've ever done in my life. The pulse is beating inside my ears so loudly I can scarcely hear anything except its pounding.

afraid of what she might say

'Of course I'll marry you, Richard,' says Sam. 'I love you.'

'I love you, too,' I say, and am unable to keep the tears from slipping down my face.

This dream isn't going to vanish.